She felt her body  er
lying dead, no, no ds
pulled her uprigh l:
'Why are you act I
thought you were

The unseen man -
she would meet her ...o
he turned out to be

Injya was led to the horse svarge. The man now turned
round to face her.

'Quite a beauty for a Gyaretz woman!' Injya stared at
him contemptuously – how dare he comment upon her! He
reached round her and for a dreadful moment she thought
he was going to kiss her, but instead he tied a rope around
her waist. He pulled her over to the fence and tying her
hands behind her back, bound her to a stake.

'Now my little High Priestess, you will be able to see
all the trouble my father has gone to for you. For he has
planned your marriage very carefully!'

Penelope Lucas lives in Suffolk with her husband and three children. She has studied world religions for all her adult life and has been writing full-time for the past six years. *Wilderness Moon* is the first novel in a series of books drawing upon her extensive research into shamanism.

WILDERNESS MOON

Penelope Lucas

CORGI BOOKS

WILDERNESS MOON
A CORGI BOOK 0 552 13647 6

Originally published in Great Britain by Bantam Press,
a division of Transworld Publishers

PRINTING HISTORY
Bantam Press edition published 1991
Corgi edition published 1992

This book is set in 10 Plantin by
Chippendale Type Ltd., Otley, West Yorkshire.

Corgi Books are published by Transworld Publishers Ltd.,
61–63 Uxbridge Road, Ealing, London W5 5SA, in Australia by
Transworld Publishers (Australia) Pty. Ltd., 15–23 Helles Avenue,
Moorebank, NSW 2170, and in New Zealand by Transworld
Publishers (N.Z.) Ltd., Cnr. Moselle and Waipareira Avenues,
Henderson, Auckland.

Made and printed in Great Britain by
BPCC Hazell Books
Aylesbury, Bucks, England
Member of BPCC Ltd.

To my husband, Paul;
my long-suffering children,
Freddie, Kirsty & Grace;
to Anita Mason who inspired me,
Jill Pitkeathley who never doubted
and to the shaman within us all.

CHAPTER ONE

The moaning wind of the high encampment shivered the skins of the sancars. Heavy clouds scudded across the tired face of an old moon and the dry stones cracked with the frost. But it was neither of these noises which woke Injya – a thud – like something hard striking the rocks outside, broke her sleep and in an instant she was wide awake. She did not move; gripped by an inner alertness she lay, ears straining above the creaking of the skins and the whistling of the wind. There it was again – a thud, just outside the sancar, and then a voice.

'It must be done – we have no option – and now *you* know, you too have no alternative. If you do not help – I will have *you* killed too!'

The thudding sound happened again, as if emphasizing the words. Not daring to breathe, Injya strained to hear the mumbled reply, but the wind took the words away. She heard the crunch of footsteps on the frost-sharpened ground receding and then the incessant wind and creaking of the sancar skins were the only sounds left.

She sat up and stared around her. Her mother, aunts, younger sisters – all still slept peacefully. What *was* she to do? I will have to kill you too – too? Who else? What else? She shook her head – this sounded like murder – but no – that was impossible! No-one . . . no-one . . . she *had* to find out more. She rose quietly and put on her outer shift, then struggled into her calf-skin boots, trying not to slip as she laced them quickly. As she reached out to take her cloak, her mother called her name, muffled with sleep. Injya froze to the spot and waited. The bundle of furs which was her mother shifted slightly, then became

7

still. Injya left her cloak where it was and took instead her mother's cloak which was hanging near the Arnjway Staff. She looked at the staff like a child looking for approval; the staff had belonged to the women for as long as memory, and its smooth painted rod, its shining silver crescent moon – even its stand – the sacred barnkop – seemed to be willing her onward. She touched the staff with her fingertips, then touched her heart. The two vibrations were the same. It *was* right to follow the voices.

Silently she crept to the entrance and hesitated – dare she go on? She lifted the skin and put an eye to the crack. Outside the night was eating away the old moon and her eye filled with tears as the cruel wind bit into it. But it brought more sounds to her: hard, low words, then again, the thud. Silent as a moonbeam Injya slipped through the skin and followed the footmarks in the fresh frost. She skirted the men's and boys' sancars, the horse svarge and, keeping low, followed the footsteps out of the high encampment as they went up the ashben, up to the Way of the High Mountain.

Hugging the thinning line of trees she gained a low rise and then she saw them – the tall, burly figure of Crenjal, Vingyar's life-long friend, and the slighter, stooped form of Grinvorst. The wind turned each strand of her hair into a razor lash, but it also carried the words – Crenjal's harsh and insistent, Grinvorst's whining, almost pleading reply. The men disappeared from view over the next crest and Injya hesitated again. She turned to the moon for encouragement but little remained to give solace. Ahni was being eaten away and many more nights would have to pass before She shone her power of rebirth on all. She shuddered as the wind wrapped her round with a winding sheet of fear. She stared at the moon, watching it being harried by the clouds, and a deep foreboding came over her. She should turn back – it was folly. Suddenly the words which her mother had used so often came flooding back to her.

'As Ahni Amwe dies to Herself, allow those things which you want to die, to go to Her. Give to Ahni Amwe all that is a barrier to your freedom.'

And for the first time Injya truly understood the words she had heard so often during her fourteen-summer life. With renewed hope she looked fearlessly into the face of Ahni Amwe.

'Great Goddess, Ahni Amwe! I give you, oh waning, dying Amwe, my fear and my black-faced uncertainty. I am a girl, soon to be woman, equal with all. I offer you my fear of men and I regain my strength as daughter of Mensoon, your High Priestess. Soon you will be reborn, powerful and strong. Bring power to me, Ahni Amwe, take away my fear, for I have no use of it!'

And though the scarce-spoken whisper was heard by no man, the liquid-silver power entered Injya and she walked fearlessly onwards into the night.

She moved quickly now, sure of her path. She left the trees far below her and gained another rise. She automatically dropped on to all fours, cutting her knees and the palms of her hands, but she felt no pain. Below her she could see the two men stamping their feet against the cold. Injya, numbed by the wind and frost, lay flat against the peak, every sense alert.

'And after the capture of the Arnjway Staff – what next? Are you sure we shall succeed?' Grinvorst's voice came as clear and shrill as the wind which carried it.

'With Mensoon dead and that damned line of hers wiped out – of course we shall succeed! Vingyar will accede to our demands and the two great tribes of Skoonjay will be united for ever!' Crenjal smote the ground with his staff and the two men turned to stare at the next peak. Injya, terror-frozen to the spot, craned forward to hear more, but the winds took the words up to the heavens and blew them away. 'With Mensoon dead' – suddenly the sense of the words hit her – they were going to kill her and her mother.

9

She tried to stand, but her legs seemed like tree-trunks. Then a sound which sickened her even more came crashing into her brain – horses' hoofs tearing at the air, as over the far rise she saw Branfjord warriors cascade. Branfjords! The tribe who had killed their priestess, who ripped open the sacred womb of Hoola, Great Mother Earth, and stole Her power and Her riches! She saw the warriors circle Crenjal and Grinvorst and the fear which she thought had evaporated returned to her. Now her feet obeyed as she turned and ran blindly down the ashben to the sleeping sancars below.

She got to the horse svarge first. Instinctively she released the horses; they rushed from their pens, their eyes wide and white with sudden freedom. As if in one body they raced up the ashben. *That* would cause a delay if nothing more. Finding her voice for the first time since the shock Injya ran round the encampment screaming at the top of her voice: 'Awake! Awake! Murder! The Branfjords!'

She ran on, tearing at the entrance skin of the women's encampment, shouting at them, her voice thick with terror: 'Mensoon! The Arnjway Staff! The Branfjords – they are coming to kill you – and me! They are going to take the Arnjway Staff!'

The women stared at her, eyes wide with awe and incomprehension. She dashed across the sancar and took the Arnjway Staff from its stand. As if released from a spell, her mother suddenly came to life.

'Injya! No!' Injya swung round, face flushed with fear.

'Mensoon – we must fight – Grinvorst – Crenjal – they are going to kill us – they are going to kill the Goddess! We *must* defend ourselves!'

And before Mensoon or any woman there could do more than draw the children to them, the sound of fighting clashed their benumbed brains awake.

The children screamed, some women wailed, while others fell to their knees, frantically praying, grasping their children close to them. Only Mensoon and Injya were unmoved. As the sancar suddenly flooded with taper-light, Mensoon tore the sacred staff from Injya's hand and spun round to face her adversary. The warrior stood, his face grotesquely flickering in the taper-light, his sword bloodied and raised. A deathly hush fell as if the spectacle robbed the women even of their terror. Mensoon took a step towards him and lifted her head high, shouting her words of defiance to the heavens.

'By the power invested in me by the Goddess, I command you to leave this place!'

The warrior stepped backwards as if the power of her words had physically knocked him. The entrance flap opened again and more warriors crowded in behind their leader. Undaunted, Mensoon continued: 'By the power vested in me by Ahni Amwe, Goddess to all women . . . '

A flash of light, a thud, a sword pulled back, gore-laden. Mensoon gasped, the Arnjway Staff trembled.

'I call upon Her avenging face. I . . . ' The sword flashed again and Mensoon clutched at her wound: 'I am the High Priestess – only my sacred mother Ahni has the right . . . '

Mensoon's body slowly crumpled as she let go of the Arnjway Staff – 'To end my' – the knife flashed once more – 'life.'

She died, claiming the word as hers and as her body fell, the Arnjway Staff remained upright for a shocked moment, then it too crashed to the floor, over the body of the High Priestess.

Pandemonium broke out as the warriors, seeing the ease with which Mensoon surrendered her power, rushed into the sancar. Children were torn from their mothers' arms and flung, like discarded skins, against the soft walls as the women were felled. Bendula, Mensoon's sister, stepped forward, tried to pick up the staff, but was killed instantly, her head severed with one swift blow.

11

Only Injya stood, unmoving, witnessing all, awaiting her execution. But no sword was raised against her, no rough hands or urgent bodies crushed her into submission.

'Just as our Mother Goddess sees all and flinches not from the flood she has created.'

Just as she had done earlier, Injya raised her hands to the heavens, lifted her head above the carnage and the screaming, wounded women and felt the pure white energy of Ahni Amwe enter her soul. She felt it course down through her body, filling her being with icy rivulets of power, but then as the tingling reached her feet, she sensed another energy rising, felt the fire in the belly of Hoola, the Great Earth Mother, boiling with rage. And then the two forces joined – the divine and the earthly – in Injya's belly. She felt it swell; her body began to shake with power and then something burst forth from within her. As if she had given birth to revenge itself, blood trickled down between her legs. Her long-awaited womanhood had begun – at such a time – at such a place!

Suddenly hands took hold of her shoulders from behind and she was propelled from the sancar. As if nothing could touch her, no sight sicken her any more, she held her head high. Once outside the place of screaming slaughter, she heard a man's voice whisper in her ear: 'Now I will take you to your father – and your husband.'

Shocked more by the words than the carnage, she stumbled and tried to shake herself free.

'As I am to meet my *husband*' – her words were sneering, contemptuous – the Gyaretz people had no use of 'husbands' – 'then I will go willingly. Remove your hands – beware of whom you hold! I now have the power of the Goddess working through me – you touch me at your peril!'

'You have yet to meet your husband!' the voice spoke again. 'I cannot let you go!'

The encampment was eerily quiet. Around the men's and boys' sancars, Branfjord warriors stood guard, swords

12

unsheathed in readiness. They stumbled forward until they came to Vingyar's, her father's, sancar where two warriors stood guard. The entrance flap was raised and Injya was pushed roughly inside. Afraid of what she might see, Injya stood with head bowed. Slowly she raised her head, saw the feet, the legs, the strong torso of her beloved father. Every atom of her being urged her to run to him, to seek consolation from his strong arms, but one look at his face told her that she must not. Vingyar, once the strongest, most fearless hunter and leader of the Gyaretz race, looked broken, his grief-stricken face creased into thousands of lines, his once noble head bowed. As the hands dropped from Injya's shoulders and she faced her father, she saw the anguish, sensed his loss, and knew that now, at this time more than any other, he needed her strength. She *had* to be as strong as Mensoon.

Injya took one step towards him and said quietly: 'Your daughter is here, Vingyar – what will you do with me?'

She saw Vingyar's eyes shine with hope momentarily, then glaze with sadness as the hope was crushed by a voice behind her, a voice she knew only too well: 'Vingyar wishes me to take you to meet your husband, Injya.'

Crenjal spoke slowly, his booming voice filling the air with authority. Knowing that she had to play her part, if not for herself, then for the pride of her father, Injya turned to him.

'Whatever my father wishes I am ready to obey.' Crenjal smiled at her and she coldly watched his eyes looking through her thin skin shift, as they probed the soft contours of her young body. He saw the blood and turned upon him who had held her.

'Who has dared to touch her? I gave orders! Who has touched her? You?'

The youth indignantly replied: 'How dare you, Crenjal! – would *I* go against my Father? No-one touched her. She stood, she put her arms to the heavens, she bled!'

13

Crenjal sensing that the youth was not lying, turned again to Injya.

'That is good – I would not wish for your marriage to be anything less than sacred, Injya. Come – you have seen your father, now you will meet your husband.'

Injya turned back, one last look, but the man who was her father was no more. He sat, slumped into himself, head in hands, oblivious to all. Injya turned and faced Crenjal.

'Beware, Crenjal – beware the Goddess!' But the strong hands pushed her outside.

The air rang with the sobbing of the women and the wailing of the children, but the screams of terror had ended. Ahead of her Crenjal strode and she, with head held erect, tripped often as they rounded the men's sancar. It was surrounded by Branfjord warriors, some with bloodied swords, but no sound came from inside. With a sickening lurch of her heart Injya thought that all the men had been murdered, but that could not be. 'Mensoon and her damned line' – that meant her, her two little sisters and Halfray. She felt her body crumple as she thought of her brother lying dead, no, not Halfray, surely not Halfray! The hands pulled her upright again, as the cruel voice whispered: 'Why are you acting like a frightened maiden, Injya? I thought you were the High Priestess!'

The unseen man's mockery brought back her resolve – she would meet her 'husband' with dignity, no matter who he turned out to be.

Injya was led to the horse svarge. The Branfjord men had rounded up the horses which Injya had freed and the beasts silently greeted her with plumes of breath which shone in the fading moonlight like feathers of love. Crenjal said something to the youth who had led her and then strode back to the encampment. The man now turned her round to face him.

'Quite a beauty for a Gyaretz woman!' Injya stared at him contemptuously – how dare he comment upon her! He reached round her and for a dreadful moment she thought he was going to kiss her, but instead he tied a rope around her waist. Relieved that she was only being tied up – like an animal, her anger screamed – the man continued to stare at her for a moment or two then, as if suddenly disinterested, he dropped his gaze.

He pulled her over to the fence and tying her hands behind her back, bound her to a stake.

'Now, my little High Priestess, you will be able to see all the trouble my father has gone to for you. For he has planned your marriage very carefully!'

The man grinned at her and touched her face, almost tenderly, with the back of his hand. 'Do not look so scornful, Injya, you will have a fine marriage. When the sun runs away to hide again, then we will bring Kraa to meet you. We will let you have a kinswoman to dress you. We are not animals, Injya, you will see!'

And he was gone, back to the blackness of the night.

As soon as it was light Injya saw the Branfjord men advancing towards her. They were all carrying staves and furs and immediately she felt the terror again. They were going to murder her. They would drive the staves into her heart . . . they would smother her with furs . . . they would each take her as her kinswomen had been taken . . .

'Sacred Ahni Amwe – help me!' she whispered through teeth chattering with cold and fear. The men stopped a little way off and began knocking the staves into the hard earth. Injya's mind raced – what were they doing? They placed the staves in a roughly circular shape, then joined them together with ropes. They were making another horse svarge – that was all. She wanted to cry with happiness at the thought – how stupid she was! But then she saw that they were covering the ropes with furs – perhaps this was a different sort of sancar construction. She shivered with cold – the horses' breath was warm on her back, but the sun was only a meagre yellow slit on the horizon and the ground was still frozen. When was her kinswoman coming?

When was she to meet her husband? She felt nauseous at the thought – husband indeed! Where was the Prental Council meeting? Where were the glade and the flowers for her hair? Where was her ceremony – her blessing from her mother . . .? She shook her head – she must not allow herself to think of Mensoon – she must be strong.

The svarge completed, the men disappeared, only to return a short time later with more staves. These were shorter, cut at an angle at one end. The men proceeded to surround the svarge with these, arranged so they pointed towards the centre. Then came a sight which froze the blood in her body: Gyaretz men, driven at sword point, carrying brushwood. None of the men looked at her. They deposited their bundles in a wide ring round the outside of the staves and with heads hung low crept back to the encampment. Her heart sank. This was no horse svarge; this was an elaborate pen. She was to be burnt alive!

Later that day they allowed Sanset, her cousin, to come and wash her. From her she learnt that with Mensoon and Sanset's mother, Bendula, her two little sisters, Prisca and Freesay, had both been slaughtered. The women had all been raped – the children spared.

'Halfray?'

'Spared.'

'My father?'

'I don't know. Two youths, Athuk and Tlö, were castrated – the rest reprieved. A few wounded. Not many came to our rescue – not after what they had done to Athuk.' Sanset did not know of this man Kraa, did not know what the plans were, knew nothing more than that her heart was breaking – but she had to go on – she had her daughter to protect. She could not show any emotion.

She stepped back and looked at Injya. She had braided her hair the best she could, washed the blood from her legs and wrapped her in her father's cape – she could do no more. Injya, for her part, stared back, eyes wide with longing for comfort. Why was Sanset – usually so loving

16

and kind – being so aloof? With a tremendous force of will she stopped her bottom lip quivering and swallowed hard, looking away from her cousin. She was already dead to her – that was why Sanset showed no emotion.

'You have done well, cousin. Leave me.' Injya's face, set like a mask, melted Sanset's heart and she went to hold her.

'Leave me!' Injya almost shouted: 'Go – look to your child, Sanset – take care of little Bendula – I am beyond help.'

And Sanset, knowing this to be true, turned away from the girl who so rudely had become a woman. She would not weep – she would be strong, as Injya was strong.

The day dragged on. When the sun was at its highest the man who had held her came back. She could see him clearly now and realized that he was only a youth – perhaps only a winter or two's turning older than she. He had the high cheek-bones and straight black hair common to the Branjford men, but his mouth was full and hard set, his eyes, glinting and malicious. What people were they, these Branjfords, that could make one so young look so evil? She shivered involuntarily and he sneered at her once more. He did not speak to her, only roughly untied her and led her by her rope into the enclosure. Injya's heart sank further as the man tied her to a stake in the centre of the arena and hobbled her feet like an animal, leaving her alone to her thoughts and fears. Slowly the sky darkened and the first star appeared. Now she would know her fate.

She stared at the place in the pen where she had been brought in – that was where *he* would come from. She strained her ears for sounds of horses' hoofs, for surely someone as important as this man was would arrive on horseback, but she heard no sound save the moaning of the night winds. As the frost began to bite Injya prayed, continuously: Let it be over quickly, please, Ahni, let it be over quickly. And as if in answer to her prayer, the skin moved and three figures came inside. Two Branjford warriors and another – this would be him! Injya drew herself up to her full height and stared at the advancing men. But no – it was only the man who had tied her up. He was carrying a goblet from which, judging by his staggering gait, he had already drunk too much. The two guards carried burning tapers whose flickering light twisted the man's face into a diabolical mask. He spoke.

'I, Galdr, son of Anfjord, do drink to your forthcoming marriage, oh Injya!' He drank heavily from the goblet, smirking in mock homage to her. 'I bring you Kraa, your husband. Do as your Goddess commands you and join with him in this sacred marriage!'

So saying, he stepped forward, holding the goblet out towards her. The guards cut her ropes and pushed her forward. She was desperately thirsty, but she would not give this man that satisfaction – even if he were the son of the chief of the Branfjord people.

'Drink it!' he insisted, holding the goblet up to her lips. Injya took a step backwards but felt the guards behind her. 'It is our sacred water – it will give fire to your womb and strength to your heart, Injya.'

Injya spat her words into his face. 'I will not, Galdr, son of Anfjord, drink from your goblet or join with your man in marriage! I am Injya, only remaining daughter of Mensoon, and as such I am now the High Priestess of the Gyaretz people. I will do nothing against my will!'

'You,' he sneered at her, 'are a frightened little girl who is about to make a sacred marriage and there is nothing you nor any moon-goddess can do about it. I will leave you this goblet, in case, just in case, you change your mind!' He bent down and placed the goblet at Injya's feet. 'You may feel the need for it in a little while!'

So saying, he turned on his heels and left the pen, accompanied by his two men.

As soon as he left, Injya pounced on the goblet, sniffed it, and hid it at the back of the pen. As she did so she heard a crackle and then a great roar. Standing up, she saw the sparks leap into the air as the kindling wood was set alight. The whole sky around her seemed to glow orange for a moment and Injya fell to her knees.

'Ahni Amwe – I am about to die – come to my aid – help me, Ahni Amwe – help me!'

But as she watched the sparks shooting she saw the furs move again. This, she knew, would be Kraa. But in the expected place of a warrior's head was a massive black curly shape bearing a horned crown. Two streams of white vapour came from where his knees should have been. Injya froze with terror as she realized in the dancing redness that the warrior was not wearing a horned crown – her husband had a horned head. Kraa was a bull!

Blind panic rooted Injya to the spot, but then the fire roared and as if its urgency ignited something in her, Injya ran to the back of the pen. The bull, seeing her for the first time, charged straight for her. She waited until he was nearly upon her before she moved and then the bull crashed straight into the wall of the pen. That was what to do – not to run – let him batter the pen down for me. Yes! She ran to the other end of the pen, desperately trying not to fall. Her body was shaking with fear, her heart crashing against her ribs. When she turned she saw Kraa shake his head and turn to face her once more. As he moved she could see clearly that vicious sapling twigs had been inserted in the underside of his great neck – he would have to keep raising his head to get away from the pain – raising his head in the attitude of a rutting bull. Scarce daring to look at the animal she allowed her eyes to lower – yes, he was a rutting bull – some animal – some man? – had already excited the creature. She felt her stomach lurch – no, Ahni Amwe – not that! Please, beloved Goddess! Not that!

She had no further time for thought as the beast lumbered forward again. His massive frame and phallus swayed with the motion, his flared nostrils sent great plumes of smoke to the ground. Transfixed, Injya stared back at him. His head lowered, his fire-reddened eyes caught hers and Injya felt suddenly powerless. She was going to die. She would be gored to death. There was no escape.

Kraa suddenly reared on his hind legs and crashed forward. His hoofs smashed against the skins and Injya ducked. The hoofs missed her by a hair's breadth and Injya, as if suddenly released from a spell, raced to the far side once more. Her foot touched something – the goblet! *Now* she would drink! If she was to be sacrificed she would drink Galdr's fire-water. The drink tore at her throat and stomach, took her breath away and in that instant, the voice of Mensoon exploded inside her head:

'Fire and air, winds and flame. Come away from the spell of the moon and the earth! Fire and air!'

That was it! Fire and air! Kraa, earth – Ahni Amwe, moon! Her only resources – fire and air!

Injya turned and confronted her fear. The fire had died down and in the dull glow from the embers Kraa seemed confused. But Injya was no longer confused. Knowing that she was facing death, she walked straight towards the beast, who, automatically, dropped his head – now he would have her!

Injya forced her eyes from Kraa's and tearing her face from his, she raised her head heavenward shouting: 'Great winds of the high places – Great God Oagist! Waken your fire-brother, Ipirün, to an even greater rage! Burn, burn your worst, take your daughter to the heavens with you. I am ready, Oagist! Take your daughter!'

Kraa seemed momentarily shocked by her voice; with head still bowed, he shook his massive body from side to side as if he were shaking the words away. He pawed the ground restlessly and moved a little to one side – no longer in the attitude of charging. He, too, seemed to be listening.

The wind, the low wind that constantly howled, suddenly dropped. The world stood still and the bull turned its head once more to Injya.

'Great God Oagist – your winds!' Injya commanded and from the silence a great roar rent the air. A thunderous, booming roar, the fury of the elements. The exalted wind, freed from its shackles, responded to the plea and from the rear of the pen came the mighty wind, the mighty Oagist, and He blew life back into His brother. Ipirün exploded into life.

Brilliant iridescent sparks flew into the black night faster than the fastest shooting-star. Kraa, terrified, tore round the ring, snorting and bellowing wildly. He lowered his head once more and charged towards Injya. Injya threw her cape over the animal's head and hung on. The cape, speared by the dreadful horns, blinded the animal and with a furious roar he dashed himself against the pen wall. In a shower of sparks the skins gave way and the fire rushed into the pen, searching out its captives. The shock of the heat took Injya's breath away but she clung on to the cape. Kraa reared and crashed through the stinking, charred furs; his mighty hoofs smashed the ring of staves. They were both free.

CHAPTER TWO

'When you fully understand the symbol of the two moons, then the terror will leave you.' The words struck the air, bridging the gap between the two – the wise and the fearful, two females, worlds apart, only joined by the sepulchral words.

Injya sat, still shaking, staring at the crone. The acrid smoke of the herbs which the Wise One had burnt stung her already tear-smarted eyes. The crone lay on her low pallet of wood, her deep, rhythmic breathing unchanged after the pronouncement.

Is that it? thought the girl as she rubbed her shaking body with fear-cramped fingers – all this, for just that? She stared at the shapeless bundle of rags which was the crone. She could feel her heart still beating wildly, the crone's enigmatic words had not calmed the pounding, and she waited. Silence.

The crone's breathing was barely audible and as Injya fought to control her terror, her breath too slowed, until the deep silence in the cave became as intense as the horror of her ordeal had once been. Fear. The grip of fear clutched at her innards like an eagle with its quarry – growing, shuddering terror – no hope – no help – no wish for more. Injya sighed as she forced her eyes to leave the sight of the silent woman. She closed her lids – pictures danced on the black canvas of memory and her stomach lurched once more. Look . . . look at anything . . . see but do not remember! her sleep-starved brain ordered her, and numbed into submission, she opened her eyes again. A glance – the crone – asleep? – the fire, thick smoke. Black walls, bones and fur, stones and twigs, sharp hurtful rocks.

Behind the crone a star shape, picked out of the blackness, glistening white. To her right – waving lines, a spiral – a serpent? A serpent surely, blue eyes winking at her. Panic, a live serpent? Tear them away, no more horror, please. A quick flicker – crone still asleep – speak to me – tell me how to be! Nothing. The fire, red, menacing, like . . . like . . . no! Force the eyes away . . . To the left, hanging from a ledge a drum, a flat, round drum, finger-marks of years shining and again a spiral. Another snake – oh no! Speak to me – Askoye – speak to me! Injya dared to close her eyes again, concentrating on that one thought, willing the Wise One to speak. She knew that the crone could read thoughts – why was she being so quiet? Could she really have fallen asleep? She laughed inside at the ridiculousness of that thought – no-one could sleep after what I have just said – *I* haven't slept for four nights! She *could* not sleep!

Askoye moved very slightly and the voice came slow and sonorous, as if already bored by the topic.

'Go inside yourself and understand why you chose to be a witness – I will be here – you have nothing to fear.' A scrawny arm creaked out of the bundle and reached for Injya's hand.

'Take one taper and place yourself at the feet of the Great Bear – allow all and all will be clear.'

The arm like the leathery wing of a bat retracted back inside its rags and a deep sigh issued from the prone figure. The audience was at an end.

Injya squatted, still staring at the fire-lit figure, unwilling to grasp what had been asked of her. She had heard tales of people having been thus advised, never again returning to normality; her mother's brother, her own brother – he of the sure spear and the swift feet, reduced to the gibbering, dancing fool who now answered only to the name of Halfray ('He who is half in the other world'). He had never recovered from his ordeal with the Great Bear – would she? She stayed where she was, struck dumb and terrified.

'Go now!' the voice commanded her, the words piercing the air like the high winds of the mountain tops. 'Leave all your outer garments here – naked you will know the truth. GO!'

Injya struggled to her feet. Her legs had gone numb with the exhaustion of her journey and she doubted that she could walk to the end of the cave. Trembling all over, her frail body mirroring the fear inside her, she knew that she had to obey – there would be no escape. The pungent herbs made her head swim as she stood up, the air at the roof of the cave thick with their penetrating smells, and for an instant she thought that she would be sick, or faint, or both. Somewhere, deep down, she instinctively knew that if she did either, she would never recover.

Her fingers seemed possessed by insects' wings; they wavered and trembled like the cotton grasses. Fumbling she tried to remove her heavy cloak. Her fingers would not do as they were told, they would *not* fasten on to the fabric, they slid and wandered aimlessly. Do it! she commanded them, do as I tell you! She drew in a deep breath and instantly regretted it; the smoke sliced her stomach like a knife and the cave swam, but miraculously, her fingers started to obey her signals. The cloak dropped on to the filthy floor, sending up a cloud of acrid dust. The bone clips to her singlet snapped open with extraordinary loudness, each sound echoing round the cave, and finally her doe-skin singlet joined her cape, falling in a grotesque heap, the beads winking at her, mocking her terror in the firelight.

As she looked at the pile of discarded clothes she suddenly realized that she was no longer shaking and from nowhere she understood – I am taking off the outer layers of my soul, she thought to herself, I *will* see and then I will know what I must do.

The dried shards of the bones which lay scattered over the floor cut her feet, but she felt nothing, it was as if she was inured to pain, having suffered so much already. She crossed over to the fire to light a taper, and stooping down as she did so, she cast a furtive look towards the pallet. The bundle of rags was still lying in a twisted, squalid pile, but the Wise One had gone, unseen and unheard, leaving only tattered shreds behind her.

Dread drained Injya of her resolve as her heart began its thundering racing once more, but Askoye's words flooded her mind: 'I will be here – you have nothing to fear', and the terror left her as quickly as it had come. She had heard tales of the Wise One moving through time and space, changing shape and form at will. She also knew that the Wise One sometimes inhabited the body of a hunter, enabling him to perform great acts of courage – she had been told, but she had never really believed. Now she dared to hope that the Wise One was inhabiting *her* body – making her strong, absorbing her fear. She stood up, clutching her lighted taper, and breathed deeply. Now she knew they had been telling the truth.

Without glancing at the pallet again, she tried to focus her eyes in the darkness. She remembered that she had seen the figure of the Great Bear somewhere in the cave when she had finally crawled into it – it seemed so long ago, that moment when, at the point of exhaustion, she had half fallen, half crawled, into the mouth of the cave. In the darkness and the dense smoke, the cave now seemed enormous and she knew that this, too, was part of the journey of understanding. Reluctantly she turned from the fire and held her taper high. The cave seemed vast, but stumbling and tripping over unseen obstacles, she reached the safety of a wall. Far behind her she sensed the fire, but the way was forward and touching the wall with tremulous fingers, she began her journey to find the bear.

Painted symbols leapt out at her as she felt her way round the cave walls: now the outline of a skeleton; now a stylized man, dancing; now serpents – again the serpents – and twisting ropes of white light leading nowhere. Nothing made sense. She came upon skins hung on the walls,

25

their sudden softness in sharp contrast to the rough cave surface, and fancied, for a split second, that the skins were still inhabited by their animal bodies. A warmth, the remembered warmth of animals, flooded through her, filling her with the longing for home, but no sooner had that feeling threatened to bring tears to her eyes than the light showed her rows of skulls, their still-glistening teeth grinning at her, their sightless eyes mocking her, as she stumbled forward, desperate to be away from the ghastly grimaces and the shining sockets.

Her light flickered as a breath of wind blew from the centre of the cave. She felt her resolve waver like her taper, when her fingers discovered something flat and cool. She swallowed hard, bracing herself for the next onslaught. It was a mirror. In the failing light she could just discern the outline of an enormous piece of obsidian, black and shining, lying in the wall of the cave as if it had grown there. Through the soot and the dim light, the magic obsidian still managed to glow opalescent as if possessed by an inner force of its own. Injya held the taper higher and taking a step back, she looked into its deep, dark face. Two burning red eyes stared back at her surrounded by matted black hair. Injya stared at herself with horror, her face seemed like a skull, and the eyes! Her eyes! Her heart started its dancing once more, her blood throbbing violently through her shaking body. I will die, if I look more, her inner voice proclaimed, and shutting her eyes against the image she crashed forward, straight into the bulk of hard, sharp fur.

She had arrived. The Great Bear stood before her. All she had to do was sit in front of it and . . . and what? Her brain reeled, *what* did she have to do? She could not remember what the crone had said. With eyes shut tightly against the vision of the bear, Injya felt utterly alone and sensed the enormity of the cave press down upon her. There was no-one to talk to, no-one to help, she was a naked girl, standing utterly defenceless, in front

26

of the most powerful beast known to man. Knowing that she had come to the end of her journey, sensing that she faced the total destruction of her former self, she opened her eyes and stared at the figure in front of her.

He towered a full two pchekts above her, twice her size. His great forearms outstretched before him, wicked claws ready to tear the air; his huge muzzle pointed directly into the centre of the cave, the eyes seeing all. As her dizzy mind slowly absorbed his magnificence, her taper finally flickered and died. With the dying of her light, Injya felt something die inside her, as she fell back into the abyss, back to the horror.

CHAPTER THREE

Injya lay perfectly still at the feet of the Great Bear. She stared up towards his outstretched arms and his dreadful muzzle. He seemed even larger than when first she had encountered him and yet, in a strange way, he no longer held the overwhelming power she had initially felt. Rising stiffly, she wondered how long she had lain there, how long it had taken for her mind to relive those awful hours. It hardly seemed to matter – they were the past. She knew that had she not relived the battle, the scene of carnage, she would not be able to do what she knew she must. She would have been held in her memory's grip, numbed with fear, for years, perhaps for her entire life. Now, she could release its hold.

Injya stood in front of the bear and touched his stiff arms. Without fear she stroked the spiky fur and felt warmed inside by the contact, as if she had returned to her father's arms. The word struck her brain and echoed round inside her skull. Father. The Chosen One. Sadness surged within her as she remembered the last sight she'd had of her father, Vingyar, and tears threatened; but almost as soon as they came, another memory washed away the grief with sunshine: her mother, arms raised to the high heavens, head thrown back, her tall willowy figure caressed by the warm breezes as she whirled round, singing to the trees and the brook, the flowers and the birds:

'Today we live, today we live, Injya, today and today and today!'

And Injya opened her eyes and closed her memory on that picture, keeping it secret in her heart. That was how she would remember her mother, singing her presence to the universe, celebrating her life.

But now . . . taking a deep breath, Injya forced herself to be aware of her today. She looked around her: the cave was still darkened, although a faint blue-grey light was emanating from one direction, showing the piles of rubble, heaps of bones, in hideous relief. The fire was out and the whole place smelt of ash and decay. Injya stepped forward, away from the bear and suddenly felt cold – of course! She was naked! Instinctively she rubbed her arms with her hands and then she turned to face the bear wishing she could return to him for warmth and protection. Looking at him directly she felt that she ought to thank him. She stared at his all-seeing eyes and feeling somewhat foolish, she said aloud: 'Great Bear, I do not know how to thank you for unleashing my memory and cleansing my soul, but from my heart I feel thanks, from my head I feel clarity and from my belly I feel warmth for you.'

The words sounded foolish and very childlike, they echoed faintly round the cave, then dropped, leaden, unheard and unfelt save by her. She looked hopefully into his eyes once more, seeking recognition, but the once all-seeing, all-perceiving brown eyes were glazed and dead. A sudden feeling of defeat came over her as she slowly stumbled towards the light – perhaps all had been a fantasy. Perhaps . . . No! she told herself as she clambered along the difficult narrow passage towards the light. She had hoped before that things were not real, that she was living in a nightmare from which she would suddenly awake. All *had* been real, hideously real, now it was time to leave everything behind – whatever had brought her to this place was, *ultimately*, for her own good, this much she must believe.

The strange grey light which she was struggling to reach turned out to be daylight, refracted along the long, low passage, the one through which, presumably, she had fallen when she had finally found the crone's cave. Half walking, half crawling, she made her way to its mouth and with a deep gulp of fresh air she stood tall again, outside the dismal place. The world before her was white, only broken by odd grey-black boulders pushing through the soft white rain like angry fingers against the sky. She could see in the distance the black outline of a forest and far beneath her, the curling smoke of a lone fire. She shivered. The world, she knew, had not been white when she had stumbled across the cave – how long had she been there? She realized that she should cover herself, but strangely she felt that the cold was merely on the outside, that inside, she was as warm as if she were still crouched in front of the winter fires in her mother's sancar . . .

'No!' she said out aloud to herself severely, 'no, I will no longer think of my mother's sancar, my home. It is no more. And it will never be the same again. I will make it anew. I will bring new warmth and light and safety to our women. It will not be the same. Different and better!'

The final words came as a shock to her – different and better! What was she saying? All that had gone before was destroyed – how could one girl, one fourteen-summer girl, possibly make things different and better?

'Ah, but you can!'

Injya swung round at the words. Askoye stood before her, no longer looking like a collection of dried bones and rags, an old woman, true, but softer and kinder.

'Askoye . . . ! I didn't hear you . . . I . . . ' She blundered to a stop – silly girl, she thought, of course you didn't hear her – she makes no sound!

'Come, follow me, you cannot expect the warmth of the Great Bear to last for ever!'

Injya followed the crone, bending double as they re-entered the cave together. For a moment Injya wondered if they had come to a different cave – she knew that the entrance was the same – but this!

There was a bright fire, kept in its place by a ring of stones, two raised wooden pallets covered in furs, bright

30

wall-paintings and torches burning all round the walls showing at one end a stone table, covered in the whitest cloth Injya had ever seen, on which were placed many beautiful gold, silver and red-coloured objects. Opposite this stone table was a slightly lower wooden one covered in fruit and cooked meats, nuts and berries! The smell of hot, cooked reindeer meat almost made Injya feel faint as she realized that she was ravenously hungry.

'Askoye!' she exclaimed and turned to the crone – 'how?'

'Eat, silly girl, and take up your clothes – it is not warm enough for you to think that it is the summer-lands in here! Go! Eat!'

Injya found her clothes, no longer all torn and bloodied, but clean and smelling of summer herbs. She scrambled into them and then stopped – she was no longer torn or bleeding. She was washed and all the cuts, all those dreadful cuts she had sustained over the journey, were healed. Her courses had ceased, too – she was perfect!

'Askoye—?' she began.

'Eat!' came the reply. ' – Later.'

Askoye did not share any of the food, but she seemed delighted that Injya could eat so heartily, laughing and smiling as Injya could remember her grandmother doing. Finally replete she accepted Askoye's offer and clambered up to sit by her side on one of the pallets. Injya had never sat on such a soft seat – like the back of a snow goose, she thought, warm and safe.

'Injya,' the old woman spoke, her sudden serious tone startling the girl from her reverie, 'I have seen what you showed the Great Bear. It was terrible. But that is a matter for the past and of no consequence here. I watched you escape too – no, let me continue' – her thin hand clutched at Injya's arm as the girl suddenly twisted round and looked at her in disbelief – 'did you think you could summon Oagist all by yourself?' Not waiting for the reply she continued in a voice which scarcely concealed the threat: 'I can only

31

help when the summons is pure – and – I can no more be relied upon than can the spring rains or the summer sun – I too am at the guidance of the Great Mother.'

She sighed and fell silent as if exhausted by so many words and waited for the inevitable accusations to come. It would be hard for Injya to understand – as would be the fact that she had already stayed in the cave for the whole of the moon's dark period. Askoye sighed, remembering how hard it had been for Mensoon, but at least she had *chosen* her path, and not had it forced upon her so brutally as Injya had. She clicked her tongue, the faint clicking of tongues that old women do who are tired of this life, but who are chained to it by unseen links of duty. How many more young men and women would have to pass through her hands before the Goddess would let her rest? She almost laughed aloud as the answer came to her: 'For as long as you ask that question!'

Injya too waited but held her tongue; the words Askoye had spoken had shocked her. If she had seen her escape – why had she not come to her help before? Why had she left it so late? She could have died – she could have been raped or gored to death by that awful Kraa. She shuddered at the thought. And if Askoye had seen her escape, why had she not made it easier for her? Why had not Askoye slain the beast, or uprooted those staves that had torn at her thighs and ankles? A spark of anger against the crone caught light inside Injya, and the flames of injustice and rebellion began to burn around her heart.

Why! It was she, Injya, who had had to hang on to that wretched bull, being torn to shreds on those red-hot spikes; *she* had had to grapple her way up the cloak until she had reached the beast's neck; *she* had been the one to plunge the dangling spears further into his neck until she had been washed with his blood; *she* had done all that, not Askoye – Askoye had done nothing! Askoye hadn't run through that pitch-black forest, terrified by the howling wolves which were maddened by the stench of blood;

Askoye hadn't scaled the sheer face of the dark side of the mountain, pulling off what few remaining shreds of skin she had left on her hands! She hadn't crawled through the wind-swept day on her belly, through the spiked marshlands and the icy rivers, afraid to stand tall in the fear that the mighty wind would blow her from the earth!

Askoye had not shown Injya the way to her cave – Askoye had done nothing! Injya had only found the entrance when she had utterly given up, when she had admitted to herself that her life would end, cut, bleeding, starved and cold on top of that dreadful mountain range. Askoye hadn't even come to her help then – she had tumbled into the cave by mistake, feeling as she did that she was falling into the dark sleep that lasts for moons. Injya believed that her flaming rage would explode inside her, but with a supreme effort of will she kept her peace. She sat, a tight ball of anger and resentment, hating the woman who claimed to be her saviour and her friend, but who had done nothing, nothing to *really* help!

The crone looked at her sideways.

'I know,' she said slowly, 'I know – one day you will understand.'

Injya looked at her, her eyes blazing with the hurt of her injustice, and bit her lip. I am NOT going to cry! she told herself, I am NOT, but her body took no heed of her head and the hot tears flooded down Injya's face.

'I know I am not Mensoon,' Askoye said, 'nor am I your father, but neither am I so far away from this world that I cannot see your pain and feel compassion – come, my child, and cry.'

Injya felt the bony arm reach round her and pull her gently over till her head rested on the crone's lap.

'It is right to mourn the loss of your childhood, but soon you will see the gift in this awful time – you will laugh and love and be healed again – now it is right to mourn.'

And though Injya was fighting with all her strength

against the 'sobs and the tears, the scalding tears hurt her wind-cut cheeks almost more than the hot spikes and the cruel rocks had.

'Bend with the wind of your passion – it will not break your frail body – and you will rise stronger for the bending,' Askoye whispered. 'Allow your fire to burn, Injya, from its ashes new life will grow.'

The tears seemed to have a life of their own. When Injya thought they had finished, they would start again, each sob seeming deeper than the last. Her whole face seemed to ripple, as if each muscle in it was weeping too. And then her throat seemed to judder, as if it too were caught in this paroxysm of pain. She drew a breath and tried to control the flood.

'Let go!' murmured the crone, 'let go – open your mouth – allow the pain to be born and to die.'

Injya opened her mouth and the howling began again, this time deeper than before, as if the sound were coming from the pit of her stomach. Suddenly it felt as if howling was not enough, as if the rage and confusion, hurts and tears were combining their power to tear her apart. She felt stifled and moved herself from the crone's lap.

'Give it to the earth – she can take it,' the old woman instructed.

Injya dropped on all fours and allowed the howling to grow. Instantly it changed, from a hoarse sound which tore at her throat, to a resonant growling roar. Her stomach too now joined in the rippling dance her face and throat muscles were performing. Great waves of nausea flooded over her and her spine seemed as if it would break in two with the rocking and the retching.

'The word! Injya! The WORD!' the crone screamed at her. 'Say the Word!' Enraged beyond all recognition that the old woman would want her to talk at a moment like this she screamed back: 'No!'

Noooooooooo echoed round back at her from the cave walls.

34

'NoNoNo!' she roared. 'Nononononono.' The word kept coming out of her and back to her until she no longer knew or cared if it were herself screaming or the walls replying. 'NO!NO!NO!NO!NO!NO!NO!' Each no getting deeper and louder until Injya felt that the word had been ripped from her very soul and never more would be spoken.

And then, the crying stopped. Almost as easily as they had started, the tears and the sobs ended. Finished. She crouched, death-still, on hands and knees, her head held high.

'Good,' the crone said indifferently, as she swept past her, 'now we can start!'

Injya dropped her head and looked at the pool of water and vomit beneath her. Sitting back on her haunches she realized with shame that that water and matter had not only issued from her mouth. Utterly exhausted she stood up and numbly followed the receding figure of Askoye.

'You must remove all that and bury it – giving thanks to our Great Mother Earth for receiving your pain – do it now!' The old woman did not look at her, but continuing her exit, said sternly: 'I will return.'

Injya watched helplessly as the figure finally vanished from sight. Feeling utterly wretched she turned inwards to the cave once more. It had resumed its former look. The fire was gone, the fine furs and tables, the food, everything had disappeared. Only one smouldering taper flickered dimly along a wall. In the middle of the cave floor lay the body of Injya's grief. She dragged herself towards it, bracing herself to do Askoye's bidding, forcing herself to face her today.

CHAPTER FOUR

Galdr had cursed long and loud when he found Kraa's lifeless body where it had fallen, among the slender ash and birch trees. Kraa, a bull creature captured two summers before, was Anfjord's prize possession – his ruddy coat with its blaze of white upon the spine particularly pleasing to his father. Anfjord would be incensed at his loss. He knelt down beside the carcass which was beginning to freeze and examined the shred of cloth which still clung to the once splendid horns. The cloth showed no evidence of human blood, only dark stains from the gore on the animal. He swore again and stared at the beast – his rutting days were over.

Galdr and his men had encountered little difficulty following the trail left by Kraa and his fellow escapee: broken trees and brambles, blood-spattered ground easily brought him to this spot. He had been sure that he would be seeing the gored remains of Injya lying near by, but there was no trace of her. A few footmarks which trailed off to nothing were the only signs she had left. He clicked his tongue in exasperation and turned to the hunting-party.

'We will have to take him home,' he announced to the four men who were still staring at him from the backs of their horses. 'Make a hyrdel for him and we will tow him back!'

Leaving the men to their work he strode out of the copse and up on to the nearest high rock. From where he stood, he could see the encampment below. He watched for a moment, arms angrily crossed on his chest, lips drawn tight and thin with annoyance, as the smoke of the fires lazily joined the mists of the dawn, then, as if irritated by the pretty scene below him, he stamped his foot and turned around.

Behind him the sheer face of the rock looked impenetrable, its massive boulders black and forbidding. He tried to estimate its size – eighty? A hundred pchekts? More? No-one could scale that – there was not a foothold to be seen. Perhaps she had skirted round it. Impossible, he decided, the shale skree on the other side was almost as steep as its sheer face – two or more footfalls and you would cause a landslide – besides, there was no evidence of footmarks. The other side? He moved slightly and craned his neck. A long way to the right of the face the rock did, indeed, break its shiny surface, but the boulders were a good thirty to forty pchekts high and halfway up there was a fearsome overhanging ledge with giant crystals sticking out from it like dreadful teeth. Impossible.

As he turned to go, something caught his eye. A flash of blue – there it was again! Directly in front of him, two-thirds of the way up the black face of the mountain, a blue bead twinkled at him. Wedged in a crevice – he rubbed his eyes – yes, definitely, a blue bead! The more Galdr stared at it, the more it seemed to wink at him, as if it had a life of its own. He blinked and stared again. The tiny speck of blue had disappeared. There was nothing – it must have been a trick of the light. It could not have been a bead from her shift – it would have been impossible for her to climb that face! He shook his head at the absurdity of his idea. The girl would have set off round to the right of the rock and would have fallen to her death down the ravine or been eaten by wolves – either way, he had more than the loss of a stupid girl to worry about.

When the party returned to the encampment the process of clearing the sancars had already begun. The oldest men and the youngest boys were huddled round the central fire, shivering with the cold and muttering among themselves. The women were taking the skins off the sancars and lying them flat on the ground in readiness to be rolled and secured for the journey. But even in the midst of all this activity, the atmosphere was thick with sorrow as if the women were wrapping skins of grief around themselves and not simply lying skins on the frozen earth. He passed a group of youths who were hacking at the meagre soil to make a grave for the dead women, their heads bowed, their faces averted from his. They did not like what they were doing and as Galdr dismounted and gave his horse to one of his men, he remembered the argument he, Grinvorst and Vingyar had had the previous evening. For some reason best known to himself, Vingyar had seemed more upset by the idea that the women were to be buried rather than exposed, than he had by his only remaining daughter being coupled with and probably gored to death by Kraa!

'If we expose them' – Grinvorst had argued to the old man who seemed to be becoming older by the moment with the weight of the argument – 'their souls will go free and return to the Mother. If, on the other hand, we bury them, their souls will be drawn down to the earth – they will spend their spirit-life with Erlik, King of the Underworld!'

Vingyar seemed not to be listening to the man whom he once had considered one of his closest allies. A far-away look had clouded his eyes. Galdr had spoken, trying to get the old man to understand.

'Vingyar, if we do not do these things, your women will believe that Mensoon will return and we will not have broken their power. We *have* to make them twice dead – only then will the women understand that to try to carry on the old ways would be useless!'

Still Vingyar had stared at the ground, swaying his head from side to side in disbelief.

Galdr had lost patience with him.

'Old man!' he had shouted at last. 'Do you want for ever to be under the control of these women? Do you want the old way to return? Never daring to do this, say that, be this, take that? Do you really want to have to offer libations to the Moon Goddess before you can even dare take breath almost? No. I see that you do not. Vingyar – their true power over you ended when we understood the truth of birth. Ever since then, they have been misting your eyes, trying to keep the power they once had, not through their divinity, but through ignorance. Now we know better and it is our turn. We have the right and the power. Without us the women would be barren. We *have* the power, Vingyar, to rule the way we want, not to take orders from women!'

Galdr saw that the old man understood. Vingyar, once the finest hunter and the most wise among the Gyaretz people, was crying like a baby. As he left his sancar he had turned to Grinvorst.

'Make sure that he *does* really understand, Grinvorst, or we may not be able to spare his . . . '

'I will, I will, Galdr.' The old tokener had interrupted him as he looked with terror in his eyes, from him, back to Vingyar and back to his face once more.

'Trust me,' he had said, fear emanating from every fibre of his being.

Now, in the cold light of day, as he strode through what remained of the encampment, Galdr wondered where Grinvorst had got to with the old fool Vingyar. Before he could reach the only remaining intact sancar, the idiot-boy Halfray came bounding up to him, hopping round and singing his usual gibberish, calling his name over and over again, his mad eyes staring out from his pallid face like pale blue taper-lights.

'Oh, get out of my way, idiot!' He tried to push the youth away with little success, Halfray clinging on to his outstretched arm and wrapping himself, snake-like, around him.

'Thtop! Thtop!' he managed to splutter, showering him in spittle.

'By the heavens!' Galdr stormed at him, finally stopping, 'what is it, half-wit? What are you trying to say?'

He looked at the boy's glazed eyes, wondering if there was any intelligence behind them at all. For a second it looked as if Halfray had forgotten why he had challenged Galdr, then, with a sudden leap he obviously remembered.

'Grinvortht with Menthoon under the earth! He thleepth like the dying and taketh them to Erlik.'

He gave a little shudder, then started his dancing again, releasing Galdr's arm and gambolling away, covering his body with dust and dirt, still singing: 'Grinrotht and Menthoon and Erlik thleeeping. Raven crying, moon dying, thun weeping!'

Galdr looked across at the young men who had been digging the earth and had stopped when Halfray accosted him. Shame-facedly they began their labours once more. Galdr turned his back on them and quickened his pace, brushing aside the two guards to Vingyar's sancar and sweeping in.

'What has been happening here?' he demanded as Vingyar and Crenjal stared up at him. Crenjal rose from his low cushion and, disregarding the question, slowly strode towards the young man, his massive arms wide in greeting.

'Galdr – welcome – you are back sooner than we had anticipated – all is well?'

'No, all is not well, Crenjal – Kraa is dead and Injya is probably at the bottom of a ravine somewhere. Why has Grinvorst been killed?'

Galdr stared up at the older man's face, searching it for the truth. In reply Crenjal put his arm around Galdr's shoulders and drew him further into the sancar.

'Because, Galdr, he could not find it in himself to persuade mighty Vingyar here of the rightness of our argument and also' – he lowered his voice – 'also to show Vingyar and all the Gyaretz people what will happen to them if they do not obey the orders of their chief – Anfjord.'

Crenjal smiled down on the youth and withdrew his arm. Speaking to Vingyar he said: 'You understand now, do you not, mighty Vingyar?' Crenjal smiled at him as the old man's head nodded slowly up and down mechanically.

'There you are, Galdr, Great Vingyar understands and agrees with us – your father will be well pleased, will he not?'

Galdr nodded silently, not taking his eyes off Vingyar. He had only been absent for a day and a night, but in that time the old man seemed to have shrunk and now he seemed dazed by some powerful herb or summer-land wine – or else, shattered by grief, he had lost the will to live. Galdr had not expected such a change.

'My father will share the sorrow you feel, Vingyar, at losing Grinvorst. He was a fine tokener and as you know, our old Colnyek was no match for Grinvorst and his tokening. I feel for you, old man.' Turning to Crenjal he added: 'My father will not be pleased with this, Crenjal.'

'Perhaps not,' he replied, 'but any bad news we bring him must be outweighed by the knowledge that we have at last united our two peoples. You would be pleased with such news, mighty Vingyar, would you not?'

Unseen, the old man nodded his head once more as if only dimly aware of what he was being asked. To add weight to his argument, Crenjal put his heavy arm around Galdr's shoulder once more as he ushered him out of the sancar saying loudly so that Vingyar might hear: 'A small price to pay for uniting our two peoples. Now, following one path, both of our great nations will go forward together to even greater prosperity and happiness.'

Galdr knew what Crenjal was saying to be true, together the two nations had the world for their taking, but as he left the sancar, he too shook his head, trying to rid himself of the dark thoughts which clouded it each time he remembered the pained old face of the man who had once ruled the Gyaretz people with justice and love.

Outside the morning mists were giving way to another bleak, sunless day. The people, silently going about the tasks of dismantling the sancars, cooking their meal and

41

attending to the few wounded among them with very little spirit. They seemed broken and listless, as if the massacre of their priestess and the lack of any real opposition they had shown to such butchery had riven the very life out of them. As Crenjal and Galdr walked round the encampment few greeted them, preferring rather to turn their sullen faces away, either through shame or scarce-concealed hatred.

Coming to a group of women winding skins, Galdr felt a sudden pang of self-loathing. Was the great vision of a united people, striding forth, conquering and claiming the earth as theirs, worth the truculent looks and the sudden hushed voices? Yes! he said to himself yes, it was. The old order *had* to go – it had gone in his tribe – well, almost – he conceded, thinking of his mother Patrec and the secret he had learnt from her, but yes, the old order *was* changing, the women of his tribe no longer practised the rituals of the moon. In one generation after the slaying of their High Priestess, the women had come to accept the true nature of man. For it was man who hunted, man who protected them against the animals of the night, man who impregnated the women and gave them children. The days of the world being ruled by moon-crazy women were over. Now it was the men who chose their women, instead of waiting to be selected by some mysterious ritual held in secret under the light of the moon in one or other of her phases. Now the men chose their partners and a lot more babies were being born. The women were happier, he insisted, they knew that they were protected, they knew that just as in the animal kingdom, it was the males who were the most dominant, the most important, not silly women praying to some unseen goddess in the sky.

Galdr reached the horse svarge and idly stroked his horse's nose while he waited for Crenjal to return from talking to the grave diggers. Crenjal was right, burial was the only way to stop the women hoping for the return of their beloved Mensoon and her sister, Bendula, but he liked it no better for all its rightness. It seemed a particularly cruel way of ensuring death, trapping the soul inside the iron-hard earth, waiting for it to be claimed by Kronos and taken down to live for ever in the underworld, slave of Erlik, King of the Dead, but those had been his father's express wishes so he must obey.

He remembered the story of Bai Ulgan and Erlik, the two brothers who first inhabited the earth. Erlik had quarrelled with his brother, had slaughtered and buried him but Bai Ulgan kept rising from the dead, until in desperation Erlik had cut him into a thousand pieces. But the brothers' mother, Hoola, the Great Mother of the Earth, had rejected the pieces and Bai Ulgan had ascended to the sky and turned into stars. He could not remember all the details, but a flood had occurred and when it had receded, Erlik had been drawn deep into the bowels of the earth and had been kept there perpetually by the power of Bai Ulgan, King of the Universe. If such a thing could happen to one of the creators of the world, was his father totally convinced that Mensoon and her sister would *not* rise again?

His thoughts were interrupted by Crenjal who arrived with several of the Branfjord warriors.

'The women are demanding that the Arnjway Staff is buried with Mensoon – I am unsure what your father commanded.'

For a moment Galdr could not think what Crenjal was talking about, then he remembered the painted staff and the precious stand, the one with the lapis lazuli – how could he forget that!

'Certainly not!' he said decisively. 'The power of the Arnjway Staff might be lessened by us claiming it, but power it still has. Under no circumstances is it to be buried with Mensoon – nothing must aid her, or her kin, in their journey to the under-world. It must be taken home with us, broken into a thousand pieces and each piece buried far apart from its neighbour – only then can we be sure that we have destroyed its power.'

So saying he strode back to the encampment, leaving the warriors and Crenjal to see to the horses.

Again he found himself shaking his head, shaking away the similarity between what Erlik had done to his brother and what his people were about to do with the Arnjway Staff. He thought that it was all superstition, but his father had been most insistent about the destruction of the staff in such a manner. As he neared the people he suddenly felt angry – they looked a pathetic tribe, disheartened women and guilt-ridden men. Galdr's anger grew till he burnt with rage; rage against the men who had not dared to fight (only two young men had raised their swords and they had been felled instantly), but more rage against the women. In less time than it took a cloud to pass over the sky, he and his men had stolen their power and they had only resisted with screams and tears – what of their great power? What of the Great Moon Goddess and her avenging black face? How stupid these people had become! Their Goddess had fled as the very blood of Mensoon had left her body. All was sham!

His anger grew to a new pitch as he looked at the milling expectant people – what use would they be in his father's great tribe? Look at them! Suddenly he turned on them and drew his sword, holding it high. The crowd flinched backwards, gasping.

'You people of the Gyaretz tribe – you "brave" warriors – look at yourselves! You are as dead as that old crone Mensoon! I ask you one question – did She come to your aid? You men – did the power of the Great Goddess fill your bellies with fire! No! She did not, because She does not exist. Look at what this supposed Great Goddess has done to you! You have no spirit, no feeling for the earth, no life – you are but clay! I have freed you from ignorance and superstition, and you are too stupid to realize what a service I have done for you! When we arrive at the home

44

of my father – you will forget all this. The way of the Branfjord people is bright and full of sunshine – you will see for yourselves! I want no downcast looks, no mourning and no shame! You have been released from the power of very evil ones and when we reach our home you will greet Anfjord, my father, as a saviour, not as a conqueror!'

He stood for a moment, arm and sword still held high, uplifted by his own words. One or two of the men had raised their heads and given him bleak smiles, but most of the women still looked to the earth, hushing the children clinging round their legs in fear.

'Ach! What is the use?' He plunged his sword back into its scabbard and stalked off to collect his cape and his prize, the Barnkop stand, from Vingyar's sancar. Behind him the silent people returned to their various duties. He felt his anger return as he approached the sancar; the two guards at the entrance did not salute him – what was wrong with everybody? As he drew closer he saw something odd in the warriors' attitude and one more step confirmed his fears. With panic rising in his throat he realized that they were dead, pinned to their places by swords which had come from inside the sancar. Automatically, he drew his sword and pulled aside the entrance flap, but he was completely unprepared for the sight which met his eyes.

In the centre of the sancar was the naked figure of Vingyar, pinned by the ends of the broken Arnjway Staff. Vingyar had broken the staff, thrust the two ends into the soft earth and at the moment of driving one end through his chin and his brain, he had fallen on to the other piece which had pierced his stomach. His grotesque, skewered body dripped gore and the stench of his ruptured intestines lent further horror to his senses. Galdr felt his stomach lurch in revulsion and for a moment feared it would give way. This news would most certainly anger his father, of that he was quite sure.

CHAPTER FIVE

Crenjal took command of the situation immediately, sending Galdr back to the people who were crowding noisily round the horses, pushing and heaving their belongings on to their backs. He was of no use at the sancar – the boy looked very white and Crenjal doubted that he would keep the contents of his stomach much longer. Fortunately, Galdr did have enough presence of mind not to blurt out his findings to the whole tribe – with Vingyar dead the people would certainly have rioted. Crenjal had silenced the milling hoards and had explained that Vingyar was being granted his wish to spend some time at Mensoon's burial mound and that he and Vingyar would catch the train up when the sun was stronger.

Crenjal knew that his commanding words and assuring smiles fooled the people, but they did not fool him. Vingyar might have been a stubborn old man, but he had been Crenjal's deepest and oldest friend and his sorrow was made worse by the, albeit necessary, lies that he told. With the tribe finally on the move, Crenjal returned to the sancar. He stood for a moment staring at the two guards, who looked for all the world as if they were asleep at their post, the dark stains circling their feet easily mistakable for shadows. Crenjal sighed at the loss of two good men and braced himself for the sight which he knew would greet him, once inside the sancar.

A sudden flutter of something black caught his eye. A great raven had landed awkwardly on top of the sancar. Crenjal eyed the bird with suspicion. The look seemed to be reciprocated, the bird twisting its head this way and

46

that, its ferocious beak opening and closing soundlessly. Raven – carrier of souls. Nonsense!

Crenjal shook his head at the thought – those damned women and their tales! – and he quickly bent over to enter the sancar. At that moment the bird started crying, flapping its scrappy wings and cawing eerily, like a babe in pain. Crenjal straightened himself up and looked again at the bird who was now walking up and down the central cross-beam of the sancar, crowing incessantly. Without thinking he bent down and picked up a stone to hurl at the creature.

'Be off with you!' he shouted, 'there'll be pickings enough in time – be off, I say!'

The bird stopped for an instant and looked at him, its bright eyes looking straight into Crenjal's heart. He responded by hurling the stone at the creature who rose in a fury of cawing, finally taking off and circling round the sancar, head down, still staring at Crenjal.

'Infernal beast!' Crenjal muttered to himself as he went into the sancar. 'Cannot wait a moment longer for his meal!'

With the entrance skin closed, the interior of the sancar was dim and for a moment Crenjal had difficulty focusing. When his eyes became accustomed to the gloom, he wished they had not. The smell and the sight cruelly invaded his senses, robbing him of his purpose and for a while he stood still, stuck between weeping for himself and for his friend, immobilized by his emotions. Mensoon and her children were necessary – but this? He should have judged Vingyar's mood. He thought that he knew Vingyar better than he knew himself; that Vingyar could have so deceived him was almost as shattering as his final act itself. Little reasoning that his own deception could have contributed to Vingyar's death, he found difficulty in comprehending his suicide. He appreciated that Vingyar held Mensoon as a special woman in his life, but he had been taken by *all* the women in the tribe – his offspring were everywhere and, Crenjal convinced himself, Vingyar had taken heart at the news that with the Branfjords he could have as many women as he wanted – and when *he* wanted them. He had brightened considerably at the prospect – why, it would be a better life – he had said so – so why this?

Crenjal looked at the grotesque corpse again, sadness mixing with anger.

'Why?' he shouted at the figure: 'Vingyar – why?' The words seemed to echo round the empty sancar and from the heavens the raven cried again.

Immobilizing his face, gritting his teeth together until his jaw hurt, Crenjal pulled the broken Arnjway Staff from his beloved friend's stomach. Shutting his eyes, he lifted the body from the upright pole which fell with a sickening thud among the spilled viscera. Working methodically he laid out Vingyar on the ground, pulled the other staff out from his skull and wrapped the body in two bear skins, securing the bundle tightly with twine. He laid the cadaver on the low cushions and returned to the Arnjway Staff. He took the two halves outside and rolled them in the short damp grass to clean them – these he put to one side. He felt nothing, he was as cold as he was when dealing with hunted game – an unpleasant but necessary task. He shut out of his mind that this was not an animal that he was preparing for curing or cooking; only the incessant grinding of his teeth, of which he was oblivious, marked any difference between one very mundane act and the one he was bitterly engaged upon.

He worked automatically, removing pole after pole from the sancar until only the main supporting frame was left. He snapped the thick sapling trunks which had made the ribbing, as if they were no thicker than twigs, carried them over to the near-extinct central fire, and stacked them carefully. Next he fetched the now redundant boulders which had served as the pathways between the sancars and from them built four pillars, each equal in height and arranged them in a rectangle round the fire. Going inside the sancar he stripped the skins from the walls and tore apart the remaining ribs. These he lashed together to make a platform which he placed on the four pillars. On top of this platform he carefully criss-crossed the broken sapling trunks and finally he carried the wrapped body of Vingyar over to the pyre and laid it carefully on top of the branches, automatically placing the body so that his head was facing east – the direction of rebirth.

It was this instinctive placing of Vingyar's cadaver in the correct position which finally splintered Crenjal's heart. He knew that at this great moment of death, when the soul would be forever freed to wander the earth, he had truly deserted his life-long friend. Vingyar would have wanted to take the same path as Mensoon, his one great love, even if it meant forever being in the underworld. This Crenjal now understood and it racked his heart with pain as he considered the enormity of his actions.

When Anfjord had first approached him and told him of his wishes to unite the two peoples, Crenjal had only seen the good which could come from such a union; as a larger, unified race they would have the strength of numbers required to sustain the group – they would be able to travel further, explore more and, most importantly, the combined forces meant that they had many more young men to employ mining the metals and precious stones at which, alone, they could only scrape.

But as he gazed at the sight in front of him, surveying his careful handiwork, his mind refused to function any longer. Crenjal could no more remember the words to be intoned to Bai Ulgan, the Great Lord of the Universe, than he could remember suckling at his mother's breasts. With mounting panic and growing desperation he searched his memory, looking up to Por, the sun, for inspiration. But Por was hidden from view, denying him access to his power. For a fearful moment Crenjal thought of the moon – terrible Ahni – black faced now, watching him. He shuddered at the thought. He scanned the heavens, relieved that he could not see her pale face and shook himself vigorously – women's cant! All was superstition and fear – how could the moon guide one's soul . . .? But he wavered and looked again into the sky, torn between relief that he could not see her and helplessness because in that instant he understood the enormous monstrosity of his actions. It was no longer solely an act of fratricide, no longer a desecration of Vingyar's wishes; Crenjal and the Branfjord warriors in one night of butchery had destroyed the power of the Moon Goddess and replaced it with what? . . . Strength in numbers? . . . Miners or metals and stones? . . . Did that matter?

He looked at the mounds of earth which marked Mensoon's and Bendula's shallow graves, at the smaller mounds which covered the three children – they at least were returning to Mother Hoola – they were giving something back – what was he doing but taking? Nothing! He stared again at Vingyar's corpse, and with a sadness he never dreamt was possible, he lit the pyre, watching his ambition of glory and greatness fly to the sky with the sparks and the smoke.

Halfray was the first to notice the thick black smoke.

'Vingyar free!' he shouted, 'Vingyar free!'

The stragglers of the group, the old men and women, lifted their bowed heads in the direction of his pointing arm.

'Stupid boy!' the eldest among them grumbled as he resumed his head-bowed trudge.

'Forek! Forek! – Thee – Vingyar free! Free!'

Forek leant heavily on his staff and turned round once more, lifting his frail white head to the bitter wind.

'What is that idiot talking about now?' he muttered under his breath. With eyes half closed against the cutting wind he looked at the smoke, which was lighter now, billowing, taking on strange, fantastic shapes. The old man was about to drop his head as the smoke took on one very definite form which hovered, motionless in the icy air. It was the form of a large raven, quite still and quite distinct.

Forek stopped dead and stared at the cloud. As clearly as he could see his wizened face in the still pools of the marshlands, he watched the vision of the raven take form and hang, motionless, over where the encampment had been. The image lasted for some ten breaths and then the wings of the beast flapped once and ascended into the greying sky. Forek grabbed hold of Halfray's arm urgently.

'Hush, boy, not a word!' he hissed at him, tightening his grip on his arm, trying to keep the dancing lad still for a moment: 'Not a sound – tell no-one, understand?'

Halfray was struggling to shake off the claw-like hand on his arm.

'Free! Freee!' he shouted, his face alight with joy, his body quivering with excitement.

'Listen, listen to me, Halfray!' the old man whispered, dropping his staff and turning the boy's face towards him with his free hand. 'Listen to old Forek.'

The boy stopped his wrestling for a moment and looked deep into Forek's face. Forek searched Halfray's eyes, seeing an image of himself in their pale blue centres. He *had* to make him understand.

'Listen to me,' he repeated, catching his breath with the effort of will needed to keep Halfray's eyes focused on his. 'If you tell anyone else what we have seen – you will join your mother underground. Do you understand? Crenjal will kill you!'

Halfray's eyes opened wider in disbelief – Crenjal was his friend, Crenjal would not hurt anyone! He stared back at the shaking old man, aware that his arm was beginning to hurt and wanting desperately to turn his head back to the spirit of Vingyar, Vingyar the raven; but Forek held his head firm and scrutinized him so intensely he was unable to move.

The old man was still talking to him but he could not hear the words – he could only focus on the old head, the whispy white hair flying in the wind and from all round Forek's body, he saw deep yellow dancing flames stretching for a full pchekt out from his form. For Halfray, who could see every person's spirit-lights at will, this was nothing surprising, but something new was happening as he watched with fascinated horror as pale blue silken strands came from the toothless cave of Forek's mouth, drowning out his words of warning. The strands snaked from his mouth and, it seemed to Halfray, began curling round his body, binding him to the old man. The threads grew tighter, cutting deep into Halfray's flesh and he felt his body grow rigid. He tried to scream, but his jaws seemed clamped together. He could no longer see Forek clearly, only an extraordinary coloured image, and when Forek's hands let go of his body, he felt the shaking take hold of him. From inside Halfray's body great shock waves forced their way out, rattling against the tight blue strands until the pain became so unbearable that he passed into the realms of the darker side of sleep.

In the blackness which now engulfed him, he saw Vingyar, now the Vingyar he knew as his father, now a greater Vingyar, Vingyar of the Raven-Spirit. He saw Vingyar soar to the top of the highest mountain in the world – the sacred mountain which takes the souls up into the sky, the mountain of Bai Ulgan, above which He presides in his glory, ruling the sun and the moon as the Great Bear of the heavens. And now Vingyar was talking with him, in a language he had not heard before, but which he understood as if it were a language he had known all his earthly life, but had never used.

'I am your guide, Halfray – forever watching over you. You no longer have need of fear on your earthly plain. Know and understand that to all you are still Halfray, Halfray the idiot. Listen to Forek, he will guide you although he will know not how. Forek will sense your powers but will touch them not. Soon you will take the road to the fire-death. You will survive. Vingyar is with you in the realms of the spirit kingdom. Remember – you and I are one. Your inside sight is the reality.'

The words stopped and the vision faded. The silken strands fell away from Halfray's consciousness and a velvet darkness overcame him as he sank, senseless, to the ground.

The trek lasted four days. Men, women, children and horses were exhausted from battling with the winds, rains and cruel rocks. All the time they kept the high range of mountains on their right, stopping often to rest in bleak caves, thankful of the respite yet fearful of waking sleeping bears. Below them black forests, now beginning to be covered in winter's white rain; above them, beyond the mountain's sheltering caves, the land where the white rain never changed, the land of ice and skin-screaming cold. Here, in the middle of the winter-lands, even the mosses and lichens had been carved into razor-edged knives and the winds played constantly their vicious game of hunt the weakest. Numbed by the horror they had left behind, fearful of the terrors yet to come, the Gyaretz people, confused and broken spirited, trudged onwards to join the Branfjords.

Sanset, who sometimes had even had to carry her eight-summer daughter, Bendula, on her back, had often looked backwards during those four days. Where their winter encampment had been had long since been obscured from view, but still she hoped that any moment Vingyar would come riding towards them, Arnjway Staff in hand, shouting that all had been a terrible, ghastly mistake, all would now be put right. But as the days progressed, her heart and hopes grew smaller. Vingyar would no more come back to them than Injya would, all was desolation.

Eventually, they reached the Branfjord encampment. It was very much like their own; a small cluster of low sancars nestling in the lee of the mountain range. This encampment had five large caves which at the moment were still being prepared. Soon the short days of winter would be gone altogether and then every member of the tribe would have to live in the caves, only the hardiest of the young men choosing to stay in the sancars to look after the horses. Even the beasts had to be covered when Por deserted the heavens and blackness reigned in the depths of the midwinter. Soon the very days would be black, as black as the shadow on Sanset's heart, as black as the thin earth which covered her beloved mother and sister and her sweet aunt, Mensoon.

But now . . . Sanset sat in the women's sancar, thankful of the skin-strewn floor and the warm fire as she stared at the sleeping Halfray, willing him to wake, willing him to be well and to come out of the sudden madness which had overtaken him on the journey . . . but now, there was still some light, some hope, and pushing the thoughts of midwinter from her mind, she rose from his bedside and rejoined the women by the fire and set about trying to count her blessings.

Halfray woke and blinked. High above him he could see smoke-blackened rafters from which hung many skins of small animals. The roof was covered in skins and from the square hole in the middle, meagre grey daylight could be seen. He turned his head slowly and looked around the sancar. It was the normal oval shape, but larger than any sancar he had seen before. In the centre was a fire around which many women were attending to the cooking and round the walls more women sat, many cradling children. Some he recognized as Gyaretz women, but the majority he had never set eyes on. The smell of food made him wonder how long he had lain there – he was ravenous! He looked back at the fire and the women: Sanset was among them, obvious in her dark blue woven gown. Most of the women wore dull brown shifts or furs and, as Halfray stared at them, he suddenly understood why they looked

54

so different to any women he had seen before – they all looked timid and subdued.

How long he had lain there or, in fact, where *there* was, he had no idea; but he did know that he felt different. The jangling, dancing spirit inside him had gone. He felt as if he were a new person, as if he could see things clearly for the first time since . . . when? Since he could remember! But he recognized the feeling – he had felt like this before, many moons ago, he had seen and not been afraid. He shut his eyes and concentrated. Slowly memories surfaced, flashes of the crone, the awful bear, the bones through his flesh, the fire. Memories of his initiation came flooding back as he touched his chest. Yes, they were still there, the scars and bumps where the bones had pierced him, where the fire had burnt him, but as his fingers explored his body he felt a new awareness of his wholeness – at long last, after so many winters, he understood that he was master of his own body. When he opened his eyes again, Sanset was standing over him, a bowl in her hand.

'Halfray?' she whispered, crouching down beside him, 'Halfray? I have brought you some broth – can you take it?'

She looked at him with great concern, her big doe eyes full of worry and doubt. Halfray struggled up and rested himself on his elbow facing her.

'My body wants to take it, but my spirit says no!' He looked at the bowl sadly, then said: 'How long have I been here?'

Sanset, taken off-guard by his lucidity, only stared at him.

'Sanset!' he urged, staring intently into her eyes: 'How long?'

Confused, she put the bowl down and looked at his face once more. His eyes were clear, his face calm, he looked – normal! Suddenly she grinned at him and turned, twisting towards the women by the fire, wanting to share her good news with the group.

'Sanset! No!' he commanded her, catching her by her arm and pulling her back down to him. 'Do not tell them!'

'But . . . but . . . you are . . . '

'Well again, yes . . . and no. Sanset, come close – hush!'

He drew her nearer to him and whispered: 'Pretend that you are covering me up or something, do not let them know I am fully awake. Sanset, you must forget all about me – *I* am no longer here – my spirit is filled with the spirit of Vingyar, Vingyar the Raven – he will guide me now. No—' He hurried on as she was about to interrupt him – 'I must not tell you more for your own safety. I am about to go on a journey. I must not eat or drink for a moon's quarter passing. If I come back, all of you will be strangers to me. Trust on Forek. Sanset – Sanset!' He could see the fear and disbelief grow in her face. He clutched her arm intently. 'Listen to me – your name means divine secret – now you have one – keep it well. You must tell no-one what I have said. Go back to the women and tell them that you cannot raise me from my sleep!'

He looked into her confused, sad eyes, desperately wanting to give her a sign, a token of his love for her and all the women.

'Sanset,' he whispered, his voice barely audible, 'I shall leave here soon – fear nothing and tell no-one; Mensoon will live again – have faith!'

He shut his eyes, blocking out Sanset's worried face and fell back into the blackness from where he had come.

Sanset stayed by his side for some time, smoothing the skins over his thin body and wondering if, now that the dancing madness had left him, it had been replaced with a deeper, more profound, insanity. But no matter what little sense she could make of his words, the fact was that his words were lucid. But she was deeply worried – he had lain there for three whole days and nights, without food or water; he was weak and thin already – to undertake a journey now, in the depths of the coldest days, would not only be imprudent, it would be sheer lunacy!

Perhaps that was it – lunacy! The dark power of the hidden moon working in him, perhaps now that the Goddess had been robbed of her Priestess, she was seeking her revenge, sending Halfray into the realms of the dark moon where no man could return. She shivered at the thought. No man can understand the way of the Moon Goddess – few enough women were chosen for that, let alone men – but, her reeling brain tried desperately hard to make some sense of it all. He *is* Mensoon's son, perhaps she could have passed some of her powers on to him, or at least, made it easy for him to understand them.

She felt the heavy stone of sorrow rise in her throat as she thought of Mensoon and Injya, Oonjya and Prisca, Bendula, her aunt, and Freesay, all dead. Mensoon! she wailed inwardly. Mensoon, beloved mother of us all, fall not into the underworld, come back to us! She let go of the grief which she had held like a dark crystal inside her heart for seven long days and the tears started to flow. Rocking backwards and forwards on her heels, she wept long and loud for the woman who had meant wisdom and power to all women. Mistaking her tears of lamentation, several women rushed over to her, thinking that perhaps Halfray too had passed into the spirit kingdom. Once satisfied that he was again only sleeping, they gently led her back to the fire and the oldest woman of the alien group cradled her in her arms, as she had done for so many children and young girls, gently rocking her in her sorrow for the death of her hopes.

CHAPTER SIX

That first winter was the longest in Injya's fourteen-winter life. The bone-drying wind was stronger, the howling nights longer and the screaming animals more terrifying than any other winter she had known. For her first three moons' passing, the days had become shorter until the light seemed only to last for a withering grey-yellow spell and be gone, as if exhausted by its brief life on earth. Injya longed for the time which her people called Aspar, that short period when the sun would waken the earth, covering her in tiny flowers and bringing life to the trees once more. Aspar was when her people would be preparing to go to the low pasture-lands, the sacred time of the new wind, the warm wind from the south, fighting back its bitter northern opponent. It would take but one moon's passing to move the camp and in that moon the Aspar would have gone on its quivering, delicate way, taking its new life higher to the top of the world, until it was reunited with its source, Por, the sun, the warmth of the heart of Bai Ulgan.

But here, far above the trees, it seemed impossible to Injya that Aspar would ever come. As the days slowly lengthened, Injya still could not quite believe that Aspar would have the strength needed to warm the frozen wastes of whiteness, she doubted that such a fragile season could last the journey.

Life with Askoye had settled into some sort of regime although Injya would often be thrown into confusion by the crone's sudden disappearances or arrivals. What continually disconcerted her was Askoye's ability to walk without sound. Mensoon had shown Injya the art of silent walking but, try as she may, some twig or stone always seemed to impede her path, whereas Askoye seemed to float on a cushion of air. She *had* told her that she had lain, senseless, for seven nights when she first fell into the cave and that Askoye had used some very powerful herbs and incantations to heal her – but what herbs, or what words, she would not divulge, saying only that when the time was right, she would know all.

For the first moon's passing, Askoye would not tell anything of her plans for the girl – Injya was to stay and rest – that seemed to be all, although she would allow her to clean and furnish the cave. Injya did this with little enthusiasm, knowing full well that Askoye could do it by her magical power in a thrice. She understood the crone was humouring her, but she pretended not to mind and although Askoye never sat down and actually taught her anything, the very act of moving, cleaning and repositioning the artifacts inside the cave, allowed a natural familiarity to overtake the often first-felt reaction of revulsion at handling bones or skins.

Within two moons' passing, Injya thought no more of moving the sacred Xiols (the tiny animal-skin pouches which contained the dried remains of several of Askoye's ancestors), than she did of rekindling the fire or sweeping the floor. The Great Bear, too, became slowly familiar to her. She discovered that his heavy pelt and head were held erect by a life-size moulding made of clay and horse-hair, and that Askoye herself had been present when the bear had been set free of his life on earth and his soul had returned to the Great Mother.

In a rare moment of intimacy, Askoye had told her about the recreating of the bear and how, for her people the keeping of a bear-cub to maturity, then killing, eating and recreating the bear as if he were alive, was of the deepest spiritual significance. As ever, she would not explain why, nor would she explain what had happened to her people, only saying cryptically that one day Injya would find them for herself. But the gentleness of the concept, that if you treat an animal with the respect it deserves to such an extent that you give it back 'to eat' its own vital organs to help it on its journey to meet its ancestors, touched Injya's heart deeply and often, during the dark winter, she would curl up at the foot of the Great Bear and sense a deep connection with the animal. She fancied that she, too, was somehow being prepared for something which ultimately would bring her veneration – she only hoped that she would not have to die to attain that!

Aspar, when she did eventually arrive, came for an even shorter time than usual and their mountain home was transformed, almost overnight, into an arid desert of searing hot winds and sudden storms. During what now passed for the night, the dancing flames of their ancestors could easily be seen in the sky, awful in their magnificence. Injya had, of course, seen these strange shooting colours before, but never with such clarity as she watched them now. In the dark indigo blue which was the night for this short summer in the mountains, the colours seemed brighter, stronger and lasted longer. Orange flames of the angry warriors, incandescent blues of the girl-spirits, greens of the animals and glorious vermilion reds of the women of creation. Injya could hardly bear to sleep during the times when the spirits played with the invisible stars, but during those long summer days much work had to be done.

She travelled extensively with Askoye, gathering herbs and roots, mosses and barks, returning to the cave after as much as a moon's quarter spent exploring, only to have to sit while Askoye prepared her medicines. Little was explained; she was allowed to watch, with the words: 'When it is right – you will understand more' spoken often.

That first short summer, Askoye taught Injya how to hunt, showed her where she could find the trees to cut her arrows, how to cut and bless the tree, how to bind it afterwards so that its life force would not be harmed and finally how to shape the arrows and bows. She became skilled in carving spears and daggers from bones, cutting her fingers and often weeping at the 'unwomanly' tasks in which she was engaged. But by the time the hot winds turned cold again and the sky once more filled with dark clouds, Injya could hunt as well as any man and had learnt skinning and curing skins, drying and smoking food, and had hunted and killed her first siaga. She had learnt too the way of the fisherwoman so that by the time the second Aspar sent the rivulets of icy water cascading over the mountains, Injya was seen, standing death-still, ankle deep in freezing water, spearing her fish as if she had been born to it.

During that second winter, Askoye had grown weaker and had taken to spending longer inside the cave, hardly venturing out even at the new- and full-moon ceremonies. It was during this time that she had begun instructing Injya in the healing properties of the herbs and roots she had collected that first summer. Askoye had over eleven hundred such plants and remedies, and Injya despaired of ever really understanding the old woman's craft – and even if she did memorize them, she honestly doubted that she would ever be able to diagnose the strange conditions for which they were cures.

But by the time Injya's third winter with the crone had passed, not only did she know all the eleven hundred plants, roots and concoctions, she knew where they grew, when was the most propitious time to harvest and how to prepare the remedies. She had learnt to trust the Great Bear too, going often to him, sitting naked as she had done that first day, and seeing the pictures unfold in her mind which showed her where she should travel or which particular tree to associate with to gain an insight. She had learnt to watch the heavens for signs and portents and she could as easily read the stars and cloud formations as see her reflection in the still pools of summer. And it was as she was watching a still pool one rare windless day in her third midsummer that she saw her brother, Halfray, standing behind her.

She leapt to her feet and swung round, her arms held wide to embrace him, her heart bursting with joy, but Halfray had disappeared! She called his name, running quickly on to a boulder, searching the landscape for his figure, her heart breaking.

'Halfray!' she shouted, weeping, 'Halfray! Come back!'

'Ack!ack!ack!' echoed the mountain tops. She ran to another rise, shielding her eyes from the sun, scouring the sweeping mountainside for another sight of him. The shock of seeing the vision of her brother threw her into chaos. A longing, which she thought had long since died, swept over her like a waterfall of lost wishes. With tears cascading from her eyes she turned and ran back to the pool, urging it to reveal Halfray to her again, the brother whom she had thought, all this while, to be dead. The pool was empty. There was no vision.

Memories of her home life flooded back to her, summer dances, long nights of stories, warmth, physical affection, tender stroking and hugging, loving – oh the loving – the need for loving! She wrapped her arms round her body tightly, hugging herself, yearning for physical love and caressing. Three winters had passed. Three hard, cruel winters of ice and skeletal touches – no warmth, no real warmth ever from Askoye. An occasional touch, a brush of hands sometimes, but always the hasty withdrawal as if touch was something wrong. No love, no genuine love, ever came from the old woman.

She sat, crying until the warm sun on her back finally penetrated her chilled heart and her sobbing gradually died. She felt exhausted by her mourning, bone-weary of keeping hidden the longings of her heart. With a hopeless, resigned sigh she splashed water over her face and arms and sat back on her heels, watching the ripples in the water slowly eddy away, telling herself over and over again that life, Halfray's life, was as insubstantial as a ripple of water, once strong, now weak, now finally gone. Her brother was dead. What she had seen was simply a manifestation of her own longing. She closed her eyes and drew in a deep breath. She must not criticize Askoye, must not surrender to these feelings, must cast them from her; life, her solitary life, must go on. She opened her eyes, about to rise and saw, in the pool, the reflection of Halfray. He was standing behind her again, his hand resting on her shoulder, though she could feel no touch.

This time she did not turn round, but looked into the pool at the vision. She tried to calm her racing heart and look at the picture before her. Halfray had grown into a fine young man, his hair as white blond as hers was raven black, his pale blue eyes shining with love. She was overcome with tenderness – she desperately wanted to speak to him, but was afraid that if she did, he would disappear again. After what seemed an age, she spoke his name. In response he smiled at her again and mouthed her name. She could hear his voice in her head as he said, over and over again: 'Injya! Oh, my Injya!' but she could not hear his voice with her ears, only see his mouth move and hear the words inside her head. She silently replied, hoping that he, too, would hear her words, though none were spoken.

'Halfray,' she said, 'Halfray – where are you? I turned round and you had gone, I came back and you are here. I see your hand on my shoulder, but feel nothing. Halfray – are you dead?'

Slowly Halfray smiled again, his blue eyes unblinking, never leaving hers in the pool, 'No, Injya, I am not dead – my body is "sleeping" at home, my spirit is with *you*. I have mastered the art of soul-walking, although,' – he smiled at her and she heard his laughter ringing in her head, – 'I am not very adept, I *am* finding this talking and showing my body to you very tiring – I might not have much time left, so I must be brief: I have learnt much of the way of the Goddess and I have come to take you home with me – you are needed with our people.'

'But . . .' Injya began, 'but – what of Askoye, what am I to do here? I am not ready yet, I cannot.'

Halfray's reflection seemed to waver for an instant and his voice became weaker.

'I know,' he said slowly and sorrowfully, 'I know – I thought you were ready, but, as you say, you are not. Askoye is old, she is taking long with you, but that cannot be avoided – I am sorry to cause you distress.' He laughed suddenly and ripples scattered the image into a thousand dancing crystals.

'I am too young and do not have the discipline of my father! Injya, I must go, I am becoming tired – watch for me in the pools and the songs of the birds – I will do all in my power to help you grow, but then, I am still learning too!'

With another quick, playful laugh, the image disappeared and the pool was once more still, deep and empty.

Injya sat, looking into the pool, long after the red sun had fallen behind the mountain top and the deep violet of the short night chilled her skin. Tonight there were no dancing flames of spirits in the sky to lighten her heart, no brilliant display of gorgeous colour, cutting swathes of hope across the sky. She heard Askoye call her name once and then the air became still, only the occasional calling of snow grouse to her young or the slow cry of a startled peewit, broke the quiet of the night. Once, a dark shadow on the pool sent ripples of fear and hope through her slender form, but it was only a silent-winged owl, searching the mosses and bobbing flower-heads for prey.

She wanted to cry, but her eyes were dry. Was what she had seen an apparition or reality? Injya had heard of 'soul-walking', but when asked, Askoye would never elucidate, only answering with: 'When the time is right.' Suddenly Injya understood why she could not cry – it was not because there were not tears there, but because they were tears of anger. All this time, three years, and Askoye had only shown her the uses of plants and how to hunt fish and deer! She was Mensoon's daughter! Mensoon, the High Priestess of their people – she had a right to know all that her mother had known – and more!

As she allowed the frustration inside her to grow she tore furiously at the innocent grasses around the pool. She had been shown the rites of the Priestess-ship, she argued with herself, but most of these she had known already; the full-moon ceremony where all the women of the tribe would sit in the open, drinking in the power of the Goddess, attuning themselves to the heavenly outpouring of divine white light, cleansing themselves of their troubles. She knew all about the quarterly moon dances, where all the women would dance around moon-wise, placing in the centre of their circle the appropriate totem; for spring, the Arnjway Staff of fecundity; in midsummer, the berries and nuts of the summer-lands; in the beginning of winter the carved wooden figures of their ancestors so that their spirits would forever be remembered and happy to stay with Bai Ulgan, and in the depths of winter the fire of the God Ipirün, to ensure that the sun would come once more to bless the earth with its life-giving heat.

Now, she was tearing great clods of earth and hurling them into the pool, rage surging inside her as she mentally continued the liturgy of what she did know: the new-moon rituals, the shining hope of each new course; the half-moon, the dangerous time for hopes, the time for care against quarrels; the full moon, the strongest outpouring of energy; the waning moon to which you gave your doubts and fears; and now the dark moon.

'The dark moon!' she shouted to the pool as her anger reached its zenith: 'The time where Ahni Amwe wears her avenging face, when all women bleed their sacred blood on the earth in remembrance of the Great Flood which Ahni Amwe in her rage sent to the earth to rid it of its evil ones. The Goddess gives and the Goddess takes away! And I too, will take away, I too will leave you, Askoye, old crone! Neither you, nor any person on this earth can make me stay! I shall go! I shall go to my people – I *shall* see my beloved Halfray in the flesh once more, I shall!'

The anger of her words could not mask the meaning from her soul – it was Halfray and her kin that she missed, not any hidden knowledge or the great secrets which the crone might know, it was simple homesickness. It was that feeling which stopped her shouting and hurling soil at the silver pool and which made her weep afresh. She fell to the ground, sobbing for her brother, her mother, her sisters and for the very earth which she had so unjustly torn apart. She wept until the first pink flush streaked across the sky and the animals and birds woke to the new day. Exhausted, cold and damp, Injya got up from the dew and tear-wet grass and walked slowly back to the cave resolving that today would be her last day with the crone.

CHAPTER SEVEN

The cave was deserted when Injya reached it. Dead ashes and stale smoke mingled with the atmosphere of desolation. There was no sign of Askoye, no trace of food having been eaten nor of her pallet having been slept on. Injya stood by the cold wood ash and surveyed the scene, turning slowly round to look at what had been her home for three winters' turning. Despondency and loathing surged up in her and crept over her skin like a slug. How she hated this place! She stared at the dead fire – like all my hopes, she thought, like all my hopes.

Hunger and the need for comfort drove her to light the fire – she could have lit one outside, the day was bright, sunny and virtually windless, but she wanted no sun to lighten her feelings, no bird-song to rob her of her resolve. She had to leave and now was as good a time as any. She kicked at the fire and a reluctant flame licked a dead log, then petered out. Crossing over the cave she found some smoked fish she had wrapped earlier in hide – the beginnings of their precious winter rations. She ate the fish in a disinterested way, hoping that perhaps the food would give her new heart, energize her to collect together herbs and dried foods, to robe herself for a journey. But instead, the fish seemed to stick in her throat and weigh her down, adding to her feelings of heaviness and loathing. She sat, huddled by the smoking fire, knowing that she would be warmer outside in the sunshine, but with the obstinacy of self-pity, preferring the meagre, poorly-drawing fire rather than make the effort to move.

Staring dully into the glowing embers she gradually became aware of another glow over on the far side of the cave wall. She kept trying to ignore this second 'fire', but in the end, curiosity overcame her and she reluctantly went towards it. As she drew closer she realized that it was the black obsidian mirror.

'Ach!' she said aloud in annoyance, 'that thing!' In all the time she had been in the cave, it had been the one article with which she had not become familiar. The memory of her first encounter with it, when it had reflected back at her that ghastly apparition of bones and flaming red eyes, still haunted her. Now she looked with renewed loathing at its black face.

'I certainly will not take *you*!' she said and turned to go back to the fire. The fire, which moments before had been dying red cinders, was out. Not a curl of smoke, not a single spark remained. Whirling round she looked at the mirror. In its centre was the fire. Panic. She turned again: the fire was out. She turned back. The fire was there. Bright red and violet flames danced before her eyes. Gingerly she put a hand towards its face. There was no heat coming from it.

Not believing her eyes she looked again towards the fire. It was definitely out. Reluctantly she looked back at the mirror, its 'reflected' fire still burnt brightly. Taking a deep breath she lifted the mirror from the ledge and trying not to look at the image, tried to force her brain to evaluate it simply as an object. The mirror itself was only half a pchekt tall and less than a third wide, but that in itself was remarkable. Her mother had used a tiny fragment of obsidian herself, tiny slivers of the shiny material were to be found dotted all over the skree slopes of the lower mountain range, but a whole piece like this was a rarity. It was flawless, its normally dense face silent and haughty as if it knew that it had been there since the beginnings of time and would be, until the earth was old and withered. It mocked the looker with its sense of history. Injya now stood in front of it, no longer able to stop herself watching the skittering flames, unable to see her reflection, seeing only the orange, red and blue picture unfolding itself before her eyes.

The flames danced their glittering fire-dance. No longer afraid, Injya watched in fascination as the flames sparkled before her, drawing her into them. Her head started to reel and she felt that she was being sucked into the very heart of the fire. A moment of terror as her spinning mind tried to fight back the inevitable and then the magic became the reality. Injya *was* the mirror! She could see her body, standing there in front of her, looking vaguely uncomfortable and uncertain, but the real Injya was inside the mirror, looking out.

A moment of blackness and then a new realization. She was no longer in the cave, but on the top of a very tall tree, from where she could view the whole world. She did not feel frightened by this sudden transformation, she felt nothing at all, as if it was the most natural thing in the world. Her body seemed to be that of a small brown bird, not a bird she could recognize, or even one she had seen before, but she felt safe and strangely happy to have acquired this form. She sat on the tree for a while, looking at the earth below her, watching tiny people scurrying about. The people looked strange to her, squatter than her own tribe, each having long jet-black straight hair and high cheek-bones; their wide, full lips never parted in smiles as they ceaselessly went about their labours.

Each one of these individuals seemed to be carrying the same thing – small round parts of a painted log. Their task seemed very arduous, because although these pieces of wood were small, they appeared immensely heavy. Injya watched, fascinated, through her tiny, round brown eyes as these minute people carried their loads, ceaselessly, back and forth, to a gaping hole in the earth, never dropping the heavy pieces of wood, never placing them anywhere, as if they were showing the hole in the earth that they had them, and then taking them away again.

Injya decided that however strange all this was, she had to try to get a closer look, and knowing and yet not knowing that it was achievable, she flapped her tiny wings. With her fluttering heart beating wildly with excitement, she momentarily faltered and then flew, straight down the tree, wheeling round its massive trunk three times, until she came to rest on the earth.

The strange people, who were, indeed, very small, even to a tiny bird, took no notice of her as she hopped and fluttered among their milling feet. Slowly she came to the edge of the hole, crowded as it was with silent people and looked in.

The sight which met her eyes made her heart lurch. At the bottom of an enormous abyss was a monstrous figure. Instantly she knew that this was Erlik, King of the Underworld. His head, that of a man, and body – which was composed of various parts of a horse, a lion and a mammoth – was covered in huge, fish-like scales. Each glistening scale barely covered the squirming body of a human being, trapped forever like a louse, close to that awful beast. His body quivered and shook with rage as if trying to rid himself of his loathsome lice. His six legs stamped the ground, pummelling the quagmire of human remains into a stinking cesspit as his tail lashed round at the sides of the hole which were encrusted with skeletons, which still seemed to be alive, their bones shaking and dancing as the awful tail smote them continuously.

The sounds which these poor souls made rent the air with anguish and pain, but it could not drown out the sound made by Erlik himself. From his mouth issued forth high-pitched screams and deep barking sounds, like those of a wolf being gored by a lion. Sickened, Injya turned on her thin legs and hopped away from the pit. That was Erlik! That was where the soul of her mother would be – condemned to live in that infernal pit for ever! Her heart lurched at the thought and with a great effort of will, she took flight again.

This time her wings did not seem to move as effortlessly and she had only gained the first of the branches of the tree before she felt exhausted. She perched for a moment, regaining her strength and studying the solemn people. It looked as if there were a thousand or more poor souls engaged on this seemingly thankless task of carrying the wood to and from the hole, and as she stared at them, slowly the recognition dawned on her: the pieces of wood were the pieces of the Arnjway Staff! They were carrying the broken staff of the Moon Goddess! They were labouring under the weight of the shattered power of Ahni!

The sudden knowledge gave her strength. She turned her body on its branch and stared up at the tree. Suddenly it no longer appeared like a normal tree – it was a birth tree, but that was where the resemblance to anything she had known ended. It was truly enormous. Its top was out of sight, hidden in the clouds, but it had only seven huge branches! In between these were cuts in the bark, seven between each branch and for the first time she saw the nests, resting precariously near the ends of the branches, each containing shining opalescent orbs, the harbingers, the very essence of lives yet to be born.

She realized this was the tree of life, the tree whose roots stretched down into the deepest part of the earth, and whose top reached into Bai Ulgan's kingdom. The shining orbs of light in the nests were the souls waiting to be incarnated, the souls of those who, through their love for mankind, had decided to incarnate in human form once more, to serve man for their highest good. It was up this tree that Injya had to fly to fully understand her purpose, and, as a tiny bird, smaller than the smallest wren, she was more overcome, more terrified of this, than any view that Erlik could show her.

She stayed for some time, mesmerized by the sight of the hundreds of shining soul forms. As she stared at them, she saw that nearly every one had a very slight imperfection, some had a slight shading, a darkened spot among the clear pearl white, while others had tiny dark crystals embedded in them. Very occasionally she could see one which was pure; these pure souls seemed brighter and lighter than the others, but strangely they felt less 'urgent' than the others, less immediate, less vital – as if their total purity lessened their longing for rebirth – they had a quiet compassion about them, an air almost of happy resignation.

A hard wind suddenly rocked the tree and Injya felt her feathers ruffle uncomfortably. A great black raven had landed on her branch and stared at her, its bright eyes transfixing hers with a stare as immediate and forceful as the very wind itself. Without hesitation, Injya went up to the raven and rubbed her head under his breast. She understood that this was Vingyar and her heart was filled with longing and love. She waited, impassive, for his thought-words to fill her mind, for him to tell her of his journeys, his death on earth, his life now, but he remained silent.

He dropped one wing low down on the branch and Injya understood that she was to climb up on it. She did so and settled herself safely on his back, her tiny wings and claws holding firmly on to the raven's body. Together they flew to the top of the tree and as silent as he had been throughout their journey he left her with no words of explanation, no words of love and no help for the rest of her journey.

He might not have spoken to her, but his very being seemed to be inside her tiny bird form. She felt immensely powerful, able to fly through the top of the heavens if needs be. She stared upwards into an array of stars and clouds which were endless, upwards into the very soul of Bai Ulgan, into the heart of Ahni, the Great Mother Moon. Injya thought she would die with happiness. Never before had she felt such ecstasy, such wholeness. She longed with all her heart to remain there, in the sight of the stars and the moon, bathing in the glory and power of the heavens, for ever. But no sooner had the longing filled her being, than she felt a great wrenching pain in her stomach and felt herself falling, through a vortex of blackness, back through the sky, through the clouds, through the earth and down, down, into a tiny form of a girl, some seventeen summers old, who was still standing, looking blindly at a blank and enigmatic mirror.

Askoye walked round the droopy, dusty strands of her web until she reached the centre. Never taking her eyes from Injya's body she rested on her web and got her breath back. She had tried very hard to follow the journey which Injya had taken, but her powers were diminishing by the moment, or so it seemed, and her attempts to go through the mirror had only resulted in a jumble of spells and incantations, the resolution of which was her present shape. Askoye was not worried – she trusted implicitly that she would resume her former shape when the time was right, but she was angered at her failing memory and apprehensive that it would be this that would rob her of her final commitment to the Goddess.

She knew that she had left it too long to instruct Injya in the way of the drum, the mirror and the soul-walking, but, she forgave herself, but she *was* old and her secrets *were* her only reason for still clinging to this life. To pass *all* her understanding of the secret ways on to Injya meant that she had to come to terms with the fact that her time on the earth plane was nearing its end and although there was no fear attached to her body's passing, a certain annoyance at the very inevitability of it all had overtaken her these last two winters and had made her hold back those things which she knew were imperative for Injya's growth.

As she sat, dirty and dusty in her web, watching the girl begin to move again, she wryly smiled to herself – why, the old Goddess still had things to teach her, wise as she was! Life was nothing more than life-long learning and now it amused her somewhat to think that even at her advanced age, new lessons were being taught. She watched as Injya shook herself and then touched the mirror; she gazed impassively as Injya felt her body all over, patting and smoothing her singlet, feeling her strong thighs, pinching her face and even pulling her toes! She hoped that whatever journey Injya had travelled on, whatever she had witnessed, she was not disturbed by it and as she thought this, she felt a pulling in her heart – a small ache which she thought had been buried many moons' passing – the ache of love for another human being. That ache brought on the often felt itching which she knew was the sign that she could change shape once more and so she thanked the spider for allowing her entrance to itself and re-inhabited her old form which was lying, on her pallet, as dirty and as dusty as the spider she had just left.

Injya was still standing in front of the mirror, feeling her body and touching now her hair, now her nose. She seemed oblivious to Askoye's presence and totally absorbed in her minute inspection. She looked pleased with what she found and Askoye knew, as she watched Injya, that soon she would be leaving her. If I taught her nothing more, she thought, the need for a man would soon overtake her.

Injya had indeed grown into an extraordinarily beautiful young woman – inheriting as she did her mother's pale skin and deep blue eyes and her father's tall, athletic body. Her eyes were wide apart, brow high and clear, and she had the high cheek-bones and somewhat square jaw-line of her people. Her mouth was full and wide, and when she smiled, the parted lips revealed white, even teeth. She was very tall for a maiden and although her frequent hunting and fishing exploits made her arms and legs muscular, she still retained her womanly roundness, hiding her strength in a deception of downy silk. Her curled raven-black hair hung in cascading waves down her long straight back, almost reaching her buttocks and framed her swan-white face and body as surely as the night frames the fragile stars. She was, indeed, a stunning young woman. Askoye involuntarily sighed as she appraised Injya

74

thus and, startled at the sound, Injya swung round, a gasp of surprise escaping from her.

'Come here, child, and tell me all.' Askoye motioned with her arm and patted the pallet beside her. Defiance blazed from the girl's eyes. 'Do not be angry with me, Injya – I am too old for your anger – come, tell me what has happened.'

'I thought you knew everything!' Injya sneered. 'You do not need me to tell you – you have seen it all, surely!'

She tossed her head and turned back to the mirror again.

'I am old, Injya, I have seen nothing. I tried to reach you, but all that happened was that I ended up in a spider's body! All I could do was make sure no harm came to your earthly form and wait. I no longer have the power to soul-walk, my child, not any more.'

There was a certain fragility, a certain pleading tone in Askoye's voice, which alarmed Injya. She had never heard Askoye ever say she could not do something – to everything Askoye had always said: 'If you want it enough and it is in the Divine Plan for you to have it, all you have to do is want with purity in your heart and it shall be yours.' Now, here she was, acting like any old woman. Injya softened and walked over to the crone. As she looked down on her she saw something which she had forgotten, the eyes of an old woman near death, like the eyes of her grandmother – soft, slightly clouded, slightly watery and gently appealing. Her heart melted, the anger gone, as tears of compassion sprang to her eyes.

'Askoye,' she said, 'Askoye – what is it?'

The old woman looked up at her again and said quietly: 'Ask no more questions, Injya, I am old and tired and I yet have much to teach you. I must save what strength I have for that. You must learn to weigh every word and every question. With someone as old as I, the time for chatter is over. Now, tell me, where did you go and what did you see?'

It took far into the night to tell Askoye everything and often Injya was afraid that the crone had died while listening to her story; her breathing seemed so shallow, her eyes so sunken into their sockets. But each time she did ask a very carefully thought-out question, the answer came strong and intelligible – as if Askoye was, indeed, saving her strength for this final instruction. Injya had been right, she had ascended to the World Tree – a feat which greatly impressed Askoye, for Askoye told her that only very advanced souls or souls who had spent entire lifetimes learning, ever reached such an exalted state of awareness. Injya was heartened to learn that Askoye firmly believed that Mensoon was not with Erlik, but was reunited with Vingyar; 'Otherwise,' she had said, 'who would have stopped those poor creatures giving Erlik what he wanted – the Arnjway Staff – only Mensoon could have power enough to stop them hurling the sacred staff down to him.' But she was unable to help Injya when she asked why, if Mensoon was alive in spirit form, would she not disclose herself to her as her father had, replying only that: 'The ways of the Moon Goddess are not for questioning.'

As the light coming from the mouth of the cave changed to pink, heralding another day, Askoye told Injya that she had known of Halfray's miraculous recovery, but that she had seen in a vision that Vingyar the Raven-Spirit was overseeing his initiation into the mysteries and she had kept her distance, choosing instead to appear to an old man, Forek by name, in a series of dreams which she knew would be passed to Halfray. Eventually they both fell asleep as the morning sounds turned into a slumberous afternoon.

Injya woke after a very deep, dreamless sleep. From the mouth of the cave came a deep orange glow – the day was drawing to a close. Rising stiffly and carefully so as not to disturb Askoye, she gently placed some twigs on the fire and blew on to it quietly. In a few seconds the fire hissed, crackled and came to life. Injya rubbed her arms, she felt chilled and very hungry. On tiptoe she crossed to the ledge where they kept their dry store and was just about to put a handful of nuts into her mouth when Askoye stopped her.

'You must eat nothing – put those down!'

The stern, hard-voiced Askoye had returned and Injya knew from her tone that she was summoning the last of her strength.

'Fetch me my drum!' she commanded as she got up from her bed. Injya took the heavy drum off the cave wall and blowing the dust from its rim, noticed a small dried-up body of a spider fly through the air and fall, noiselessly, to the ground. When she turned round with the drum Askoye had undergone a total transformation. She was dressed in a collection of skins, each one covered in symbols and feathers, bones and animal tusks. She had on her head a small woven cap which Injya had never seen before, which was decorated with a picture of the sun on one side and the moon on the other. From this cap hung a long strand of twine, itself carrying feathers and a collection of stones which cascaded down Askoye's back like vertebrae. Feathers also adorned the hem of her garments as did the pelts of many small animals. Injya had to suppress a sudden desire to laugh – Askoye looked like the contents of a jackdaw's nest!

'Come here, Injya, and place the drum on the ground near my feet.'

As Injya drew nearer she could see that the shift was only one singlet, with long sleeves and not many as she had previously thought. It had looked as if there were many garments, as on the front of the singlet and along the arms were paintings which represented the skeleton of the wearer, which, in the weird orange light and dancing firelight, she had mistaken for differing layers. As she inspected Askoye closer she realized that the decorations on the singlet were similar to the markings on the drum: spirals, serpents, antlers, star and moon shapes, but all slightly obscured or altered deliberately to confuse the looker. Injya's desire to laugh vanished as quickly as it had come – this singlet, which she had never seen before, was a manifestation of a part of Askoye which was of the profoundest importance.

Askoye watched Injya scrutinize her and her clothes, then bade her to sit at her feet. She bent over to pick up the drum and hesitated momentarily – she truly did not know if she had the stamina for this, the final part of Injya's initiation. Injya glanced up at her, her fresh, open face clear and pure, hand ready to pass her the drum, trust shining from her innocent eyes and Askoye felt the slender golden cord which had imperceptibly joined her heart to that of Injya's fall away. Instead of picking up the drum she touched Injya's head, smoothing her glossy hair and said simply: 'Close your eyes, girl. Wait until you hear a leaf fall, then put on the clothes and drum. The power is yours.'

Askoye heard herself say these words, saw Injya obediently close her eyes and felt only mild surprise. So, *this* is what the next step is! How extraordinary! Slowly and silently she removed her clothing, the clothing she had spent three summers keeping from Injya's sensibility and allowed herself one look at the girl. She sat, face still upturned towards her, eyes patiently, unflickeringly shut, simply waiting. For an instant the word goodbye formed in her mind, but she knew that there was no goodbye. Without a sound she left the cave and paused momentarily at its mouth, then descended the rise to find the tree which would take her to her mother, Ahni Amwe, protectress of all life. To her surprise, she felt pain in her feet as she walked, naked as a babe, down the bare mountainside, but after a little while, the pain stopped. As soon will this heartbeat, Askoye thought, as she walked through the dappled late evening sunlight towards her future home.

With her eyes closed, Injya heard the singlet fall to the floor and then nothing save the crackling of the fire. She too felt something fall away from her heart, but she did not know, or care, what it was. For a long time she sat, eyes darkened to the outside world and then something touched her hand. It was a curled, brown oak leaf. She knew before she opened her eyes what it was. She knew also that the nearest oak tree was some three days' journey away. She knew, too, not to be surprised.

CHAPTER EIGHT

Injya waited, staring at the oak leaf, listening for the sound she knew would never come. She hoped that the leaf was Askoye – that once again the crone had taken on a form not her own – but she knew it was a vain hope. She felt curiously unemotional – she ought to have felt like weeping at her loss – or happy that she was now free. But she felt nothing as she stared at the curled brown leaf. Eventually, with a sigh only half-regretful, she allowed the leaf to fall from her hand and got up. Askoye had told her to put on the clothes. This much she had to do.

She put on the curious singlet, adorned her head with the cap and sitting cross-legged on the floor, began beating the drum with the carved bone which had been placed on its face for that purpose. Without knowing why or how, she began to beat the drum slowly and rhythmically. It made a curiously dead sound as if the beat was not carried on any ordinary air, but kept itself somehow inside the very drum itself. The cave did not respond either, its friendly echoes silenced. The light from the mouth of the cave turned from orange through magenta, to violet and as if the very light itself was directing her, the tempo of the drum slowly increased. The drummer and the drum were becoming one and as the rhythm became faster and faster, Injya began to feel the power of the animals whose many pelts adorned the hem of the singlet, grow in strength.

Quicker and quicker the drumming became, the drummer now absent. The stars and the moons, the suns and the bones, began to inhabit her, bringing with them their mysteries. Injya wanted to dance, every atom of her being ached to dance to the drum-song, but she was restrained by a power which she could not understand – another force was working through her which she did not fight – her trust in the divine was total. Suddenly she knew that she should stand. Still drumming she got up and immediately the turning began for her. Just as the drum was drumming itself, the drummer being absent, so the dance too was dancing, but *she* was not there. Round and round she swirled, still drumming, the beat faster than her flying hair, quicker and surer than her stamping feet. Around in her head flew the animals and symbols of the singlet, faster and faster came the song of the drum. Injya felt again the ecstasy she had experienced with Bai Ulgan; knew again the oneness of the universe.

In that moment the drum dropped. The silence was absolute. Then the power began.

She realized that she was possessed with the spirit of an animal. Injya knew that she was no longer Injya, but a proud bull reindeer – she could feel his weighty antlers, knew his sure feet and strong back. Lifting her head she roared the reindeer cry to the roof of the cave and as she let the sound escape, she heard the animal-spirit respond.

'I am the spirit of Ch'ankwé, I will give to you the strength and endurance of my thick coat in winter and my proud rutting strength in the spring. Call me when you are needing – I am part of our universe!'

No sooner had she heard these words and understood the language of the reindeer, than another beast entered her, this time a white wolf, silent and cunning as the frost in winter; to her he gave sight in the dark and the ears to hear a thousand pchekts distance. She became possessed by animal after animal; now a hare giving swiftly running feet; now an eagle, giving her the greatest gift of all – flight. Round and round her body still danced, the dance without the dancer. The bones on her singlet spoke to her, showing her the ways of the dead, revealing to her the realms of the underworld where she would have to travel to find the souls stolen by the forces of darkness, allowing her to see the great rivers she would have to cross to bring back the spirits of the sick. As the beings were leaving her, as the dance was dying, she saw at last Mensoon, shining from the centre of a full opalescent moon, her face serene, her eyes radiating tender love. She had no words for Injya and Injya asked no questions as slowly the vision faded and the dance quieted, until the dancer fell into a deep sleep.

When the winds turn around and the sky is riven with grey-legged geese, when the cotton grasses dance wildly and the red moon sinks low, then winter is about to bite your heels and dry your bones. Injya could read all the signs, knew well enough that soon the clouds' tears would turn white with sorrow at the passing of the brief, hot summer, but she felt incapable of moving. Since Askoye's disappearance Injya had been overtaken by a sadness which she likened to the colour of long-dead wood – deep brown and mournful. She felt that she was infused with a stale, dark heaviness which left her listless and lifeless.

After the first week of frantic searching for Askoye's body, Injya had returned to their cave, hope dying in her. A mood of desolation enveloped her and although she knew that she should move, quit the cave and say the unspoken goodbye to her mentor, she felt unable to act. It was as if, having been granted her freedom, she now could gain no real sense of it. She could not find that feeling of oneness that she had only so recently experienced. Her sense of isolation, instead of making her yearn to find her people, only made her want to stay in the warm, womb-like safety of her cave. She remained, not daring to hope for a sign or a return, just waiting, sitting and waiting. What she waited for she had no clear idea – she did not *expect* anything, nor did she look for anything, she was immobilized by her own inaction.

She did the absolute minimum – she did not harvest the few remaining fruits of the summer, nor catch and dry fish and game for the coming winter. She ate little with the result that her body took on a dried look; her firm, brown arms and legs looking cracked and parched, her magnificent hair taking on a dull, matted appearance. She no longer cared for her body or her soul; she felt consumed by darkness. She would sit in front of the Great Bear for long stretches, hopelessly looking into his all-seeing eyes, and she broke the habit of seventeen summers by disregarding the rituals of the full moon for two whole moons' passing.

It was as the third full moon shone, cold and bright, that Injya finally came to her senses. Since Askoye's disappearance she had taken to sleeping at the feet of the Great Bear and as she tossed and turned, listening to the gathering winds outside and the howling of the wolves far below in the valley, a tiny flicker of hope grew in her heart. Perhaps her *own* mother could help her, perhaps the Great Mother of all could help ease this pain of dank torpitude? She almost dismissed the notion as quickly as it had come, choosing instead the path of inertia, but the flame persisted, and with a feeling tantamount to annoyance, she rose from her crumpled bed and wandered aimlessly over to Askoye's pallet.

Disconsolately she fingered the garments piled upon it; the full-length moon-ritual gown, the shorter shift of the animal powers. She picked up the heavy dark blue over-shift which she had so painstakingly woven that first summer with Askoye. Memories of its making came back to her as she felt its weight, remembering her aching fingers as she had struggled to separate the strands from the birch bark, how she had soaked and dried the gelatinous mess, never believing Askoye's insistent urging that it would, in the end, come out as manageable silken twine. She had spent long back-breaking hours combing the dull threads and weaving them, only to find them all falling apart because she missed one or other complicated process. Her mother had woven all their garments from rabbit fur – a process which seemed comparatively easy compared with this. But she had persisted and eventually the long, heavy fabric was ready for dyeing. Again, Askoye would not allow her to use saxifrage flowers or bilberries – she insisted on dyeing it with a strange leaf which had to be fermented in urine! Injya suddenly remembered the smell of that dye and once more she felt the anger rise in her – Askoye had made her do so many things which she could not understand and which she would not explain!

She lifted the moon-gown high and it fell heavily over her slender body. In the dying light of the fire the beautiful silver crescent moons and brilliant star shapes Askoye had magically sewn into it seemed to leap out at her. Her dress looked as black as the interior of the cave, but the symbols gleamed and glistened, making her feel almost giddy. She picked up the woven cap she had worn when she had drummed, staring, mesmerized at its shining crescent moon crest and intricate woven pattern. Since Askoye's disappearance, she had wanted desperately to wear something of hers – the cap, the singlet which had shown her animal powers – but each time she had approached any of these sacred items something had stopped her; now as she fingered the cap with its long trail of bones and feathers, she knew that it was right for her to wear the moon-gown and the animal-cap together.

Injya brought herself up to her full height and inhaled deeply. The long-forgotten rush of energy immediately came to her aid and she stood, eyes closed, breathing slowly and consciously, nourishing herself in the feeling of power that the garments gave her. After a few moments she stepped cautiously outside the cave and stood at its mouth, bathed in full moonlight. The night was crisp, bright stars seemed very near and the shining, radiant moon stood full above her head, bathing her in its glory. Lifting her arms to the heavens she began the long incantation to the Goddess, the secret and sacred words coming easily to her mind, the sounds issuing forth as if coming from her soul, flowing from her

84

heart, as the rivers flowed joyously to the mother sea in the summer.

Oblivious of all around her she allowed the song to the moon to grow from her yearning spirit:

> Ahni Amwe, Ahni Oomwha
> Beloved Goddess, Ahni Amwe,
> Come to my soul, oh Ahni Amwe
> Come to my soul, oh Ahni Oomwha.
> Ahni Amwe, breathe your light,
> Ahni Amwe, breathe your life,
> Ahni Amwe, stir your waters,
> Ahni Amwe, stir your power.
> Ahni Amwe, fill your daughter,
> Ahni Amwe, fill your beloved,
> Ahni Amwe, Ahni Oomwha,
> Come to me now in my need.
> I am open to your desires,
> My heart yearns for your love,
> My body aches for your power,
> My womb is receptive to your seed of life.
> Ahni Amwe, breathe your light,
> Ahni Amwe, breathe your life,
> Stir your waters,
> Stir your power,
> Fill your daughter
> Give me my desire.

Injya sang the sacred words over and over again, releasing the power contained in them to drive deep into her soul, allowing the desire to consume her, until she *was* the desire. She craved nothing more than what the Goddess wished for her – to become an instrument of Her will – to be allowed to act only in the way that the Goddess wished, to fulfil Her plan on earth. As the words stirred the pool of emotions in her heart, filled her being with moon-sent, moon-blessed power, Injya could feel herself being consumed by the Goddess. Wave after wave of pure white energy pulsed through her body, coursing down through her breasts and belly, stirring the waters and blood of her womb, filling her with a power so urgent that her whole being pulsed and spasmed in ecstasy.

She sang, thus, until the last vestiges of night had gone, until the sky was streaked with the sun-rays and as Injya finally dropped her arms and looked gratefully at the violet sky which was now concealing her spiritual mother, she recognized her power; understood that whatever should befall her henceforeward, would be because she had ordained it, because she was acting out her part of the Divine Plan. She sank to her knees and closed her eyes, feeling the sun touching her temples, bathing her in love.

It wasn't until the crashing sound became so close to her and the chorusing birds ceased their morning exaltation that Injya opened her eyes. Not ten pchekts distance stood a mother bear, her eyes intent upon Injya, her two cubs hiding behind her great hind legs. Injya gazed at the beast, fearing nothing. The bear, equally still and fearless, regarded Injya for a moment and then as if reluctant, stalked off, stiff limbed and swaying, her cubs still dancing round her heels, back down into the valley, down the path which Injya now knew she herself would travel.

Although clear headed, Injya was still deliberating which clothes to take with her on her journey when the she-bear returned. Injya had heard her approach for some time, but it had not hastened her departure. She knew that she would have to leave one set of sacred clothes, either the skins and the drum, or moon-gown and the head-dress. She could not take both and as the heavy lumbering footsteps became louder, she became more muddled – to leave the skin-shift and drum would mean that perhaps never again would she experience the animal powers it showed her; but to leave her moon-gown would mean certainly a loss of her power and perhaps many more months making a new one – if, in fact, she could make another. The gown was heavier than the skin and drum and less practical and with winter fast approaching she doubted that it would keep her warm, even if worn over her normal doe-skin shift.

She had so much to take – two of the most important xiols, most of the herbs and unctions for healing and she desperately wanted to take the obsidian. It wasn't until the first of the cubs skittered down the sloping entrance to the cave that Injya finally made up her mind. She quickly placed the mirror, drum and shift on a high narrow ledge, hoping that it would be too narrow for the mother bear to climb on to and too high for the cubs, and thrusting her moon-gown and cap hurriedly inside her father's cape, she clambered out of the cave. The mother bear stared at Injya, Injya smiled back and as she walked away, the bear entered the cave with the certainty of one returning home.

Injya made good progress that first day and when evening fell, she had already caught a hare and eaten it, cooking it over her fire which she had lit in a little depression in the bare mountainside. As she lay in the hollow, curled up by the bright, sparking fire she felt truly nourished. For the first time for three moons' passing she had eaten animal flesh and after giving thanks to the animal for its ultimate sacrifice, she felt replete and strengthened.

Her head seemed full of words, words from her mother and Askoye. She did not understand with her reason how she had become so integrated with the Moon Goddess, but she knew in her heart that she was filled with divine power. She could feel the moon coursing through her body as it coursed round the world, nourishing and bringing life and light to all. Injya surprised herself at *not* feeling surprised by the mother bear's arrival; she was reclaiming her rightful place on earth, taking to herself the power of the Great Bear, as Askoye and her people had once done.

She gathered her father's cloak round her more tightly as she gazed into the fire, fancying now that she could see the spirits of her ancestors dancing in front of her eyes, urging her onward, keeping her safe from harm. Warmed, unworried and satisfied that she was doing the work for which Askoye had equipped her, she shifted slightly and gazed at the stars. Straight above her she could see Arcturus, Guardian of the Great Bear in the heavens, Guardian of the thousand pieces of Bai Ulgan which surrounded her on every side.

She felt an overpowering sense of belonging – she was one with the earth, the moon, the stars and the sun. Her body sank slowly and heavily into the earth, which, in turn, was supporting and cradling her in its bosom. She was a child of the universe, a child of the heavens and of the earth, of mother born and father spirited.

And as she slept she dreamt of her father, brave Vingyar, at last reunited with Mensoon – their children, Oonjya and Prisca, playing happily around their feet, picking sweet smelling herbs and wild, delicate flowers from the garden of the soul. She slept the sleep of innocence, safe in the knowledge that she was playing out her part in the Divine Plan.

CHAPTER NINE

Halfray felt a sharp stab of pain in his solar plexus, he rubbed it cautiously, making his movements slow and methodical. Each time he went soul-walking, it hurt him less. He lay on his bed, staring at the hole in the sancar's roof and watched the summer sunlight filtering through the trees, playing games with the shadows on the inside of his sancar wall. Outside he could hear the children laughing and playing and the murmuring of the women as they went about their work. He closed his eyes and remembered Injya's face. How shocked she had looked – and how she had grown – quite a beautiful tall young woman – the men at the camp would be fighting over her when she came back. His smile turned to a frown as he thought of the brutish way the Branfjord men treated their women, but it eased when he thought of Injya's return – she would teach them differently.

He raised himself on one elbow and thought about getting up, but the droning of the bees outside and the humming of the women made him decide against it. He flopped back down again and stretched idly. His body felt pleasantly tired – he ached slightly and the pain in his stomach was still there – better not move too quickly, he told himself, you can never be too careful! He laughed – to the rest of the people Halfray was an idle, lazy dreamer, who professed to 'see' things and who was, on occasion, quite 'mad'. To everyone except Sanset, his cousin, and the old man Forek, he still played the stuttering fool, although when his real 'madness' had left him, he found he was almost incapable of turning somersaults. He moderated his singing and cavorting as it exhausted him and so it was, that at nineteen summers old, he was accepted as a harmless simpleton by the Branfjord and Gyaretz peoples alike.

Only Forek knew of his true calling and even then could understand little of what had happened to him. Not that Halfray could, at first, appreciate what had occurred. As he lay on his fur-covered bed his thoughts wandered back to his dreadful initiation. He had not been wrong in telling Sanset that he was about to go on a journey, but she had been mistaken in thinking that he would be travelling outside the confines of the encampment. His spirit certainly did leave the sancar, but his body remained, twisted and convulsed, as his soul underwent its hazardous walk. He only learnt much later that Sanset and the women had, at one point, tied his body with thick ropes to stop him cutting himself with knives and trying to throw himself into the fire. He had shuddered when Sanset had told him that the women had stayed up with him for seven whole nights as his raving filled the air.

All he had known, after he had fallen into that deep sleep, was that his father, in guise of a raven had summonsed him and he had flown with him to the very centre of Erlik's kingdom where he had watched his body being cut up and boiled, then chopped up and fed to the most hideous underworld creatures that Halfray had ever half-imagined in his worst nightmares. His torture was not over, as he then had to slay each and every one of these creatures to regain the pieces of his body and then bind them back together. Had he failed in his task his earthly body would have disintegrated and his soul would have forever remained in Erlik's kingdom. When he had regained his body, Vingyar had then taken him to the World Tree and shown him not only the mysteries of the incarnating souls, but the myriads of tukris and anatukris, the evil spirits of souls bent on destruction and evil, who also were waiting for incarnation.

Vingyar had shown him what great evil these discarnate spirits could achieve and had given him many spells for casting out the evil anatukris, for they liked nothing better than to inhabit people's bodies or try to steal their souls away from them while they were sleeping. Finally he had been shown the face of Bai Ulgan – such an intense, brilliant white light that Halfray feared he would be blinded. Halfray had seen the son behind the sun and His presence not only blinded him, but turned him mute with wonder. No words could express the bounteous beneficence of His presence, no sound could describe the harmonious outpourings from His heart – Halfray had felt more in awe, more terrified of this than any meeting with the tukris, anatukris, or even Erlik himself.

When he had finally left Vingyar, he returned to his earthly body with such force that he added to the scars on his breastbone, and an open wound to his stomach which had taken many moons to heal. His foreboding that he would return to his people as a stranger was truer than he had predicted, for not only did he not recognize his people, he could not speak, or move for many weeks. Everything seemed new to him – he had lost all the words which named things and had to be taught again, like a child, the names of trees and utensils, people and animals. He had lost his ability to token and since the death of Grinvorst few had the ability to teach him, but Forek and Sanset had been patient with him and by the time the first Aspar had warmed their bodies and clothed their harsh mountain tops with flowers, he had regained his strength and his mental capacities.

Forek constantly urged him to be vigilant against displaying any of his new-found talents and it was only when the people moved to the summer marshlands that the friendship between Forek and Halfray became so noticeable that Galdr decided that Halfray should be moved out of the women's sancar and given one to share with the old men of the tribe. And it was in such a sancar that Halfray lay, dreaming of his walking and his, as yet, untried powers of healing when a sudden change in the droning sounds from outside finally roused him.

An argument was going on, that was obvious by the men's harsh voices. There was nothing particularly disturbing in this, the Branfjord men always seemed to be fighting each other, but Halfray could distinguish the voices of Anfjord and Galdr and that was something unusual. Galdr had grown into a young man of uncommon strength, he was the most cunning of their hunters, the quickest and most able rider and by far the most lascivious of all the young men. He was now, like Halfray himself, only nineteen summers old, but there, any resemblance to Halfray ended. Halfray was tall, willowy with almost-white blond hair and pale blue eyes surrounded by short, reddish coloured lashes; Galdr was taller still, standing two full pchekts to the crown of his head, with skin bronzed by the summer sun. Halfray had the straight nose and high forehead of his mother, his mouth, always parted in a smile, was small and pale-lipped; Galdr's face showed his prominent bone structure, his cheek-bones were high and square, jaw-bone too, square and strong, his nostrils flared wide over an equally wide, full mouth and above his nose, eyes, so dark brown they could be mistaken for black, glistened behind long, curved black lashes. His hair, too, was jet-black and hung in swathes around his thick neck. Where Halfray was sinuous and slender, Galdr's body was muscle-bound and strong, where Halfray's voice was soft and low, Galdr's was harsh and often loud, haughty and commanding and it was this openly contemptuous voice that Halfray could now hear raised in anger against his father. Most of the time Crenjal managed to keep the peace between the two men, but obviously, whatever had ensued was out of the province of the silver-tongued Crenjal.

Sighing deeply Halfray rose and went outside; how he wished he could summon one of his spirit-guides to interrupt this childishness, but that would have been out of the question, not only would the people have been terrified but he would have been killed immediately as having been overtaken by an anatukris himself. With a slight feeling of boredom he adjusted his eyes to the bright sunlight. Very quickly this feeling left him – there was something new and very threatening in the air. Halfray could see father and son, standing in front of Anfjord's sancar; Anfjord, purple with rage, was brandishing his sword in the air and Galdr was facing him, square on, hands on hips, defiance and contempt radiating from every pore. The women, who up to a moment before had been happily cleaning skins and playing with the children, had disappeared inside their sancars and the old men stood huddled in a group, near the oblivious grazing horses.

Suddenly Halfray knew why the atmosphere was so charged: all the young men, whom he had assumed were out hunting, were in fact, standing some way off, watching intently. Every one of the young men had their hands on their hunting spears and every one of those spears were pointing towards Anfjord.

'You will *not* – you will *never* take over the running of this camp – you do *not* know everything, young man – you do *not* know my plans and while you act like this, neither will you!'

Anfjord was shouting at his son, his mouth covered in the froth of fury, the arm holding his sword shaking with anger. Galdr stood his ground and sneered at his father.

'You? You don't *have* any plans – you are one of the old tribe – you follow the same paths, you take the same old ways – you are too old and too stupid to try anything new! *I* know where we can mine copper, *I* know where the seals and the reindeer are – I know better ways and I can and I *will* show our people!'

Anfjord was almost speechless with rage – he lowered his sword and smote the ground with it, sending up a great clod of marsh grass as he did so.

'You cannot travel further east – it is impossible, I *know*, I have been further east than you could ever consider – there is nothing there but marshes, more marshes and then the mighty river of the end of the world. There *is* no copper, there *are* no herds of reindeer!'

Galdr suddenly laughed, laughed in the face of his father and hissed so low that only Halfray could have heard the words he spoke: 'I know, because your wife – your precious Patrec told me – she saw it in a dream and she told me while I laid with her!'

The old man looked as if he had been turned to stone by the words. Patrec, his most favoured wife – Patrec, the woman who had been with him for almost half his life, Patrec, who had born him many fine children, but none who had caused him this much anguish. Patrec had lain with Galdr! As Galdr's words struck they almost took the old man's breath away. Galdr had just admitted lying with his own mother!

For an instant, Halfray thought that Anfjord would cleave Galdr's head from his shoulders. He stood, veins throbbing in his crimson temples, his weather-beaten face sanguine with fury. Suddenly he turned about and strode into his sancar. The silence was riven with one long anguished scream and then fell again as Anfjord stepped out of his sancar, blood dripping from his sword. His mighty frame was shaking like an aspen leaf as he threw his head to the sky and shouted to the heavens: 'Take my son, Great Oagist, take him on your mighty wings and destroy him! Bring Kronos from his fiery hole to take Galdr, my son, and give him to your brother, Ipirün, King of Fire, to consume him! Let him burn forever in your flames of revenge!'

The young men dropped their swords and looked aghast at Anfjord as the words of the curse rang out in the soft air of the summer day. Anfjord turned slowly towards Galdr.

'Go, Galdr – you have no home here – you will forever roam this earth alone – you are motherless and fatherless and Kronos will stalk you all the days of your life until Ipirün finds you and condemns you to everlasting torture by flame!'

So saying Anfjord wheeled round and re-entered his sancar, leaving the men shamefaced and downcast, and Galdr thunderstruck with the words.

He had been cursed. He had been banished and no-one, not even a chieftain's son, could live in banishment. Galdr had signed his name to his death the moment he had lain with his mother and the prospect of banishment meant that his death would come more slowly than the avenging sword of his father, but come it would.

He attempted to smile, but his mouth only twisted slightly at the corners. He looked over to the group of young men, then at the old men cowering by the women's sancar. He hung his head and shuffled uneasily, perhaps he was hoping that his father would relent, perhaps he was ashamed, but Halfray dismissed that thought from his mind – never, in all the three summers that their two peoples had been together could Halfray ever remember a time when Galdr had been ashamed of any action he had committed. He watched as Galdr ceased his shuffling and slowly straightened his back and raised his head to assume the familiar attitude of haughty self-confidence. Galdr stared straight ahead of him then quickly turned on his heels and walked, stiff-backed out of the encampment, taking nothing with him save what he was wearing, never wavering in his footsteps or turning back, walked over the flat marshlands until his dark head was no bigger than the lazy bees which now continued their droning to the midsummer air.

Halfray slowly closed his eyes, and, ignoring the crowding women and men who had come to watch the receding figure, he prayed for Galdr. He prayed that Galdr would meet his end swiftly and painlessly, that the Goddess would relent and not treat him as cruelly as she had treated others, but it was a forlorn wish – he, more than most, understood the just laws – as above so below, what you do to others will be done to you, if not in this lifetime then in the lifetimes to come, but above all he knew that love could change all, could alter the wheel of life – if only . . . His thoughts came back to Anfjord and Patrec. With a shudder he felt the dual emotions of anger and compassion as they wrestled in his heart. Anger at the act of murder committed in rage, and compassion for the state of man who could act so.

Halfray walked slowly over to Anfjord's sancar and looked impassively at the two men who were always on guard at the entrance. Fear was clouding their eyes and culpability was written clearly on their faces. The blood letting would not be over with Patrec's death. From inside the sancar he could hear Anfjord sobbing and he had little difficulty imagining the scene; Anfjord would be cradling his dead wife in his arms, overcome with remorse and Patrec's lifeless body would be limply swaying, the blood still running, the pain still evident on her face. He turned his back on the guards and closed his eyes. Immediately he saw the vision of the two people engulfed in intertwining colours; from Anfjord's form came the dull red-brown emanation of guilt and sorrow, from hers came the violet quivering light of a soul trying to release itself from this earth, but held back on its journey by the stronger shadow of grief.

Whatever sin Patrec had committed, she did not deserve to be held back. Halfray knew Patrec, he knew her as a fine mother and a wise, patient woman and he knew that she would not have enjoined in the coupling with Galdr unless he had some peculiar hold over her, some power of persuasion which made her commit the greatest taboo known to their people. Keeping the vision close in his mind, he slowly walked up to the top of a small hillock which overlooked their summer encampment. From where he stood he could still see Galdr's head as he weaved in between the many small rivulets which crossed the marshlands, but he turned his back on it – Galdr would live or die without intervention from him! He sat on the ground, his back supported by his favourite birch tree and closed his eyes. He focused his mind on the image of the

96

two people far below him, locked together in their grief as he stilled his breathing. He waited until his body calmed to the state of no breath, that moment when the spirit, heart and mind are in perfect unison, and then he brought the vision closer to himself until he felt as if he was engulfed by it, he *was* the vision.

He could see among the merging colours of brown, red and blue, the thin golden strand which held these two souls forever bonded together. It was the same golden strand which binds all peoples on earth together, the strand which ensures that life after life, they will incarnate in groups, that in one life they may be brother and sister, in another mother and son and yet in another, no blood relation but bonded by a strong mutual feeling of either love or hate. For a second he hesitated – what he was about to do was an awesome responsibility and one which man should only ever leave to the Gods. In that instant of hesitation he felt a stirring of the air and knew that the Raven was with him. This was the sign that he had not even recognized he had been waiting for. Now knowing and trusting utterly in the rightness of his action, his own form of opalescent white light insinuated itself between the two forms and with an action which felt as if he were wrenching his own physical heart in two, he tore apart the golden thread which bound the two people.

Instantly in his mind he saw the spirit form of Patrec turn from a rosy violet to a purer amethyst and then fade to a shimmering pale blue, the colour of forgetfulness. Its form hovered above the crumpled body which it had just left and then slowly ascended, like the tiniest wisp of smoke from a dying flame, to the pale blue summer skies and was gone. Anfjord's colour deepened momentarily and then was suffused with a darker red. There was little Halfray could do about this – Anfjord would, and should, discover the horror of his act. The scream of rage which emitted from his sancar brought Halfray suddenly back to his physical body – the vision left him and he sat on,

97

breathing deeply, watching with a sickened stomach as he saw Anfjord tear from his sancar and without warning raise his sword and despatch first one guard and then another, their heads rolling on the soft earth even before their bodies crumpled and the blood flowed.

CHAPTER TEN

Galdr, of course, knew nothing of Halfray's intervention between the souls of his mother and father, he only heard the terrible sound of his father's anguish and pain. The roar of his rage carried over the still air and panic seized him as he thought that his father had changed his mind and was even now mounting his fastest horse, in hot pursuit of his son, to smite him down as he had so brutally done his mother. His first instinct was to run from the sound, but his pride would not allow that. If Anfjord was to come to kill him, then so be it! He tried to laugh at the idea that a man of over forty summers could match his twenty-summer strength, but failed miserably. Anfjord was still the strongest man in the whole country of Skoonjay, land of the reindeer, land of the summer-spirit skies.

As he thought of his land he suddenly felt a heavy sorrow fill his heart. He had relinquished his inheritance – the inheritance of leader of the known world, for what? For a few nights' delighting in his mother's body? He had known, inside himself, that what he was doing was wrong, was the greatest taboo he could break, but finding out that Patrec was secretly invoking the power of the Moon Goddess to aid her and her women *avoid* their duty of bringing forth many children – that had been a gem too sparkling and bright to ignore. He had hoped that by lying with his mother she would become with child – his child – and when the child had been born, he would have gained the right to become leader of their people! Why – the proud Branfjords would never have allowed Anfjord to claim that *he* was their uncontested and uncontestable rightful lord, when his own wife openly lay with his son! He would have been laughed into obscurity and shunned by all – it would have been him, Anfjord, who would now be walking into banishment and certain death!

Cursing his loose tongue which had let slip his secret and cursing his envious heart for being incapable of holding its hatred of his father a few more moons' courses, he stumbled onward, not knowing where he was going, not caring which direction he took, only needing to put as many pchekts distance as possible between himself and the object of his hatred. By nightfall he found himself wading through tall reed-like grasses, his ankles and feet covered in slimy mud, his legs torn by the sharp-edged grasses, hopelessly lost and very hungry. The tall grasses seemed to extend for ever and in the strange, indigo-blue, half-night that marked their summer, everything took on a menacing shadowy appearance. He knew that he had to get out of the marshlands, but could find no guidance – the stars glimmered very faintly and it was impossible to pick out the brightest – he could not even discern the Great Bear of Bai Ulgan to help him.

With growing desperation he tore at the razor-sharp grasses, hacking at them with his short hunting knife, wrenching them from the sodden ground with his bleeding hands as he tried in vain to build up a reed-bed on which to lie. The sun had already risen by the time he had covered the wet ground sufficiently and still filling the air with invectives, he had eventually thrown his body on to the crushed, water-filled stems and fallen asleep, only to dream of his mother, who, at the moment he had given her the fruit of his manhood, turned hideously into his father.

When he awoke, the sun was at its highest in the azure blue sky and Galdr was wet through with sweat and itching all over. He rose stiffly and surveyed his body; his bare arms and legs had been bitten by hundreds of insects which whirred about him as he rose from his reed-bed. His desperate need for water was aggravated by seeing water all around him, but none fit to drink. His protesting stomach reminded him loudly that he had not eaten since daybreak yesterday and cursing loudly he scanned the horizon for evidence of safer ground. His sun-blinded eyes saw nothing save a vast expanse of dark green and brown reeds. He swore furiously at his misfortune and scratched himself vigorously. Damned woman! he thought, she *was* lying, there *is* nothing here, but water and marshes, reeds and insects! Still cursing he stumbled on, turning back hopefully inland.

He had stumbled and fumed his way through the long hot day when the sinking sun gave his exhausted body some respite. He fancied that the ground which was now underfoot was marginally less waterlogged than that of the morning, but he was beginning to doubt his reason as the short blue night overtook him. Eventually he stumbled once too often for that day and lay where he had fallen, not caring to make a bed, no matter how perfunctory, oblivious to all except the burning itching of his body. When the ruddy sun burst forth for the third morning, Galdr could contain himself no longer. He scrabbled at the earth and found brackish water some half a span under its mossy covering. Bending on all fours, he lapped the acrid water like a dog. It tasted as he imagined the earth would taste: acid and rotten, and, although it did little to assuage his thirst, he felt marginally better for it.

Scanning the horizon for the first time that day he saw, far into the distance, a slight rise and what looked like trees. His heart leapt with joy – if only he could get to trees, he would be safe – trees meant game, higher ground meant the possibility of fresh water! For the first time for three days Galdr allowed the thought that he might live race through his veins: 'Trees mean game, ground means water,' he kept saying as he continued on his graceless, lumbering journey.

By the morning of his fifth day, when the vision seemed no nearer, Galdr contemplated cutting his throat but as he lay, full length on his stomach, a slight movement above his head caught his attention. A tiny bird had alighted on top of one of the reeds over his head. Inching his hand slowly, trying to keep his outstretched arm steady, he moved his arm a fraction at a time, his fingers opening wider, slowly until yes! He had the scrap of life in his palm! With a surge of triumph he ripped the tiny head from its body and scarce bothering to tear the feathers from its minute form he ate it. When he came to dig once more for water, he had to go down a full hand's span depth before he came to the brown life-giving liquid. He was getting near.

Galdr also felt the wind turn around. Almost overnight the storms which had buffeted his fragile camp in the trees and threatened to smash it once more on to the rocks below ceased, and in their place came the cold wind from the north. He was almost glad of the drop in temperature – at least that meant an end to the tormented nights he had spent scratching and slapping his now sore-encrusted legs, although with the coming of the wind he knew his resting place in the trees would no longer be safe. His home of three moons' passing would soon have to be abandoned as before long the freezing whiteness would inhabit his tiny self-made kingdom and he would have to journey further north, to the land where safe refuge could be found in a cave. He had prepared for this time well, using his fine skills as a hunter to catch many more animals than his appetite demanded and though he had endured many failures with curing the meat, he had finally managed to dry nearly the whole of one reindeer carcass and many more rabbits and hares than he imagined he would need. He was still reluctant to leave his home, putting off his departure daily, pretending to himself that he was not afraid of his journey, just being sensible and staying as long as he could. It wasn't until one full-moon night when the sounds of the wolves had become too close for the deception to go unencountered, that he finally accepted the inevitable. He had to go further north.

The tree-line was two days' journeying below him and he had already regretfully discarded half of his dried meat when he saw a thin plume of smoke, halfway up a slow rise. Fear gripped his heart. Another traveller! That could only mean another outcast – or, his frantic brain raced, his father? To the best of his knowledge, no other people inhabited this world – the two tribes of the Gyaretz and Branfjords were now one huge roaming people, a tribe of over two hundred souls. Could someone else have been banished while he had been away? Could his people already be in the hills? He dismissed this idea as unlikely – they would, indeed, be in the hills by now, but always they kept to the same trusted routes – this land was new to him – his father would not have brought such a large group of people on untried ways. Perhaps it was a newly banished person – perhaps they were sick – perhaps they were mad?

His mind raced, now fearful, now exalted at the thought of human contact. With the silence learnt from hunting, he quietly laid down his heavy load of dried meat and expertly covered it with mosses. Although everything urged him to swiftness he forced himself to be methodical – he needed to be able to retrieve his food – not give it willy-nilly to the animals of the night. He stopped frequently, looking again and again at the steady plume of smoke, trying to quieten his wildly-beating heart. He had convinced himself that this was the smoke of another outcast, preferably a woman (though his rational mind kept reminding him that women were *never* banished – a fact he chose to ignore), and that they would meet and join together and form another race, *his* race, the race of Galdr!

He only dropped on to his hands and knees when the scudding clouds showed the face of the moon and the whole mountainside was bathed in her eerie light. For the rest of the journey he walked quickly and quietly, searching the ground for anything which would alert the keeper of the fire to his presence. The way had been longer than he had anticipated and he regretted burying his meat so early in his journey – he could have easily and safely carried it much further. When the smell of the burning dried mosses reached his nose, the first few rays of the risen sun hit the cold ground and the dawn's mist began to rise. Galdr silently swore at the swirling miasma as it clung to his knees and obliterated the ground from view – he nearly tripped more than once on an unseen obstacle and his feet seemed to catch every dried twig, every frost-crispened leaf on the whole mountainside. But slowly he came nearer to the plume of smoke.

He could see clearly now that it came from a small depression in the side of the mountain; he stumbled once more as he gained the rise and looked into its hollow. The huddled form still sleeping, curled by the fire, stirred and then fell back into slumber. Galdr stood and watched the figure as it slowly moved with each breath. Whoever it was was not of his tribe – of that he was sure – he had never seen such a fine cape and there was something else – a dark blue hem of a gown, a slender naked foot. It *was* a woman!

Galdr descended the rise and skirted round it until he could see the sleeping form from the other side of the fire. Her face was framed in glorious black curls, her long body curved and womanly – whoever she was, she possessed an uncommonly beautiful face. As he gazed at her, something stirred in Galdr's heart which had never lived before – he had taken many women, he had fancied he had loved a few of them, but this creature – what he felt for her was unearthly . . . yes, he decided, that was the only word for it – an unearthly longing. He was unsure what to do, but finally he decided that if he sat by her fire and made no sound, perhaps she would not be too startled when she woke. He dropped on his haunches and watched her sleeping, impassive face. A familiar ache in his loins stirred – how he wanted her! He felt his organ grow and begin to throb with desire, almost painful in its intensity. He shifted his position to ease the ache in his engorged sex and in that instant Injya opened her eyes.

She moved not an inch, her breathing did not change from its slow, gentle rhythm as she stared impassively at Galdr's face. She recognized him instantly – how could she ever forget *that* face? But she felt no fear, no surprise even. Her only thought being: 'So the Goddess has sent *him* to me – he, too, is part of the divine plan!'

Galdr, seeing her open eyes immediately blurted out: 'I saw your fire – I, I—' he tailed off, stuck for words.

'I thought I would come and see who it was?' she suggested to him, not taking her eyes off his face.

'Yes, yes, I, I am a traveller,' he began quickly, 'I am travelling to, to find—'

'An outcast you mean—' Injya corrected him impassively, 'an outcast.'

'No! Yes – No!' he affirmed loudly. He fell silent and looked at her beseechingly. By the Gods, he thought – I must have this woman – I must! As if Injya could read his thoughts she suddenly rose and said: 'You are Galdr, son of Anfjord – you are not welcome at my fire. No man may share my fire. I am Injya, High Priestess of the Moon Goddess, Ahni!'

Galdr looked as if he had been struck with a bolt of lightning, his jaw dropped and his eyes widened with fear. Feeling stupid and at a disadvantage, he too stood up. Injya was almost the same height as him – and she had the bearing to match his. Suddenly he felt an onrush of anger – she might be Injya – she might be some mad woman cast out – she might be a tukris come to plague him for all he knew, but yes, damn it, he was Galdr, son of Anfjord, and as such he would have this woman, if that was what she was.

'You are right, I am Galdr, son of Anfjord, but I doubt your name. Injya perished some three winters ago – you can not be her.'

Injya looked at Galdr, noticing how the proud and arrogant youth had turned into an even more proud and arrogant man. She felt utter contempt for him and for his people – how she wished she had not left behind those herbs – she would soon show this loathsome man who was the Goddess's rightful heir on earth! The two stared at each other for a long time – he defiant and flushed, she cold and impassive. Finally Injya broke the silence.

'I am travelling to meet with my people, I will find them before the earth turns white and I will be reunited with them to teach them once more the true way. I do not wish you, Galdr, to come with me. I will leave this place now and you will go on your journey. We will never meet again in this lifetime!' Having said this, Injya fixed him once more with her cold contemptuous eyes and turned her back on him. She began gathering her bundle of furs together, annoyed with his intrusion, annoyed that she would have to journey a while before stopping to eat, but it could not be helped – she had to be rid of this man!

She did not have time to turn round at the sudden sound before Galdr was on her. Her arms were pinned to her body and she could feel his urgent sex thrusting against her back. She twisted and turned, desperately trying to reach the tiny hunting knife which was strapped to her thigh, but he had both arms held close to her body. She tried to break his grasp by bringing her arms up quickly, but the hands seemed locked together, the weight of his body forcing her nearer the ground. She bent her head this way and that, trying to reach his arms to bite them, but she could not reach. They struggled for some moments like this, Injya desperate to keep her ground and not be pushed over by his superior strength, but suddenly he shot a foot out and kicked against her ankle and she fell, face down, pinned on the ground by his body.

She knew only too well his intention and she understood that further fighting at this level would be out of the question. She was desperately afraid, her heart pounding in her body, her stomach a tight hard knot of terror. She had to outmanoeuvre him, for she was no match for his strength. His body was crushing hers, his arms trapped

106

with hers underneath her body, bruising and pressing the very breath out of her. Suddenly she let go of the fear which was binding her as tightly as were his arms and body – she must not be afraid – he was only a man – she could outwit him. Instantly she dropped her resistance and became limp in his grasp.

Almost immediately she felt his hold loosen. With a sudden movement he moved his trapped arms from underneath her body and banged one hand firmly down on the back of her neck while the other began tearing at her gown, roughly moving it higher and higher. He was sitting astride her back and she gauged that to gain access to her womanhood he would have to shift his position, if not lift his bulk completely. In that moment, she would be able to reach her knife and thrust it into his knee. The movement of the cloth suddenly stopped as Galdr shouted triumphantly: 'What is this, my little Priestess? A knife?!'

He patted almost tenderly the place at the top of Injya's thigh where the small sickle-shaped knife was secured. Injya tensed as she felt his fingers circle round the top of the knife and then dig into her flesh hard. She cried out with pain as he pulled at the knife and the leather thongs strained and then finally snapped. She felt his body tense as he raised his arm and threw the knife away, far over her head and she sank deeper into the earth as he pressed down harder on her neck – her only chance of escape gone, lost among the soft mosses and brackens of the mountain. She knew she was defeated.

As the pressure on the back of her neck increased, breathing became even more difficult and she thought her neck would break as he slowly shifted his weight on to the tops of her legs. Her arms were still trapped underneath her body and the combined weight of their bodies only added to the terrible feeling that she would suffocate. She felt his body tensing and straining as he shifted uneasily, trying to part her legs with his and she knew, that unless she could

107

summon more than sheer physical strength, Galdr would succeed. She forced her body to relax once more and as she did so, Galdr hesitated. Quicker than a bolt of lightning Injya arched her back and twisted her body. Galdr faltered in his grasp and lost his balance. His hold on her throat loosened momentarily and she sprung to her feet, kicking out wildly at the prone figure. Struggling away from the grabbing hands, she scrambled on all fours and then stood up, but she had taken no more than five or six breathtaking leaps, when Galdr felled her with an iron-like grip on her ankle. Down she fell on to the hard earth with such force that it knocked the last of her breath from her body and once more he clambered upon her, this time holding his hunting knife to her throat.

The hard earth took her screams and her blood, as Galdr forced his searing, urgent sex into her. The pain of the act was so intense that Injya prayed that she would lose consciousness, but oblivion was not granted. She had known that it was right to be afraid of this violation, but she had never imagined how terrible, how painful and how long the act would be. Her secret place was raw as the brutish action continued, ripping and tearing, bludgeoning and beating her until finally she felt a hot onrush of something pulsing through her and his body finally fell, exhausted, over her. He lay for some time, his sweat dripping on to her torn and bruised body, but his grip never loosened its hold on the hilt of the knife which lay perilously near her throat. Eventually he withdrew from her body and straddled her back once more. Sheathing the knife he turned her over to face him.

'More,' he said almost sweetly to her, 'I will have more!'

CHAPTER ELEVEN

Injya shivered. Although Galdr had roughly covered her with her father's cape, her bound body was naked and the wind which had blown out the fire, now lifted and shook the heavy garment as if it were reed grass. She lay on her side feeling the wind cutting her flesh, watching the glowing embers become greyer as the day wore on. Galdr had left her to retrieve his dried meat saying that he would return before nightfall. She did not know which she dreaded most, his return or the freezing whiplashes of the wind. She had tried shuffling to an upright position, but had fallen, again and again. Her hands had been tightly bound behind her back and attached to the bands which secured her knees and ankles together. She cursed Askoye and her gown making – the torn shreds from her moon-gown were as strong as the trees from which they had originally come – the only difference being that in the great winds of winter, the trees would bow and bend with the gales – here, torn into sharp-edged strips, they only seemed to tighten and become more inflexible.

She did not cry until the sounds of Galdr's footsteps had long gone and then the flood of emotion hurt her battered body more than the memory of her violation. She eventually stopped and tried her fantastic dances in an effort to stand. She gave that up too when the repeated falls only contributed more cuts and bruises to her earth-covered body. The wind gusted stronger and Injya watched with hope fading, as the greying sky turned a menacing dark blue. The rain, when it started, appeared to relieve her hot aching body, but gradually it turned her pain-seared form cold. Her cape became sodden, her hair plastered over her face and the once dry, unyielding earth turned into mud. Bound as she was, she could do nothing to warm herself; if she rocked about, it only sent oozing mud lapping over her body and she felt that by so doing she was digging her own grave. When the sun finally went to rest, the rain continued and the wind blew with even greater ferocity. Injya convinced herself that she would be dead before Galdr returned – if he returned at all.

The sight of the rising moon filled Injya with hope, but almost as soon as her spirits lifted, they crashed again. How could she invoke the help of the Goddess, trussed like a reindeer on a carrying pole? She must be unworthy to carry on the Priestesshood – there could be no other explanation for it – otherwise, this could never have happened. She tried in vain to reach the source of her power, but each time she focused her attention on her heart, and delved deep into her core, she felt Galdr's body inside hers and fresh sobs racked her body.

She must have fallen asleep for she was abruptly awoken by a loud crackling sound. Galdr was hunched over the newly lit fire, the brilliant flames reddening his face and making it dance with shadows. She shuddered involuntarily and closed her eyes against the sight. Galdr had seen her and slowly rose from his squatting position.

'Will you eat?' Injya opened her eyes again and saw the piece of flesh he offered her.

'I cannot – not like this – you must untie me.' Self-hate filled her – she had not meant to say *that* at all! She had meant to say 'No – I will never eat your food – never, I would rather die first!' but her head seemed to take little direction from her will – her stomach spoke its need first! Galdr suddenly laughed, the sound hitting the air incongruously, like bird-song at midnight! He looked at her hobbled figure lying in the mud – she did not look so grand now, he thought, just like any other woman, but pity of a sort overcame him and he took out his knife and advanced towards her. Injya's heart stopped beating with fear, but all Galdr did was cut the strand which bound her tied hands to her feet. He picked her up roughly by her shoulders and set her down again on a drier patch of ground, resting her back against the mound and straightening out her legs in front of her. Her body tingled all over as the blood rushed unimpeded through her veins.

'I am cold and wet!' she announced, looking up at the dark face of her captor as he stood, face silhouetted by the firelight.

'Yes,' he agreed solemnly, 'yes, you are.'

He turned his back on her and went to the other side of the fire. In the dim firelight Injya could see him unwrap a great bundle of fur which he shook and then brought over to her. He laid it, skin side uppermost, close to her and then gently lifted her on to it, gathering it round her shoulders and patting it to her form. The fur was wet, but it warmed her and she looked at Galdr with appreciation for the offering.

'Now you will eat?' he asked again as he crouched in front of her. She did not reply, but watched silently as he cut thin slithers of dried rabbit flesh from the bones. He offered her the meat off the end of his knife. She looked from the meat to him and back to the meat again and shook her head. With a sigh he put the rabbit down in her lap, took the meat off his knife and put it to her lips. The smell of the meat made her mouth fill with saliva and she swallowed hard before opening her trembling lips. Never taking her eyes from his, she felt the meat being slid into her mouth which she chewed at slowly, watching his face and his dark eyes, watching his mouth as it changed to a smile. As soon as she had swallowed the morsel he offered her another. This time she took it hungrily, chewing quickly and swallowing it before it was thoroughly masticated. Again the meat was offered, again she took it, chewing and watching silently as he now fed her, now himself.

111

The rabbit's bones lay in a sinewy mess on her fur-covered knees as she saw him lick his fingers and slowly sheath his knife in his waist-pouch. He stood up and began to walk over to the other side of the fire when something made him change his mind. He resumed his squatting position in front of her and gently wiped the grease from round Injya's lips and chin. He went to put the grease-smeared fingers in his mouth when he seemed to think better of it. He offered his fingers up to her mouth. Injya turned her head away violently and clamped her teeth shut. Immediately his right hand caught her round her chin and forced her face towards him, exerting pressure on her jaw-bone to open it.

'Yes!' he said under his breath, 'yes – you *will*!'

She stared at his face, but could not see clearly, she could only feel his fingers insinuate themselves into her mouth, as they slid over her tongue, along the top of her teeth, round the inside of her cheeks. Each time she tried to twist her head away from his hand he forced his fingers further into her throat, making her gag and retch.

She almost felt relief when the fingers were replaced with his tongue, but the taste of his mouth and the smell of his skin made her stomach retch anew. She slid down the mound in an effort to escape him, but stopped as she felt his hand clamp down on her womanhood. Now his fingers were probing inside her and she struggled violently against his onslaught. The meat had not only filled her belly, it had filled her spirit too and at the moment that his fingers thrust inside her she bit his tongue with all her might. She tasted his blood in her mouth as he immediately shrank away from her and in an instant she had rolled on to her side, stuck her head and shoulder into the mud and used them to lever herself off the ground. With arms tied behind her back and legs hobbled together she attempted to run.

When she felt the crashing blow on her head, her body crumpled. She felt him lift her by the waist and then kick at her knees, as if she were a wet skin. Her body obeyed and she stayed, head down in the mud, knees bent, waiting for what she now knew would certainly come. She gritted her teeth against the inevitable, tasting as she did so the warm sickly taste of his blood in her mouth.

Injya had not cried out when Galdr had drawn more blood from her as he clawed at her back, nor had she cried out when he entered her; she felt that there could be no further degradation. She had been wrong, but she had made no sound when he mounted her again, this time gaining access to her unnatural passage. Then she knew that her vitiation was total. She had remained mute when he had finally withdrawn from her and kicked her over, leaving her where she had fallen, in the mud and blood-spattered ground. Her humiliation was complete.

The long night had finally given way to a brilliant azure-blue dawn, the rose-tinted clouds adding ironical insult to the picture of corrupt ruination which Injya felt her body showed to the world. Unlike Galdr, she had not slept for what had been left of the night, she seriously doubted that she would ever sleep again in this lifetime, and for the first time throughout all her ordeals in her brief life, she wished for death. She shut her eyes against the beauty of the day; tried to shut her ears against the singing birds far below in the valley; and tried to shut her heart from yearning for escape as she invoked the terrible name of Kronos, bringer of death. She imagined she saw his black-bull form, carrying her down to Erlik, on his great bull back, but nothing happened to her, save a quickening of her heart. Next she imagined the World Tree with all its wonderful souls ready and waiting to re-incarnate: 'Come to me – take me!' she implored, but nothing happened except the sun suddenly burst forth from the horizon sending its splendid carmine rays over the chilled earth. She wished she could weep her life away, let it spill from her as her precious blood had been spilt, but she was more frightened of waking Galdr than allowing her tears to flow.

She tried to entice the spirit of Halfray to her side, but again she failed and when, at last, she exhausted all her possibilities she heard a rustle in the air. Looking up, far away in the heavens, she saw a raven wheeling high over them. The spirit of her father!

Her heart sang with joy – of course! Straightening her body out as best she could, she rolled over on to her back and stared hard at the bird. The raven circled slowly twice and then swooped down towards her, coming to rest on the mound of earth which sheltered Galdr and the fire. She looked into his bright eyes, hope filling her and bringing with it the strange rush of energy she experienced every time she thought in the right manner. She willed the bird to come down to her, to peck at her bonds, but the bird stayed still, hopping up and down the mound, looking at her first this way, then that. She rolled over on to her stomach and waved her bound wrists at him frantically. The bird did not move. She tugged and pulled at the bands.

'Come, unleash me!' she beseeched him as she pulled, wriggled and twisted till she felt the first drop of blood fall from her wrists. 'Oh come, come now!' she implored, but still the bird eyed her, hopping up and down on top of the mound. The bird was not her father – it was just a stupid raven! She looked with loathing at the creature and it flew away. She was just about to scream at it with rage when she realized that the bird had been perched, not just on the mound, but on a specific part of the mound. He had been hopping on a quartz crystal which now gleamed and glinted in the sunlight, showing her her route to freedom!

Injya rolled over to the mound and with great difficulty levered herself on to her feet. The crystal was level with her shoulder-blades and to use it as a knife meant that she had to stand on tiptoes, raising her hands behind her back in an extremely painful position. This pain she *could* endure. Her near-naked body was drenched with sweat by the time she broke the bands, but the activity had warmed her. Not only had it warmed her body, but now her soul cried out for revenge! Quickly she untied the bonds from her knees and ankles and rubbed them urgently to restore the blood. Galdr's regular snoring could still be heard behind the mound, she had not woken him and without stopping to think, Injya ran round the side of the mound and dropped into the depression. Galdr looked warm and snug, wrapped as he was in *her* father's cloak and resting on *her* bear-skin fur. She saw her torn doe-skin singlet, trodden into the mud, but she picked it up and wet as it was, she slipped it over her head. Her beautiful moon-gown lay where it had finally been flung, its long skirt shortened by the tearing knife as Galdr had slashed at it to make the instruments of her bondage. This too she put on, tying the hem up around her waist to make a pouch and bundling inside it a dried rabbit carcass. Now she did not worry about the noise she was making – she cared not if he woke, she knew that she would escape him – no matter what he managed to do to her – he could never own her soul!

She hesitated for a moment, wondering if she should try to take his knife, but decided against it – powerful again she might be – foolhardy never. As she decided against trying to steal his knife a glint of something bright in the heather caught her eye – her own tiny sickle knife! She skirted round the prone figure of Galdr and retrieved her knife, tucking that also into the skirt-pouch. She turned and looked back at Galdr's sleeping body – she could cut his throat right now! He was so deeply asleep he would never know – she could murder him as easily as her mother and her sisters and her aunt had been! For a second the instinct for revenge took hold of her, but she knew that she could safely leave matters of revenge to the Goddess – Galdr would be taken care of in Her own good time, not Injya's.

Injya fled with the swiftness of an eagle, indeed she felt as if she had wings on her feet as she raced down into the valley. She found a brook and drank heartily from it. Despite the coldness of the air she again removed her clothes and bathed her sore, cut body, washing away the stench of Galdr, the mud and his seed from her body. She dried herself by dancing round in the sun and then donned her damp clothes. She knew that she must wash and dry them, but to make a fire this close to her hunter would be madness. She ate some of the rabbit and carefully securing the rest round her body, she ran on in a wide circle, hoping that when she came out of the valley it would not be back near the place of her captivity. She ran until the sun set and then she climbed a sturdy birch tree, using the last of her energy to bind herself tightly to its trunk. At last she slept, tied up once more, but this time free, her spirit joining the tender spirit of the tree, her heart resting secure in its branches, her aching limbs supported by the outstretched arms of the benign birch.

She woke before dawn, her body as stiff as the tree which supported it. Carefully she unbound herself and looked around her. From where she sat, midway up the birch, she could see the thin line of trees going far away into the direction of the rising sun, to the west she could see the trees thin out and then the marshlands begin. Injya clambered down and hugged the tree in gratitude. She sat and ate the rest of the rabbit, carefully burying its bones and then she continued her journey. It took her most of that day to reach the end of the tree-line and by evening she regretted having eaten so heartily. There was little chance of catching game at this time of night! She climbed another tree and securing herself as before, she slept, exhausted and hungry.

When she woke she climbed the slender tree until she no longer felt safe. There was no plume of smoke, no sign of man anywhere. Below her the woods thinned out and ended in marshlands, above her the bare mountain range climbed impassively. There was something in the texture of the hills which seemed familiar – something in the pattern of the colours of the lichens, mosses and the occasional stunted tree-form. She shut her eyes on the picture, holding it fast in her mind. When she opened them again she was certain. This was the beginning of the mountain range that her people always took to meet the caves – this was her path – soon she would find her people.

CHAPTER TWELVE

Anfjord had insisted that Patrec's body should be burnt. Although the normal practice for their people was to expose the body, only cleaving the skull to release the soul, Anfjord would have nothing less than cremation. Crenjal had not argued with him, but the elaborate ritual brought back memories which he had tried to silence for the past three summers. He felt an anger grow in him against Anfjord – all these arrangements – Anfjord was only making them to make him feel better – as if by giving Patrec a complex funeral could change the fact that he had slain her!

Anfjord mourned excessively, then, once the funeral was over, spent days bemoaning his dual loss. Not only did Crenjal have to listen to how wonderful Patrec had been, but also endless stories of how Galdr was so gifted at taming horses, how strong and gifted his three children were and always agreeing with him, humouring him, never showing him anything less than gentle concern. Soosha, Anfjord's eldest daughter, he shied away from, demanding, and getting, only Crenjal's attention.

And Crenjal hated him for it – how much longer would he have to present this double face to the tribe? How much longer *could* he hide the fact that he was secretly overjoyed at the removal of his one strong rival? For with Anfjord now discredited in the eyes of the Skoonjay people and with Galdr gone, he was the next obvious successor as chief. Bran, Anfjord's younger brother, had proved to be more interested in communing with trees and birds than hunting or protecting the women and children and of Anfjord's remaining nine children, six were maidens and of the three boys one was lame, one acted like his Uncle Bran and the other was a mere babe. But Crenjal was used to biding his time, to keeping his anger and impatience hidden. He had waited three winters for this moment, now, with power within his grasp, surely he could wait another season's turning?

A moon's cycle had passed since Patrec's funeral and Anfjord was still steeped in sorrow. Crenjal and he were walking through the encampment, Crenjal only giving half an ear to Anfjord's litany of woes when they came upon the seated figures of Forek and Halfray who, deep in conversation, did not notice their approach. Anfjord stopped in his tracks and looked at them so obviously enjoying each other's company. How much he missed Galdr! He caught hold of Crenjal's arm: 'See – the old can learn from the young, Crenjal!'

Crenjal laughed out aloud – Forek was as much of an old fool as Anfjord – the only thing Forek was learning was the art of not-listening! At the sound of the laughter, Forek and Halfray looked up and fell silent. Forek struggled to his feet.

'M'lord,' he said, bending his head low.

'M'lord,' Halfray likewise echoed.

'Forek!' Crenjal greeted him. 'You seem to be in hearty converse with Halfray here – are you learning much? Lord Anfjord says we have much to learn from our young men – is that true, Forek?'

Crenjal laughed as the old man stared at the ground, not raising his eyes. 'What think you, Halfray? Are you passing on your wisdom to the old – or, do you believe, as I, that the young learn from the old?'

Halfray lifted his face from staring at the ground and stared levelly into Crenjal's contemptuous eyes.

'I think the moon cries when old men look afeared,' he said quietly.

Crenjal guffawed and turned to go on: 'Why – you and

your riddles – you think the moon cries, do you? Who are you to know what the moon does?'

Halfray lowered his eyes and stared at the ground once more.

'What think you, my lord – does the moon cry when old men become frightened?'

Anfjord did not answer, he looked instead at the bowed head of Halfray and said slowly: 'Do you *know* the moon, young man? Do you see her crying?'

Halfray became very frightened – he did not dare answer truthfully, but knowing Anfjord's rages and sudden tempers, he dared not delay in answering either.

'Sometimes I feel that I *am* the moon, lord.'

He hoped that this would be preposterous enough to make them laugh at him and so dismiss him. Crenjal did laugh and started to walk on, but Anfjord stayed his ground.

'And can you *see*, like the moon, pray?'

'Why, yes, my lord, I can see the whole earth far below me, sometimes. When I am the moon I can sing and weep at the same time. Shall I dance for you, my lord?'

He struggled to his feet, trusting that he had done a passable impression of a lunatic and started hopping up and down on one leg, waving his arms round and giggling inanely.

'Be still!' Anfjord commanded. Halfray froze in mid-hop. 'Come here.'

Halfray half walked, half skipped, over to him.

'If you *are* the moon, if you *can* see the whole world, then you would know where my son is, would you not?' Halfray gulped and crossed his eyes – he knew what was coming.

'And if you knew where my son was – you could bring him back to us, could you not?'

Halfray pretended that he did not understand, as he scratched his head, uncrossed and recrossed his eyes once more and smiled stupidly.

'He would know – would he not, Crenjal?' Anfjord

bellowed at Crenjal's receding figure. Crenjal half turned round and shouted back: 'I doubt that Halfray knows where his backside is, my lord, let alone your son! But if he *says* he is the moon – then he ought at least *try* for you, my lord!'

'Yes, yes!' Anfjord clapped Halfray on his back, and with something which approached a smile, he continued: 'You *shall* go, Halfray, you shall go and find my son and bring him back to us – perhaps we have a use for the lunatic after all!'

So saying he left the stupefied Halfray and hurried to catch up Crenjal, pleased that the Gods had shown him a willing scapegoat for his guilt.

After his initial incredulity, Crenjal, too, felt pleased. The young man would not survive two moons' passing outside the encampment, certainly he would not find Galdr and would perish in the attempt, thus ridding him of the last of Mensoon's line without recourse to further bloodshed. Yes, it all fitted perfectly and it was yet another sign to the Skoonjay people that Anfjord had lost his reason – Halfray indeed!

Halfray sat alone in his sancar preparing himself for his journey. He knew that he would have little difficulty finding Galdr – all he had to do was summon his raven-spirit; his father's spirit would scan the earth until he found him, but how he was to bring Galdr back, when every atom of his soul rejoiced at Galdr's banishment, was a more profound difficulty than mere hundreds of pchekts travelling.

He closed his eyes and stilled his breathing, waiting for the familiar cawing sound which heralded the advance of his spirit-father. Quickly the image of the raven filled his brain and he waited for the question to come to him. The questions he asked his spirit-father were never the ones he thought he needed to ask. It was as if underneath each obvious question there lurked another one, which was always the true question, but which often surprised even Halfray. The question he had in his mind was: 'Why should I bring Galdr back?' but the silence of the raven showed him that this was not the correct one to be asking. He sat and concentrated upon the vision of the bird: 'How can I bring Galdr back?' – again silence. The vision faltered and began to fade. Halfray tried harder to grasp the right question, but the more he struggled with his work-a-day mind, the fainter the vision became. He gave up and opened his eyes. He could hear the noises outside which told him that the people were dispersing from the evening meal – soon the sancar would be filled with men. He made one last attempt, imagining this time that he had been taken over by his spirit-father, that he had become the raven. Instantly the question came to him: 'What gift has Galdr for me?' Immediately he felt as if his body was being bathed in white light and he started to shake as the figure of Askoye suddenly appeared before his eyes. Askoye the terrible, Askoye the crone, Askoye the knower of truth, Askoye the seer! He caught his breath and opened his eyes. It was not a question of what Halfray could do for Galdr, it was more what Galdr could do for Halfray!

Only Forek and Sanset came to the edge of the encampment the following morning. As he took his leave of them he suddenly knew that when he returned Forek would be no more, he would have joined the spirits of the air. He hugged the frail old man as he blinked away the tears which he felt pricking at his eyes.

'And remember' – the old man was saying – 'never take the life of the snow hare unless you are truly starving and under no circumstances eat the liver!'

'Yes, yes!' Halfray said quickly, glad of the old man's nagging – it lightened his heart.

'And do not lose my singlet – you will be glad of the warmth even if you do not want to wear a woman's clothing.'

'I know, Sanset, you have been very kind giving it to me.'

'Lending it!' she retorted, 'I will have it back when you return!'

Her quivering bottom lip belied the words – she felt sure in her heart that Halfray would perish – it mattered little that she had given him her finest, woven rabbit-shift – what did that matter when compared to a human life? She caught him roughly by the arm and kissed him briefly on the cheek.

'Be gone then, Halfray, and the Gods be with you.' She turned and ran back to the encampment, her tears flying in the wind, her heart heavy with foreboding.

Forek stood watching Halfray and as he slowly turned and walked away, he too knew that he would not see Halfray again. As Halfray's figure diminished, he saw the end of his life's usefulness – he could no longer ignore the calling – he would not be making the journey to the mountain home when the winds turned around.

Apart from the sadness he felt at saying the very final farewell to Forek, Halfray felt curiously excited by the prospect of tracing Galdr. He was convinced that he would have no difficulty, either in finding him, or travelling alone. He knew that the Goddess of the Moon and the Great Mother of the Earth would provide for him and although he had never been seen fit enough to accompany the men on their hunting, he instinctively knew how to find food for himself. Unlike the other young men who were only interested in proving themselves great hunters and warriors for the sake of the women, he had learnt the ways of the plant kingdom from the women and Forek, and he doubted greatly that he would ever have recourse to kill Forek's much maligned snow hare. He travelled east all day, not stopping until he came to an outcrop of moss-covered stones, and there he made his first night's camp. As he lay on his back and surveyed the vast canopy of stars, he imagined he could see mapped out in the heavens the route which would take him directly to Galdr. He fancied that Galdr was hiding at the heels of the Great Bear and that Arcturus, the Watcher, was keeping him within his confines, safe from harm. He prayed to Ahni and to the spirit of Mensoon, his mother, for guidance and strength, and feeling comforted and secure, he fell asleep.

The next day did not yield any signs, nor the next, nor the next full moon, nor the next waning one. The winds turned around and the howling coldness bit through Halfray's skin cloak and his doe-skin shift and when the rain turned white and Halfray was shivering in the low foothills, it ate its way inside Sanset's woven singlet as well. Halfray had spent three moons' passing now in despair, now full of hope, always convinced that he would find Galdr, as convinced as he was each time he reached the top of the next rise, that this would be the last, and always bitterly disappointed as he saw, not the top of the world, but yet another snow-covered hill, barren of all signs of life, save that of the snow hare.

Travelling had not been easy for Injya either. She imagined that she would find her people very soon after she recognized the land, but it had taken her another two full moons to be sure that she was even heading in the right direction. As the long cold winter drew on, she made several homes in small caves, each time abandoning the cave with reluctance, fearful of not finding another in which to shelter. She knew that by not moving she was only increasing the likelihood of perishing, to stay in the foothills with winter approaching meant almost certain death. The longer she left it, the worse the travelling would become. Already the rain's white tears covered her ankles, soon it would be impossible to climb higher. Injya knew that her people would already have decamped to the mountains long before the white rains had come. To travel at such a season was utter folly – surely she would perish!

Each day she rose, ate and walked, always looking upwards, hoping to spot smoke in the sky which would be the sign of habitation. Each day the light got shorter and the distance she was able to travel diminished. She had killed several reindeer, not for their meat, solely for their skins and as she added layer upon layer of skin to her skin, the weight pulled her down as surely as the crystalline rain. One night a monstrous blizzard blew and Injya watched, terrified at its ferocity, from the mouth of her cave. She *had* to find her people, she had to leave the cave the next day, to stay longer would be catastrophic.

The storm raged for three days and nights and when the keening wind finally died away, a blanched carpet covered Injya's entire universe. Not one single black rock stood proud on the hillside, not one hillock remained visible. As far as Injya's eyes could see, the tender white tears lay, clothing the world with their gentleness, protecting the earth from the freezing nights and the cruel winds. But Injya had no choice. She had used all the wood she had brought with her and had only kept warm on the third night by burning precious reindeer meat.

She wished she had paid more attention to the men when she was younger; she had a dim memory of watching them tying sticks and skins on to their feet whenever they had to journey through white rain, but she was a child then, and she never believed that one day, she too would need such a skill. As she bound her feet with skins she felt as if she was binding her spirit with them. There had been days before, of course, when she doubted that she would find her people, but none as desolate as this.

Six steps outside the cave she sank up to her thighs in a drift and exhausted herself totally getting out of it. She crawled back inside the cave, lay on its wet, blackened floor and wept. With supreme effort she ventured outside again, giving the unseen dip in the ground a wide berth. She scrambled and clawed her way up the mountainside, the freezing air hurting her lungs, the heavy furs dragging her down. As the wind rose again as advent to the coming night, Injya had covered less than a hundred pchekts. Like the mountain hare or the sly white fox, she began digging at

125

the snow and by the time the first mocking star appeared in the inky sky she had made the first of her white-rain homes. Her breath turned the tiny cubicle into ice and the heat of her body gradually returned as the deep cold covering insulated her against the wind's whip.

Through the tiny hole which she had lined with a scrap of fur she could see the black night. This hole was her lifeline – through it she could breathe and could see if more white rain fell. Weak as she was with the exertion of the day, she forced herself to stay awake, fearful of the white rain and the sound of the white wolf in the distance that her solitude-sharpened ears had picked up; but the howling of the wind and the wailing of the wolf sang a lonely lullaby to the night and despite her better intentions, Injya slept.

She dreamt of Erlik and the fearsome creatures she had glimpsed during her soul-walking, they became entwined in her mind with the white wolves who were now bounding towards her. In her dream the only avenue of escape was straight into the hell of Erlik himself as the wolves grew larger and came closer, their evil red eyes hungry for her flesh, their slavering mouths gaping as wide as the open arms of Erlik himself. She felt herself stumbling backwards, into the chasm and on the point of falling she clearly saw the figure of Askoye beckoning her, calling her towards the voracious jaws of the dogs of death. As Injya clutched at the air as she fell into the depths, the words of Askoye came singing through the night:

The great truths lie far away
in the lands of desolation.
The way there is through suffering and loss.
Privation alone can open the mind
to the secrets hidden from others
less brave than yourself.
Be brave and trust totally your universe
only then will you know your truth.

126

The dream finally left Injya and she slept as warm and content as a babe in arms. She woke chilled and damp, and the next day made much better progress. The ground hidden beneath her feet was rising sharply and often during that second day she had to climb up sheer faces of ice, but as she made her second home from the frost-crispened whiteness, she knew that with luck, she would reach her goal.

It was the smell which reached her first, the faint aroma of cooking on the air. She froze in her tracks, using all her energy to calm her pounding heart. On the wind came the sounds of men – far off to the right of her, indistinct at first but definitely voices, the first she had heard for nearly three moons' passing! She thought she would die with happiness as she dashed through the snow, slipping and skating her way nearer to the blessed voices. And then she saw them, strung out along the next rise, dark fur-clad men, the men of her people!

'Aieeaiee!' she called loudly. 'Aieeaiee!'

The small line of figures halted and looked in her direction.

'Aiee!' she called again in greeting, raising her arms and waving distractedly at them: 'I am Injya – I have come home!'

Injya slept for what was left of that day. When she eventually woke, she ate hungrily and silenced the women's insistent questions with her gaunt face and red-rimmed eyes. She would allow only Sanset to be with her and even then, rejected her many offers of love and guidance. Again she slept throughout the long night, dreaming nothing, feeling nothing, lost in an oblivion of blackness. She woke, saw Sanset's concerned face above her and felt Sanset squeeze her hand. From the sounds around her she knew that she was in one of the women's sancars and from the grey light realized that another day had dawned; but she did nothing but return the squeeze and fall into a deep sleep once more.

127

When eventually she woke fully it was in the gathering gloom of early evening. In the flickering light, she reached out her hand and touched Sanset, who was still squatting by her side. Sanset jumped, for she had fallen asleep and then smiled broadly.

'Now, will you eat?'

Her voice was low and soft, the first gentle feminine voice Injya had heard for three winters and as Injya looked at her cousin's round comely face, tears began to fall; tears of gratitude, joy and love. Sanset too began to cry as she reached out and took Injya into her arms.

'I thought you were dead!' she cried, over and over again as she rocked Injya to her.

'Injya, sweet Injya, you are home!' Ordinary words, ordinary emotions, one who was lost is returned. Injya thought she would cry for happiness for ever. Real warmth and affection, gentle loving. Her heart sang with joy.

Eventually the two women stopped crying and Injya was able to wash and change from her sodden skins into a shift that one of the women had given her. Food was brought to her and slowly, one by one, the women returned to the sancar, to tell of the fate that had befallen them since she had left. Apart from Sanset who sat close by her, Injya felt herself to be a stranger, not only from the Branfjord women, none of whom she knew, but from her own people – the little girls she had left behind had blossomed into women, the women had become older and there had been many deaths, for the journey to the mountain had been hard for the Skoonjay people. Never before in their combined memories could they tell of a worse trek. The white rains which made their summer-lands uninhabitable had come early, the marshlands freezing seemingly overnight and the expected dry mountains had turned into a nightmare of ice and white rain. Some of the Branfjord women blamed Anfjord himself for the catastrophic weather – it was the Gods' revenge for the slaying of Patrec; others thought that Galdr's soul was cursing them for his banishment. Whichever it was, they had lost fifteen of their oldest women and five children.

The men had suffered greater losses, nine of them being swept away by a snowfall at one time and a further eight had simply died of the cold. Four young men had perished in attempting various feats of bravery and two had been lost on a hunting party. There had been many babies born too soon and two young women, carrying their first child, had perished in the act of giving birth. As Injya listened to their sorry tales she detected a deeper sorrow in the women, unconnected with the freezing deaths and the stillborn babes, a sorrow born from their loss of spirit.

She had heard the story of Patrec's death, of Galdr she knew more than the women, but she kept that secret to herself and she listened with a heavy heart as they related his father's wild and brutal couplings with whomsoever he chose. She now understood where Galdr's brutality sprung from – if that was the norm for the Branfjord men, small wonder that babes so conceived died before their time or that the women bore them with such suffering. Nothing that the women could tell her lightened her foreboding. Of Crenjal they knew little – he was always by Anfjord's side, had seldom taken a woman of either tribe and was greatly feared. Since Patrec's murder he had seemed to have a stronger hold over Anfjord, very often speaking for him and it had been darkly hinted that it had been at Crenjal's insistence that Galdr was banished.

As night drew on and the stories told slowed from their excited gabbling to a more orderly pace, a messenger from Anfjord came to the sancar. He hoped that Injya was now rested and bid her come to him the following morning. With not a little dread in her heart, Injya once more slept, but this time it was not the dreamless sleep of the exhausted, but the fitful sleep of a woman who knew that when she woke, she was to face her destiny.

CHAPTER THIRTEEN

As Injya washed and oiled her body the next morning, she wondered how she would be received by Anfjord. She was surprised that he had left her so long undisturbed – to find out after all this time that she was, indeed, alive must have shocked and perhaps frightened him. Crenjal, no doubt, would have hardened his heart further towards her and as she allowed her hair to be brushed and braided she wondered again about these two men. Having listened to the women and all that had befallen them, having watched their scared faces and picked up on the air their frightened whisperings she knew that she had to restore the power of the Goddess to these women or else perish in the attempt; but how, precisely, she was to do this, now eluded her.

All through her journey, she had gone over and over the meeting with Anfjord, imagining first one scenario, then another. She had rehearsed her words and actions, weighed every possibility, but this, this allowance, this tolerance of her presence, she had not foreseen. She had planned, naïvely, to bewitch Anfjord; she had half-convinced herself that Crenjal would have perished or been slain before now. But now, faced with the prospect of two men, who seemingly had the total control of all the tribe in their hands, she no longer felt sure of her path and a deep fear arose in her which was not dispelled by prayer or reason.

Finally dressed and suitably cleansed, Injya was taken by the women through the encampment to Anfjord's sancar. Injya had scarcely been aware of the size of the encampment when she had first been enfolded by it. It looked as if there were twenty or more large skin-covered sancars, protected by the circling mountain. The mountain

130

itself gave shelter to more than a hundred of the most vulnerable of the group as a labyrinth of caves wound in and out of its base. The journeying may have been hazardous, but the encampment was secure and would serve the people well throughout the long hard winter. Sanset and her daughter, Bendula, now a frank-eyed child of eleven summers, left Injya with swift embraces at the entrance to Anfjord's sancar. Injya felt that, perhaps, those would be the last tender embraces she would feel and she had to fight with herself to let go of her gentle cousins.

Steeling herself against her fear, Injya, not looking at the two men standing guard, had to bend almost double to gain access to the chieftain's sancar and as she did so, the memory of the last time she had done this came back to her. Then she was a child-woman of fourteen summers who had just witnessed the cruelty and carnage of this man's wishes, now she was a woman of nearly eighteen winters, and one who had studied with Askoye, one who had been to the centre of the earth and the zenith of the heavens! The words she had used to Galdr came flooding back: 'I am Injya, only remaining daughter of Mensoon, and as such I am now the High Priestess of the Gyaretz people and I will do nothing against my will!' The words brought with them the familiar tingling of power – she *was* the High Priestess – no man – or men – was worth her fear!

The inside of the sancar was opulent compared to that of the women, its rock floor covered with many furs and hung on the walls were many twinkling gems. The room was lit by the central fire and by tapers round the skins; dried flowers hung from the rafters giving a sweet, musky smell to the air. This was not as Injya had expected. Anfjord and Crenjal were seated on fur-covered daises at the opposite side to the entrance and neither of them moved as she stood and took in her surroundings. Deliberately she avoided looking directly at either man and for a long moment the three people inside the sancar were as still as the now frozen lakes of the summer-lands. Eventually, Anfjord rose from his skin-covered pallet, took two steps towards her, then stopped and looked at her. Crenjal remained seated, his eyes taking in every detail of her dress and manner.

'You are Injya – the daughter of Mensoon – the last of the Priestesses?'

Anfjord's question was a statement of fact and required no answer. He slowly walked towards her and then stared hard into her face. Looking back at her, Injya saw a man much hurt, not by the journeying, not by the lines of the many winters which had etched themselves into his face, but a man much hurt by himself. He stood of equal height to her, his long black hair oiled and combed sleekly, his dark brown eyes heavily hooded, staring intently into her face. His nose bore a resemblance to Galdr's, slender at the ridge, flared at the nostril and his mouth, though puckered with age, still looked full and sensuous. Like all the Branfjord men, his cheeks were hairless, his high cheek-bones and square jaw-line glistening in the light as his face slowly creased into a smile, as a look, which Injya instantly recognized as the look of desire, crept into his eyes.

'You are beautiful – like a fine young colt.'

He touched her face with the back of one gnarled hand and then held her chin, twisting her head to inspect her features more closely.

'I will enjoy riding you one day!'

He suddenly dropped his hand and, laughing loudly, turned his back on her and regained his seat.

'What do you think, Crenjal, shall we let her live, shall we share ourselves with her, or should we find another Kraa for her to sport with?'

He laughed again and stared at Injya. Crenjal sighed and slowly stood up, fondling Anfjord's shoulder as he passed him.

'I know not, my lord, we must ensure that she gives up something of herself – she is still proud, still defiant – I do not think this colt has been broken yet – there is

132

more than the common spirit about her – perhaps she is still practising her mother's evil ways. Are you, Injya?'

These last three words were spoken directly into Injya's face as Crenjal bent over her. Injya looked into the deep black eyes of the man she hated more in this world than even Galdr. She looked impassively at his much-scarred face, his cruel twisted mouth, his straggling beard and unkempt dung-brown hair. She could smell his strong breath as his face came yet closer to hers, she could feel the overpowering presence of his body as it towered over her and suddenly she knew what she must do.

'No,' she said quietly and sweetly to him, 'No, Crenjal, I am not practising my mother's evil ways. For three winters I have wandered alone, searching for my people.'

She looked deep into his eyes, the eyes of the treacherous, the eyes of the murderer of her hopes and dreams. She drank in the bitter-sweet perfume on the air and inwardly chanting a spell of enchantment, she continued in a low voice.

'And in that time I have come to realize the lies my mother told. In that time I have come to understand the lies that my grandmother told. Crenjal, there *is* no Goddess! The moon *has* no power save that of scaring the children with her sudden appearances and ghostly light! I have come back to my people, I have come back to be with you – you, Crenjal – if you will have me – I am yours!'

She stared deep and long into his eyes and blinked slowly, knowing that when she opened them, Crenjal would be as blinded to her true intentions as a newborn rabbit and as bound to her as the bear-cub is to its mother.

The roar of laughter which came from Anfjord broke the spell.

'Crenjal, what say you now? What say you about this woman who you would have had me despatch from this life while she slept this very night? What say you now?'

133

Anfjord rolled about on his seat, clutching his stomach and bellowing with mirth. Injya looked into Crenjal's eyes and saw her spell working as his face softened and his own eyelids closed slowly.

'Nothing, my lord Anfjord, nothing.'

He suddenly hung his head and stared at Injya's feet – what was happening to him? He shook his head and looked at Injya again. Before him he saw a beautiful young woman, shining with love, love for him! He felt his heart sink to his stomach and rise again, expand in his chest until it almost hurt. Love for him poured from Injya's face and he felt stupid, confused, and, suddenly, ridiculously happy. He stared at the ground again, his mind reeling as it tried to make sense of his emotions. He had taken few women before – he found them tiresome and the act of mating unsatisfactory. He understood the young men's hunger for women, but had taken a secret pride in the lack of desire he felt for them himself. But suddenly . . . his heart leapt as the enormity of Injya's words struck him . . . suddenly Injya was offering herself to him and she was the most beautiful, fragile creature he had ever seen. He shook his great head in disbelief – how could he have not seen this before – how could he have plotted her death? He felt tears of remorse prick the back of his eyes as he raised his head once more and took in the delights of her face.

'Injya!' he whispered gruffly. 'Injya!'

As if transfixed by her own spell, she lifted her hands towards his face and took it between her own. Rising on to her toes, she kissed him slowly and deeply on his mouth: 'Crenjal,' she murmured at last, 'be my husband!'

Sanset's heart was heavy with secrets. She lay on her bed in the red darkness, listening to the light snoring of the women around her, the wind as it whistled through cracks in the sancar skins. In less than a moon's passing the wind would die, and silence and ice would smother their world. Death. A word familiar; the death of the year, the death of the wind. Silent brilliant coldness would soon envelope her and everyone of the Skoonjay people, but now there was still a whispering and inside Sanset's head the secrets rose and fell like waves on an ocean of consciousness.

She knew Injya's plans for the future, knew that her return to them heralded the beginnings of change – for her, her child and the entire tribe and she was afraid. Injya had emerged from her meeting with Anfjord changed. She had become aloof, looked at her as if she were a stranger. Sanset understood that the marriage Injya had spoken of was not what Injya herself wanted, knew that Injya was plotting, but was afraid for her, she was playing an awesome game, the outcome of which she saw only as death. That word again. She felt as if Injya was dying to her, that her old relationship was dying, and could not shake off a growing feeling of resentment towards her cousin.

Injya had spoken to her as if she were no more to her than the rest of the women. Perhaps the gulf which Injya was putting between them was for her own protection – but she did not *want* to be protected – she was not a child, she was a woman of twenty-three summers, older by four winters than Injya, and here she was, being treated like some child as if she were incapable of confidences.

Divine secret, that was what her name meant. Was she to be always and only the receptor of others' secrets? Was she to have none of her own, or be party to none of the greater secrets that Halfray, Injya and even old Forek knew? She felt warmed by the heat of anger – why had she not been fit to inherit any of the powers of the Goddess? Anger turned to petulance as she thought of the inequalities of life. Bendula, her mother, was beautiful – as beautiful as her sister, Mensoon – she was gifted with a keen mind and a warm, loving nature, but she had none of the powers of Mensoon. Sanset had none either, neither had she inherited the beauty of either her mother or her aunt, she was as short as Injya was tall, as plain as Injya was striking – the list seemed endless!

Sanset snuggled close to the slender body of Bendula for some comfort from the feelings of impotence and unfairness. She felt her stir in her sleep and as she lay, trying to keep her restlessness to herself, she began to feel calmer. She could see the outline of her daughter's profile by the glow from the fire and sensed the deep, peaceful sleep that the child was enjoying and slowly, slowly, an understanding grew in her.

Her path was as different from Injya's as her own mother's had been from Mensoon; her path was the path of the nurturer, the path of Hoola, Great Mother of the Earth. She sighed deeply and allowed herself to be comforted by that realization: Sanset the nurturer, Sanset the mother. She touched her sleeping daughter on her downy shoulder, drew the fur covers around her and found herself thinking of Galdr and Injya, of what little nurturing Injya had received in the past few years. Her heart became cold as she remembered Injya's whispered account of her meeting with Galdr and she felt a sob rising from her as she thought of the child which Sanset knew was growing in Injya's secret place. Cold fingers of fear clutched at her stomach like ice creeping along a grass blade. How could Injya hope to keep her secret from Crenjal? How could she possibly believe that Crenjal would not see through her deception?

Sanset knew, even before Injya told her of the rape, she knew that Injya was with child, she could read it in her face, could see it in a certain heaviness of the breasts. Injya's figure was still lean from travelling and her belly showed no signs of swelling, but her breasts had the heavy darkness which presaged that milk would soon flow from them. Crenjal would know too, before long, everyone would know and then surely Injya's true intentions would be clear to all. She remembered Injya the last time she had seen her, an orphaned maiden, scared, awaiting a 'marriage' of bestiality and now Injya, by her own volition, had put herself in exactly that position once more.

'Beloved Hoola, take pity on poor Injya,' Sanset prayed as silent tears fell on to her pillow, 'poor, poor Injya! Have pity.'

As Injya lay, listening to Sanset shifting around uneasily in her bed, she was feeling as equally sorry for her cousin as she was for her. Poor Sanset, she really has no idea how important a role she is playing. Injya smiled bitterly to herself as she remembered Sanset's grief and anger when she had described her ordeal with Galdr and the awful loneliness she had felt those three long winters' turning spent with Askoye. But she had felt nothing for herself as she related it to her. She felt nothing but the stirring in her body of Galdr's child. She had known almost immediately after the second coupling, that she was carrying his seed and the thought of her child growing inside her had added fire to her resolve to reach her people before the birth. She could not feel the child quicken yet, but she had not put the cessation of her courses down to the hardship of the journey and she, too, could see the changes in her breasts and feel the changes in her belly. She thanked merciful Hoola that Crenjal had been blinded to the fullness of her belly and prayed that indeed, he would stay ignorant of that, and her true purpose, for several moons to come.

She had not known until she saw Crenjal and Anfjord together that it would be Crenjal whom the Goddess sent to her. Now, that too felt comfortable. Crenjal had been treacherous, it was only fitting that he should be the recipient of treachery – it was all in the divine plan, the law was absolute: as you give so shall you receive! She knew that under the guise of being a good wife to Crenjal, she would be above suspicion, secretly she could share the knowledge she had learnt with Askoye with the women. Crenjal would protect her from Anfjord, she would be in no danger from him and slowly, as the men understood that what Injya was teaching was not a return to the ways of the female-dominated society of her mother, but a fusion of all the powers of the universe, they, too, would be no threat. Perhaps even Anfjord himself would be won over! She had no doubt that this could be achieved. Crenjal was besotted with her, blind even to the lechery of Anfjord and it mattered little to her who took her to be his wife – both men were repugnant to her, but to make the rest of the men and women of the Skoonjay people follow her, she must have standing and prestige – she must be seen to be powerful.

She closed her eyes once more and stilled her breathing. Tomorrow she would enter into a sacred marriage with Crenjal, she must rest and gain her strength. She snorted quietly at the words – a sacrilegious marriage would be more suitable! She felt her heart sink as the thought and memories of the degredation she had suffered at the hands of Galdr came flooding back. She fought against her thundering heart and forced herself to calm her breathing; Crenjal would have no power over her, her incantation had worked – he could not touch her as Galdr had – and taking comfort from that thought, she eventually slept.

Only Crenjal seemed to have slept well that night. He had fallen instantly into a deep, dreamless sleep. A certain surety had come over him as he had gazed at Injya, all his frantic scheming and need for power had left him. Nothing mattered any more to him, save that he could be allowed to be with Injya. He felt perfectly at peace, at ease with himself and his universe. He loved and was loved. He needed to know no more.

Unlike Crenjal, Anfjord had been kept awake by desire. He had taken two women, but nothing could rid him of the vision of Injya. It was as if she had invaded his senses, had got inside him and was creeping along every muscle of his body. He needed her, he needed to be inside that woman as she was inside him. She had a power over him that was greater than anything he had ever known before, greater than anything of which he had ever dreamt. He had to have her, own her, know her power. His hand touched one of the women he had taken earlier. The feel of her flesh only served to enforce the aloneness he felt. Only Injya could make him complete. His fingers tightened their grasp on the woman as he tried to imagine that she *was* Injya. His manhood rose again urgent with the memory of her face and he was about to mount the woman who had barely stirred, when anger overcame him. This fat sow was not Injya! Rage overcame him and he smote the woman a blow which squealed her awake.

'That's right!' he shouted at her, 'squeal like the hog you are!'

The terrified woman shut her mouth and endured his onslaught, biting her knuckles with the pain, clinging on to the furs, waiting for the act to be over, but his thrusting manhood found no release inside her and after what seemed an eternity, he cried aloud: 'Damn you, Crenjal! Damn you!' and racked with rage he withdrew from her and flung her from him, oblivious to the fact that as his cry had torn at the mantle of the night like a beast in agony, it had been met only with a slow smile upon Injya's face.

Injya accepted with good grace the soft grey woven gown which Patrec's eldest daughter, Soosha, gave her. It slipped over her long body like a glove, it was warm and comforting – something of which Injya did not doubt she would be glad. Many of the Branfjord women had given or loaned her things for the marriage and as they huddled around her, admiring her strong body and her wondrous curly black hair, Injya began to pick up something on the air which amounted to excitement. It was as if their own marriages were such mundane matters, ones which they did not enter into joyously, that they took greater delight in the preparation for her own. Her own women, in contrast, were solemn, the memories of the summer groves still too fresh, to share in this parody.

Eventually, when the meagre winter sun was at its highest in the heavens, Injya walked away from the sancar and stood alone, waiting for Crenjal, in the centre of the encampment. She did not have long to wait. She heard the drum begin to beat behind her in one of the caves and the deep voices of the men chant in unison the name of Crenjal. She stood, watching the entrance to each sancar, wondering from which sancar he would emerge. The chanting grew and echoed round the caves behind her and suddenly she saw the top of his head appear over the rise beneath the encampment. He was wearing a fine helmet which flashed in the sunlight, the gems embedded in it winking at her, its coppery surface shimmering with an almost unearthly light. As the rest of his body came into view, dressed in fine silver furs and leather singlet, Injya wavered in her resolve. He was, indeed, a mighty man, standing almost as tall as the Great Bear himself in Askoye's cave and as he stretched his arms out to her in greeting, she was reminded again of the similarity between the two. But it was Crenjal's helmet which fascinated her most, and as he approached she suddenly knew why. It had been made from the metal of the Barnkop – the sacred stand of the Arnjway Staff, the Barnkop which had been fashioned into the likeness of a woman's sex and which had held the most sacred object known to her people for aeons! And here was Crenjal, wearing it on his head! Injya did not know whether to laugh or cry – the profanity was too great!

The drumming was reaching a crescendo as Crenjal strode over the ground to embrace her. Injya felt that she would faint with the noise and the blazing helmet burning her eyes. She felt fused with the power that this object contained – it mattered not that it had been rebeaten into another shape – whatever its shape, it still held enormous power. She felt her skin tingle and her heart race as Crenjal drew closer to her. She forced her eyes away from the helmet and into his eyes. All she could see was a pure shining love reaching out from him, as she blazed back the message with her own eyes and heart.

'You will love me no matter what I do – you will love me until you die!'

As Crenjal reached Injya the drumming and the chanting stopped. In deathly silence Crenjal took both of Injya's hands and pressed them to his chest.

'I give you my heart – for it has no other desire but to love you!'

Moving her hands to his forehead he said: 'I give you my thoughts – may I have no others save those of you.'

(Fool, Injya thought mercilessly, you *have* no thoughts!) Then moving her hands to rest on his loins he said softly: 'I give you my manhood – for without you I have none!' (And *with* me you will have none either, Injya thought cruelly.)

Suddenly he flung her hands from him and embraced her, clutching her with such force and such longing that the breath was nearly crushed from her body. As soon as he embraced her, the women began ululating with joy and ran from their hiding places in the sancars and caves, throwing precious seeds at the entwined couple and dancing round them, their faces shining with emotion and, as Injya followed Crenjal to his sancar, she caught herself thinking that he was not the only fool in the encampment.

Crenjal's sancar was not as lavish as Anfjord's, and only half the size but it was warm, the floor covered in skins as Anfjord's had been and if anything it smelled sweeter. Injya was very surprised, she had expected this great bear of a man to live like the animal he so closely resembled. She was also very surprised by his demeanour – he seemed more like a shy maiden than a man of nearly forty winters. He bade her sit upon a great heap of furs as he busied himself removing some of his finery and finally he sat with her, offering her a silver-coloured goblet.

'Will you drink this? It is the sweetest wine from the nectar of the bees in the summer-lands – it will warm your soul.'

He looked so eager, so desperate to please that Injya's heart softened and she took a sip. The sweet liquid coursed down her throat gently, it was very good indeed. She took another long drink and passed the goblet back to him.

'You too, my husband, you too!'

He smiled the tenderest smile and tears welled up in his great dark eyes.

'Oh, Injya!' was all he could say, as his choking voice gave way to the tears of love he felt for this divine woman. Eventually he sniffed loudly and then sipped at the goblet as if he had never tasted wine before, sipping and never taking his eyes off her face.

'I need no wine, when I can drink in your beauty, my sweeting,' he whispered, his voice scarce audible through his emotions. He carefully placed the goblet on the floor and put one giant hand on her thigh. Instinctively Injya recoiled from his touch.

'More wine?' she said quickly and hopefully, reaching for the goblet.

'I have told you – I do not need wine with you.' His voice sounded harsher and his hand clutched her thigh more intensely.

'But – perhaps I would like some?' she said as sweetly as she could and answering her own question she took a large gulp of the liquid. Instantly she regretted it, for her head began to swim. She dropped the goblet as he pulled her towards him. Now! she thought, now his manhood will leave him, now he will be unable to continue, now! But as his grip tightened she felt the sancar begin to spin round her: now! she screamed inside herself, now, magic-making Askoye, come to the aid of your daughter, rid this man of his manhood! But as the room began to spin faster and faster inside her head, she knew that her power had left her the moment she had drunk the wine. All the years of preparation were for nought – she had no more power over him than the crickets had over the sun.

142

CHAPTER FOURTEEN

Crenjal grunted and turned over as Injya endeavoured to disentangle herself from under his massive heavy body. Her head throbbed and ached as did her womanhood. As she slowly stood up, she felt his life dribble down the insides of her legs and for a terrible moment she wondered if the act would have harmed her baby. She rinsed the goblet, took a long drink of water and then washed her legs. *That* must never happen again! she resolved. She looked at the sleeping hulk of Crenjal and caught herself wishing that he were younger and smaller – perhaps then she could love him . . . No sooner had the thought crossed her mind than she immediately censored it. No man would ever take her again – no matter how young or handsome he was! She wrapped herself in a large fur and crept from the sancar. All was still and calm, the wind for once was silent and the full moon bathed the whole encampment in its ethereal light. How she wished she could do the full-moon ritual, but it was too dangerous, she must be careful. Instead she settled for a grateful look into the face of the Mother and crept back inside the sancar.

She put some more wood on the fire and squatted on her haunches, looking deeply into the dancing flames. It had not been so bad with Crenjal, she decided, not like . . . and she shivered as she remembered Galdr. Crenjal had tried to be gentle with her and from what she could remember, he had not hurt her as much as . . . that man! She shook her head with annoyance, it seemed to her that she was unable to rid her mind of Galdr, that at every moment when her mind was not actively engaged upon

143

praying, plotting or just surviving, Galdr came into her head unbidden and unwelcomed.

'May the flames of the underworld take him from me as surely as these flames are consuming this wood!' she hissed spitefully to the fire. From nowhere the words of Anfjord's curse came upon her and she found herself saying out aloud: 'Take my son, Great Oagist, take him on your mighty wings and destroy him! Bring Kronos from his fiery hole to take Galdr, my son, and give him to your brother, Ipirün, King of Fire, to consume him! Let him burn for ever in your flames of revenge!'

She began to shake as the words were wrenched from her mouth – they were not *her* words – the words of another had entered her! Crenjal snorted and stirred and suddenly Injya felt terribly afraid – there was a power here over which she had no control – a power perhaps greater than that of the Mother. She knew that the words had come from Anfjord, that those were perhaps the last words he had ever spoken to his son, but why would they come through to her? What demon of the night was taking those words and putting them into her head – what evil tukris lived in this sancar?

She jumped to her feet and stared at the floor where she had been squatting and on it she saw a blue gem wink back at her. She bent down and picked up a small piece of lapis lazuli. She fingered it for some time, turning it over in her hands until she realized that it must have fallen from Crenjal's helmet. Silently she crept over to the helmet and saw the hole where it had once been. As she fingered the gem and tried to put it back into the tiny indentation, the helmet became first hot and then freezing cold in her hands. It appeared that it had a life of its own and she stared in fascinated terror, as the hole from which the gem had fallen slowly reddened and seemed to melt, filling up with a dark red substance. She could not stop the cry of fear as a single drop of blood, warm and viscous, fell from the hole.

She turned to Crenjal, her cry had not wakened him. Reluctant and fearful she looked at her hand. A well of deep red blood lay in her white, upturned palm. She looked at the helmet. The sliver of lapis lazuli was where it ought to be. And again Injya found herself asking – what magic was this?

Galdr jumped awake, the sound of his father's curses ringing loudly in his ears. He lay for a moment wondering where he was and then he remembered. A thin whitish light was coming from the entrance to the cave and he guessed that it was moonlight. Struggling to his feet he crawled through the long, low passage towards the light. A beautiful serene full moon quivered high above him, an halo extending from it shimmering with faint iridescent pinks, violets and pale yellows. Galdr took a deep breath of the cold night air and surveyed the scene which unfolded before his eyes. Crisp white rain lay everywhere and far below him he could see the trees, standing like a patch of frost-covered fur. As he watched the picture of night beauty he saw a pair of darting orange eyes flicker and then disappear into the trees. Wolves. More tiny flame-bright eyes darted in and out of the blackness. Galdr involuntarily shivered – bears he could cope with – wolves he was not too pleased to encounter.

He turned around and bending low re-entered the cave, slipping yet again on the steep narrow incline which led into the cave. Cursing, he finally stood upright and looked round in the gloom of his home. It was a strange place – the symbols painted on the walls with white ash, blood red and black soot meant nothing to him, although when he had discovered the drum, skin shift and mirror, tucked high up on a narrow ledge, he knew that the cave had been inhabited by not just a mad man who had eked out his time by daubing the walls with incomprehensible nonsense. He had tried to make sense of the drawings many times, looking for similarities between the swirls and dashes on the drum and those on the walls. Each day he understood a little more, now seeing clearly a man with reindeer antlers, now a highly stylized tree, now a star, now a circling path, but as soon as he had thought that he had the symbols fixed in his mind, next time he looked they seemed to represent something new, as if overnight they would change their shape deliberately to confuse him.

He kicked at the dying fire which sent fresh billows of smoke up to the charred roof of the cave and coughing, he squatted down in front of it, staring into the flames and feeling very alone. The sound of a wolf howling in the valley below did not arouse fear in him – he welcomed the sound – it meant that he was not completely alone. He regretted now having burnt the effigy of the giant bear he had found – he was quite a friendly sort of beast in his own way – but having spent two sleepless nights, convinced that the bear was staring at him, he had felt incapable of doing anything else. He half-regretted killing the two bear-cubs also; perhaps he could have kept one for a pet, only killing him when he became a dangerous size. But the slaughter had seemed necessary, he convinced himself, he would never have been sure that the cub would not have held the killing of his mother against him and that one night, while he slept, it would have decided to maul him to death.

He looked at his arms and hands, the great weals cut in his flesh by the mother bear's talons had healed remarkably quickly . . . although . . . He looked again and felt the raised spot in the centre of his left palm where the mother bear had caught his hand, spearing it in her mouth with a huge incisor, although . . . perhaps not! . . . He rubbed the spot which seemed suddenly tender. He tilted his palm nearer the fire and watched as, without any pain, the spot opened and one large drop of dark red blood slowly oozed from it. He watched, fascinated as the drop trickled slowly down towards his fingers and finally fell on to the floor of the cave, leaving no trace of its slow journey behind. He examined his hand again. The spot was completely closed and healed – there *was* no break in the skin from which it had come! He rubbed his palm, the tenderness gone; he turned his hand over and examined the back of his hand – there was a dent and a scar, but the skin was healed. He looked at his right hand – nothing! Finally he decided that he must be having a strange waking dream and rubbing his hands briskly together, he bundled himself back into his bed, gathering his furs round him tightly as he tried to shut out the moon and the cold and the sound of the wolf.

The next day was a perfect day for hunting, Galdr decided, as he scanned the cloudless sky and noticed the high wisps of cerise-tinged vapour – a good omen of fine, clear weather. He had set his mind on hunting today and the fine heavens confirmed that this would be auspicious – if he did not manage to return to his cave tonight, no ill would come to him – it would not snow again and the air was still. He breathed in deeply. He knew that there were reindeer, probably sheltering in the woods below – he could smell their warm animal earthiness. They would be driven out of their cover soon, if not by the wolves, then by their need for salt. The black boulders which dotted the mountainside contained the salt they so desperately needed in this midwinter season and Galdr knew that if he secreted himself down-wind beside one of the bigger boulders, it would not be long before the animals came to lick the sides of the rock, satisfying their curious craving.

He went back inside the cave and chewed slowly on a piece of last night's snow hare. It was tough, its thin stringy texture cloying and dry. Galdr wished that he had picked more berries and nuts when he had had the chance, but, he shrugged his shoulders to himself, he had not done badly. He was still alive and fit. Wiping his fingers on his fur singlet he heaped moss on to the fire to dampen it and collecting his sling and spear he left the cave.

He was halfway down towards the biggest outcrop of rock when something caught his eye. Instinctively he dropped down into the snow and looked again. On the blanket of white rain, some one hundred pchekts distance was a large black cross of immense proportions, some six or seven pchekts wide and two to three long. It seemed to waver on the snow, shifting slightly, shimmering almost. Galdr felt his stomach tighten and a knot of fear form in his throat. The image shifted and then thinned and wheeled away. With a startled yelp that was born out of relief, Galdr looked upwards to the heavens. All it was was a shadow, a shadow of a large black bird! Feeling very stupid, Galdr laughed to himself as he watched the bird circle the spot and then fly towards him. He could see clearly now that it was a large black raven – an old one too by the look of its ragged wings. Galdr wondered about trying to kill it, but thought better of it – still, the sight heartened him – an early messenger of Aspar? As he continued his journey the bird seemed to be following him, circling him high up in the blue air, wheeling round and round his head. He started several times to load his sling, but each time he did so, the bird would caw loudly and wheel off, only to reappear some few moments later.

After a long time, Galdr reached the rocks which he had set his sights on and thankfully sat down, resting against a sun-warmed boulder and waited. The bird seemed to have tired of its game and disappeared, and as the sun rose to its highest point, the warmth lulled Galdr to sleep, its golden rays touching his dark figure with gentle brushstrokes of saffron-coloured slumber.

When he woke, stiff and cold, the sky was already darkening and the setting sun showed that he had slumbered long. He shook his head with anger – how stupid could he be? He picked up his spear and swore softly – the chance of game had passed – if they had come out at all that day, they would have either passed onward or gone back; either way, he would not catch anything *this* night! He rubbed his flesh vigorously to restore the blood and then scrambled to the top of the rocks. From his look-out point he could see a thin line of hoof-marks moving from the trees towards a rock, then out towards his left and finally disappearing over a ridge. He cursed again – they had moved and he had missed them! He *could* try following their hoof-marks – perhaps he could reach their night resting-place before total darkness fell. His stomach rumbled its disapproval, but he studiously ignored it, telling himself that if he did not follow the tracks, it would soon show more than mere disapproval!

He did not step in the tracks themselves, but kept always to the higher ground a little to their right. The sun gave a final flourish and sank from view, as the moon rose with speed. The white world beneath her took on a silver, shining light and Galdr found no difficulty in following the prints made by the beasts. He was cheered when he saw them skirt by the mouth of his cave, he could smell the dung easily – it was still very fresh – they could be no more than a few hundred pchekts ahead of him. He resisted the temptation of going back to his cave and resuming his trek on the morrow – reindeer could travel over many hundred pchekts a day once they were on the move – he had to follow them.

As he gained the rise which was just below his cave, he suddenly saw them, a large group of perhaps twenty or more does with four or five bucks among them. They were sheltering in the lee of some rocks and in the strong moonlight they were clearly visible, two big bucks standing, their proud heads and massive antlers pointing outwards from the group as the rest lay, presumably sleeping. Galdr silently crouched down, removed his fur boots and leggings and dropped his heavy bear-skin cape noiselessly beside them. The cold air bit into his bare arms and the frost-sharpened white rain felt like knives under his feet as, silent as a shadow, he hugged the ground, drawing ever closer to the resting herd. He skirted away round them, finally stopping altogether on top of the rocks below which they were resting. There was no movement save an occasional stamped foot by one of the bucks. Stealthily as a reed-snake he silently removed a small but very heavy round stone from his pouch and placed it in his sling. Very slowly he stood up, his naked feet gripping the edge of the craggy rock and then with a whir which sent all the deer struggling to their feet, he spun the sling round his head and sent the stone flying through the air, whistling down towards the unsuspecting animals with impressive force.

The missile hit the forehead of a large doe and she dropped instantly. The herd dashed away in all directions in their frenzy, slowly regrouped and cantered a little way off, then stopped and turned to face him. Galdr jumped down from his lofty perch and expertly cut the doe's throat. The soft plumes of breath ceased from the gentle animal's muzzle as her carcass twitched convulsively for a few moments and was finally still. The moonlight showed the bright blood black upon the ground and Galdr almost felt sorry for having spoiled such an idyllic scene, but hunger and the need to survive the rest of the winter could not be sacrificed on the altar of the picturesque. Watched by the standing animals he expertly gutted the beast, saving its liver, and with an effort hauled the doe on to his shoulder and staggering slightly under the weight, stumbled back to the cave, only stopping to retrieve his clothes and adjust his burden.

By the time Galdr eventually got back to the cave he felt utterly exhausted. Thankfully he dropped his quarry on to the floor and then he flung himself on to his pallet bed. His back felt as if it were breaking in two and his neck and shoulders were sore from the frost-crisped fur of the animal. He yawned and stretched, straightening his shoulders and rubbing his neck, but finally he turned over and fell into a fitful sleep. He woke from a nightmare of charging reindeer bucks, only to stare into the glazed eyes of the dead doe, lying in a crumpled, bloody heap upon the floor. A weak shaft of sunlight entered the cave and Galdr reluctantly got off his bed and stretched again. His whole body ached and his feet were cut and bruised. As he hobbled and winced his way over to the still smouldering fire, his heart stopped. Sitting calmly on the other side of the fire was Halfray!

Galdr opened his mouth to speak, but the shock of the figure robbed him of his words. After what seemed an age, his heart, now pounding in its confining rib-cage, gave him the wit to speak.

'You!' was all his astonished mouth could utter.

'You!' he said again, looking incredulously at the smiling figure before him.

'I have been sent to bring you home,' Halfray said quietly, as if he had only talked with him the day before. 'Your father sent me.'

He smiled up at the astonished young man, his crystal-clear eyes shining in the pale yellow light.

'I . . . ' Galdr began, clutching his brow and looking as if he would fall over with the shock.

'Come, sit down – look, I have brought you some berries—' Halfray extended his hand towards him and showed him a few plump, pink berries.

'How . . . ?' Galdr stuttered again – the questions racing round his befuddled brain.

'Oh,' Halfray started, 'I know a potion for keeping them fresh – they are good – try some!'

'No! Not the berries, fool!' Galdr shouted at him, frowning and finally sinking on to his knees, 'not the berries – how did you find me?'

'I was guided,' Halfray answered simply.

When Galdr had recovered sufficiently, Halfray told him of his journeying and something of his precognitive dreams which had helped him on his way. He did not inform him of the part his spirit-father had played in his successful hunt – Galdr would know of this in his own good time. As he talked and watched Galdr's reactions, he became aware of a subtle transformation in his demeanour. It was as if, by relating his own hardships and sufferings,

151

something of the awesome responsibility of his actions had begun to fall into the mind of Galdr and he detected a certain softening in his face, a slight loss of arrogance, as he listened intently to his tale.

It was not easy relating to Galdr what had happened to him. He had to censor not only the part played by his spirit-father, but also his own thaumatology which had extricated him from certain death at the jaws of a mountain leopard, and had quietened the fiendish anatukris who attempted at every turn to draw him from his true path. Eventually his story was told and he fell silent, waiting for Galdr to share his already half-known story with him.

Galdr kept his silence, lost in confusion and wonderment. He, like so many others, considered Halfray to be what his name meant: He-half-in-the-world, but here, sitting in front of him, was a man of his own age, who had set out on a hazardous journey, without even the practice of hunting that Galdr had received and who, to all intents and purposes, was an imbecile! Certainly Halfray's story was not without incident, but compared to his own, he had experienced few difficulties or real hardships. This was reflected in his face – Halfray looked, if anything, fitter and less haunted than he remembered him, whereas the six moons' passing had taken an all-too-obvious toll on his own looks; his face had become cracked and dried by the elements, his eyes were permanently red-ringed from the sunlight reflecting on the white rains and his ebony hair was already beginning to show signs of greying, more befitting to a man of forty, not twenty summers.

Eventually, after they had both told their tales, they abandoned the dying fire and went out into the day. The fresh air hit Galdr like a stone and he thought for a moment that he would faint like a woman as he took in deep breaths of pure, sun-warmed air.

'You must eat,' Halfray said anxiously as he saw Galdr sway. 'I will prepare the doe for smoking – come – I have some food for you.'

He gently led Galdr back into the cave and gave him some dried meat from his pouch and more berries.

'Eat these!' he commanded, 'they carry the power of the sun – they will give you the life-essence which you lack.'

Galdr, too confused and too weak to argue, ate the offered food and gratefully accepted a drink from an ingenious skin-pouch which Halfray had secreted around his waist. He had scarce swallowed the sweet-tasting liquid before the cave began to swim before his eyes. As he sunk to the floor, he managed to gasp: 'Halfray! You have tricked me . . . !' and Galdr knew no more.

CHAPTER FIFTEEN

As the world around Galdr began to sink into oblivion, his last sight was of Halfray's benign face smiling at him and then all was blackness. He felt his body crumple like dying birch leaves in autumn and as he fell to the hard rock-bed of the cave he was conscious of the pain that raged throughout his body. He seemed to be sinking further and further into the earth. Then total darkness overwhelmed him. No thought, no sight, no sound, no pain, the void.

Soft, ink-filled blackness. A blackness which had the quality of deep caverns, almost tangible in its totality, a blackness of death. Galdr tried to think, but no words would form in his brain. He clutched desperately at various words which he tried to string together into some coherence, but his brain threw up nonsense. He opened his mouth to speak but no words came. Instead, his world was suddenly filled with the reeking stench of death and then another sensation – his body seemed to be composed of tiny crystals and each crystal was now crumbling, dissolving and falling away into the void. He was utterly powerless to stop it – powerless to do more than just recognize the feeling. He was disintegrating!

A searing pain to his throat changed that feeling and suddenly, from out of the death-blackness, a shining figure was standing before him. Patrec. She stood, a shimmering figure, incorporeal, yet hideously real. Her right hand covered the wound in her neck which was gushing forth her life force, and she smiled. Galdr felt a shooting pain in his heart as if the spear which had so cruelly cut her throat had now pierced his soul. She began to speak. Slowly and quietly she talked to her son who could do no more than listen, without thought, without reaction, as if these were the first words he had ever heard.

'You, who are my earthly son, you, who are now before me as helpless as the babe you once were – listen to me. Take my words to your heart – you will not again be blessed with my presence. You will return to your people, but you must not stay long with them. Seek council with Soosha – Soosha of my womb who is even now a woman with powers as strong as yours. Her path is the one of the Moon Goddess, although she knows it not. You must heal the breach between you. She will wear the dark face of the moon until you release her from her anguish. If you do not heal the chasm of hatred which she feels towards you, the dark aspect of the Ahni Amwe will reign forever on our earth. You must do this and then you must leave. You will journey to the land of the yellow race, those of the straight eye, the land of the high deserts and then you will travel for many moons' passing towards the rising sun. You must find this land – and you must do it soon – the way will not forever be open to you. You will know when you have reached your destination, red mountains and red trees taller than the stars themselves will greet you. It is a land of great beasts and many shining metals. The greatest of these metals will open a door for the universe – treat it with respect and awe. It is a new land – treat it and everything it contains with courtesy – for you are but a guest upon the earthly plain. Every blade of grass, every tiny insect, every bird and every four-footed animal is your brother. You are its son and guardian, its lover and its keeper.'

Patrec's voice trailed away and the luminous figure slowly faded from Galdr's sight. He felt curiously at ease, as if the vision had given him a benediction. He felt no fear as he became aware of the blackness engulfing him again. He lay in the silent womb-like void, the smell now seeming to comfort his senses as the long-forgotten remembrance of the flowers of childhood.

Slowly the smell became stronger again, but the quality of the scent had changed. The air became thick with the vapour which seemed to attack him from all sides. If he had been able to think coherently, if his brain had allowed those thoughts to be transmitted to his body, he would surely have retched at the stench which now assailed his senses. Slowly, from the deepest part of the void came a hideous figure. A woman, a being degenerate in decomposition, a bilious, rotting cadaver. The woman's red hair was plastered to her skull, showing up in sickening relief the decaying flesh still clinging there. From the holes in the stinking skull where bright blue-green eyes once smiled, lay worms, their blind, writhing bodies, dancing in mockery of the orbs on which they had feasted long ago. Tattered remnants of cloth still hung to the gangrenous corpse and the whole being shifted and crawled almost imperceptibly with the creatures of the soil. As the spectre came closer to Galdr, all his senses suddenly returned and his mind reeled with the sight as his powerless body retched as the stench of decay overcame him. A terror such as he had never felt before, gnawed at his stomach as the very worms were gnawing at the dead woman's flesh. He broke out in sweat as the awful apparition came closer and still closer to him. He could feel the droplets running over his body as he looked at the sight which so overwhelmed him and he wished again for the death-like void which had first encompassed him.

'Bai Ulgan!' he cried in terror, 'save me!'

The woman stopped and the sightless face seemed to stare at him. Slowly the skull creaked and the mouth opened, rotting teeth falling from it and the tongue rasped its message to the writhing form which Galdr, in his terror, had become.

'Did you think you could remain unfeeling, unsensing, here for long?'

156

The voice crackled and grated from the corrupted body. Galdr shut his eyes but the woman was inside his eyelids – he could not escape the picture.

'Did you think you could escape your sins so easily here? Here in the Kingdom of Erlik? No, Galdr, not here, here you will see what you have done. I see you do not know me – I am Mensoon, mother of Injya. This is what you have condemned me to – an eternity of decay. I have seen, though, Galdr, even from here I have more power than you can ever imagine! I have seen what you have done. I have seen you violate my daughter and I can see now. I can see that she is carrying your child, *your* child, Galdr, and I can also see that without you – both she and your child will die. You will not die here, Galdr, oh no, for reasons best known to the Goddess you are to be saved the fate which you so willingly gave to me. But hark my words well, Galdr, if you do not now love Injya with your total being, if you do not now embrace the way of the Goddess, not only will Injya and your child die but the whole of the world will be put at risk.'

The voice stopped and Galdr dared to look at the figure without fear.

'I see you understand,' the voice continued, 'but this too, you also have to understand, only through love can you achieve this – and this includes me. You will have to love me, now, as I am, as I stand before you, you will have to find it in your heart to love me before either of us can be free.'

With the words barely out of her mouth the figure stepped forward. Galdr felt the icy touch of her fingers on his cheek and for an instant thought that he would pass out at the touch, but he held firm and stared at the ghastly face without fear and without judgement. For a moment the form before him changed into that of a woman in her prime, round, soft, her fair white face framed with abundant chestnut curls, her green-blue eyes shining and radiant, her full red lips parted in a warm smile and the touch on his cheek became warm and tender. Now Galdr recognized Mensoon, the Mensoon whom he had heartlessly murdered and buried. He felt that his heart would break under the weight of the sorrow he now felt as he gazed into Mensoon's lovely face, but as quickly as it had come, the vision faded, both ghoul and woman gone from him. For a brief moment a moon – round, serene and luminous, filled his consciousness; in the centre of the orb he glimpsed Mensoon's face but as quickly as it had come, this too faded and the blackness returned.

A dusty spider weaves its web across Galdr's mind. Into it she threads many pictures. As if she is a maiden putting out washed shifts in the summer sunshine to dry, she hangs the tapestries from the threads of his mind. Here – Galdr's sister, Soosha, muttering as she stirs a large urn, her face cracked and blackened with soot. In the place where her heart should be, a dry bone, carved like a tree, hangs upside down. The picture wavers in Galdr's mind as he listens to the incantations of his sister. Nothing stirs in his heart, for Askoye the crone has taken it away from him – for it would surely break if it felt all that it could feel when the pictures of life are painted. And here, a little further along the web, another image, Injya, swollen with child, screaming his name. The bottom picture drips blood – the birth blood of his child and now, another vision threads its way along the web . . . his father – yes! he can clearly see his father, Anfjord. He observes him as he rides on the back of a young naked woman, drinking something from a goblet in one hand and striking the woman with the other. Other young women are lying all around him sobbing and asking for mercy but his father takes no notice; guards stand around a great hall and laugh at the sight, guards who are not of Anfjord's race, strange, tall, blond-haired men, laughing maliciously at his father and the young women.

The picture is suddenly swept aside as he sees another unfold before him: a large picture, painted on rock, a scene of hundreds of people, not like his people – strange brown people – crying and wailing to the heavens, the people all wet with rain which is pouring down upon them in torrents. They stand there, arms stretched upwards towards the relentless rain as the rivers break their banks and the seas rise. The picture dissolves in a flood of tears and another is spun, a picture of a shining man, hanging, semi-naked on a cross, silhouetted against a storm-laden purple sky and then another, this time of metal-clad horsemen riding fast into deserts, swinging long swords, carrying banners and crosses, crosses like the cross on which the shining man was hanging, their baggage horses ladened with vast sacks spilling jewels and precious objects all around them on to the dry earth. In the background are many fine buildings, such as Galdr has never seen before and as the background turns into the foreground, he sees fat men and women in strange clothes, running in and out of the buildings, ringing bells and screaming, some trundle carts behind them, on which are piled the bodies of those who have died, bodies covered in sores and black buboes. And in another picture, men lying in wet earth, blackness all around them, the terror of warfare etched into every face as they all watch a sudden blaze of orange light up the sky and the picture shatters as the orange ball comes towards them and they break into bloody bits in the rain and the blackness of their dug-out homes.

The black rain washes away the picture and slowly it is replaced with one which looks as if it is made on dried parchment; it does not dance in the breeze of his mind as the others did, it unfolds stiffly and through it he sees many people; people wandering aimlessly in a desert, people everywhere dying of hunger and thirst and, as slowly as it had unfurled, it crumbles from view to reveal yet another masterpiece. An old woman, seated in a cave, impassively waiting for the return of something. Her body shudders slightly as a dusty spider drops from the roof of the cave and laboriously inches its way up her black clothes. She does not wince or brush it away as the spider carefully navigates the crevices in the old woman's skin and finally comes to a halt in the middle of her forehead. Slowly she opens her eyes and the picture becomes larger, so large that it now fills the entire space in Galdr's mind. The spider's web has gone. Askoye the crone has come.

'I do not need to explain the web – all you have seen will come to pass – and more. Halfray will help you, but you must help him too – he is a good boy – but limited.'

Galdr lay, eyes closed, the vision of the crone filling him, her piercing words cutting like knives upon his exhausted mind and heart.

'For reasons best known to only the Goddess you are to be entrusted with the next part of Her unfoldment. You must take Injya as your life partner and you must do whatever you can to bring understanding of the true way to Soosha – without that, what you have just seen will be a hundred times worse. You have already been touched by the Goddess,' the crone continued, 'you will be instructed about your part in bringing about her wishes on earth. You yet know nothing and understand nothing. You must die to be reborn. You must not forget your experiences or the pictures which have been shown to you. Much will frighten and worry you. You will come to no harm if you do as you are bidden. The spirit of Por, the God of the Sun, works through you as the spirit of Ahni, the Moon, works through Injya – together you will create the true spirit of Bai Ulgan. You will now see one more picture and then you will awake unharmed by what has happened. Never again will you lie and never again will you kill your brother man. This I say also to you: never fight against the will of the Goddess or resist Her supreme wisdom. This last picture will show you the manner of your death. Heed it well, for in it is the manner of your rebirth.'

The figure faded from Galdr's view and in its place he saw a tiny picture, no bigger than his thumb-nail. He waited for it to grow large, but it did not. He squinted

160

and concentrated hard on the tiny scene. In miniature he saw himself running from a great black shadow, a shadow which was gaining on him and with his restored heart pounding in his body, he saw the shadow overtake him and seem to consume him. He heard himself scream horribly as the shadow seemed to turn to ice and he saw himself spread-eagled, frozen, but with the silent scream that filled his soul he heard the screaming of an eagle. From the drained strangulated body he saw a mighty eagle rise, silver white and gold of eye it flew straight towards him. Galdr could feel the air vibrate as the great wings trod the air easily, its clear orange eye fixing him straight in his own. In the eagle's eye he saw himself again, this time seated, cross-legged, upon a high, red mountain. Warmth surrounded him, his body was bronzed and dried-looking and as he looked upon his form once more, the eagle arose. Clear upon shining blue skies the eagle ascended, his cruel downturned beak opened once and a long scream issued from deep inside the bird's throat. In that instant Galdr's senses left him and he returned with a shuddering, bone-withering pain to the floor of the cave.

Pain and the smell of woodsmoke. Pain in Galdr's back – stinging in his nostrils. Aching – a deep boulder-shaped ache between Galdr's shoulder-blades and the pain! Pain deep inside his chest as if a stake was sticking straight into his heart and coming out through his shoulders. With eyes still closed, Galdr shifted his head slightly, away from the smoke. The movement did not ease the ache, his matted hair was no protection against the rough stone floor of the cave. Tentatively he lifted an arm and stroked his chest. It felt as though he were moving against a heavy weight, as if simply to raise his hand off the floor and on to his chest required as much strength as lifting a tree or a boulder. Thankfully he rested his hand on his chest and felt above his heart. There was no stake, but the pain! He allowed his arm to drop to his side and touched the earth. Dust.

His fingers stroked the dust, feeling each grain as if it were precious to him. He allowed his palm to relax and to feel the cool, gritty texture of the cave floor. He shifted each leg in turn slightly, feeling the rough floor under him and again experienced the heavy dragging weight of each limb, moving as heavily and as tortuously as if clad in wet furs and wading through mud up to his thighs. He sighed deeply and groaned with the effort. He dared to take a deep breath, but the smoke-laden air seemed to scorch his lungs and spluttering he sat up, choking and gasping for air.

'Welcome back!' Halfray was squatting opposite Galdr, the fire before him burning brightly, sending orange and black dancing shadows across his ingenuous face. He smiled, acknowledging Galdr's inability to answer him, as Galdr coughed, and angrily waved away the water-bottle that Halfray offered him, as slowly his spluttering ceased. Eventually Galdr was able to speak.

'By the heavens, not *that* again!'

Halfray laughed and rising from his place went over and rubbed Galdr's shoulder and back.

'There – better now?' he asked innocently. Galdr stared at Halfray's face in amazement – he could be enquiring about a child who had just fallen over and hurt his knee – did he really have no idea of where he had been and what he had seen? Galdr stared at Halfray's face for an answer and finding none looked down at his feet. The pain in his heart had gone, but he still ached all over. He closed his eyes again and hugged his knees close to his chest. He felt Halfray's hand leave his shoulder and sensed him returning to his seat.

'I was a little concerned for you at one point – did you know that you screamed out: "Bai Ulgan – help me!"?' Galdr did not reply. 'I hope you did not hurt yourself overly when you fell down, your head made an awful crack when it hit the stones – I moved your feet – I thought you could do without being burnt alive as well.'

The conversational, everyday tone which Halfray was using annoyed Galdr more than he could express – this man really *was* an idiot! No sooner had he thought that, than a picture of the rotting corpse of Mensoon flooded his brain and the words of the crone came crashing back to him: 'Halfray will help you, but you must help him too.' He shook his head against the memory and looked at Halfray sullenly. Halfray's face expressed nothing save a slight look of puzzled concern and vague amusement.

'Do you really have no idea what has happened to me?' he asked incredulously.

Halfray smiled broadly and said frankly: 'No – no, I do not know what has happened to you. I know that you have been deep inside yourself – what you found there – I am waiting for you to tell me.'

Galdr shut his eyes and rested his head on his knees. How to tell the horror? How to explain to another person something which he could not explain to himself? And what had happened had *not* happened inside himself, as Halfray had put it, it had happened *to* him – he, Galdr, had not been there – he had been somewhere outside himself and yet, in a way, inside himself at the same time. He shook his head once more and sighed.

'Halfray . . . Halfray, I do not know how to tell you what happened to me.'

Suddenly he felt like crying, suddenly feeling very small and very afraid, like a child, frightened to tell in case he was not understood, in case the person to whom he was speaking would laugh at him, ridicule his experience.

As if he could read his mind, Halfray said softly: 'Just tell me, Galdr – I will not interrupt or comment in any way – I will just listen. You need to know that I will give you my full attention – I will simply listen.'

Galdr searched Halfray's face for any trace of sarcasm or deceit. He found none. He looked long into Halfray's clear blue eyes and saw himself staring out of them. His dark, hooded, troubled eyes; his grief-distorted mouth.

Swallowing down the tears which rose in his throat he quietly began his story.

Halfray listened with eyes half closed as the young man before him spilt out his guilt and grief. Halfray had to concentrate hard on ridding himself of his emotions when the dreadful apparition of his mother was described to him, but the tears and remorse that Galdr showed while recounting this part, helped him overcome his natural feelings of anger and resentment towards the man who had been so instrumental in her death. If Mensoon herself could forgive him – who was he not to? He felt curiously distanced from his feelings when Galdr told him of his carnality with his sister – somewhere, deep inside himself, he knew that she was only working out the plan of the Divine Goddess – she would be taken care of, of that he was sure. He was not surprised in the part that Soosha would come to play in their lives – he had known ever since he had first glimpsed the girl that she had the powers – her spirit-lights were as strong as those of his sister, mother and now Galdr's – the only difference being in the quality and the colour. Injya, Mensoon and now Galdr, shone gold and blue – their spirit-lights extending from their bodies for almost a pchekt. Soosha was surrounded with an equally strong light, but since the murder of her mother it contained a deep sanguine which was almost black at the nearest point to her body. Halfray had assumed that it was grief which so discoloured her spirit-form, but on hearing the warnings given to Galdr from Askoye, he feared the worse. Soosha was immensely powerful and it was a power of evil, not good, which led her.

After a long time, Galdr stopped speaking and wiped away the tears which he had unashamedly shed.

'I do not know what to do, Halfray,' he said in a half-pleading, half-pitying way. 'Tell me what to do now.' Halfray sighed and looked at him, suddenly drained by the effort of giving him his total attention.

'I think you must forgive yourself,' he said simply. 'I think you have to forgive your old self and start anew.'

'But how?' Galdr looked at Halfray's impassive face, tears welling up in his eyes once more. 'How can I forgive myself for what I have done? It is impossible – I am just evil – all evil!' He sank his head on to his knees and sobbed loudly.

'Galdr,' began Halfray, 'Galdr, listen to me – you *have* to let go of your guilt – you have to let go of your former self – your old self has to die, if you like, so that you can be born afresh, from new, from now.'

Galdr stopped crying and looked again at Halfray. How could he remain so impervious to what he had just said? Why is he not angry? Why does he not hate me?

Halfray spoke again: 'I need to sleep now, Galdr. It is up to you to decide how best to take up your new life. Your old one is already dying, but you need to let it go completely – it will feel like a death to you – in fact, it *is* a death of everything you once held to be true and right. But *you* must do it – *you* must die to the old. And be careful – this letting go – this death, may hurt more than anything you have experienced yet. You have started to cut out the bad part of the apple – but the rot goes deeper and the cuts hurt more, but with it, your apple will surely rot. Do it cleanly, a sharp knife is needed, the sharp knife of truth and forgiveness.'

With that, Halfray closed his eyes and lay flat on his back. Galdr watched with astonishment as Halfray's chest rose and fell rhythmically and slowly, and within two or three breaths, a faint snoring issued from his slightly parted mouth. Galdr listened in amazement and shock as the truth slowly dawned on him – Halfray had simply gone to sleep – like an animal, he had just felt tired, lain down, and gone fast asleep! As Galdr watched the figure, his words came back to him – he was right, he *was* rotten, rotten to the core, but it would take more than a metaphorical death to cleanse him of his evil. He would take a knife all right, but a knife to his throat!

The resolution sank into his consciousness with the clarity of ice. His former self-pitying gone, he suddenly felt very strong. Moving quickly he lit a taper from the fire and went over to the ledge where the mirror and the strange doe-skin shift lay. A fitting end, he thought, I shall wear magical clothes for a magical death.

Quickly Galdr removed his clothes. He realized that he still had the blood of the doe on his hands. It seemed so long ago now, since he had killed that animal. At the thought of his quarry his stomach rumbled and he remembered he had not eaten for two days . . . three? He did not know how long he had lain there, seeing what he had seen. It was still daylight, but which day? It did not matter, he told himself, time and the cravings of his stomach no longer mattered. He was surprised that he could even think of something as prosaic as food when he was about to commit the worst sin of his life – that of ending it.

He shook out the dust from the shift and put it on. By the light of the fire the mysterious symbols leapt out at him with renewed brilliance. No, he told himself firmly, I will *not* try to sort these out again! Whatever they mean will forever remain a mystery to me – I do not deserve to know. He picked up the drum and touched its taught surface. The painted markings seemed raised underneath his fingers and he slowly traced the shape of a spiral reaching towards a star which was in the centre of the drum.

'Let go!' he said out loud, 'let go of this life!' and with great restraint, he placed the drum back on the ledge. He resisted the temptation to look into the black mirror – he no more wished to look at his face – soon he would not see anything – whoever, or whatever he was, would be gone. He crossed over the cave and drew out some lengths of rope, pulling, as he did so, on each long strand to see that they were firm and strong.

'Yes,' he muttered to himself, 'these will do, they will hold me firm, they will stop me from running.' Casting a long look at the sleeping Halfray he crawled from the cave.

The sun was majestic. A low, fiery, almost molten-looking sun quivered on the horizon. The sun is setting on my world, Galdr thought, how apt! Fearlessly he stepped forward into the gathering dusk. He clambered down the mountainside quickly and headed straight for the forest far below him. The sun had long since gone to its home under the world when he reached the trees and the night winds had begun to howl as Galdr examined first this tree, then the next, looking for the right one to show itself to him. The sky was blotted out by the creaking branches of the forest and eyes, sinister orange eyes, seemed to dart at him from every direction. Finally he stopped. In front of him was The Tree – his tree. He looked upwards into its mighty whispering branches and knew, instinctively, that this was the tree to take his life.

He looked at the tree long and hard and then suddenly knew what to do. Quickly and methodically he cut two lengths of rope, one he tied around the trunk at roughly waist height, the other, approximately neck height. Next he took two pieces which were a little shorter in length than each arm and tied noose knots in both ends. These he flung over two branches and threading the loose ends through the nooses, he pulled them tightly which left the short ropes hanging down, their nooses free. Pleased with his efforts he bent down, tied his feet together, hopped over to the tree and rested back against its cold, damp trunk. Mechanically he took the first rope and tied it securely around his waist and the second round his throat. He did not tie the one which was round his throat very tightly – he did not want to spare himself the agonies of death by simple strangulation. Finally he threaded each hand into its awaiting noose and pulled the ropes taught.

There was no way he could escape his binding. He could not bend his head far enough to see his feet and although he could swing his arms to and fro, they did not meet each other, let alone his body. His fingers could not undo the slip knots which were already beginning to cut into his wrists. Perfect! Suddenly he laughed aloud – he was like that shining man he had seen in the pictures the spider had woven for him – did he, too, nail himself to a cross like he had hanged himself? He dismissed the notion as untenable and laughed again at the workings of his stupid brain – trying to work out minutiae when any moment could be his last, when any moment the shadow of death could come for him. As if the thought itself produced them, Galdr heard the far-off sound of wolves. So it was to be wolves, the hunters of the night, they were his soul-shadows. Smiling, he closed his eyes and waited; wolves were to take him to the shadowlands – well, so be it.

The moon was barely visible through the tangled branches above his head, but he knew that she was there, shining down, impassively, on her son. The cold winds were not so biting as out on the mountainside, but the cold relentlessly crept up Galdr's legs and through his shift. He could feel his skin tightening as the moisture froze on it and his body prickled all over. His arms ached mercilessly and he wished, more than anything in the world, that he could lower his head and sag at the knees. Shortly he could no longer feel his hands or feet. He longed for the wolves to come – prayed to them, willed them to come and tear his heart from his body and put an end to this slow, self-inflicted torture. And as the night deepened, the slow numbness crawled along his body until finally he felt no pain and his eyelids closed as he waited for his death to overtake him.

CHAPTER SIXTEEN

Injya had sat for a long time looking at the drop of blood
on her palm. It was a sign, a portent – but of what?
She shivered. Her head ached from the wine, her body
ached from the coupling. Beloved Ahni – tell me what
this means, help me understand, she prayed silently. But
no words came to her – all she could hear was Crenjal's
breathing, the low hissing of the fire, the wind creaking the
skins of the sancar and a lone wolf howling at the moon.
She was beginning to get colder – she had to move. Injya
inclined her hand and the blood which had fallen from the
helmet dribbled slowly down her palm and fell between
her middle two fingers. It left no trace behind. She got
up stiffly and turned to the fire, rubbing her chilled arms.
As she turned, the firelight glinted on the helmet and for
an instant she thought it had taken on its former shape,
the shape of the Barnkop Stand. The stand was a replica
of the gentle lines of womanhood: the outer lips were
decorated with precious stones, fluted inner lips glistened
as if damp. Secreted at its centre where the most sacred
object of her people, the Arnjway Staff, had once stood,
a large oval moonstone lay, mysterious and compelling
in its luminosity. Almost before Injya had time to draw
breath, the sacred object once more assumed the shape
of the helmet. Injya wanted to cry, could feel the tears
pricking behind her eyes. Was her power like that of the
Barnkop – transient and fleeting? Was that why her spell
to rob Crenjal of his manhood had failed?

The fire, covered as it was for the night, gave little
heat and reluctantly Injya climbed back into bed. The
body of Crenjal was hot next to hers and moving very

cautiously she inched her way nearer to him, stopping
a hair's breadth away from touching him. Very slowly
the warmth from Crenjal's body warmed hers and sleep
descended mercifully quickly, but it was a sleep riven
with dreams. She saw herself as young, thirteen, perhaps
fourteen summers. She was in a sunlit glade picking herbs
which she knew were for Mensoon. Sunlight was filtering
through the canopy of silver-green birch leaves overhead
and she felt happy, untroubled, full of natural love for the
earth and mankind.

She wandered deeper into the wood and although the
sunlight no longer penetrated the leaves, she felt neither
hesitation nor fear. Nor did she feel these emotions when
she came across the spread-eagled form of Galdr, hanging,
arms outstretched, tied to a trunk of a tall tree. She stood
and gazed at the figure, registering nothing else but a mild
surprise. She began to weave the herbs she had gathered for
her mother around his head, when a movement high up in
the tree attracted her attention, and still wide-eyed, she saw
Galdr now standing on the topmost branch, arms raised in
greeting to her. Beside his figure was her father and by
Galdr's other side, Askoye stood, whispering something
into his ear. Behind the three a full moon was pouring
down her melody of white light. Enthralled, Injya watched
as behind this moon a large sunset-red sun rose. It came to
rest behind the moon, turning her cool moonbeams into
rays of the deepest orange. The three figures now turned
to her, beckoning her to join them and overcome with
happiness at seeing Askoye once more, she stepped back
from the picture blossoming in front of her eyes with the
intention of flying upwards to meet them. As she prepared
for this flight she became herself again. In her dream she
saw herself, now eighteen summers old, covered in grey,
belly already swelling, hatred in her heart. She looked
at the trio, hating them all, consumed with anger. She
wanted to run away, to hide from the truth – that here, in
this place, Askoye's prophecy was being acted out. Her

170

words rang again in her brain: 'When you fully understand the symbol of the two moons, your terror will leave you!', and suddenly the feelings of hatred melted, once again she was the innocent child she had been. But her flash of anger had acted upon the three and the vision was fading. An overwhelming sense of loss struck her heart. As the picture of her loved ones receded into blackness, Injya sobbed out loud: 'Come back! Oh come back! I love you!' and with tears streaming from her eyes she tried to run after the dream, the tree, the feeling of love and warmth, she tried to recapture those feelings of innocence and belonging; but the harder she ran, the further away the tree became and the louder her crying. Her dream-crying woke Injya. Her hair and face were wet with the tears which still fell. She felt bereft and confused and not in the least comforted by the large rough hand of Crenjal who was stroking her head and cheeks, whispering in her ear.

'My precious, my sweeting – what ails you? Come, let me comfort you, my wife.'

It took a long while for Injya to stop crying. She was fighting not only the feeling of loss at seeing Askoye and her father once more, but desperately trying to fight off the truth which the dream had shown her. Her destiny was inextricably linked with that of Galdr – Galdr the hated – Galdr the despoiler of virgins, the murderer of her mother! As clearly as she could feel Crenjal's hand on her brow or hear his words of comfort, she knew that somehow, Galdr held the secret – it was the wish of the Goddess that the power of the sun was fused with her power of the moon – that this was the path forward. Every atom of her being wanted to deny this truth – she would *not* take Galdr to her – whatever else might befall her – surely the Goddess could not be that cruel – to tie her to that man – that man of evil!

Crenjal solicitously did not try to stop his wife crying, he simply carried on stroking her hair and shoulders, wiping away the tears from her cheeks. He did not know what it was that had made Injya so tormented – whatever it was he simply wished to love it away. She was the most beautiful, precious being he had ever encountered and when he could find out what it was that made her so upset, he would do everything in his power to change it. Eventually the crying and sobbing ceased and she turned round to him. Her face was swollen with tears, her normally clear forehead puckered with lines of pain. Crenjal's heart melted even further and he folded her into his arms as tenderly as he would have a new-born infant. How long had he denied those feelings? So many years of hardness, where his only thoughts were those of advancement, conquering new grounds, mining new metals, fighting anyone who stood in his way. All his life he had acted thus and within two days his life had totally changed, here, now, in his arms, lay the woman who had transformed his soul – oh, how he loved her!

As Injya lay in Crenjal's arms she no longer felt the revulsion she had once felt for this great bear-man. He was being kind and gentle with her. He asked her no questions, he did not try to stop her feeling thus, he was being just like her father had been, strong and loving. Fresh tears fell as she remembered Vingyar – and here she was, taking comfort from the man who had killed him! She struggled with these dual feelings, but like the feelings she had when she thought of her union with Galdr, she could not sort them out into a clear-cut set of emotions, all was chaos, all conflicting. She calmed her crying and tried to focus on what was happening now: Crenjal was caressing her back and shoulders, rocking her slightly as if she were a colicky baby. It felt nice, being held thus. She relaxed some of her tension and burrowed her head into his shoulder. The hand began moving more slowly, up and down her spine, up to her neck, down to the rise of her buttocks, round her shoulder, down to the curve of her hip. When Crenjal's hand moved to her belly, panic rose once more: her dream had shown her that surely, Galdr was dead, but,

172

as the warm, rough hand circled her breast and his fingers became tauter as they moved inexorably towards her sex, Galdr was alive too – alive in her womb.

Inwardly she spoke the words to render Crenjal impotent: she called upon the avenging face of Hoola, the Mother who could release her child, Ipirün, the God of Fire, at will, the Goddess who could move mountains and rent her precious skin asunder with fire. But Hoola was deaf to her pleas and as she was overpowered by Crenjal, as she felt his strong body enter hers, she understood that she had created a schism in her world. She had lied. She had used her powers to ensnare another human being, to change the natural course of events – now, she had to reap the harvest of her deception.

Anfjord woke to the sounds of the morning and stared at the roof of his sancar. His bed was empty, the two women had abandoned him. He lay, listening to the wind and the dull sounds of voices and felt desolate. He thought of Patrec, the only woman who had ever been close to him and hated her memory. Liar, cheat, traitor – that was what she was. He had shared his life with her and she had repaid him by taking her own son to her arms! He used to cry over her, he used to wail over the loss of his son. All along the winter trail he had cried, mourned their passing, but always Crenjal was there to support him. Now Crenjal was no more. Crenjal had what he had once had, one woman. He thought of Injya – a strange, beautiful woman. He let out an involuntary moan of longing which turned into a groan of despair as before his eyes the vision of Injya and Crenjal mating formed. He saw their writhing bodies, imagined Injya's soft and strong body close to his, tried to feel what Crenjal would be feeling – how he would feel inside her body. Suddenly he brought his closed fist down upon the furs of the bed.

'No!' he shouted aloud to the empty sancar. 'I will not have this! I will not feel this! I am a man, a chief, the

173

only chief in the world! I have under my control two hundred people. I am powerful, I am the one – not Crenjal, not Injya. Me!'

He threw the clothes from him and leapt from his bed. Hot with rage he doused his head with freezing water and roughly pulled on his shift and furs. As he scrambled frantically into his clothes he felt as though he was armouring himself, wrapping himself up to fend off the feelings of loss, envy and lust. He had lost Crenjal – Crenjal, his right arm, his friend, the man out of all the men he knew who meant something to him. Now he was besotted with a woman! Now he no longer cared for Anfjord, now all the friendship was as if for nought.

He struggled into his boots and tied the thongs around his ankles furiously – to lose Crenjal's friendship and to such a woman! He saw Injya in his mind's eye: tall, beautiful, haughty – and he wanted her. *He* wanted her, he wanted her as he had wanted no other woman before, more than he had wanted Patrec. Injya *had* to be his! He felt he would go mad – to lose Crenjal to a woman he wanted! To lose Crenjal if he *took* the woman he wanted! To take Injya from Crenjal would take Crenjal away from him for ever – he could not have both – indeed, he could not have either! He felt torn in two by his emotions: jealousy, lust, pride all pulling him this way and that. And it hurt – it hurt him like Patrec's death, like Galdr's banishment – would the pain ever stop? Gathering his cloak around his shoulders he went to leave the sancar, changed his mind and called instead for his guard: 'Amjund! Enter!'

A moment later, Amjund bowed his way into the sancar and stood before Anfjord. He was used to Anfjord's rages and was fearful of what command he would be given. He stared at Anfjord's feet, head bowed, and waited.

'Bring Soosha here – now!'

Relieved that it was no more than a simple errand he backed out of the sancar and ran across the encampment.

She stepped out of her sancar as he approached, as if she knew already that Anfjord had sent for her.

'Your father . . . ' he gasped, catching his breath.

'I know, I am going!' she said somewhat imperiously as she strode past him.

Soosha had known, and known the instant that Injya returned to their people, that Anfjord would summons her. Since he had banished Galdr, he had called for her more and more. He had taken little comfort from her – Crenjal was the only one whom he would allow to give him that – but he had listened to her and he had *used* her. He had used her to find out what the women of the tribe were saying, had relied on her to be his eyes, as once he had used Patrec. But Patrec had been a stupid woman; she had not used the power she had over Anfjord, she had not even recognized that she had power. But Soosha understood it. Soosha knew also that there would come a time when she could use that power for her own ends. But for the time being she was content to let Anfjord think that he had the power of the tribe, that he was the chief. But her day was dawning, her day would come when she could wreak the vengeance her heart called for, vengeance for the banishment of her brother, vengeance for the death of her mother, vengeance against the man who called himself her father but who thought little of her needs, who, though he professed love for her, could not show it, whom, all her life she had loved and never had that love returned. Oh yes, the day was coming when she would have her revenge!

But Anfjord knew none of this; he knew only what Soosha wished him to know and she, acting out her part as his eyes in the women's sancar, told him only what he wanted to hear. If Anfjord had not been aware of all the women were saying, what little plots and intrigues were happening, he would not have remained chief for one moon's passing, let alone twenty winters' passing. Like all the Branfjord men, he thought power lay in strength and the ability to impregnate women. How little he really understood – how small was his reason, how weak his true power; for he did not appreciate that his very power was his tragic flaw. His need of women was his undoing and would be the undoing of every man. But, it suited her for him to be ignorant of this. It suited her well and she played the submissive daughter only and exactly for her own ends.

'Soosha – what are the women saying?' he blurted out as soon as he saw her enter the sancar. Soosha's thin lips parted as she smiled, her dark, heavily hooded eyes flashed as slowly she crossed the sancar and put her rather bony hands on his shoulders. She looked hard into his troubled eyes, smiled reassuringly and patted him on his arm. Sighing faintly she said in her odd, deep voice: 'The women are saying that now Injya has returned, she will try to bring back the old ways. They are frightened, Father.'

Anfjord sat down heavily and sighed: 'Is this what you, too, believe?'

Soosha did not reply for a moment, preferring to stand, one arm outstretched towards him, as if imploring him not to question her further.

'Well?'

Soosha dropped her head, and then, as if reluctant to speak said slowly: 'I have no doubt. Father, Injya has tricked Crenjal – how else would he take her to his bed? You know Crenjal as well as I – he has never been interested in women – he would much rather ride or hunt – then suddenly, Injya comes back, tells him that she has been searching for him all this time and marries him! Surely, *you* do not believe that, do you? If *your* father had been murdered by a woman, would you then happily take that woman as your trusted wife?'

She suddenly fell silent and dropped her head upon her bosom. Slowly she removed the hood of her cape and shook her head, tossing her oiled black hair on to her shoulders. In a softer voice she continued.

'It is all nonsense. She has used magic to ensnare him and there are rumours that she will use her power to overthrow you. Think, Father – the Gyaretz women are not as content as our women – it has only been three winters' turning since they lost their priestess – even though they may be frightened of the old ways returning, they are *their* old ways. Injya knows this and she will ensnare the women – and with them – their mates, and before long, she and Crenjal will try to take over your position.'

She watched Anfjord closely as she said this, saw the logic of her argument sink into his understanding.

'But Crenjal' – Anfjord began – 'Crenjal is not stupid – he would not allow a simple girl to take away his reason – he—'

'He cannot help himself, Father!' Soosha interrupted him hotly. 'I am sure that Injya has cast a spell upon him . . . and—' Soosha suddenly stopped, dropped her head, as if unwilling to continue.

'And – and what, Soosha – what are you hiding from me?'

'Oh, Father, do not be angry with me – I am being foolish, forgive me!'

'What – what are you not saying, what are you thinking – what else have you heard?'

Anfjord rose quickly from his bed and took Soosha's slight shoulders between both hands. She lowered her eyes once more, her face clouded with secrets. Anfjord shook her slightly, fingers digging into her delicate arms; she was keeping something from him, of that he was sure.

'Father, please, it is only my evil mind playing tricks, do not be angry, please, Father.'

She felt his grasp tighten and let out an involuntary cry. 'Father, please—'

Anfjord released his grasp a little. 'Well?' he demanded again, his eyes blazing into hers.

'It is probably nothing, but for a moment I thought that perhaps Crenjal might be using Injya – not the other way

177

around – that perhaps both of them have a plan, a plan to take the chieftainship away from you. Father – don't!' she cried as Anfjord raised his hand to strike her. 'I have said, it was only a passing idea – of course Crenjal would not plot against you – he loves you as you love him. Father, I am sorry. It is just that I cannot bear to see you so unhappy, I am sorry!' Soosha covered her face in her hands and wept like a child. Anfjord turned his back on her, turned away from the sight of her tears – she was weeping the tears he needed to shed.

Soosha stopped her crying and like quicksilver was by his side. They stood, facing the wall of the sancar – he towering above her, she silent once more, submissive. With a sigh Anfjord slowly turned and slumped down upon his bed, covering his face in his hands. Soosha too turned, but this time did not attempt to be near him. She drew herself up to her full height and said in a voice barely above a whisper: 'Father, we are not to know the future: we do not know that Crenjal will not tire of Injya, or her him. If, *when* that happens, you still want her, Crenjal will give her to you – she is only a woman, and' – she continued hastily, seeing him shrink as she called Injya 'only a woman' – 'think of the respect you will earn from the men when they see you sacrificing your longings for the sake of your friend – think how noble they will see you to be, how wise and caring you are. That will surely outweigh any mischief Injya may try – she is young, she will soon be with child, Crenjal's child, then any trickery or magic will fall from her. Believe me, Father, in a few moons' passing you will laugh at this.'

She looked deep into Anfjord's eyes and saw that her words had worked. He stared back at his daughter and said, gruffly and somewhat grudgingly: 'Of course, Soosha, how wise you are!'

And as she turned to go she smiled and said almost sweetly: 'Now think no more of Crenjal as a traitor – he loves you all the more for letting him have the object of your desire.'

Anfjord nodded his head in agreement, then looked up again quickly – what had she said? Traitor? But Soosha was gone from him, leaving only a whispered scent of treason in the air.

The sun was already high in the heavens when finally Crenjal and Injya emerged from their sancar. Smiling faces greeted them and Injya did her best to smile back. She had to carry on the deceit, she had to continue to look as if she was now enjoying her position – the place of wife to the chief's right-hand man. A whole reindeer carcass was roasting on the great central fire – a luxury in honour of their marriage and the air was thick with the smell of cooking meat. Everywhere Injya looked people were busily scurrying around. Some of the sancars were being taken apart – some to be stored, some to be reconstructed inside the largest, most open cave. They walked through the biggest cave, accepting the shy smiles from the women, the broader, more knowing grins from the younger men and as was the custom of their people, Injya kissed the maidens who ran up to her, for a kiss from a woman just taken in marriage imparted some of her fertility power to the children who themselves would soon be wives and mothers.

A tall young Branfjord warrior whose name was Vronjyi approached Crenjal and whispered something into his ear. Crenjal flushed slightly then taking Injya's hand said, 'Vronjyi is to show us our cave.'

Injya felt confused – what did he mean, *their* cave – surely they would be united with the rest of the tribe now – the marriage night was over, surely she would be allowed back into the women's sancar? An awful foreboding began to gnaw at her stomach – what new terrors were in store for her? Vronjyi led the way down a narrow passage which opened into a chamber. Tapers flickered round the walls of this cave and furs had already been scattered on the floor – was this *their* cave? Apparently not; bending almost double they followed the youth down along a narrow passage until they came out into a very small cave. Tapers had already been set up around the walls which rose at a slight incline to a lofty roof which was no more than a crevice in the rock face some twenty or thirty pchekts high. This small space, only four or five pchekts in any direction, was further confined by pillars of rock, rising from the floor, falling from the ceiling, like frozen wax from a taper. It had a small high ledge running two-thirds the way round one side upon which were already laid many furs and although there were no visible cracks or gaps between the rocks, running water could be heard. Injya shivered as she understood that this was their marriage-den. She remembered, among all the things that had been spoken of when she had first come back, one of her own women talking about this strange ritual of the Branfjords, but among the whole welter of news, she had given it little importance. Now, as Vronjyi, with eyes downcast, left her and Crenjal to be alone, the details came flooding back. Although the Branfjord tribe had long since abandoned the rituals of the priestess-ship, they still held the belief that a newly married couple should spend one whole moon's passing in seclusion from the rest of the tribe. For the Gyaretz people, this had meant that the couple lived together in a separate sancar, but such was the joy at the coupling that they were looked after by the rest of the tribe for that special time. They were held in great regard and exempted from normal duties, but they were very much a part of the whole community for it was believed that the love they shared should also be shared with the whole tribe. A marriage was a great time of celebration for all. For the Branfjord tribe, they had turned this time of seclusion almost into a period of incarceration. Crenjal seemed overjoyed at the prospect, Injya full of dread.

She sat down on the ledge and looked at Crenjal. He, mistaking her eyes, almost bounded over to her and kissed her exuberantly. When she was able she held his hand in hers and said in a voice which belied her sinking heart:

'Tell me, beloved, I know that we are to stay here for a moon's passing, but so that I do not anger you, tell me what I must do.'

Crenjal looked mildly surprised at the suggestion that anything she could do would anger him, but he answered simply: 'Injya, the ways of the Branfjord people are good. They are wise – wiser than . . . ' he hesitated, unwilling to speak of Vingyar or the ways of the Gyaretz people. 'What they believe is that women, being so attuned to the moon's courses and therefore the water's ebb and flow, need the spirit of the fire to counteract that of the moon. They also know that it is the spirit of the fire which enables man to bring forth children and so it is your task, and only your task, to keep the fire. You have to light it and you have to ensure that it does not die for this month – or else my seed may die in you.' He cast a sideways glance at her: Injya's face was impassive, showing nothing of the astonishment she felt at this belief – her people had always shared such an obviously mutually essential task, but she nodded her agreement and feigned a smile.

Crenjal squeezed her hand and continued: 'You are allowed to leave the cave only to fetch wood. You are not allowed to speak to any other woman – if you need anything, you may only speak to maidens. You may not speak or look at another man – you must avoid them at all costs – not even letting your shadow fall on men. You will not have to prepare food, all the food will be brought into us, but you will have to feed me. I know this may seem strange, Injya, but your hands will have touched my seed and so, by feeding me, you will be giving me back some of my strength. After I have been fed, you may eat whatever I leave for you – so do not look alarmed, I will leave you enough!' His tone lightened and almost laughingly, he said: 'The practice of the people is that I may only leave the cave for obvious bodily functions, for the rest of the time I must rest, for it is also the belief of the Branfjord tribe that it is my duty to couple with you as

181

often as I am able. So you see, my sweeting, all we have to do is love each other – often!'

He stopped and gave her shoulders an encouraging hug. Like a child, having just been given some bauble, he hurried on, quite oblivious to Injya's inner sorrow.

'They are fine laws, are they not? You have nothing to do but tend the fire, and I have nothing to do but to love you and give you a child . . . and . . . here, in this little cave, we will be safe from danger – no wind can reach us in here, Injya, and we are totally supported by the rest of the tribe! What more could we want?'

Injya tried desperately hard to stop the tears of desperation which filled her eyes but to no avail.

'I . . . I . . . I am crying with happiness, Crenjal . . . ' she finally managed to blurt out. 'They are only tears of joy, beloved, only silly women's tears!'

CHAPTER SEVENTEEN

The glorious full moon of her wedding had waned. Two quarters had passed and now the black face of Ahni, hidden by the mantle of Bai Ulgan brought forth the courses of the women of the tribe. Each day Crenjal asked, and each day Injya had to admit that her courses had not come. For two quarters' passing she had suffered the advances of her husband, but now, when the air of the caves was suffused with the sweet strong smell of the women and the herbs they burnt to cleanse the air, Injya could not hide her pregnancy from Crenjal. She told him that she was carrying his child, that, indeed, she was almost sure she could feel the child move within her, so strong was he, so great was his virility! Crenjal became euphoric at the news – his child – and moving already – two quarters' passing and strong already! A miracle, a wondrous miracle! He was so infused with joy that he broke the taboo of not leaving the cave save for bodily needs and dashed from their den, shouting for Anfjord. Injya watched his bumbling figure as it lumbered down the passageway and felt almost sorry for her naïve giant of a husband. She sat, head cupped in hands, by the fire, waiting for his return, and although she felt a compassion of sorts for the deluded man she still prayed with all her might that her pregnancy would give her another excuse to avoid coupling.

During the awful first two quarters with Crenjal she had used every wile, every possible excuse to avoid mating, but had failed. The spell she had used to capture his heart was strong – stronger than that to take away his manhood and Crenjal was acting in the prescribed manner for new husbands; the law was to mate with her as often as he had

183

strength, and Crenjal was, if nothing else, a very strong man. Injya sat staring into the fire. She felt as if something was dying inside her, not growing. Soon the moon's course would be new and she would be released from captivity, but how long could she hold the deception? She stroked her belly – already it was beginning to show signs of her child – would anyone else, apart from love-crazed Crenjal, believe that this child was his? Again she wondered, as she had wondered endlessly, should she tell Crenjal the truth? Tell Anfjord?

She shook her head, it was impossible to believe that the people would not see through her deception – even if they suspended belief and accepted her story, once the child was born, three moons too early, one sight of the child would show that it was not Crenjal's. Crenjal had a low brow, a slender, straight nose, like her own and a slightly pointed chin – even if the child was a girl, she would have something of Galdr's high brow and cheek-bones, something of his flatter nose, and if the child was a boy, almost certainly it would inherit the chiselled square jaw-line of his real father. Her heart grew heavier as she reasoned thus. Everything since her return had gone wrong; her spell on Crenjal had not worked, she had been robbed of speaking with her women, indeed even her ploys at meeting with Bendula had come to nought and now, Crenjal was busily telling Anfjord that she was carrying his child! She tried to pray, tried to recapture the certainty she had once felt, but this too was denied her.

Crenjal returned to their den, bringing with him wine which he consumed eagerly and quickly. As had happened before when he had drunk the wine of the summer-lands, he became very talkative, very affectionate but mercifully very suggestible. As he lay, drowsy and warm, Injya whispered about her child, told him that she thought the child would be brought forth early into this world, that indeed, it was a sign from the Gods that the child was already big within her and finally, when he fell into a heavy drunken sleep, Injya felt sure that she had once more fooled this great oaf of a man. As she too fell asleep, she dared to hope that Anfjord, too, would be as easily duped.

Anfjord too was thinking that Injya had made a fool out of Crenjal. Although his daughter had urged patience, his mood was as dark as the face of the hidden moon. Soosha had brought him wine, evening after evening, which she had said would decrease his longing for Injya, but it had only served to send him into a drugged sleep, where all night long dreams and visions of Injya gave him no peace. Each morning he woke with such a strong desire to mate with her that he felt as if he was fighting with himself throughout the day to stop himself from breaking the taboo and rushing into the marriage den to take her then and there. He took to his bed maidens who had not yet lain with a man in a desperate attempt to quell himself of his need, but all to no avail. As the days wore on, he took a young girl from her mother, a girl not yet a maiden even and coupled with her, trying hopefully to imagine that Tyanka, the girl of twelve summers only, had some of the illusive quality that so attracted him to Injya.

When the new moon came Anfjord married Tyanka. Crenjal was allowed to witness the marriage, Injya was not. In her tiny cave she heard the songs, the music, the dances and inwardly wept for the child who was Anfjord's latest victim. Crenjal returned to her, drunkenly describing the girl's beauty, Anfjord's joy and expressing surprise when Injya had blurted out: 'But . . . it is against *all* the taboos, Crenjal! All of them! She is not yet a woman – she is a little girl still – Crenjal – you must try to stop this!'

But Crenjal had only patted her thigh as if she, herself, was a petulant girl and as he rolled over to sleep said only: 'There is nothing I can do, Injya, and at least it makes Anfjord happy!'

In the darkness of the night Injya prayed for the girl, prayed for her and for herself, asked forgiveness of the Goddess – if she, Injya, had not been so rash she would have reasoned that it should have been Anfjord that she should have married, not Crenjal. She was, in part, to blame for the far-away screams and pleas for mercy that even here, Injya could hear from the marriage den of Anfjord and Tyanka.

When the full moon came again, Injya and Crenjal left their cave. The encampment had changed. All the people were now living in the caves, only one long, low sancar stood outside, abandoned – its inhabitants, the horses, too, had been brought into the caves. Ice was everywhere. It hardened the thin soil which covered the almost bare rocks and turned the short bleached mountain grasses, where they were able to keep their tenuous hold on the earth, into razor-edged knives. The pale midwinter sun gave no warmth as the ice held each person in its grip as they fought the wind and the crushing cold, using precious energy in an exhausting effort to maintain some inner heat. The wood that they had so laboriously gathered which fuelled their meagre fires gave little respite. The sancars creaked as the wind tried to ruffle the stiff skins and at night the crackling of the sancar poles sent a fear deep into the hearts of the people. Death and illness took the weakest – the elderly whose time-worn teeth could not eat the hard dried reindeer meat, the youngest whose fragile bodies succumbed to the cold as the searing winds dried up the milk in all but the healthiest of women's breasts.

As was their custom, Injya and Crenjal now would sleep apart, unless Crenjal wanted her, in which event he would send a boy, who was not yet a man, into her sancar to bring her to him. Injya made a passable show of looking sad at the parting, but with her heart leaping with joy she was returned to her cousin and her women.

Sanset had spent the moon's passing torn between two sets of emotions: expectation and despair. She knew that Injya would try to bring about a moral and spiritual revival to her people, but the means by which she would accomplish this mammoth task filled her heart with dread.

186

The majority of the women saw Injya as a threat: they could sense her power and were frightened of it. The forty or so Gyaretz women had divided loyalties: some had coupled with Branfjord men, some were happy, others had coupled with their own men and had borne children. Although many missed the sisterhood that the rituals to the Goddess gave them, most were too frightened to change their lives, no matter how dreary they had become.

During the three winters that Injya had been absent, Sanset had confided in only four women: Ullu and Djyana, who were Branfjord women, and Oanti and Aywe, young women from the Gyaretz tribe. Sanset's daughter, Bendula, had been almost inseparable since early childhood from the younger of the two Gyaretz women, Oanti, and had subsequently become firm friends with Ullu. It was these women who sat whispering round the fire when Injya burst into the sancar flap on the morning of her release and it was these women who shyly kissed Injya.

Injya sensed many pairs of eyes, not all friendly, watching every move she made. She had to behave impeccably, pretend to be the loving wife of Crenjal, so conversation with Sanset and the women was peppered with innuendoes which she could only trust to the Goddess, would be recognized by those who understood her true motives. She listened more than she talked, watching the four friends of Sanset and Bendula intently, hoping against hope that from this tiny nucleus somehow the power which she wanted to restore to her women would grow. Ullu fascinated her, she was a maiden of fourteen summers with an open, honest face which, even in this dark winter time, was coloured with freckles. She bore a strong resemblance to Soosha so it was without much surprise that Injya found out that she was, in fact, Soosha's half-sister. Her mother had died giving birth to her, and Anfjord, her father, had given her up too for dead. She had spent all her early life with an old woman of the tribe, who had died on the journey to the caves. But it was not this personal history or her physical appearance which attracted Injya to her, but her spirit-body. Ullu had, Injya knew, the clear-sight of the Goddess. Ullu, herself, knew nothing of this, but Injya knew, beyond all shadow of a doubt, that soon, Ullu's powers would manifest themselves.

Djyana, the other Branfjord woman was the same age as Injya – eighteen summers, but there, any resemblance to Injya ended. Outwardly she was a slow-moving giant of a woman, taller even than Injya, stronger than many a man. Her muscular body was browned by the sun and her short-cut black hair shone with health and vitality. She moved as gracefully and as slowly as Aywe, but where Aywe's eyes were the blue of calm, reflecting water, Djyana's were like the unfathomable brown depths of the very earth itself. Like a fuller, more profound version of Aywe, Djyana weighed every word, only speaking when her somewhat ponderous mind had fully reasoned any likely reaction.

The two Gyaretz women, Aywe and Oanti, Injya only remembered as children; now Oanti was fifteen summers old and firm friends with Aywe, one summer her senior. Oanti was short, strong bodied with black curled hair as luxurious as Injya's own; she had a quick, receptive mind, something which showed itself in her sure, fast movement of her slender body; she chattered like a bubbling stream, her eager mind swift to grasp and assimilate the smallest nuance. Aywe, by contrast, used few words and if Oanti was a bubbling stream, Aywe was as reflective as a still pool in moonlight. Aywe was as tall as Oanti was short, as graceful as a larch tree, and as pensive as Oanti was impulsive. In short, they complemented each other like sunshine and showers.

Her women. Injya kept repeating these words to herself as she watched and listened: her women. She would have to impart all her knowledge to these women, would have to be as Askoye had been, detached yet connected. Little Ullu, scarce out of childhood, unknowing yet gifted, blessed yet cursed; little Oanti, sparkling, vivid, sure-spirited, vital; pensive Aywe, slender of form but strong of heart; Djyana, laborious Djyana, heavy earth-woman; Sanset, nurturing, unselfish, suffering much for others, taking little for herself and little Bendula, still a child, still a being washed along by the tides of events, unable yet to know her energy, feel her power. Injya wanted desperately to talk with these women about her life, share with them the plans she had for the future of the tribe, tell them all that had happened to her, all that she had learnt, but to be private was to bring suspicion.

Privacy in this winter encampment was almost impossible. In the summer-lands many sancars were made, the tribe splitting into blood-related groups of women and children, men and youths, but in this deep midwinter, heat became the criterion for life and only two large sancars had been made, crammed together inside the largest cave. In these lived nearly all the members of the tribe, so the women's sancar in which she was now seated was home to nearly sixty women and children. The smaller caves had been taken by animals, the infirm and Anfjord, Soosha, Anfjord's brother Bran, and of course, Crenjal. Injya had been horrified to find that the very elderly and ill had been excluded from the more able-bodied of the tribe, but once again the laws of the Branfjord people had overcome those of the Gyaretz. Sickness was seen by the Branfjords as either weakness or evil. Weakness, they believed, could infect people as easily as bad water could induce sickness and if the illness was caused through an evil tukris taking away a person's spirit, it could attack continuously. So it was that only Gyaretz women dared to tend the elderly and frail, only the Gyaretz women who caught any disease which was contagious, and obviously it was the Gyaretz women bore the main brunt of the illnesses. With each Gyaretz death the sagacity of the principle was underlined: only the strongest survive and only the strongest deserve to survive. Injya knew that she would have an almost insurmountable task ahead. Eventually the women settled for the night, sleeping closely together, but it took a long time for Injya to sleep; a long time before her sense of isolation from the majority of the women was dispelled by the love she knew her women had for her.

Injya woke abruptly in the middle of the night. She felt very hot; the air in the sancar was thick with the smell of human sleeping bodies, but it was not the lack of clean air which woke her. She felt ripples on the atmosphere, ripples of fear. She lay in the darkness, listening intently. She could hear a muffled female voice, but it sounded a very long way off. She was about to sit up when a tightening in her abdomen stayed her movement, her womb seemed to suddenly become rock-hard, a tight, fearful ball. For an instant she panicked – the baby – it was coming – she would lose her baby but then a scream echoed round the caves, a deep, blood-curdling scream and soon the sancar was alive with frightened women.

'Ucatt!' someone shouted. 'Ucatt – quickly!'

The sancar immediately turned from a hushed, frightened silence into a crush of excited women. Everyone got up, various children were handed to women as three of the oldest women of the tribe rushed out.

'What is happening?' Injya turned to Sanset who herself was hurriedly dressing.

'Ucatt's child is coming too soon – hurry!' Injya followed behind Sanset and the old women along the dark tunnel which led to Ucatt's cave. She shared it with two other pregnant women and three women who had just given birth – one of whom, Toonjya, had only three days before delivered a stillborn child. The atmosphere in the small cave was electric with foreboding.

Injya crept forward through the milling women until she stood before Ucatt. One glance at her face was enough to tell her that she would not survive the birth. Already her eyes were bloodshot with myriads of tiny broken blood vessels ruptured with the effort of her labours. She had

190

bitten her lip badly and it was obvious that she had lost much blood. She looked at the three elders and knew from their set faces that they, too, believed that Ucatt was doomed. Knowing that it was already too late to save this woman only increased Injya's resolve – she must save the child – the whole tribe was dying and here was another babe about to die if something was not done! In the flickering taper-light Injya looked from one face to another – each one registering little else but a certain defeated, crushed look. She knew she had to act – even if to do so would mean certain discovery – she had to show these women that a dual death was not an inevitability; that they *did* have the power to save, if not Ucatt, then certainly her child. She turned her back on Ucatt and the three old women who were now supporting her and addressed the women.

'All of you – gather round – all of you, come, be with Ucatt, share her pain – help take it away from her.'

The three old women stared at her in disbelief – who was she to order them what to do? The other women looked at her with fear in their eyes.

'Sanset – who was the woman who lost her child?' Injya's voice was calm and commanding – she would use any means at her disposal to make these women regain their power – even if by doing so she hurt them. Sanset pointed towards Toonjya. Toonjya, who had been sitting hunched against the cave wall, looked up quickly as Injya approached her, then hid her head in her folded arms.

'Toonjya – Toonjya – look at me!' Injya's eyes blazed, forcing Toonjya to look at her.

'You, you who have so recently and so cruelly been robbed of motherhood, you, out of all of us, know what Ucatt is feeling – Toonjya – tell these women to listen to me – tell them to follow me or to leave this cave. We will deliver Ucatt of her child and you, *you* Toonjya, will help!'

Toonjya's darting eyes showed her fear, but Injya's words seemed to strike at her heart. Reluctantly she stood up and looked intently into Injya's face.

'Yes' she whispered, 'I will help.'

The words were hardly out of her mouth when the air rang with screams as the pain gripped Ucatt once more. The contrast between Toonjya's whispered response and the terror-filled scream gave Injya new strength. She turned on the women and raised her hands to the roof of the cave. Lowering them slowly she turned her hands palm-upwards and spread her arms wide, circling them all with her energy.

'All of you will help!'

The women looked from one to another then back again at this commanding woman.

'Now, each of you, squat on your haunches and when Ucatt's pain comes again, you must imagine that you, too, are giving birth.'

Reluctantly the women did as they were bid acquiescing to Injya's compelling voice.

'Good,' Injya said at last and then turning to one of them ordered her to get some iced grass, some icicles and any water she could find.

'The men!' Injya called after her, 'they will still have some water – take it from them – we must have water!'

More frightened of Injya than of the consequences of going to the men, the woman ran from the cave.

'Good – now, women, all of us, together, we must all push forth this child from Ucatt's body – she is too tired to do it herself. Do not be afraid, you women with child, this will not bring your children forth, for you are pushing with your heart and spirit, not your body.'

The oldest woman who was squatting behind Ucatt relinquished her place to Injya and kneeling on the ground behind Ucatt she took the weight of the woman on to her, resting her head on her abdomen and stroking her wet forehead. Her pains seemed to stop for a few moments and Ucatt panted, her head lolling from side to side on Injya's belly as Injya prayed silently for the safe delivery of the child.

'I have some grass and a little water – I could not find any icicles – the men had broken them off,' the woman blurted out as she ran back into the cave.

'You did well,' Injya said gently as she took the goblet and the grasses from her. She could feel Ucatt's body tense as once more the pain came upon her. Injya pressed the freezing grass to her brow and held her head firmly.

'Work, women, work!' she shouted to the waiting women and with one voice, they all strained as if they too were giving birth. Injya bent her head over the labouring woman and said, very slowly and very clearly: 'Sacred Ahni Amwe – beloved Goddess – help this woman in her labours, give her the strength to bring forth new life!'

At the words some of the women faltered, but Injya carried on, sensing their fears, but knowing only that she must do whatever was needed to save the child.

> Ahni Amwe, stir your waters
> Ahni Amwe, stir your power
> Ahni Amwe, fill your daughter
> Ahni Amwe, give the child life!

Ucatt struggled in her pain, trying to shake off Injya's hands.

'Leave me,' she whispered hoarsely, 'let me die – the child will not come.'

'No!' Injya returned. 'No, neither will I let you or your child die – you will live, by the grace of the Goddess, you will live. When the next pain comes, call on Ahni, call on the Goddess, she will help you.'

Ucatt had no time to reply as the next pain ground down into her body.

'Ahni Amwe, fill your daughter!' she screamed to the heavens: 'Ahni Amwe, give the child life!'

The chant was taken up by the women and soon the air was filled with the words of the sacred mother of all women:

> Ahni Amwe, stir your waters
> Ahni Amwe, stir your power
> Ahni Amwe, fill your daughter
> Ahni Amwe, give the child life!

Over and over the words were chanted. Above the cries of the pain the words rang out, the sounds of the chanting women drowning out the screams of agony, the sounds of the sacred age-old chant, over and over the name called upon:

> Ahni Amwe, stir your waters
> Ahni Amwe, stir your power
> Ahni Amwe, fill your daughter
> Ahni Amwe, give the child life!

Then the moment! A child, slithering down the secret dark place of mystery, a child, spluttering and squealing, crying and shivering, a new soul, shining with life.

The chanting stopped as quickly as it had started, the women now knew what to do. Quickly Ucatt was laid on clean furs to rest, the babe was covered in furs which had been warmed by the fire, and was laid on her breast as the second-birth was delivered and placed in the spirit-bowl. Water now came from everywhere, women freed from their fear of the men by the power of the miracle they had witnessed, ran to and fro, demanding and obtaining water from the men. But the spirit of the water, the spirit of life which had been frozen in the precious substance, came too late. As the last star of the deep midwinter night faded, so too did Ucatt, giving up her slender spark of life.

As Ucatt breathed her last, Injya whispered the words which Askoye had taught her, into the woman's ear.

'Take flight to the shining ones, spirit of Ucatt. Fear not the sights you will see, heed not the passages of past lives, past pleasures, past fears. Look only to the Goddess, look only to the white light of pure love. Ahni Amwe will guide you to the Great White Spirit, Bai Ulgan. Let nothing hold you back.'

She nodded to Sanset who gently removed the child from Ucatt's breast. As she laid Ucatt's head upon the furs she looked up at the silent women standing round her.

'Do not be frightened,' she said calmly, 'Ucatt is at rest, she will not harm you.'

Sanset looked towards Injya and saw her eyes flicker towards Toonjya. Sanset understood and held the child out towards the woman. Toonjya recoiled as if Sanset was offering her something abhorrent. Injya saw the look, saw the other women look, open mouthed, as Sanset began walking towards Toonjya, and she said gently: 'Take the child, Toonjya. In honour of all women, take the child. You still mourn your own loss, do not make us mourn a double loss. Your milk is within your breasts, milk for your babe – give your life to this child of Ucatt's.'

Toonjya hesitated, turned to look at her one remaining child, a boy of four summers called Potyami, and glanced again at the tiny boy-child which was being held out to her. For a moment Sanset and Injya thought Toonjya would begin wailing as conflicting emotions of fear, hope and sadness all flashed across her face.

'Take the orphan of the wind, Toonjya, honour Ucatt's passing with the milk of your body. The Goddess wills it so.'

For an instant, Toonjya looked terrified at the word 'Goddess', then something seemed to change in her and she stepped forward and took the child into her arms. Now the tears of the women fell, tears for Ucatt's death, tears of relief, but tears of fear also for they had, in that tiny birth cave, returned, if only fleetingly, to the ways of the Goddess and this, they knew, could spell disaster.

Injya and Sanset quickly left the cave, leaving the women to attend to the rites for the second-birth and the dead. As they passed swiftly down the long passage towards the women's sancar they saw the hooded figure

of Soosha retreat into her cave. In the shadowy light the
women stopped and looked at each other, one with fear,
one with a nodding acceptance; Soosha had witnessed all
that had happened. Soon Anfjord would know; soon all
Injya's protestations would be for nought. Sanset put her
hand out and touched her cousin's arm.

'Yes – I saw her too,' Injya said. She had no need to say
more – all, too soon, would be revealed.

CHAPTER EIGHTEEN

Whispers. The meagre day seemed filled with whispers. They vied with the wind for access to the people's ears. Upon their return to the sancar, Sanset and Injya had told none of the other women anything more than Ucatt had died giving birth to a boy-child, which Injya had called Wa-Oagist and that Toonjya had taken the child to her breast. But the old women whispered the words Injya had used and soon silence fell when Injya or Sanset were near. Both women waited – for what they were unsure, but as they worked at their daily round they could not rid themselves of a feeling of dread, as tangible and as threatening as the death of Ucatt herself.

The two women who had taken Wa-Oagist's second-birth to the tree-line came back to the encampment shivering with tiredness and cold. They had found a birch sapling, had buried the spirit-bowl along with the second-birth and they were sure that Wa-Oagist would grow as the birch sapling would grow, into a fine, strong adult. They wished only for food and sleep. Injya watched as the women were drawn into the group now that the questioning was over; from the corner of her eye she saw the women being fed, saw the old women whisper to them, knew without hearing that they, too, were being told of the secret words Injya had used to bring forth the child and watched as their eyes turned wide with fear and their mouths opened with alarm, and as she turned away from the group and prepared to lie down for the night, she knew that the same whispering, the same fear would be abroad in the men's sancar. Anfjord had his proof, Soosha would have ensured that. Now that he knew that Injya *was* still practising the ways of the Goddess, he would have to act.

The following day dawned in a brilliant whiteness. Overnight the rain's white tears had fallen softly, turning the hard, frozen land into a gentle roundness. Injya looked at the ground and wanted to weep – it was as if the innocent earth, clothed in purity was mocking her dark mood. On the horizon an orange sun wobbled and for the first time since waking she thought of Galdr. The sun reminded her of her dream – moon and sun combined, the power of Galdr and herself fused together. She shook her head angrily – it would never be! The morning wore on, but the business did nothing to lighten her doom-clouded reasoning. Anfjord would call for her shortly, Anfjord would act, something would happen, but all around her the quiet day-to-day activities of the women hummed; even Sanset seemed to have brightened. Injya had no appetite for food, but accepted the meat offered to her – she was being given meat when all the other women had only broth – as was fitting to her station. She wanted to throw the meat back into the pot, wanted to tell the cowed women not to look at her thus, not to be afraid of her, but how could she when she herself was terrified?

Injya had taken only one mouthful of the meat when the whole of the sancar frame shook. The women who had been sitting in circles all leapt to their feet in apprehension. Again the sancar shook as someone crashed against its skin walls. Startled children began whimpering and ran to their mother's knees. Injya's mind raced . . . Anfjord . . . It was Anfjord come to kill her! With heart beating wildly in her chest she stood up and faced the entrance – now she would know her fate. She wanted to walk to the entrance, to stand tall against her enemy, but her pounding heart made her limbs shake with fear. The entrance flap was torn apart. Injya stood transfixed with horror as a figure swayed towards her. The figure screamed out to her: 'Injyaaaa!'

It was Crenjal – not Anfjord.

She took a step towards him and saw him lift his great head as once more he screamed out her name. It echoed round the cave and now she ran towards him. He was doubled over and swaying slightly, his huge shoulders shaking and then she saw. From his loins bright scarlet blood pulsed through his fingers. The women squealed and ran to the walls of the sancar, covering their children's faces, as Crenjal lumbered nearer to Injya. He reached out for her with a blood-covered hand and Injya tried to support his toppling frame, but sank under his weight to the ground. Crenjal's blood spurted from his loins in a relentless, pulsing stream, covering her body as she grappled with him, desperately trying to staunch the flow.

'Injya!' his cracked voice called to her once more: 'Injya – Anfjord did this – hold me – Injya!'

As his near sightless eyes searched for hers in the gathering gloom of death, he opened his blood-soaked palm – in it was his severed manhood.

'Injya, I am cold! Injya, make me warm . . . ' His voice trailed away as she tore her eyes from the horror of his hand and tried to cradle him in her arms.

'I will always love you, my Injya, always,' he whispered. 'Kiss me!'

Blindly, not knowing what she was doing, she lowered her face towards his – this much she owed him – but as her lips met his, his body suddenly convulsed and then crumpled. He lay heavy in her arms, bled white, a death-cold being whose life had been ended because his body had enjoyed hers. His life had been taken instead of hers. Anfjord had acted.

As the women began to keen, Injya's sobs were taken to the heavens and stirred an old raven, who was frozen half to death, perched on the top of a tree under which a young man was hanging. The raven knew the sound as well as he knew the sounds of the mountains, and as his black old heart cracked, he cried to the heavens in response.

It had been hard for Injya to hold on to any feeling of integrity or self-worth. She was forced to stand by and watch the freezing deaths overtake the weakest of her peoples, as the darkest part of the winter blackened their lives. Four moons had passed since Crenjal's death, four moons spent as little more than Anfjord's slave. And as such she was restrained from administering comfort or help, unable to use her power of healing. Cut off from the source of her creativity, she, too, longed for death. It was only the quickening in her body that kept her, too, from freezing. She had been taken by Anfjord the evening of Crenjal's death and now, although her belly was large with a child he knew was not his own, his need of her had not diminished.

Injya, Tyanka and Anfjord spent their time together in one of the small caves off the large central cave. Anfjord rarely left the two women alone together and both were becoming weaker. Soon it would be time for the trek to the summer-lands and Injya, exhausted by Anfjord's demands and her growing child, found no magic potent enough to rid her of this man. Her power seemed useless – she felt it had died with the death of Crenjal and day by day she became weaker. She longed for death and it felt that it was only her hatred of Soosha and Anfjord that was keeping her alive. She knew that Soosha was drugging the old man, knew that his sexual powers were not of this earth and knew that she was but a part of Soosha's plot of revenge. But knew, also, that she was powerless to change it.

That night, Anfjord took her once more. She lay, feeling nothing, sensing nothing as Anfjord's body pounded against hers. Tyanka was lying stiffly beside her, eyes tightly shut against the sight, breath held in fear. Injya felt so tired and weary that she gave up, gave up not only the desire for the brutality to be over, but gave up hope. In the instant of no hope, when she felt herself fall deeper and deeper into the black abyss of self, the swirling started, just as it had done all that time ago when she had looked into the black face of the obsidian mirror in Askoye's cave. For a moment she confused the feeling with that of fainting, but as quickly as that thought passed through her mind, she instinctively knew what was happening to her was different. The swirling blackness had a quality of self-hood which was different to fainting and with a great sigh of relief, she gave herself up to the void. Down she swirled until she finally came to rest, a small white dot in the vast blackness of eternity. The dot slowly grew as her consciousness did and then she knew that for the second time in her life, she was soul-walking.

She could see herself lying on the bed, a twisted heap of writhing flesh, Anfjord heaving his life into her, but she, Injya, was safe, bodyless, far above the tableau of flesh, far above the roof of the cave. Her spirit was free and she had the whole of the heavens to choose from. But no sooner had she recognized the fact that she was apart from her body, than she felt it pulling towards her again, could feel the pain in her solar plexus. She tried hard to stay detached, to keep the space and the clarity but as surely as her child was linked inside her with the cord of life, so she, too, was linked to her own body with a cord equally as strong and as tangible as that of her child's. She could see a slender, silver cord coming straight out from the solar plexus of her earthly body, right up into the heavens where her soul was, and no sooner had she seen it than she felt the tugging, the life pulling at her consciousness until she could no longer restrain it. She felt herself give in to the drag of her body and slowly slide down the cord until once more she was back inside her flesh, inside her body.

Eventually Anfjord left her body and stumbled away – how she hated him! Injya held out her hand and touched Tyanka's trembling arm.

'It is all right, Tyanka, it is over for now.'

Tyanka sniffed loudly and the shaking increased.

'Come, come here.' She felt in the dark for the child-woman's body and Tyanka came to her, shivering with fear and emotion.

'There,' Injya soothed the girl's head. 'There.'

Tyanka cried softly and allowed herself to be comforted in Injya's arms. Eventually Tyanka's sobbing subsided and she slept as Injya cradled her. If only she could teach Tyanka how to leave her body, Injya thought as she listened to her shallow breathing, then she could be spared some of this. But she knew that the girl was not long for this world – when a child is desecrated in such a manner, something of their spirit dies and unless they are nurtured again with a great and giving love, the spirit does not recover and slowly it surrenders its hold on life. This, she knew, would happen to Tyanka. Injya shuddered with loathing for the man who called himself the chieftain of the Skoonjay people – if only Crenjal had given to him the treatment he had meted out to Crenjal, there would be hope for the people once more! With an effort of will she stopped that train of thought – there is no profit in reliving old hurts if nothing could be learnt from them.

Injya sighed deeply and relived the experience of soul-walking; the problem was one of time – how could one extend the time when one was out of the body, without the body dying, how could one *not* feel the pull of that silver cord, and how could one move through time and space when one was disembodied? Halfray had learnt how to do it – he had appeared to her by the pool all that time ago, and he had his body with him! Somehow, she knew, she must practise leaving and re-entering her form until she could do it at will, and then, perhaps, the ability to truly soul-walk would come to her. Still racking her brains for answers she eventually fell asleep, cold and tired, bruised and uncomfortable, but with more hope than she had felt for many a moon.

Another moon passed and then it was time for the journey to the summer-lands once more. The going was

202

hard for everyone. The children cried almost incessantly – poor food and lack of sunshine made their bones brittle and their skin cut and bruised easily – and the women were dispirited. All hope died when they witnessed Injya's degradation, and now, when they were most in need of this woman who had once seemed so shining, so powerful, here she was, struggling down the slippery mountainside, heavy with child and burdens, just as they were.

Sanset choked back the tears as she watched Injya and Soosha in the train ahead of her. Soosha, head erect, wrapped in thick furs, riding on one of the few horses which had survived the winter, commanding and giving orders, and walking by her side the bowed figure of Injya, only the beauty of her raven hair making her distinguishable from the hoards of other laden women. She pulled Bendula closer to her and in answer to the child's enquiring look she ruffled her hair.

'I am sad, that is all, Bendula – Injya – what does lie ahead for her – for any of us?'

Bendula stared at her mother solemnly and dropped her eyes. *She* knew, *she* knew what would happen to Injya, she would die giving birth to the child of Crenjal, that was what lay ahead of her, a painful bloody death, like Ucatt and so many others. She let slip a long sigh and stared hard at the ground. Life was hard, she decided, but with the swiftness of an eleven-summer child her dark mood changed as she spied a very tiny pale green tuft of new grass managing to cling on to a slither of life on the dried barren rocks.

'Sanset, look!' she shouted in glee. 'Grass!' Sanset stared at her feet, she could see nothing.

'Look!' the child insisted, 'there!' Sanset dropped her bundle and stared at the rock. Between Bendula's feet was a minute crevice, no thicker than a strand of her hair and in it was growing a few blades of spindle-grass.

'Thanks be to Hoola, Great Mother of the Earth!' she whispered to herself, adding, as if thinking aloud: 'You are growing again, despite our cruelty.'

A sudden shout from the men ahead of her broke her prayer. They were pointing upwards as a great flock of geese flew effortlessly overhead, the noise of their slowly undulating wings and the call of their leader almost masking the shouts of glee from the men.

'Aspar!' Sanset sang with joy in her voice, 'you have brought the birds back to us!'

Stones whistled upwards, but fell with sharp reports on to the rocks beneath their feet – the geese were flying too high for slings and stones to stop their majestic journey and though hungry as she was for fresh meat, Sanset was pleased that the stones missed their quarry. She knew that there would be plenty of fresh meat shortly.

Injya remarked the passing of the geese without comment save that of a fleeting thought that she wished that she, too, could fly, fly away from the burden in her belly and the pack on her back. She stared resolutely at the horses' hoofs cracking on the hard rocks beside her and the resentment in the pit of her stomach sank deeper. Ripples of anger flowed through her body as she thought of the woman sitting so imperiously astride the horse. Soosha was powerful, as powerful as herself – the only difference between the two women being that Injya had been trained to use her power, to empty herself of self-will and become as a reed for the outpouring of the divine. Soosha was as a child, wide open to all power good and evil, and all the while that she sought to further her own ends, the power of evil would triumph over the good. In a peculiar sense Injya felt almost sorry for her, for she knew that there is no action without reaction, that no matter how long, how many lifetimes it took, Soosha would reap the harvest of what she was now sowing.

The line of men and horses ahead of her suddenly stopped and thankfully Injya flopped on to the earth. Her back had been aching all morning and even the removal of the furs she was carrying did little to take away her discomfort which now settled in the small of her back and clung there like a dull brown sorrow. As the tribe scurried round her to prepare food and go foraging for precious wood, Injya closed her eyes to the scenes of business and drank in the air. In it she could detect the faint smell of new leaves and grasses and the slightly salty aroma which told her that they were no more than two days' travelling from the summer marshlands. Above the noise of the children, she heard faint bird song and her spirits lifted – the geese, the harbingers of summer, had woken the birds from their winter quarters and she knew that shortly the skies would be filled with the beating of their precious wings and the songs of their hearts.

Very carefully she lay back on the earth and automatically put her hand on to her swollen belly. The babe inside her had been very quiet for the last three days, the churning around was conspicuous by its absence. For an instant, panic lurched in the pit of Injya's stomach – what if? – she stopped the thought – some thoughts are better not finished. Her rational mind told her that there was precious little room for the child to be moving around, that he was settled, waiting for the time when he could draw breath. She stroked her bulbous stomach and fell into a deep reverie.

Pictures of flower-strewn glades, sunshine and bright blue skies formed in her mind, and in it she saw herself cradling her child who was gazing up at her with the trusting clear blue eyes of innocence as he suckled at her breast. Around her came the creatures of the young woodlands, spindly-legged fawns dappled in the sunshine, gambolling rabbits with tails whiter than cotton grass and young snow grouse, all fluff and feathers, their as yet flightless wings as brown and dappled as the fawns, making them safe from the birds of prey. They, too, were waiting, waiting for their pretty feathers to turn white for the winter which now seemed many more than five moons away. Slowly she opened her eyes and gazed at the high white clouds in the pale azure sky. High, high up she saw a dark V and knew that it was another flock of geese travelling northwards – she hoped that they had had a better winter in their far-away homes than the tribe had lived through and once again, she found herself thinking of Galdr – Galdr, far away in a home about which she knew nothing. She wanted to believe him dead, as she had seen him, hanging on that tree, but she knew this was fallacious. As surely as she knew that her child would soon be born, she knew that some time, in some place, he would be with her again. She closed her eyes against the skies and tried to picture him with her in her leafy glade, but no comforting pretty pictures filled her mind, in their place came confusion and doubt – how could she ever, *ever* imagine loving the very man who had so cruelly treated her? Her mind was tired of trying to reason, whatever would be would be for her ultimate good, of that she was sure even though she knew not what that would be, and as the gentle breezes lulled her to sleep she resumed her stroking and comforting of Galdr's child. The child who lay coiled and curled and calm inside her body, who would soon, like the tender leaves of summer, unfold himself and live apart from and a part of her.

Galdr, too, lay on the grassy hillock, stroking his full stomach, eyes shut against the sunshine and the high white clouds. He could hear Halfray gently snoring by his side – it had been a long journey and they had both begun to doubt their senses at undertaking such a trek into a place which they both knew would cause them much pain and many heartaches. But now, a full moon's passing since they had left their cave, with the sun shining and their bellies full, good feelings washed over him. All would be well. Galdr chuckled quietly to himself as he remembered his self-inflicted torture – just what *was* he trying to prove? Oh, the needing to die had been real enough, but to die for whom, and for what? His smile faded as he recognized the answer – he wanted to die to avoid the responsibility of his actions, to avoid having to put right his wrongs, but more than anything he had wanted to die because he was afraid. The path which had been shown to him was one of constant truth – to live his life by the rules he had learnt, to live without deceit, fear or avoidance, to consistently meet life openly and greet her and her opportunities trusting that all was, ultimately, for the good of his soul.

How much he had learnt! He smiled again as he thought of Halfray – the hours they spent together, he learning in four short moons' passing all that had taken Halfray half a lifetime to learn about: plants, herbs, infusions and the clarity and concentration necessary for soul-walking. But he had been able to teach Halfray things too, or rather, they had discovered together the use of the drum and the mirror. When Galdr had recovered from the injuries the ice had done to his fingers and toes, one of the first things he showed Halfray was the drum. Now he understood the strange symbols on the walls and the shift and the drum – they were the pictures of a man's journey towards his creator. The spirals were the many convolutions one makes as one progresses along life's journey; the star or the sun, the ultimate goal, the reuniting with the source of all life and the strange antler shapes showing how one has to harness the power of the animals and become as cogent with the earth as they are. Only then could one use the feathers which symbolized man's flight to the heavens.

Flight to the heavens. The words resounded round his brain – how he had wished, at the last, that he too could fly. He had been wrong in wishing that brother wolf would kill him, been wrong hoping for some savage bear to miraculously awake from his deep midwinter slumber and put an end to his paltry life. Brother wolf had come, many of them in fact. They had woken him from his unconsciousness with their howling, but they had not torn him limb from limb; as if held by an instinct stronger even than their hunger, they had gathered round him as he had hung from his tree, only their slavering jaws and red eyes hinting at their baser instincts. It had been as if Galdr was looking into the very eyes of death and this too was being denied him. A cruel irony.

He had hung on his tree of self-destruction for two devastating nights; the first when the cold froze his flesh and the wolves first appeared, he thought was the worst. By the time the short day had succumbed once more to the ink-filled terror, he had lost all sense of pain, time and most of his fear. A saying his mother used to say kept going round inside his head: 'There is nothing to fear, but fear', and when, in reality, he had put himself in a place of total fear he found that there was nothing more. Then he had faced who he really was.

He had cried for the return of the pictures, the torments which are supposed to engulf one at the moment of death, but that was denied him. In their place came a true reflection of his inner self. Sorrow and grief had no part in it – he was already sorry for his actions and grieving for the harms and hurts. A deep clarity, an undeniable inner knowing slowly dawned as he had hung there. Then he knew the true purpose of the black mirror – with it you could see yourself as you really are. With the understanding, compassion arose, compassion for himself and for others. As he gasped at the thin air and the rattle which accompanied each breath grew until he felt the whole of his chest vibrate, he knew that he not only had to forgive himself, but everyone else who had been part of his life. He had been unaware, that was all, and so he could no more blame his father, mother, sisters, Injya herself, for anything they had either done or not done – they simply could not help themselves.

As the pink and violet sun had risen on the third day, Galdr had found himself standing on the very top of the tree. Unharmed, unhurt, no longer cold or afraid. He knew that his body was dead and wondered that he still felt a body around him. He looked straight into the eye of the sun and for an instant thought that he saw the moon in front of it, changing the violet rose into the warmest orange, but when he blinked and looked again, the vision had passed. He looked down through the branches of the tree and saw his own body hanging, stiff with frost, the wolves silently watching it. He wanted to do something for it – such a sight should not be left to frighten a chance traveller, but he did not know how to proceed. He knew that the body he was inhabiting was not a real body – how could a real body stand weightless on the apex of a slender birch tree? But he seemed stuck fast and unsure. Again the wish to have the ability to fly came upon him – if only he could simply glide down, remove the ropes and cover his body with branches or stones – but . . . no sooner had the thought formed in his mind than he heard the beating of wings, felt the rush of wind as a massive white eagle, larger than any he had ever seen before, flew past him, circled him and then hovered in front of him – its bright yellow eyes looking straight into his own.

This was his power! This was what the crone had pointed out to him – this was his spirit! He raised his arms out wide and closed his eyes. He felt the eagle's breath entering his body, felt the cool silky feathers caress him, felt the power of the glorious creature fill him anew and when he opened his eyes again, he *was* the eagle. Triumphantly he moved his wings and the slight movement made him soar to the heavens. Far below him he could see the trees, the bare rocks, the smoke billowing from the fire that Halfray must have lit at the mouth of their cave. Another movement and he was higher still, the trees now just tiny dots far, far below him. He was free! He was an eagle! King of the skies!

He twisted his head and caught sight of his lifeless body, a mere shadow only, disfiguring the graceful lines of the stately birch – at least he could peck through the ropes which held it fast. With another turn of his head and a flick of the tiny feathers at the far end of his wondrous wings, Galdr the Eagle flew down to his body. He landed on its shoulder and stared at its face. Already it was turning grey and cold, soon it would be stiff. Quickly he tugged at the knots in the rope, sinking his sharp talons into the cold flesh to keep a good grip, tearing at the ends of the ropes and pulling. His wings beat the air furiously as he tugged at the last of the ropes, but finally it snapped and the body which was once him crumpled to the earth. In that moment Galdr the Eagle felt a pain as searing as if his heart was being torn from his body. It ripped through his chest like a spear through a tiny fish and his wings gave way. He fell like a heavy blanket of white feathers on top of his lifeless body and he felt the power streaming out from his heart into the heart of Galdr, son of Anfjord, and he knew that his brief life on earth, either as human or bird was truly over.

Galdr laughed out aloud and woke the snoozing Halfray.

'Galdr?' Halfray muttered, rubbing his eyes and propping himself up on an elbow. 'What is it?'

'I was laughing at myself!' he said, 'Laughing at how I was, sure that I had died on that tree, and laughing because it is good to be alive – really alive – you know!'

Galdr stretched, yawned, scratched himself and stood up, offering a hand to the still perplexed Halfray.

'Come on – you have slept enough – we still have many pchekts to travel.'

Halfray took the offered arm and pulled himself upright.

'Indeed,' he agreed. 'At least all today and tomorrow, if not a third by my reckoning.'

'No,' Galdr said quietly, 'it will not be that long.'

Halfray fell silent – when Galdr spoke thus he knew whatever he said to be true. Galdr knew, instinctively almost, how long journeys would take, where they would find food, where they could seek shelter for the night. Halfray bent down and gathering his furs together slung them effortlessly over his shoulder, picked up his walking-rod and gazed before him. The land gently unfolded itself before his eyes, great sweeping plains already covered in the bright green of Aspar, a pleasantly undulating landscape, soft and curved like a woman, where hidden brooks and trees would suddenly surprise the eyes with their sparkling water or their deep shade. Far beyond them he could see the flat lands, the flat marshlands of summer where the salt-waters came far inland and the seals and the fish were plenty. Shielding his eyes from the sun he fancied he could see the sparkling of the great salt waters and remembered swimming in her cold gentle waves.

'Galdr . . . ' he murmured. 'Isn't she beautiful? – Our mother earth, so—' he paused for breath and for words to describe the feelings of joy he felt. A sharp scream of pain from Galdr broke the spell of beauty like a lightning bolt and Halfray dropped his belongings and ran to him.

'Galdr! Galdr! What is it?' Galdr had sunk to his knees, clutching his stomach, sweat already forming on his brow.

'It is begun, Halfray!' he whispered through clenched teeth. 'My child is being born!'

CHAPTER NINETEEN

Injya's scream of pain shocked those nearest to her into silence. She cried out only once – it was the shock that made her scream, not the pain itself. One moment she was happily day-dreaming, half awake, half asleep, stroking her unborn child – the next the dull ache in the small of her back had turned itself into a set of bird's talons which tried to rip her apart. It did not last more than a moment for which she was grateful, but she had never expected such a tearing, renting pain. Sanset and Tyanka were by her side before she even had time to stand up.

'Sanset!' she said shakily.

'Has it begun?'

She searched Sanset's frightened eyes with her own, willing her to deny it, hoping she would reject the possibility. Sanset said nothing, but, dropping her gaze from Injya's face she looked at her swollen abdomen and without speaking put a hand on to the top of the rise. She could feel the taut skin and the womb beyond it, hard and unyielding. Eventually she said: 'I think it could be, I am not sure – tell me what the pain felt like.'

Injya told her, all the while rubbing away at her back for the ache had returned, worse this time and slightly higher. Sanset listened in silence, head bent, staring at the ground.

'Well,' she said at last, 'it could be – we can only wait and see – if you have another one, then you will know for sure – I think you should rest – I'll get you some broth.'

Leaving her with the small crowd of women who had gathered round, she marched off to the cooking fires. Injya sat down again, grateful for the smiling faces of the women round her. So, she thought, this is it! Birth! She surprised herself at how calm she had suddenly become – the long waiting was over now, soon the child would be born. Looking around at the rest of the tribe who were busily cooking, grooming themselves, eating and resting, Injya wondered how they could be so prosaic – so unaware of the momentous occasion. She watched with a curious sense of detachment as Sanset, bowl of broth in hand, stalked over to the place where Anfjord, Soosha and several young men were sitting eating. She saw their heads all turn in her direction and then back at Sanset. With amazement she saw Sanset stamp her foot hard on the ground and point at Anfjord who instantly lowered his head – what *was* she saying? She watched as two young men left their food with obvious reluctance and sauntered off in the direction of the tethered horses. Sanset said something more to Anfjord whose head nodded slowly up and down in agreement and then she suddenly spun round, face gleaming with triumph and swiftly strode back towards Injya.

'That is *that* organized then,' she said with obvious pride, 'they are making you a hyrdle *and* you have two horses to pull it – *he*' – she cast a contemptuous backward glance in Anfjord's direction – 'wouldn't allow four men to carry you, so I insisted that you had the horses – Soosha can walk like the rest of us! Now, sit up and drink this – come on!'

To say that Injya was surprised at Sanset's sudden forthrightness would be an understatement. She acquiesced completely to the woman who had seen her through so many trials, so much heartache and sorrow – of course Sanset would look after her.

Nothing else happened to Injya for what seemed a very long time. She dutifully drank her broth, the women one by one slowly went back to their various tasks and Injya watched the rest of the tribe eventually finish their eating, cover over the fires and get themselves into some sort of order for the resumption of the journey. She watched the high white clouds being chased away by more ominous looking heavy dark-grey ones and felt the wind pick up, but no other thought crossed her mind. Neither did the arrival of the hastily constructed pole and skin hyrdle prompt much response – Injya was lost deep inside herself, lost to a place of secrecy and power. She had heard of women in labour being called moon-mad – now this, too, was happening to her. She felt utterly at peace, completely at one with the earth and the elements, waiting, as the moon waits for her time to rule the heavens.

The crowd ahead of her started to move again as Injya allowed herself to be helped to her feet. She did not need the help, but accepted it graciously as slowly she walked over to the waiting hyrdle and the patient horses. Carefully manoeuvering herself round the two animals, she patted the gentle beasts' muzzles and whispered into first one, then the other's pricked ears: 'Go carefully, my friends – you are bearing the future chief of the Skoonjay people.'

Mildly surprised at what she had said, she cautiously picked her way round the animals and with particular gracefulness placed herself gingerly on the hyrdle. So *that* is who my child will be, she thought to herself, well, so be it. She closed her eyes to the threatening clouds and wrapped herself very carefully around with the furs. Gently, gently, she said to herself as the horses started to move and she felt the unfamiliar bumping over the rough ground. The sun-warmed furs were soft and the steady footfalls of the horses soothing. She fancied that she would sleep now, rocking slightly, the steady droning of the people before and behind her making a travellers' lullaby. She felt calm, safe and nurtured.

'Ah,' she said to the heavens, 'how gentle and good is the earth.'

The pain that shot through her made her gasp and clutch at the sides of the travelling bed. It shuddered from the base of her abdomen and then relentlessly clawed its way over the mound of her child.

'Great Hoola!' she muttered through gritted teeth: 'Not now!'

The pain took no heed, over the top of the babe it went then down again, down by her spine, back to the root of her womanhood. A stab of pain in the middle of her back made her gasp for breath and arch her back, but as suddenly as it had come, the pain disappeared, leaving Injya trembling and shocked to her bones. Gradually she became aware that a hand was covering hers and slowly turning her head she opened her eyes.

'Sanset,' she whispered, 'don't leave me.'

The moon hung, as impassive and inscrutable as ever in the mid-heavens. The stars, intoxicated by her splendour, twinkled their appreciation and in recognition she sent dancing beams of silver light to play upon the lonely earth. Exhilaration was felt everywhere: from the smallest creature of the forest who quaked as the eagle-eyed owls used her light to seek them out, to the blinking, still sleepy, bears who, thin after their winter's long sleep, cavorted in the waterfalls and streams, hungry for fish. The night was alive with the sounds of the animals, the snorting of the horses and the crackling fires. The travellers gathered round the fires, whispering quietly. None seemed to want to sleep, even though the make-shift travelling sancars had been erected long ago. The squealing, river-thrilled children were for once all sleeping, wrapped in furs and their mothers' arms, exhausted by the journey and the unexpected icy river which had suddenly compelled them to throw themselves in screaming with cold and excitement.

Injya looked often into the enigmatic face. Cold and unfeeling, the moon stared blankly back at her. Another pain juddered through her body as she clutched at Sanset's shoulder and held fast to the trunk of a larch tree.

'Ahni Amwe – help your daughter,' she whispered faintly through a dry mouth. The pain slowly reached its peak and then subsided. The women resumed their walking.

They walked round the encampment, along the side of the river for a long time, but the Moon Goddess was still not commanding Injya's waters to flow, still keeping the tides in her power. As the moon slowly relinquished her position to the struggling sun, Sanset slept at last, exhausted by the trial of watching another's pain. Bendula and Tyanka supported the walker, stopping frequently as the pains stopped the relentless moving. They saw the sun rise, yellow beneath the purple clouds, they watched the thin line of light prick out the grey shadows of the low sancars and the sleeping animals and then, as if afraid of what it might see that day, saw the sun retreat quickly behind the solid bank of grey-black, rain-filled clouds.

The tribe moved quickly that morning, hurried onwards more by the need to leave the threatening clouds than any desire to reach the summer-lands before another nightfall. No sooner had the scout shouted his long awaited, 'Aiee – it is over this ridge!' than the heavens opened and the deluge of icy rain doused the fires of the midday stopping place.

Robbed of the means to eat hot food, Anfjord decided to carry on with the trek – if they could keep up this pace, they *would* make permanent camp that night! As the driving rain beat upon the backs of the travellers Anfjord urged them forward, galloping up and down the thin line of the soaked tribe, shouting, cajoling, threatening and very occasionally entreating them. Injya and her women he ignored, they had fallen quite a distance behind – well, let them! Anfjord thought angrily – perhaps a good drenching would encourage Injya's waters to fall – they might not have been caught as unawares by the weather if the horses had been freed to carry the skins! He cantered furiously along the line of people, splashing them with mud and clods of earth, cursing the rain, the sicknesses, Injya and her retinue. He hated birth – hated everything to do with it – loathed the women and their stupid rituals – why could they not be more like the beasts of the fields? Eventually he became so enraged he abandoned his tribe altogether, galloping off to join the scout, to savour the view of the summer-lands by himself.

It was nearly morning when Injya arrived at the encampment. Smoke and steam rose from the wet skins and fires, covering the whole scene in a fine grey mist. Thankfully she drank in the picture and closed her eyes once more as the pain came again. The respite between the pains was almost negligible now and the intensity of their grip unbearable. Sometime during the final mud-covered descent the Goddess had relinquished her power and Injya's waters had deluged her already sodden body, but that had brought no relief, no sudden change in the back-breaking torture, only a deeper, more concentrated agony. Later, she could only look at the freshly caught and cooked fish and slowly shake her head – and later still, when Bendula brought her the tansy she had so meticulously described to her, she refused the infusion of leaves which had brought forth many a babe. The rain thrummed stolidly on the skins of the sancar as persistent as the pains themselves and as Injya fell deeper inside herself she felt that the rain was as obstinate in its desperation to get inside, as the child was to get out. Rain drumming, child pounding, womb pulsing, back breaking – oh, how tired she was!

With the first light of dawn the pains stopped. For a moment Injya thought it was all over – the child must have died – there was no pain – nothing. But the moment passed very quickly.

'Bai Ulgan!' she shrieked. 'Help me!'

The urge to push out the child overwhelmed her, it held her in its grip and forced every atom of her body to obey the laws of birth.

'Push!' the women shouted, 'push!'

Supported on all sides, Injya pushed with all her might. She pushed with her elbows, thighs, abdomen, even her

voice joined in, roaring like a wounded snow-leopard she
bellowed for her babe to be born. Her roaring hushed the
men who were shaping sturdy sancar poles, it reduced
the cooking women to whispers, it frightened the dancing
children in the brooks and made them run to their mothers
for comfort, but it did not bring forth her child. As the
smoke of the evening fires twisted lazily up to the crimson
heavens only tiny whimpers were heard from the direction
of the birth-sancar. It had gone on too long, all the old
women agreed, no woman could survive that. They shook
their greying heads and looked knowingly at each other –
unspoken they silently held the thought that Anfjord had
killed yet another of their kind.

'The child must not be allowed to die!' hissed Soosha
angrily. Sanset shook her head. Exhausted by the nursing,
lack of sleep, coping with the interminable old women
who offered first one remedy, then another, until her head
was swimming in confusion, this last suggestion, the final
solution, was too much. She rubbed her red-rimmed eyes
and raised her head.

'No, Soosha, no. If it is the will of the Goddess . . . '

'Don't talk to *me* about the will of the Goddess!' Soosha
said angrily. 'The will of the Goddess has nothing to do
with it – if we do not remove the child, he will die as well as
your precious Injya – what possible good would that do?'

Sanset dropped her head into her hands again and tried
to smooth away the lines of worry furrowing her brow.

'Soosha,' she said quietly as she raised her aching
head once more and looked at her levelly: '*You* will
then be taking on the role of the Goddess, *you* will
be responsible for Injya's death. Do you want that?
Even if the child does somehow survive – who will
nurse him?'

'I am not interested in the whos and the whats of the
situation!' Soosha rejoined hotly. 'The only thing that is
important is that the child should live.'

Sanset, tired as she was, frightened as she was of Soosha's words, managed to retort: 'And why, Soosha, are you so particularly anxious that this child be saved? Since when have *you* ever had Injya's interests at heart – or the interests of any of the women here? What makes *this* child so important, Soosha?'

Quaking at her own words, Sanset stared deep into Soosha's dark eyes. Hate glistened back at her as Soosha hissed her reply.

'Because Crenjal has never fathered a child before – he will be a magnificent creature. I want the child for the tribe – for me!'

Sanset's mouth dropped open in amazement but further arguing was stopped by another blood-curdling scream from inside the sancar.

'That is it!' Soosha said triumphantly. 'I am not delaying any further – I am Anfjord's daughter and I will cut that child free – it is my father's wish and there is nothing you can do to stop me!'

With that, she turned on her heels and strode over to the men's sancar. Sanset closed her eyes and felt something die inside her. There was nothing further she could do – she was not strong enough to stop her. The warm yellow sun mocked her dark mood as she turned round, turned away from the glistening light of early morning and went into gloomy, dark birth-sancar.

Lying on a fur-covered pallet, Injya was a pitiful sight. Her hair, matted and straggling, clung to her sweat-rung face: dark brown shadows surrounded the blood-shot eyes, livid against her ghostly white skin: her lips were cracked and her body was shaking still from the last pain. The ring of white faces of the women who surrounded her looked up expectantly as Sanset entered and, sensing her defeat, looked quickly away again. Her daughter, Bendula, alone among the women, looked sorrowfully into her mother's eyes. It was over, the role of the women redundant, Soosha and her butchers would take over. Tears brimmed in her deep brown eyes, bottom lip trembling she stroked Injya's brow. She watched her mother take in a deep breath and then softly walk towards her.

'Bendula, beloved, leave this place – I will stay.'

Bendula faltered, hand still gently caressing Injya's temple. Sanset crouched down beside her and put an arm round her shoulders. 'Leave, my daughter, you must not stay.'

Bendula looked deep into her eyes and saw the look of utter hopelessness there.

'No, mother, I will not leave her – let me stay, let me.'

A slight movement under her hand brought her attention back to Injya.

'Mensoon?' Injya gasped, 'Mensoon?'

'She is slipping away,' Sanset said quietly. 'She is seeing her mother – we can do no more.'

The women who had nursed, supported, calmed and cried with Injya, bowed their heads. They knew what Sanset said to be true. There was nothing more their prayers could do. Stiffly, one by one, they rose and left the sancar, leaving Bendula, Sanset and Injya alone.

'I am staying!' Bendula announced calmly, 'I—' She was cut short by Soosha and four young men entering the sancar.

'Get out, child!' ordered Soosha. 'This is no place for maidens – Sanset, you may stay if you have the stomach, otherwise take your daughter with you and go!'

The harsh words shot out into the air like the knife she was carrying, sharp, unyielding, unwomanly. They were the hardest words Sanset had heard for more than three days and nights. For three whole days and nights only gentleness had surrounded Injya, now, here was Soosha, eyes glinting with hatred as the firelight glinted on her instrument of death.

'I will stay!' Sanset said defiantly. 'I will stay.'

220

She knelt down and stroked Injya's brow. Injya seemed to be sleeping, her breaths coming soft and regularly. Sanset could hear and sense the men moving around her, knew that they were positioning themselves, each holding a limb. She saw out of the corner of her eye Soosha lift the sodden shift from Injya's abdomen, but all the while she concentrated on Injya's face, willing herself to be inside Injya's head, calming her, comforting her.

'Take hold!' Soosha commanded. The young men immediately obeyed and gripped Injya's arms and legs. Instantly Injya's eyes shot open.

'Sanset!' she cried. 'What is happening, what are they going to do – what are *men* doing here?'

Her terror-filled eyes searched Sanset's face for an answer.

'Injya,' she said softly. 'They are going to free the child – fear not – you will feel little – I will be with you.'

Injya knew she was lying, knew that the moment of her death was near.

'My child,' she whispered, 'my child!'

Tears streamed freely from her eyes: 'Take my child – take good care of him, Sanset.'

She sighed a long sigh and her eyes glazed over once more as a pain deep within her urged the babe forth.

'Now!' screamed Soosha. 'Hold her!'

Sanset gripped Injya's head tightly. With all her might she grasped Injya's head, pressing inward and downward, bracing herself for the screaming pain which would soon envelope her cousin, her beloved Injya. She prayed as strongly as she grasped the sweat-slimed skull and the pallid face between her hands.

'Ahni Amwe – take your daughter!'

The knife glinted in the firelight once as it flashed through the air.

'Ahni Amwe – receive her soul!'

221

Injya's eyes opened, wild with terror, as the cold blade touched her skin. She opened her mouth to scream.

'Ahni Amwe – bless your beloved!'

Another cry shattered the sancar.

'*NO!*' A man's voice boomed out in the gloom.

'NO! I, Galdr, command you to stay . . . *NO!*'

CHAPTER TWENTY

Galdr's dark figure was silhouetted in the sunlight, his arms breast height, pulling apart the skins of the entrance, making him look like a black cross against the gold. The room and its occupants had frozen at his words. Sanset stared hard into his shaded face, unsure for a moment who this strange figure in such strange clothing was. Could this man, dressed as he was in a profusion of ragged animal skins, really be Galdr? She stared in dumb amazement as the figure came towards the group. It was Galdr – no manner of strange painted shifts, no amount of animal pelts, could change the man. Involuntarily, Sanset shrank from him.

Soosha did not shrink from him. Without turning round she dropped her knife and bowed her head slightly, as if admitting defeat. The young men shamefacedly let go of Injya's limbs and she took in the figure dressed in the clothes of the animal powers, screamed out his name once, and then passed into oblivion.

'You!' was all Soosha was able at last to say. She raised her head slightly and slowly turned round to face him. Brother and sister stared at each other for a moment, then Soosha turned back once more to face Injya. Sanset could see her face turn black with rising rage and her body tense as her hand slowly reached out for the knife.

'Galdr! Stop her!' Sanset screamed and in a flash Galdr crossed the sancar and caught his sister by her arms, raising her from her squatting position and turning her round to face him.

'Sister' – he said very quietly and calmly – 'no! *This* you must not do.'

223

His eyes left hers for a moment as he scanned the sight before him, his face becoming set with determination. He pushed his sister away from him and held her firmly at arm's length.

'Take your men and go, Soosha. I will bring forth the child. If you value your life, go to our father and keep him away – do anything to keep him from this place. If you fail me in this, the knife you were about to use on Injya will be turned on you. Now go!'

Soosha faltered for a moment and then without another glance motioned for the men to join her.

'I will leave you – but you will have no more success than these stupid women here – come!'

She tossed her head and stared defiantly into his eyes as the young men, not daring to look at Galdr, meekly followed her out into the sunshine and bird-song of the early morning.

Saying nothing to Sanset he came nearer and sank to his knees between Injya's spread-eagled legs. Sighing deeply and closing his eyes, he rested his hands upon her abdomen. Sanset and Bendula watched in fear-filled expectation as Galdr dropped his head and started intoning strange words in an alien language. Sunlight streamed in momentarily as another figure ventured into the sancar. The golden hair of Halfray was unmistakable as it shone like a halo around his head.

'Halfray!' Sanset cried with joy. 'Oh, Halfray – you too!'

Tears of happiness poured down her cheeks as Halfray moved silently towards her and touched the crown of her head.

'Be silent, Sanset,' he murmured, 'there will be time for talking later!'

He knelt down beside her and removed her hands from Injya's head. No visible signs of emotion passed over his face as he looked at his sister, only a deep sigh issued forth as slowly he shook his head and gently traced the lines of pain etched deep into her furrowed brow. Rising again he crept towards Galdr and placed both hands on his shoulders. He threw his head to the heavens and swaying slightly, closed his eyes.

'Spirits of the mountains, spirits of the earth and the underearth; spirits of the waters and winds, come to your son. Come away, out, from this woman. Work through your son only. Spirits of the mountains, spirits of the earth, manifest yourselves, inhabit once again the flesh of your animal selves. Behold, Galdr, son of the earth and the heavens is waiting for you. Come to him, let go your hold on this woman and her child.'

Halfray and Galdr seemed locked together, Galdr bent huddled over the figure of Injya, hands pressed upon her swollen belly, Halfray, tall and rigid, hands gripping Galdr's shoulders tightly. All was silent for a moment, then Halfray began using the language Galdr had first used, as both of them began shaking. At first, the shaking was no more than a slight tremble, but as Halfray's voice grew stronger, the shaking became more violent and Injya too began to tremble. Sanset, terrified at the scene before her eyes, drew Bendula close to her and hugged her tightly, desperately trying to stop the shaking of her panic-filled body. Great Hoola, she thought, stop this madness! Ahni Amwe, come to our aid. As if the prayer released something, Galdr suddenly stopped shaking and began braying like a horse. Halfray increased the grip on Galdr's shoulders, shouting now with words Sanset could understand: 'The child has the spirit of the deer and the horse – the deer and the horse.'

Halfray threw back his head to the roof of the sancar and screamed out: 'The spirits are here! Free the deer and the horse from this woman, Galdr!'

Galdr wrenched himself free from Halfray's grip and suddenly jumped up, kicking and throwing his arms and legs wildly, thundered round the sancar like an unexpectedly freed colt. Halfray fell to his knees and

225

placed his face full on to Injya's abdomen. In a trice, he was on his feet once more.

'Mountain leopard! Mountain leopard! I see you, I hear you. Come out from this child. I command you to leave this soul!'

Immediately, Galdr dropped on to all fours and began leaping and tearing at the walls; his lips drawn back tightly in a fantastic grinning, his eyes mad and bright, his breath coming in short, sharp gasps. Instantly Injya's body contorted with pain and her eyes opened bright with terror.

'The leopard!' she screamed. 'The leopard!'

Sanset could stand it no longer, she almost threw the quaking Bendula from her and in one bound was once more squatting at her head. She held Injya's head, concentrating all her power into her hands, almost crushing her skull in an effort to hold her head still. Injya's back arched until it was as taut as a bow, her lips parted showing her white teeth ground together as the pains shot through her.

'*NOW!*' she growled. '*NOW!*'

'NOW!' Halfray screamed in unison with her. 'NOW!'

Galdr roared, a deep roar that joined with Injya's until the whole sancar was filled with a raucous cacophony of animal and human sounds.

'The head!' screamed Halfray. Not understanding him, Sanset automatically grasped Injya's head once more as she sank back, gasping for air, her face livid, sweat and spittle mingling with tears. Galdr dropped to the floor as if dead, silent at last, as Halfray gently pushed down on Injya's abdomen.

'One more push, my dearest, one more,' he implored as Injya shook her head slowly from side to side, grimaced and sighed long and deep. The baby slithered out, sticky, white, blood-covered and trembling.

'Waaaa!' the tiny baby screamed angrily, her arms and legs spasmodically thrashing the air, 'waaaa!'

*　　*　　*

226

As if hearing words down a long tunnel, Galdr could hear his father's voice. Although the words were indistinguishable, his tone was instantly recognizable. From a long way off he heard the barked instructions presumably to Sanset and the other women and then the softer, quieter voice of Halfray. The harsh tones of his father made the child cry and he heard the gentler voice of Injya as she soothed the baby. One phrase he heard clearly before once more the deep sleep overtook him: 'It is only a girl – you would be better looking to my son. Tend *him*, women. Tend my son!'

The day was already beginning to fade when the low mumbling voices slowly became more distinct as consciousness awoke in Galdr. Gently he pulled his aching body up and tried to support his head with his hand. He failed and sank back on to the furs upon which he had been laid. How long he had been there he had no idea. He turned and looked around him: the sancar seemed full of people, all too busy talking to notice him. After a few moments, his eyes became accustomed to the darkness and in the flickering taper-light he could discern Halfray and Sanset and a very wide-eyed Bendula, deep in conversation – and in the shadows two other women sat huddled, each stitching small garments for the child, their agile fingers drawing the invisible thread in and out of the material with the ease of a spider making her web. Far beyond the smoke of the central fire, in the deep shadows of the sancar lay Injya, her pale white face framed by her tumbling black curls, her long lashes resting on drawn cheeks, deep purple shadows under her eyes a sad reminder of her pain.

He thought his heart would burst at the sight of her and the pain which the leopard-spirit inflicted on his body as he drew it out from her, stung his flesh once more. Tenderly he stroked his arm, though he knew that no sign of the attack would be visible. It had been a fierce spirit, it had clung to the soul of the unborn child with a rapacious grip and tearing it free from his child had cost his spirit-body dearly. This had been the first time since his meeting with

227

Bai Ulgan that he had encountered the spirits of the animals and he shuddered with the memory. When Halfray and he had used the drum, all that time ago, and Galdr had descended the nine layers of the kingdom of Erlik and ascended the seven steps to Bai Ulgan, then he had met not only animal spirits, but spirits of women who had lain with him and then devoured him, spirits of men who had cut his flesh from his bones, had cast it into cauldrons of flaming water until he saw his skeleton and understood the magic of his bones. But the pain he had felt then was as nothing to the pain he had undergone battling for the life of his child. He stroked his arms and legs again, gentling the pain from them, never taking his eyes off Injya's face.

As he watched, Injya's eyes slowly opened and she gazed straight at him. A tiny, hesitant smile played across her lips for a moment and was gone as the heavy lids fell and she resumed her sleeping. His vision was blocked as Halfray quietly approached. Galdr attempted a smile at him as Halfray squatted before him, touching his shoulders and arms.

'You are back with us – for a time I thought you would sleep for ever – how is it?'

He touched Galdr's chest, signifying concern for his heart and soul – the unspoken question – are you whole? – implicit in the touch. In answer Galdr only smiled weakly and nodded his head.

'The child . . . ?' he began.

'Is fine!' answered Halfray smiling at him. 'A little girl, with legs as long as a colt's and hair as red as the sun – come, see for yourself!'

He stood up and extended an arm towards him. Galdr allowed himself to be helped to his feet and stretched himself – how he ached! He ran his fingers through his hair and automatically adjusted his clothing. Surprised, he realized that he was no longer clad in the shift of the animal powers, but in doe-skin leggings and a rough woven top.

'How . . . ?'

'Your father' – Halfray began solemnly – 'I took the liberty of redressing you before he saw you – no need to provoke unnecessarily.'

Galdr smiled at his friend – how typical of him, and he had known nothing!

The two men skirted the fire and stood by the side of Injya's pallet-bed. The child lay sleeping, wrapped in furs, its pink and white face peeking out from a thick mass of dark red curls. Galdr saw the unmistakable nose and high cheek-bones, the full, pretty lips pouting, the black lashes fluttering beneath the delicate violet lids. He sank to his knees.

'My child,' he whispered, 'oh, my precious child!' Tears came unbidden to his eyes as he lowered his head – that something so beautiful should come from such a brutal coupling! A faint rustle made him look up again. Injya was staring at him, her pale face opalescent in the glow from the fire.

'Galdr,' she murmured, 'you have come, as I knew you were destined to.'

She raised an arm and dropped it heavily back upon the furs, too exhausted to do more. Galdr touched the back of her hand, the veins standing out, showing deep purple through the white skin. Almost afraid, he took the limp hand in his and squeezed it gently. Her response was faint, but she too tightened her hand round his. Not trusting his voice to words he sighed a deep, tear-repressing sigh and stared again at Injya's hand. Delicate and frail, like the pale violet bell-shaped flowers of the mountainside in summer. Injya's voice, as soft and secret as a fawn's breath broke the spell.

'Galdr, I cannot talk many words – I am so tired, so weak. I know that the Goddess wishes us to be together – I have had so many strange visions, so many dreams.' She squeezed his hand again in acknowledgement of his nodding head.

'I cannot talk now, Galdr. I know you have just saved our lives – mine and Pentesh, for that is to be her name, the Goddess wills it so.' Her voice faded until it was barely audible. At length she resumed.

'When I am stronger we will talk. Until then, we must both leave it to the Goddess – only She will know what is right for us. That much also I know.'

Injya closed her eyes and almost immediately the slight grasp of her hand in his fell away as she fell into a deep sleep.

Anfjord strode about the near deserted encampment, a broad grin creasing his weather-beaten face. So, Galdr had returned! That idiot Halfray *had* found him after all! He wanted to sing, wanted to run about like a child – his son had come back! He felt boundless exhilaration – he had not felt like this for many a moon's passing. When Soosha had run into his sancar, flushed and angry looking, telling him that Galdr had returned, it had taken his very breath away. He had wanted to run to him immediately, but Soosha had stopped him, explaining that he and Halfray were trying to deliver Injya's child. His son – delivering children – whatever next? He feared that his exile had robbed him of his senses. Soon, people were trying to crowd into his sancar, more fearful of the noises coming from the birth-sancar than of breaking the established etiquette. For what seemed an age, the crowded sancar and those outside listened as the sounds of the animals raged through the soft air of the day, until finally the cry of the new-born had broken the spell. Even then, Soosha had implored him not to go near the sancar until someone, anyone, came out.

'You are too precious, Father, to be put in danger – please!' and she had been so earnest, so childlike, that he had stayed the impulse to rush and see his son. But now he had seen the man his son had grown into, he was overjoyed.

He smiled at a group of tiny girls playing with stones in the clearing, making patterns on the grass with coloured pebbles – soon Crenjal's tiny daughter would be doing that! The thought of Crenjal touched him not – with Galdr back he had no need of the Crenjals of this world. He grinned broadly at the old woman who was watching the children, who, startled by his unaccustomed warm look, flushed and bowed her head.

'Old Taronyak!' he called to her. 'Take good care of the little ones – they are *all* precious to me – even the little girls!'

Taronyak did not look up – she knew too well that the joy that was evident in old Anfjord's face could change as quickly as the wind, into rage and hatred.

As he walked aimlessly round the encampment, he thought of Injya's child and felt a stab of pain – how he would have loved the child to have been his and not Crenjal's. He could never forgive him that. But – he shook his gnarled head and looked at the sky . . . perhaps it just was not meant to be. He thought of Injya as he had last seen her, pale and drawn, and something akin to shame grew in him. He had treated the girl badly – he had misused her, he decided. And for the first time since Injya had returned, he was able to think of her without longing or fear. She was a mother now, he reasoned, all that stuff about the Goddess would go – she was only another woman and now she had a child to rear . . . an idea suddenly formed . . . what greater gift could he bestow but to give Injya to his son! Yes! As his mind raced onward his fantasy grew: Galdr would be so grateful, giving Injya to him would show him that he had truly forgiven him, Galdr and Injya would bring up Crenjal's child as their own – the child would know no difference and soon, Galdr would sire children from her too, the line of Anfjord would go on, Galdr would take over when he became infirm and would care for him because he had sacrificed his lust for Injya . . . yes, that is how it would be . . . Galdr and Injya and himself. Suddenly he stopped in his tracks, lifted his hands to the heavens and cried: 'A feast! – We will have a feast – Soosha? – Find me Soosha – we will have a feast for my son – everyone – prepare for a feast, this is the happiest day of my life!'

He felt his heart singing inside him as the birds sang in the clear white-blue sky and a great weight of grief fell from him as he thought of Galdr and Injya, his other girl-children, his family.

'Find me Soosha, child,' he called to a little raven-haired girl of six or seven summers. 'Bring my daughter to me, we have such joy to share!' But the child could not find Soosha for she had long since run away to find her own comfort and joy.

When Soosha could restrain her father no further, she had watched him almost run to the birth-sancar. So – how quickly her influence waned! When everyone else was crowding round the entrance to the birth-sancar, she had stolen away and now she lay back in the umiak and dribbled the cool water between her trailing hands. She needed the water to calm the flame of white-hot anger which she feared would consume her. The icy water gently lapped at the stretched seal-skin umiak and the faint breezes, humming and buzzing with insects, played a gentle melody on her frowning face. How she hated him! The thought of Galdr quickened her breathing once more.

'I hate you!' she mouthed silently to the blue skies and innocent birds. 'With all my heart, I hate you, brother mine!'

The clear azure skies and golden sun mocked her murderous mood. Even the weather was against her, she thought ruefully, it should be raining, it should be blue-black with venom, not this glorious day. Disconsolately she idly paddled the water with her palms, turning the small boat in a gentle circle. What to do? She lay prone for a few moments more, then sat up quickly. Tall brown-headed reeds marked the semi-circular bank, ahead of her lay a clear expanse of water, dancing blue and white, twinkling clear and free. She bent forward and picked up the broad double-ended paddle – she would show him, she would show the world who was the rightful heir of Anfjord.

Paddling furiously, head bent almost to her breast-bone with effort, she cut through the glinting water until the drone of insects was left far behind. Ahead of her she could see the rising-falling water of the great sea-swell and a little way to her left, a rocky island around whose shore-line great tusked seal-fathers lay basking in the sunshine. There, she decided, I shall find some peace. Carefully she navigated round the boulders surrounding the island and, keeping a very watchful eye on the tusked beings whose deep brown lashless eyes blinked widely at her, she secured the umiak by wedging it between two shell-encrusted rocks and clambered ashore.

A fat, dappled beast, almost twice as long as she was tall, angrily belched at her and humped himself inelegantly down to the water's edge and glided effortlessly away. With the movement of the king, his subjects also flappered and flopped their way into the water, honking and belching their annoyance at her. Soosha watched the tusked seal-fathers go with satisfaction – now, perhaps, she could think.

She climbed higher up the rock and sat, uncomfortably, on a granite ledge. Fulmars and guillemots wheeled overhead, as angry at the invasion of their territory as the walruses. She put a hand out to steady herself as she watched the crying birds and then quickly removed it from the slimy patch in which she had thoughtlessly rested it.

'Great Bai Ulgan!' she swore out aloud, 'what more?'

Wiping her filthy palm on her shift she stared gloomily into the crystal water below. The animals, so ungainly on shore, were diving in and out of the water, sleek and beautiful, bearded muzzles rising from the water, white tusks shining, playing with each other and the water as if life itself was a game.

'I hate you too!' she shouted at the sporting beasts, oblivious to all but their splashing frolicking. She closed her eyes and bringing her knees up to her chin rocked gently to and fro. She had done everything she could, she thought comforting herself, everything to ensure that she would finally take over the tribe. She grimaced as she picked at her bare feet, lost in self-pity and recounted her triumphs to try to raise her spirits. That fool of a tokener, Colnyek, had managed to teach her to read and token before she had finally overdone the poison and he had died – thankfully before he could tell Anfjord what she had made him do! Now the sacred history of the Skoonjay people was in her keeping and she had almost finished retokening it. Anfjord now consulted her about everything, she had so befuddled his brain with strong herb teas and wine which made the old fool rut and couple all day long with that Injya woman, that he no more knew or cared about what became of his people, and now, when she finally thought that power was within her reach, Galdr returns!

She snorted aloud at the twists of fate. Now all her plans were for nought. Damn him! Angrily she stared into the water. The walruses, tired of their cavorting, cumbrously made their way ashore again and having heaved their way on to the rocks lay panting, luxuriating in the sunshine. Something in the way the animals moved touched her; there they were, so heavy with fat, so ugly on shore, yet once in the water they became one with the tides, sleek, silver beings, as graceful as the birds who were still wheeling around her head. She too must become as distichous as they – presenting an ingenuous face to the world, while all the time secreting her other self, the self which is as profligate as the outer is pure. She rose from her ledge somewhat unsteadily and lifting her hands to

234

the heavens cried: 'As Bai Ulgan is my witness, I *will* have my way!'

The crying birds fell silent at her words and for a moment the very sun seemed to darken. She bent down and picked up a rock, clutching it to her breast so hard that it marked her flesh.

'I will become as hard as this rock and as strong as the fire in Hoola's belly that made it!'

She stared at the rock then hurled it into the ocean. As the foaming waves consumed it, she shouted to the winds and the seas and the unblinking animals.

'And that is how my rock will be – no-one will see it, it will be hidden until I choose to bring it to the surface again. For I, Soosha, will hide my rock from all, but it will be there, as strong as the earth, as terrible as the fire under the earth until one day I will release its power and then *I* – not Galdr, not Anfjord and certainly not Injya – will be the power on this land!'

CHAPTER TWENTY-ONE

When Soosha returned to the encampment, she found the preparations well under way for the feast celebrating Galdr's return. A massive central fire had been laid and the women were frantically skinning the does which had been caught. Some of the men were still away hunting and fishing, some still cutting wood. Everywhere she looked people smiled at her – they all seemed so happy that Galdr had returned and yet, only a winter's turning previously, none had shed one tear for him when he was exiled. She smiled and nodded back in response, but inside she was far from happy. Stupid people she thought, such short memories, such little reasoning. But as the evening drew on, more fires were lit and the smell of the roasting meat began to make her feel hungry, some of her hostility faded. From now on, she vowed as she prepared herself for the festivities, none must see my face in any other guise but ringed with smiles.

'My son has returned!' Anfjord shouted in triumph, when all the people had assembled. He held one of Galdr's hands, clasped firmly in his, up to the heavens and the people cheered.

'And the boy, now man, who found him – Halfray!'

Another cheer rang from the crowd as Halfray had his arm nearly pulled from its socket as the jubilant chief raised his aloft also.

'Where's my Soosha?' he bellowed, 'where's your lovely sister, Galdr? She, too, must greet you.'

'I am here, Father.' Soosha came forward from the crowd.

'I have been waiting until Galdr had recovered from his journeying; can I welcome you now, Galdr?'

The light, innocent tone, so different from that of the hissing, hating woman he had encountered earlier that day, quite shocked him; what deceit was she planning now? But his voice, as he answered hers, was as ingenuous as her own.

'Sister!' he shouted to her. 'Delay no further!'

Soosha tripped lightly through the crowd and ran towards him, arms outstretched.

'How I have missed you!' she murmured in his ear as she threw her arms round his neck. 'I have so much to tell you – how happy you make us by your return. I thought . . . I thought—' She bowed her head as if unable to continue and he felt her gulp as if she were swallowing tears of joy. He almost wanted to congratulate her acting skills, but instead said tenderly: 'This is no time to cry, sister, this is a time for joy!'

He raised her head with his hand and smiled into her glittering eyes as if completely unaware of the malice behind them. He gave her a big bear-hug, lifting her feet off the ground and whirling her round. Another cheer rose from the people at the sight of brother and sister so obviously united.

'That is the way!' Anfjord clapped his arm round the nearest available woman. 'Look how they love each other! Look how happy they are!'

Anfjord embraced both his children and turned them round to face the eager people.

'Now, we will drink and sing and dance!'

The people cheered once more as he held Soosha's and Galdr's hands up high. 'Come, you two, make an old man happy!'

And with faces wreathed in smiles, they joined the thronging people and led them in a huge circular dance around the great fire.

The celebrations continued right through the short night and for a while the women felt that some of their power had been restored to them as one, and then another, young woman took the man of her choice to the grove to lie with him. No-one could do wrong, Anfjord was laughing and singing with them all round the great fire, nodding his gnarled head to the women and men who danced around it. He kept Galdr and Halfray close to him, asking questions of first one, then the other. Much was explained to him, but far more was omitted, but the old man seemed happy enough to listen to the travellers' tales, shedding genuine tears as they recounted their hardships and sufferings. Eventually the questioning ceased and Anfjord announced that as Galdr had saved the life of Injya, it was his wish that he took her as his wife. Galdr made a passable attempt at sounding disinterested, but at the news his heart leapt with joy. The feeling was soon dispelled as Anfjord continued.

'But, mark my words, Galdr, it is a mixed blessing. She has strange effects upon a man – why, she so befuddled Crenjal that he killed himself – and she must have woven a great spell upon me, for I myself fell under her charms for a while! But she is a fine young woman for all her nonsense and she will give you many fine sons. Have her with my blessing and if she does not please – or' – he added darkly – 'she starts any of that damnable Moon Goddess worship, you have my full permission to finish the job you bungled three winters ago – but none of this now – have her when you will! I am giving you a rare gift, Galdr, for she is a rare woman and I have loved her in spite of myself!'

Galdr's mind reeled at what his father had spoken. Crenjal? Anfjord? What evil had gone on here? He tried to hide the pain that his father's words caused and stared into the fire, frantically fighting with the urge to strike his father. Anfjord had taken Injya? No – it could not be! He got up suddenly and instead of striking his father, patted him reassuringly on his shoulders.

'Father – thank you for such a gift – a sacrifice indeed!'

Anfjord solemnly nodded his head – the boy had understood and was pleased, well – that was what he wanted, the boy to feel gratitude – good!

'Father,' Galdr began again, 'we have been travelling for many days and nights – I am exhausted, I need – we want—'

'Son! Of course! Though after such an absence do you not want a woman? There are many here who have been waiting for your return, Galdr – and you, Halfray, is it not time you too took a woman? Why, this is a feast of celebration – enjoy! Enjoy!'

Halfray stared at his feet and blushed to the roots of his hair. Anfjord saw his discomfiture and roared with laughter.

'So – you want to sleep! Come then!'

He struggled to his feet and clapped both men round the shoulders.

'Use my sancar – tomorrow is time enough for women!'

Feeling as if they had both just escaped from the jaws of death, Galdr and Halfray removed themselves from the crowd and crept into the sancar. And while the people outside continued their dancing and singing, Halfray told Galdr the truth that he had learnt from Sanset. As the stars faded from the heavens the two men finally slept, disturbed and disillusioned. This was more than they had expected, this was treachery and murder more foul than their most dreaded nightmares.

Soosha also had little sleep that night, but had risen early to find half of the tribe still sleeping. She amazed those who were awake by gathering the small children to her and overseeing their squealing swimming in the myriads of tiny streams which meandered throughout their summer home. She had been more than surprised to learn of Injya's safe delivery and had listened intently to the hushed rumours of animal spirits helping with the birth. This Injya was obviously more powerful than she thought – unless . . . her gaze wandered over the delighted naked children as her thoughts wandered freely, unhindered by the parameters of normality. Galdr *was* changed, and it was a more profound change than would be warranted by spending nine moons in the company of Halfray or wandering lost in the wilderness of the mountains. His spirit-lights were different, not just a different colour, but a different intensity – she had seldom seen such lights – they extended for almost a full pchekt beyond his body making the whole of him shine, and the colour! – brilliant pale orange-gold, the colour of the newly-risen sun! Perhaps *he* had conjured up the animal spirits. She vowed to find out how.

She knew that he did not trust her – she had given away too much when he had first seen her – if he had only come a few moments later, both Injya and the child would have been dead. She had to find an ally, someone who would be trusted by both Injya and Galdr. She thought of all the young men of the tribe, naming them and counting them off on her fingers. Eventually she decided upon one, who out of all the young men to come from the Gyaretz people fitted the criteria she had mentally laid down. Xynon. She let out a deep sigh of contentment and with it suddenly realized how tense she had become – of course! Why hadn't she thought of him earlier? She massaged the tension away from her shoulders and neck and laughed out aloud – he was perfect. A contemporary of Injya, of Injya's own people, a strong healthy warrior, noble of looks – no-one would be surprised if she chose him as her consort and he fitted perfectly – he was fearless, one of the bravest and most cunning of hunters. She thought more about him – he was intelligent – that much she had gathered when she had overheard conversations he had had with the other menfolk and his friend – what *was* his name? – the fat man, strange voice – Igrat! That was it, Igrat and Xynon, inseparable from birth but as different as eagles and elms – and when the time came – when she no longer needed him, she could play one off against the other and so dispose of living evidence. Perfect!

She sank back into the grassy bank and idly watched as a scrappy raven circled overhead. Go and find your mate, old bird, she thought – I've found mine – you find yours. She shut her eyes to the croaking bird and collected her thoughts; with Xynon's help she would find out how Galdr had come by his power and then use it against him. If that did not work, she could easily persuade Anfjord that Galdr was plotting against him – with Injya by his side, of course Anfjord would be wary of that – then, with Galdr and Injya and that cunning fool, Halfray, safely out of the way, she could take over leadership of the tribe – then life would change.

She bit her lip in excitement, she would transform the Skoonjay people. When they heard of her new history, saw the inevitability of her plans, they would settle, here in the summer-lands. They would build strong houses against the winter's white rains and howling gales. No need for the unnecessary trek to the mountains every year, it cost more in life than lives saved, of that she was sure. She felt the grass under her, warmed with the heat of her body, touched the grass beside her – *her* grass. Soon every man would feel that, would know that ownership of the world. With the tribe settled in a permanent base, each man having one or two wives whom he *owned*, the men would want to work and explore, because she would make them totally responsible for their womenfolk. But first, she had to read them the history. No, she argued with herself, first she must learn the source of Galdr's power, then she must read them the history. Armed with the knowledge of his power and the might of the history, none could stop her. She tugged at the grass, snapping its tender shoots with excitement. The pictures she conjured before her eyes danced as the ripples on the water danced in the sunshine. When I read them the history, she thought, when they understand – none would notice the changes – it has been many a winter's turning since they have been read – no-one will know! She opened her eyes and gazed at the splashing children – they were her real hope for the future. They knew nothing of the old ways, all the nonsense of the Great Goddesses of the Earth and Moon, not being allowed to plant crops, not being allowed to claim a part of the earth as one's own. The earth was there to serve man, as the animals were – the children would see the sense in that!

She warmed to her ideas; within a winter's turning she would have the most motivated army in the world, then she would travel away from the cold mountains, away to where she knew the world would be warmer, to the land of the soft gold metal of which her mother had spoken. She did not believe, as Galdr did, that this land lay towards the rising sun – their mother was wrong – the whole way forward was south, away from these frozen mountains and insect-filled marshlands. With her army of strong young men, she would overcome any tiny wandering tribes she might encounter, she would gather them all to her, create a new nation, based on land ownership, each man and his family settled in one place, owning the earth and her fruits, living off and for it. And she, Soosha, would be the chieftain, she would rule with justice and strength – and perhaps she would keep Xynon with her – he was the most able of the people and there was a certain something about him. A sudden splash of icy water on her face broke her reverie: 'What the . . . ?'

'Soosha, Soosha . . . ' the wide-eyed shivering child shook water and fear all over her. 'It's Jya-Finrik – she went down to the bottom of the water, Soosha, and she has not come back again!'

'Damned child!' Soosha muttered angrily as she tore off her clothes and waded into the icy stream where all the children were standing, pointing at a spot in the centre where the little girl had gone under. 'Damned child!'

The commotion eventually died down and Soosha was generally hailed by all to be a heroine. Little heroics, actually, had been called for; Jya-Finrik had been hauled free from the river weeds which had held her fast in the swift-flowing stream with relative ease and she rose, gasping for breath, more afraid of Soosha's slapping hand than the death she so innocently courted. As the late evening sun settled like a giant pulsating ball on the horizon, Jya-Finrik's grateful mother came to Soosha bearing a necklace which she had made from tiny coloured stones as a token of her gratitude. Soosha eyed the offering suspiciously. She quelled her first impulse which was to give back the gift – such a paltry thing – more of an insult than a show of appreciation – a stone necklace for the life of a child! Instead, she smiled sweetly and demurred her tongue. The woman seemed abashed at this unexpected behaviour – Soosha was not only renowned for her icy heart but her acid tongue and falteringly she took her leave.

They will soon come to love me, Soosha thought as she brought up both hands to her still damp hair and ran her fingers through it, spreading each fingerful to the dying sun. She stood for a long while, facing the sun, combing her hair with her fingers, drinking in the breezes, bathing in the soft warm light, and, for the first time since Injya's arrival, she felt calm. Stretching luxuriously she looked straight into the deep red sun and felt sure of her path; now she felt powerful and knew that the power she craved was within her grasp. Dropping her arms she smiled to herself; she could afford to be generous – afford to pretend to be pleased with trinkets. Lazily she let her gaze wander over the evening scene; smoke from the fires curling cautiously to the deepening heavens; women sitting, caressing their sleepy children; men settled already round two of the largest fires, lounging or sitting cross-legged as the stories of the day were being told; long purple shadows making the outline of the circle of sancars blurred, the parameters of the encampment suddenly vastly increased by them. Soon, the shadows of our people will cover the whole of the earth, Soosha told herself, and I will be their leader!

A sharp crack of a twig being broken behind her made her spin around, shattering her peacefulness.

'I am sorry . . . ' Xynon began, looking abashed, 'I did not mean to startle you.'

Soosha swallowed the irritation she felt at being disturbed. She had forgotten that she had sent for Xynon, forgotten that she had instructed a child to bring him to her, here, on the edge of the copse overlooking the encampment – forgotten also what a splendid specimen of manhood he was. She dropped her gaze as if it should be she, not him, begging pardon. For a moment she kept her eyes firmly rooted on the ground, trying to calm the rapid beating of her heart, then slowly brought her eyes upwards to meet his. Her heart had not been calmed by signals coming from her eyes to her brain; bare strong feet, flat upon the earth, high insteps brown with the sun, slender ankles giving way to shapely calves and taut knees, downy, well-thewed thighs visible almost to the mound of his manhood, scarcely covered as it was in a thin swathe of coarse material. His flat abdomen and muscular chest were patterned with dark hairs, glinting in the last rays of the sun, his strong neck holding his angular face and gently curved head in an attitude of unashamed frankness. Involuntarily, she caught her breath and then held his dark blue eyes with her own. You will be mine, her eyes said to his, mine.

'Xynon,' she said, trying to keep her voice level, fighting the sudden onrush of desire in her, 'Xynon – it must be you who are surprised by me – disconcerted that I asked for you to be brought to me – no?'

She surprised herself by giggling like a naughty child. Turning her automatic reaction immediately to her advantage, she allowed the giggle to turn into what she hoped would pass for light-hearted laughter.

'You look so solemn – do not be afraid!'

She smiled at him and turned from him slightly, taking a measured step towards the copse.

'I am not afraid, Soosha.'

His deep voice rang true – no, this man would not be afraid of anything! 'I simply do not know what you want of me – have I done something to displease you?'

Displease me? thought Soosha, I doubt that you will do that!

'I want simply to talk with you, Xynon – I want you to tell me of your life – that is all.'

She laughed again and held out a hand towards him. 'Come, walk with me and talk with me – I am tired of women's talk, it is time I knew more about all our people – too long I have been in the company of women, I want to know about the men – what they feel, what they enjoy doing most – what they want from life!'

A faint cloud of doubt flickered over Xynon's face as Soosha started to walk again.

'Oh well – if you do not *know* then—' she began.

'No!' Xynon said eagerly as he rushed to join her, 'no, I *do* know, I was just—'

'Amazed and flattered that I asked you?' she answered for him, turning to him and smiling broadly. 'Well, do not be. Oh!' she sighed, turning from him once more and continuing her walking, 'I know what my father *says* the young men want, but I am not so sure – do you not feel that there is more to life than just hunting, fishing, making the sancars and wandering to and from the mountains each year – is there not more that you want?' She turned and faced him squarely – how she wished he would raise those strong arms and pull her towards him – how she wished that he would dare to kiss her, right now. Instead he stood darkly before her, his brooding face clouded and full of doubt.

'I want—' he began, then instantly dropped his eyes, a flush creeping over his bronzed face. Yes, thought Soosha, I know what you want, but you dare not ask for it, dare you, Xynon?

'Yes?' she prompted.

245

'I *do* feel that there is something missing in our lives, Soosha, how perceptive of you to see it too, but I do not know what it is,' he added lamely as the walking got under way again. They walked side by side in silence for some time, each lost in their own private thoughts.

Eventually Soosha said quietly: 'Do you miss very much the old rituals, do the men of your people still miss that?'

Xynon laughed unexpectedly – a generous, childish laugh.

'No, Soosha, we men do *not* miss them! So much was unexplained, so much was kept secret from us – and anyway, I was only a child when your father' – he stopped abruptly when he realized that he was about to say 'murdered Vingyar' – 'when our two tribes joined,' he added hastily, looking at Soosha under his lashes.

'But what of the older men, Xynon, do *they* miss it?'

'I do not think so,' he answered slowly. 'They remember the bad days, the days when the High Priestesses could castrate young men to appease the Goddess – or so they said – I do not know, all of that was long before their time too, but they still live in fear that the sacrifices *might* return. It is strange how things have changed – once the chief only reigned for one year and then was sacrificed to Hoola – then the women altered that into the sacrifice of a mountain goat, or, if they could get one, a cow, then they changed it again so that no sacrifices were made – only prayers and rituals; but all the time, there was this fear for us men, that although the offerings had changed, the reasons for them had not and perhaps, once again the women would rule with cruelty and fear.' He stopped talking suddenly, lost in the memory of garbled stories of old men.

'So,' he said at length, 'in answer to your question, *no*, the men do *not* miss the old ways, it is so much better to be . . . what can I say? . . . ' he searched for the right words.

'Free?' Soosha asked gently, 'free to choose – is that what you were going to say? Free to choose?'

Again the flush, again the faltering in the step.

'Yes,' he said simply, eyes firmly fixed on the leafy ground.

'But what if a maiden *did* go back to the old ways – I don't mean the sacrifices and nonsense like that, but what if a maiden did decide to choose a man to lie with her, because *she* wanted it? Some did you know, only last evening. What if a woman was to ask you, now, to lie with her, what would be your reaction?' Again the boyish laughter rang out to the trees.

'Well, if I liked her, I would have her – but it would be *my* choice – I could not be forced through fear, it would still be *my* choice.'

He swung his arms as if to show his freedom and touched the slender branches overhead.

'And if *I* asked you?' Xynon froze on the spot, one arm still outstretched to the leafy canopy overhead. 'Would you still have the choice – if the chieftain's daughter asked you? What of your choice then?'

Slowly Xynon's arm fell to his side and he stared at the ground. After a long moment he said quietly: 'That would be difficult for me – I think I would feel that I had no choice, that because of her position and her power, I had no choice.'

His voice had dropped to a barely audible whisper as he continued staring at the earth. Soosha was so close to him that she knew that one movement of her arm, one twitch of her finger and she would touch him. She stayed very still, feeling the air between them vibrate, as if it held invisible threads of emotion pulsing with expectation.

'Xynon,' she said eventually, keeping her voice low and calm, 'Xynon, can you imagine a time when a man chooses to take a woman to be his wife and who lives with her, who lives in a sancar with her alone? Could you imagine those two people loving each other, raising children together, staying in one place, owning the land that they cared for and only sharing with others

247

who they wanted to share with? Can you imagine a time like that?'

Slowly Xynon raised his head and looked at her dumbly. She continued, ignoring his perplexed look.

'Can you imagine what that would mean – what wonderful changes that would bring to all – each man owning his wife, owning one woman – or maybe two if he so desired – each man his own chieftain, chieftain of his home, his part of the earth, his quarry?'

His puzzled eyes searched hers for the answer she so obviously had, his mind reeling at her words. She touched his shoulder and a charge of energy passed through his body as if the earth itself had shaken.

'Xynon – *this* is what I have been sent to bring about – I know it now, as I know my own heart. We have wandered over this land as a collection of men and women who are rootless, trekking up to the mountains each year to avoid the white rains, living lives no better than the animals we hunt. If we brought about the changes I spoke of then each man would live by his merits alone, he would not be at the whim of his desires or those of unwilling women. We could change the face of the earth!'

Her face shone up to his, glowing with her inner vision.

'Oh, Xynon, can you see it? Can you not see that we could take from the forests the plants we hunt for and move them to our own piece of land so that they would grow where *we* wanted them to grow, instead of having to arrange long foraging parties? Do you not see that we could catch our own stags, our own does and keep them like we keep the horses so that we always have meat to eat instead of hunting? That we could dam the rivers and catch the fish we need – can you not see that – that vision?'

Now it was Soosha's turn to search his eyes for an answer – had she cast the spell? Could this man accept her plan for the future? Cautiously she let her fingers glide gently from his shoulder and down his chest, finally letting them drop from his body as they reached his taut belly. Xynon closed his eyes for a moment, feeling the caress stirring his loins.

'I . . . I . . . ' he stammered, 'I *want* to see it, Soosha, I want that vision.'

Suddenly he grasped her hand and placed it palm down on his chest above his wildly beating heart.

'I want that vision as much as I want you,' he said gruffly as he dropped his head and stared at the ground once more, overcome with shame at what he had said – afraid that she would reject him, afraid that the vision would fade, pass and fall away.

'I knew I could trust you, Xynon,' Soosha whispered as she gently removed her hand from under his and traced the pattern of hairs over his chest with her fingertips. 'I knew that you alone would see the vision.' Her fingers moved over his belly as she drew closer to him. 'I knew that you would understand.' She brought   other hand up brushing against his manhood and spread both hands over his belly and round his waist. 'I knew that you alone were worthy of me.' Her voice was so thick with desire that it was barely audible, her insistent hands now holding his pulsing manhood as slowly she sank to her knees and took him deeply into her mouth. She felt his hands grasp the top of her head, then sink down on to her shoulders as his manhood filled her mouth. She heard him moan deeply as she grasped his buttocks and dug her nails deep into his flesh.

'Soosha!' he gasped. 'Soosha!'

She felt him slowly take himself from her mouth as he sank to his knees.

'I want you,' he said as he grasped her shoulders and pulled her towards him. 'I want you *and* your vision.'

His hands gripped her shoulders as he pushed her gently backwards on to the grasses and the leaves.

'I need you – your home – your body – your harvest.'

His fingers found her secret place and slowly insinuated themselves into her. Soosha did not know whether the

249

pain was pain or pleasure as they found the inner entry to her being. She pressed herself against him, her mouth covering his as the pain reached a breath-gasping pitch and was gone. Hot tears fell unbidden as very gently he entered her and as she sank into a warm darkness she felt his body inside her body, his heart pounding against her heart, his mouth searching for hers as the flowering of his body pulsed inside hers. He rose slightly and tearing his mouth from hers he hungrily bent his head to her breast; she clung on to his shoulders and back, her hands quick and urgent as he slid his hands down behind her and clenched her buttocks together, raising them from the ground as deeper and deeper inside her drove his burning manhood. Now the pain became exquisite as the aching need inside her took hold of her body, tightening each muscle.

'I want you!' she screamed to the skies and the trees and the birds, 'I want you – now!'

The aching screaming muscles responded to her cry, lifting the small of her back off the ground as she felt each fibre of her body concentrated in her loins, as suddenly she felt herself explode in a pulsing, bursting climax of convulsive shuddering. In the instant that she felt the world fall away from her into silky blackness, a second explosion burst within her as Xynon's manhood swelled and spilled in a turbulent tarantism of love that gentled away the last eddies of desire.

CHAPTER TWENTY-TWO

While Soosha and Xynon slept the slumber of sex satisfied, Injya and Galdr talked quietly to each other. Pentesh lay sleeping upon the shoulder of Injya, having suckled lustily from her breast and Injya, though still pale from her labouring, showed the same rosy tint in her cheeks as her child. Galdr sat on the floor, occasionally touching the downy head of his daughter. Injya told Galdr all that had happened to her since she had returned to the tribe: her 'marriage' with Crenjal; the awful retribution meted out to him by Anfjord and of the dreams and visions she had had about Galdr. He listened to her story intently, often shaking his head in sorrow – seeing in his mind's eye all she had spoken of. When at last she had finished Galdr felt that his heart had been wrung dry.

When falteringly Galdr told her of his trials, Injya wavered between disbelief and amazement – she had seen it all, in dreams and visions. The synchronisity pointed to only one thing: they were destined to be together. Both Injya and Galdr had seen the vision of the fusion of the sun and the moon and both understood the new energy thus released; both, in their differing ways, knew the power of the drum, the strength harnessed in the animal spirits waiting to be tapped and brought to fruition; and both knew that it was only by uniting the total force of the earth, sky, sun and moon could man live in harmony and rightness – but more than that? It was Injya's turn to shake her head when eventually Galdr fell silent. She looked at her sleeping girl-child: if both of them could be so mistaken in believing that the child they had made would be a boy, could they not also be mistaken in following this uncharted path? Was it possible that Injya had simply fallen into a trap laid by Galdr? His will was strong – she frowned as she remembered his physical will – perhaps the will of his mind was equally as strong – perhaps he had willed her to see those things – perhaps all of this was a ploy to ensnare her. But then she remembered what Galdr had said about Askoye and the pictures she had woven in his mind. Galdr could not have imagined that – he had never met Askoye – he could not have conjured her out of thin air! Askoye – everything seemed to start and finish with her. Perhaps it was Askoye's will all along – perhaps she could see their destinies as clearly as Injya could see her infant . . . perhaps . . .

Injya bit her lip, she felt suddenly very frightened and close to tears. Why was everything so confusing? She looked at Galdr whose head was bent over their child. This man had saved her life, had saved the life of her daughter, but, if it had not been for this man, none of that would have been necessary! She felt her anger rise as she stared fixedly at the top of Galdr's head – he was compliant, contrite, bowed before her, and she? All she felt was anger and hate! No matter what visions they had shared, no matter what magic Askoye had woven, she would never succumb to this man – she hated him more than she hated Anfjord – he would never enjoy her body again, she would rather die!

No sooner had Injya resolved her mind than Galdr raised his head and looked straight into her eyes.

'You hate me – I know.' He dropped his head as her eyes flashed. 'I know that there is no way that I can prove to you what I have said to be true, that there is no possible reason for you to change your mind about me. I have acted abominably. Injya—' he reached out for her hand which she snatched away, staring at him with blazing eyes, her mouth set in a straight line of defiance. He gazed hopelessly at her. 'I have no right – no reason – to expect you to act any differently to the way you are behaving now.

All I know is that somehow it is in the divine plan that we should be together – perhaps it is not meant for this lifetime, perhaps many lifetimes will have to elapse before what you and I have both seen will come to fruition. But please, Injya, try not to hate me. It has been willed that I return here, it was ordained that I arrived when I did – and I know that it is also destined that we leave this place and try and find the land of the golden sun-metal of which my mother spoke, but more than that I cannot tell. Injya, please' – he hurried on as she was about to speak – 'hear me, if only this once. My father has given you to me, as you know. To safeguard you from him, I will accept – but I will not become your husband until you wish it.'

Injya snorted her reply as she turned her face away.

'And that will never be, Galdr, never. I will never take you for my husband, I would rather die first and that much, too, you know!'

As Galdr forlornly made his way to his sancar he saw two shadowy figures descend from the copse. In the dark violet which was heralding the dawn, he swore he could make out the figures of his sister and a tall, nearly naked man. Shaking his head in disbelief he crept into the sancar and fell heavily on to his bed. Sounds of Halfray's snores mixed with the first bird call as sleep claimed his consciousness, but he slept fitfully, waking often, dreaming of Soosha, of his father, the old tokener Colnyek drinking poison, his daughter and Injya, always Injya, until he finally awoke, heavy of head and heart.

Eventually Injya too slept, but not before her aching head had clarified some of her thoughts and emotions. She resolved finally that she would have no part in Galdr's plans: his ideas of forming a new tribe and travelling to the land of which his mother had spoken were nonsense. If he wished to leave his people – so be it, but she would do everything in her power to stop Halfray and anyone else going with him. He was as egotistical and power-crazed as his father – a new land indeed! She resolved that she would never again leave her people, no matter what the danger. As she drifted into sleep she comforted herself that the only thing that really mattered was sleeping and feeding her child – she would *not* think of matters so immense – her sweet daughter needed all her energy, all her love and attention.

Pentesh stirred in her sleep and threw out a soft pink arm; all thoughts gone save those of her child, Injya twisted around and stared hard at her baby. Pentesh's tiny bud-like mouth puckered and suckled in her sleep as if she were at her breast; her tiny fist twitched as if she were already clutching at Injya's skin and the violet-lidded eyes fluttered with the sweet dreams of babyhood. Injya thought her heart would break at the sight of such perfect innocence and she swallowed back a tear as the child once more became still, her gentle breaths calm and regular, her downy skin pink and clear as the first rays of sunshine in midsummer.

At first light she was woken by Sanset and Halfray. Anfjord had just roused the whole encampment and announced that Soosha was to marry! Injya was not as amazed at the news as her cousin and brother, saying only: 'Why Xynon?'

As she nursed Pentesh, she talked over the previous evening's conversation with Galdr – what did Halfray feel? Was Galdr really so changed? To find that Halfray not only believed Galdr wholeheartedly, but had been sucked into his plan of journeying to a new land, frightened Injya greatly – that her own brother could be so fooled! She was beginning to feel isolated – no sooner had she found some constancy, some respite from the finger-pointing fear of those around her, than her new-found security was under threat – and Soosha's impending marriage was part of that threat – of that she was convinced.

'Why Xynon?' she asked of Sanset. In reply she only shrugged her shoulders. 'But I have known Xynon since I was tiny – surely Soosha knows of his love for Igrat?

Xynon would never take a woman – surely he could not go against his nature so?'

Both Sanset and Halfray shook their heads – how to explain the inexplicable?

'She is plotting,' Injya warned them. 'This is all part of a plot – she is using Xynon for her own ends – though what they are, Great Hoola alone knows!'

She looked at her brother and cousin, then down at her child. In a voice hardly above a whisper she said: 'Sanset – use Ullu – she will know what Soosha is planning – she is her half-sister after all. Halfray – can you find from Igrat what is behind this? Oh, beloveds, I feel a great fear – something is about to happen which neither you nor I have any power to withstand. Please, leave me to rest now, but seek out the truth, for all our sakes.'

Sanset took Pentesh from her, kissing her gently on the cheek.

'I will send Bendula in to be near you, Injya, do not fear so – nothing Soosha can do will harm you, or your little one, of that I am sure.'

But Injya knew that Sanset was only saying these words to comfort her. Sanset knew as did Halfray, that Injya's prophetic words came only from her deep insight and not from any fear she had for herself. As she laid the sleeping child next to Injya, she turned to Halfray whose face was shadowed with worry.

'Will you show Aywe how to prepare the comfrey – I must find Bendula.'

And before Halfray had time to ask why, she was gone from the dark sancar. He turned to Injya but saw that she, like her daughter, was sleeping. He crept from the sancar and out into the brilliant morning sunshine – perhaps Injya was wrong – perhaps this marriage meant nothing more than Soosha wishing to take a man to her bed.

Halfray sat, cross-legged in the sun, carefully stripping the leaves from the gathered flowering comfrey scattered around his knees. Aywe was silently attentive, handing him the tall, slightly furry-leaved plants, speaking seldom. Occasionally they looked down into the encampment at the people who were variously rushing around or standing in small groups, talking excitedly of the news. The very air seemed to tingle with the collective anticipation of the tribe – so, 'ice-heart' had melted, she had decided to take a mate! The young men wavered between jealousy and pity – Xynon was a strong young man, but was he man enough for Soosha? A few wondered of what now was to become of Igrat, Xynon's life-long friend. More innuendo, more doubt.

Xynon's relationship with the still baby-plump Igrat had always been a matter for whisper and cruel laughter. Igrat the soft man, Igrat the half-woman – well, time alone would tell. Anfjord had declared that the marriage would take place on the morrow and had called, once again, for a feast. But the young men who inwardly scoffed and outwardly smiled went happily off to the seas to fish and into the woods to hunt, a feast was a feast – no matter what rumours were whispered.

When the pile of leaves in Halfray's lap threatened to spill over on to the ground, he carefully gathered them together and placed them on the waiting doe-skin. The discarded white and mauve flowers on their long dark green stems looked like so many fallen warriors, sad heads on limp bodies. Halfray gently agitated the leaves on the doe-skin, separating them out so that they would dry evenly, and sighed, well satisfied with his morning's work. Dropping both hands into his lap he looked again at the scurrying crowds and thought, not for the first time, of the wasted frenetic energy that man expends on trivia and how life would be better for everyone if we were more like the plants and animals of this world. However, he thought, as he gazed at the plant heads, certain things must be done.

Lazily he started brushing the stems together, gently raking the soft grasses with his fingers to free the already dying flowers; but suddenly he stopped and stared at the pattern which the stems and their wilting heads made. In front of him was laid out a picture as clear as if it had been painted in soot on stone. His heart seemed to leap into his mouth as, with a voice strangulated by fear, he pointed to the flower stems before him: 'Aywe – look!'

Aywe bent her head and looked at the stems, then up at Halfray.

'I see nothing – what is it?'

'There, look see, these have fallen in a ring, look, like people standing around watching, and here, in the middle, oh, Aywe – cannot you see?'

Aywe's eyes darted from Halfray's wildly blinking ones and she stared at the picture spread out on the grass before her – she could see a circle, but in the middle? She stared hard at the pattern the stalks and flower heads made. Suddenly she saw it and clutching her stomach with one hand, shooting the other out for support towards Halfray, she cried: 'Beloved Mother – yes! Halfray, what does it mean?'

'It means' – Halfray began with a voice which had become hard; all traces of fear gone – 'it means that you go now, to Injya and you do not leave her side until I return. I need to work!'

Aywe fled from the rise upon which they had sat and Halfray watched her as she entered Injya's sancar. Leaving the leaves to dry, he gathered up the flower stalks and made for the shore.

The two young men's laughter as they struggled to stretch the dried seal skins over the wooden frames was comforting. Halfray sat on a rock by the water's edge and threw again the flower stalks. They landed on the crystal white sand in exactly the same order as the last time he had thrown them, which was exactly the same as the first, second and third time. Inside the ring of 'people' five 'stalk-people' stood – four were tall, one small. Three

257

of the tall ones and the little one stood in a straight line. In front of them stood one who had a thin, sharp branch extending to one side.

He picked up the four stalks and felt again the same fear which he had experienced the first time he had seen the picture; for he knew that these four innocent flower stalks on their heavy drooping heads represented himself, Galdr, Injya and the small one, Pentesh. He tried placing them somewhere else inside the ring of 'people', but something stayed his hand, nowhere, except where they had fallen, three times now, was the right place for them. He placed them back inside the ring and with fingers trembling, picked up the tall 'stalk-person' with the branch. The stem of the leafless stalk seemed to burn his hands and he knew that he was looking his murderess in the face. This flower-person was Soosha, the spiked branch, her weapon. He placed her back, in front of the line of four and looked around the ring; but all the stalks had their heads bowed. The Skoonjay people would not save them as they had not saved Mensoon and her kin – they would bow their heads with shame and watch the slaughter.

He tried again, concentrating hard and looking through half-closed eyes – was there any space in the picture for escape? Any inner feeling that would show him where to place an animal, a bird, another person who would save them? He picked up a stick, holding it lightly between his fingers and moved it slowly backwards and forwards over the flower picture. Wherever his stick wandered in the ring of people there was blankness, a resistance. As surely as he knew that the one with a branch was Soosha carrying a weapon, he knew that he could not make this picture change – there was nothing he nor the Gods could do except flee from the murderess.

With an anger he rarely felt, he picked up the flower stalks, clawed at the sand until it became moist and hard under his hands and buried them; as Soosha will bury us, he thought ruefully.

A sudden yell of pain from one of the young men startled him from his angry thoughts. The youth ran howling down to the water's edge holding a hand out before him, as if it no longer belonged to him, the blood pouring from it leaving a brilliant scarlet rivulet in the white sand. Halfray was by his side in the icy, salty water, even before the youth's companion was. Both young men jigged in the freezing water as the wound was held under the surface, Halfray now grasping the young man's wrist firmly just above the gash.

'No more!' the injured man pleaded to Halfray.

'A little longer,' he replied softly, 'just a little longer.'

The uninjured youth made hasty apologies and quit the water – even after such a brief immersion his toes were already turning blue – and he sat on the sand massaging warmth back into them as he watched the scene in front of him.

'Enough now,' Halfray finally said and holding the injured hand high above the youth's head he led him from the water. 'Fetch me that pouch lying on that rock – go – quickly!'

The other lad scrambled to his feet and raced to where Halfray had been sitting, returning in a flurry of sand which coated his seated friend.

'Open its ties!'

Dithering with cold and the shock of Halfray's tone, Torben opened the pouch and held it near Halfray's free hand.

'Do you know nothing?' he shouted, 'take out the bundle – carefully now – and press the whole of it on to Eabran's wrist – oh – give it to me!'

Quieting the exasperation within him, Halfray applied the thick wodge of leaves on to the cut, pressing it hard against the gash.

In a gentler voice he said: 'Now, Torben, hold this just as I am – do not worry, it should not bleed again. Eabran – I am going to leave you for a moment – do not attempt

259

to rise – you will faint – you have lost much blood, the cut is to your bone.'

Eabran's white, horror-struck face, shot up to look at Halfray's.

'Fear not!' he almost laughed at the look of abject terror on the young man's face, 'you will not die – now, Torben, hold fast – I shall be back before you know I have gone.'

So saying he picked up his pouch and ran to the rock upon which he had perched. Sitting on the sand, the rock hiding him from view, he removed the smaller objects from his pouch; tiny leaves wrapping the most precious of herbs, hollowed reeds containing unctions, salves and the seven stones which protected the seven centres of his spirit body. These he laid out carefully in the shade of the rock and covered them with sand, smoothing the sand flat and sending a quick, quiet prayer to the heavens to protect them from harm. Next he shook the pouch vigorously and stretched its neck wide. This done he closed his eyes and mentally pictured a rod of light reaching from the zenith of the heavens, through his spine and into the very centre of the earth. Almost immediately he felt his stomach relax and his head clear. Taking a deep breath he quickly unsheathed his knife and, bracing himself against the rock, cut his wrist. The poppy red blood spurted from the cut as Halfray in an instant dropped the knife and covered the wound with the open neck of his pouch. Breathing very slowly and deeply he counted, one, two, three . . . ten, eleven, twelve.

'Close wound!' he commanded. 'Close!'

Holding his pouch in his teeth and clutching his still bleeding wrist firmly with his free hand, he walked carefully back to Eabran and Torben who looked solemnly at his advancing figure as if they were boys caught stealing another's meat.

'It has healed!' shouted Eabran to him. 'The wound – it has just closed!'

Considering that Torben had never done anything like it before, he made a very good job of binding Halfray's wrist with the leaves. Eabran was not so enthusiastic about drinking the blood which Halfray had shed for him, but after two attempts, he reluctantly drank the sweet sticky substance. The inevitable questions came thick and fast – what to say? How to explain? After a long time Halfray decided to stop being evasive, to trust the inner feeling he had about the young men – what did he have to lose by telling them of his life and the skills he had learnt? If the picture could not be changed, it mattered little now if he was vilified – his life was measured in a matter of days, not moons.

Eabran and Torben listened, only their open mouths and wide-eyed expressions showing their incredulity. At last Halfray had finished – he had told all, including the part in his life being played by Injya and Galdr and their shared understanding. Eventually he fell silent, expecting laughter or ridicule or worse, just plain disbelief. But that did not come – what did was totally unexpected; both young men wept! Through their tears they pleaded to be accepted by Halfray, pleaded that they too might be allowed to join with them on their journeying to the new world. With the simplicity of eighteen-summer men they shrugged off the dangers, discounted completely the inevitability of the fate shown by the flower picture and embarked on long personal histories of their own to show how good they both were at hunting, fire-making and trekking. Eventually Halfray silenced them with cries of, 'Enough! Enough!', then continued darkly: 'I believe you – but remember – tell no-one unless you are completely sure of him – secrecy is of the essence – if we do have to leave here before we planned, we must not give warning of it, for that way death surely lies.'

When Halfray returned to the encampment he looked for Galdr, and not finding him in their sancar, he went next to Injya's. As he entered Sanset and Aywe ran to his side: 'Tell me – tell me you have changed the picture?'

Aywe's voice was thick with pleading. In answer he put his arms round both women's shoulders and shook his head. As his eyes became accustomed to the gloom of the sancar he saw that Galdr was kneeling at Injya's bedside, arms around her. They had both been weeping.

'Galdr, I have some news, some comforting, some' – he hesitated and lowered his eyes – 'not so.' He could not see Galdr's face, hidden as it was in Injya's shoulder, but could see from Injya's expression that much had passed between them. She looked at him through eyes awash with fresh tears and her mouth trembled again: 'Halfray – tell me it is not so!'

Halfray hung his head – there was nothing more he could say. Galdr disentangled himself and turned to him.

'You have thrown the flowers thrice?'

Halfray nodded. Galdr sighed deeply and stood up.

'This is sooner than I had wished for, but there can be no changing our fates. We must leave this place, and leave soon!'

Injya began crying again as she reached out her hand towards Galdr's back: 'Can you not see that I cannot leave? I must stay, I have only just given birth, Galdr, I must regain my strength – I could not go with you.'

Galdr swung round and grasped her hand, sinking to his knees before her: 'Dearest Injya – we will not leave before the winter trek – you will be strong by then, what I meant was that we must be prepared, we must act now, not leave it for moons and moons. Soosha's marriage *is* part of a plot, of that I am as convinced as you, but I fear for our safety after what I have heard from Aywe. If the marriage fails to further her own ends, Soosha will, in cold blood and broad daylight, contrive to kill us, and with the blessings of Father and the whole tribe. We must prepare, we must make ready. If you stay, you too will be slaughtered.'

Injya looked into his deep brown eyes and knew that he was telling the truth.

262

'But if I go with you and Sanset and the rest – will not the outcome be exactly the same?'

None in that sancar could say that the journey to a new land would not mean the deaths of not only Injya and her child, but all of them, and they hung their heads, like the wilted flowers of Halfray's omen.

CHAPTER TWENTY-THREE

'No, I don't!' Igrat's red face quivered with emotion as he stood over Xynon. 'I do *not* understand – and I do not think *you* do either!' Xynon slumped further down on his fur cushion and held his head in his hands in an attitude of despair.

'Look,' he began in a tired voice. 'We have been over this – cannot I rest now?' He closed his eyes and rubbed them hard like a tired child.

'Rest? REST?!' Igrat shouted at him, 'you tell me all this and you expect to rest? What do you think I am made of? Earth? Mud? Do you really expect me to say: "All right, Xynon, my life-long friend, carry on, get bedded with your adored Soosha, spy on her brother and *your* kinswoman, Xynon, so that you can find out what this so-called magic is all about. Carry on, tell your new woman so that she can use the magic too – to what ends you have no notion." Is that what you want me to tell you? Go ahead, sleep happy in your bed – you are still a good friend, I still love you! Is that what you want to hear? Is that the sort of response someone who *truly* loves you will give?'

He dropped his hands with a heavy slapping sound on to his thighs and looked with despair at the bowed head of his companion. Xynon hugged his knees with his arms and sighed deeply – how could he make Igrat understand? What words to use to explain the vision that had enfolded him? Like a lost child he slowly raised an arm and held his hand out towards Igrat.

'Hold me, Igrat, come, be with me, let me explain once more.'

Igrat looked at the outstretched hand as if he had never seen it before and stood his ground. Every atom of his being wanted to hold that hand, to touch that bare arm, to lie next to Xynon and hear the whispered words of the grand plan; his heart ached to be close to Xynon once more, to feel those strong arms circling him, that taut flesh, next to his own soft body, to be talked to, to be gentled through the gate of understanding. With a feeling of sadness that he barely managed to hide, he slowly shook his head.

'No. No, Xynon, no matter how much I want to, no.'

Xynon dropped his arm with a sudden thud and stared dejectedly at the floor. Igrat looked upon his friend, at his attitude of total defeat and something inside him broke. He felt the unwelcomed tears well up from his cracked heart, the hot pricking sensation stinging the already red-rimmed eyes and knew that he, too, was defeated. He could no more deny Xynon than he could his own life – wherever Soosha was leading him, whatever Xynon did from now on, Igrat knew that he had to be close by, had to be near – to pretend to himself that he could leave his life's love simply because of a scheming woman was a denial of that love.

He silently took a step nearer and laid his pink palm on the top of Xynon's black head. At the touch of his beloved's hair a great tear splashed on to the back of his gentle hand and trickled on to Xynon's still bowed head. Soon, it was joined by many more before he finally sank to his knees before him.

'Hold me—' his voice, cracked and hoarse through the tears, sang quietly through the still night air and filled Xynon's heart with hope. 'Tell me again,' he murmured as their bodies entwined, hot salt tears mingling with their kisses, tingling on their flesh as they gently fell together on to the soft furs. 'Help me understand.'

Soosha did not need any other person to help her understand. Her instinct about Xynon was right. A thrill shivered through her body as she remembered their love-making, remembered his sleepy assent to her wishes, the soft grey-pink dawn light playing upon the nape of his neck, as she played with the small hairs so secretly growing there. How easy it had all been – Xynon had understood directly what her wishes were and there had been no hint of doubt in his face when he agreed to try to discover from Galdr where his power lay. She smiled to herself as she remembered the fear she had felt, fear that he would reject her, that her instinct was wrong – but now? Now she had no doubts for on the morrow he and she would be bound together, and then, even should doubts arise, she would so encircle him, so enthral him, that he would do whatever she wished!

Power! Silently she mouthed the word in the darkness of the sancar. Power! She had it within her grasp: power to use Galdr's secrets against him, power to overthrow her father, power to lead her people! She mouthed the word again, opening her mouth wide, breathing the sound into the dark air. Power! Her fingers idly played upon her bare stomach and thighs and among the springy hairs on her mound of womanhood. The word resounded deep inside her abdomen and as her fingers, no longer idly exploring but urgently seeking, found her tiny nub of pleasure and felt it growing and swelling between the lips of her sex, she imagined the word forming a shape: a strong black shape which was rising from the bowels of the earth and penetrating her as Xynon had penetrated her.

Power! The word moaned through her parted mouth as the black force overwhelmed her. Power! Her head sank deeper into the pillows. Power! The word forced her fingers inside her body, forced her shaking form to pulse and sweat with longing and as the urge gripped her until she felt that her body would break with the tension, she knew that it was not Xynon who could raise her to such a pitch, but power itself. It was the power secreted deep inside the earth, the power of Erlik himself, King of the

266

Underworld, King of Darkness – He was the root. For a second the knowing frightened her, her thrusting fingers were suddenly cramped in a paroxysm of fear – but say the word only: power! Her body responded, as naturally as it had responded with Xynon and it shook with the intensity of its yearning. Power! Now she was no longer alone, now her bed, her body, her soul was covered with another, a black beast, a black-skinned being entered her, until she knew not whether pleasure was pain. Her head no longer responded, only her body pulsed and strove nearer and nearer the centre of the earth, deeper and deeper into the realms of her master. At the point of climax she saw Erlik himself standing before her, his massively swollen scarlet phallus in his scale-clad hand, his beast-like features broken by a leering laugh. Then she knew that she had discovered the source of her own power – Erlik was her source, her husband – now and for ever.

*　　*　　*

If the short silky night had murmured with stealthy secrets, the sun-kissed morning dismissed them with its wild tossed roof, clear to the sun itself. With the fading of the final stars the whole encampment became alive with activity; children, weaving flowers into long strands with which to entwine the couple, sat in giggling groups or ran round the skirts of their mothers who in turn were busily cutting vegetables, chopping meat or desperately trying to sew with their fine bone needles a tuck here, a bead there. Before the sun had even turned from his red robe to the fine gold one he would wear which would serve him all day, a fishing party had been despatched to scour the seas and inlets for plump pink fishes and beady-eyed crustaceans. Many fires were lit and much water carried to and from the streams for cooking. Soon the whole encampment was filled with the smells of meat, herbs, fishes, flowers, wood-smoke and the salt-encrusted bodies of young men, tired and yet exhilarated by their labours on the white waves of the icy ocean.

Injya sat outside the entrance to the sancar, watching the bustling people, remembering with sadness her own 'marriage' to Crenjal, all that time ago. She wondered if Xynon would appear to Soosha crowned with the Barnkop-helmet as Crenjal had once done – would that now be taken into the tribe and its true origins lost? Today she felt better, she had slept heavily and well, little Pentesh had only woken her twice for food and each time after nursing her child she had once more fallen into a deep, dreamless sleep. Bendula was combing her hair and chattering away to herself and anyone who would listen – sweet Bendula, thought Injya heavily, how little you know! But as she sat, bathed and caressed, child in arms, hair being combed in the sunlight of such a perfect day, she allowed a little love to fill her heart – perhaps Xynon would love Soosha, and the love would change her heart and her spirit-lights. No one person is totally evil, of that she was utterly sure, and no matter how Soosha had misused and abused her, no matter what plans Soosha had for the future, love could and would change them, if not completely, then subtly.

She could not help but be changed by love – it would overwhelm her and warm her heart, towards herself, her child and Galdr. The picture Halfray talked of *was* worrying, but he was only a man – no matter how adept, he did not see things the same way as her – of course there was a way out from the danger so graphically represented, but it would not be found upon the path of fighting or running – those are men-things. Soosha and Injya, when all else failed, had their sex in common and it was a sex based on love, trust and understanding. They could work this all out, there *could* be a place for a new religion in their tribe which would not threaten any one – why, what *could* there possibly be threatening about each person recognizing and living their life as if they themselves were divine? Let the people see that there would be no more discord or tension – happiness and a new caring for each other could only arise from such a concept.

Her attention was distracted from her musings by the sight of Galdr, Halfray and Centill, the son of Colnyek, a man of some twenty-five summers who, like his father, carried his slight frame with the springy agility of a mountain deer. They were walking up the slight incline towards her sancar, deep in conversation. Galdr looked dark, great furrows cutting swathes of fear across his brow, his long, black hair framing his worried face and casting more shadows around it. Her heart sank. From thirty paces or more, she could feel the despondency and gloom exude from the trio as if they had just taken a beloved to the death-stone.

The three sat before her, finally silent, waiting for Galdr to speak.

'Igrat is missing!' Galdr announced. For a moment Injya could not connect their sad faces with the news, then suddenly the gravity of it hit her. For Igrat to desert his friend – at such a momentous time? Her thoughts raced with her heart and her stomach lurched sickeningly.

'Are you sure?' was all she could find to say. Each one nodded their silent answer.

'I saw him go myself,' Centill said in his deep, clear voice. 'I heard a noise in the horse svarge and was outside quieting them, when I saw . . . Injya – he was naked!' Centill disconsolately picked at the grass.

'And Xynon? What of him?'

'Oh, he is so besotted with Soosha he would not notice if his right hand had gone missing!'

'But what do you want *me* to do? I can scarce walk – let alone go hunting after naked men – Halfray – *you* must know where he is – can you not . . . ?'

The question was not finished, obviously Halfray had asked his spirit-guide for help, and so, too, would have Galdr – that could only mean that it was not to be; that Igrat was beyond the help of the spirits of men. Suddenly Injya understood – perhaps he was beyond the call of the spirits of man, but woman? She said quietly: 'I will see

269

what can be done – go now, it would not be seemly for three men to be seen paying homage to me on Soosha's marriage day!'

Galdr helped her to her feet and kissed her lightly on the cheek. The kiss startled her and she found herself blushing.

'Do you . . . ?'

'No, I do not need you – this much I can manage on my own.'

The men descended the rise and were lost in the throng of people – sweet Ahni Amwe! thought Injya – four days only and you call on me again! Passing Pentesh to Bendula she went inside the sancar – thankful once more that at least the birth had given her privacy. She touched the place that Galdr had kissed – how strange to feel gentleness from him, how odd to accept this man when only two days before she had vowed to hate forever! She did not know whether it was their shared fear that brought them suddenly together or whether her rational mind had finally given up arguing with the inevitable, but since Halfray's flower picture something had changed in her heart towards Galdr, but what it was exactly, she had no clear idea.

She forced her attention to do what she knew was expected of her. *She* had to find Igrat – the men could not. Carefully she sat down and gingerly crossed her legs – how she ached still! Closing her eyes she found the small, still place inside herself where her consciousness lay and drawing herself up straighter, calmed her mind and her breathing till she was as unmoving as the great ice-sheets of the mountain country. She felt the pull in her stomach as she willed her soul to leave her body and then, before she had time for doubt, she was free, her spirit-body floating high above the encampment.

Keeping the image of Igrat firmly before her she craved knowledge of his whereabouts.

'Bai Ulgan, if it is for the highest good, allow me to see Igrat.'

270

Quicker than she had dared hope, suddenly he was before her, weeping, sitting naked as reported, his soft skin besmeared with mud, horror and torment writ large upon his keening face. He had his feet in a tiny stream and his fat body sat uncomfortably upon the water's edge – abject mortification transformed his plump, good-natured face as tears streaked away the mud with pale lines of sorrow. Far around him, Injya could see his spirit-lights, normally of the palest greens and blues, now suffused with browns and deep reds – this was more than the sorrow of losing a friend, more than a jealous reaction. She knew that she must show herself to him but feared the consequences – such torment! Steeling herself against the shock to her own system, she drew the energy of the spirit world to her and clothed herself in a mantle of flesh. Placing herself behind him, she allowed the thoughts to flow from her.

'Poor Igrat,' she thought, 'poor, poor Igrat.'

Igrat heard her thoughts and swung round alarmed, covering his naked manhood with his hands.

'Injya,' he gasped, 'how did . . . ?'

She put her finger to her lips to quieten his speech and concentrated hard.

'You must tell me what caused you to run away, Igrat,' she thought and knew that he had heard her voice inside his head as he immediately turned from her and shook his head. All she could sense from him was the words.

'You do not know, you do not know!' repeated over and over again.

'What do I not know, Igrat? What?'

Igrat looked up and sighed a long, despondent sigh. He turned from her and sank his head into his hands once more. His thoughts rang in Injya's head: 'You do not know – you do not know!'

Something in his attitude, something in the urgent yet helpless words made Injya sense that he was not talking, or thinking, of *her*, but talking rather to Xynon – it was *Xynon* who did not know. Intuitively Injya knew this to be right as she carefully formed the question in her mind.

'What does Xynon not know, Igrat? What?'

Igrat's body shuddered as his mind received the question and for a moment he obviously fought with himself, rocking to and fro, clamping his teeth together, shaking his head from side to side in utter misery. Then suddenly the words came, tumbling, pell-mell from his lips, devoid of coherence. Injya could feel the chaos of Igrat's mind as his swirling images of darkness tumbled from his mouth, a jumbled cacophony of disjointed sounds and words.

'Soo . . . Erlik . . . sha . . . murder . . . Injya . . . Hal . . . moon . . . death . . . fray . . . Galdr . . . Xy . . . Galdr . . . love . . . Xynon . . . death . . . love . . . Sooo . . . Erlik . . . Sha . . . '

On and on the words poured from his mouth as Igrat rocked in his confusion and wretchedness.

A dreadful cold foreboding fell in Injya's soul as she tried to make sense of the crying torrent of words. Iced fingers of fear clutched at her as she watched, helpless, as Igrat sobbed his words to the marshlands.

'No!' she commanded him after what seemed an age of crying. 'No more, Igrat, no more!'

She willed the words to stop, willed him to be silent, but the madness and inner turmoil were too deep – too entire for thought-words to still. Her own body started to shake as the fear of his trapped mind began to influence her. With a supreme effort of detachment she took a step backwards from him and very consciously shutting out his thoughts and words, she drew into her soul the life-force of Por, the healing golden energy of the Sun. As warmth began to flood her being, she methodically started to cleanse Igrat's spirit-lights. Her frail fingers, each one emanating pure white gold light, began their task of combing away the evil from his spirit-body. It felt as if she was putting her hand into a hot, putrid substance as on and on her fingers combed the air around Igrat's body, pulling the heavy red-brownness out of his spirit-body and replacing them with gold and white, the ultimate colour of love.

It took a long time before Igrat stopped shaking and sobbing, before the words stopped and the fear left him, but eventually she was able to stand before him and look into his pale, red-rimmed eyes.

'Can you tell me, Igrat? Tell me what you saw – what you know?'

Igrat stared at her for a moment and then slowly shook his head.

'Pictures, pictures, Injya, that is all,' he whispered, dropping his head once more into his hands.

'Are they still there?'

'No.'

'Are the words still there?'

'No.'

'Do you want me to leave you now?'

'No.'

'Will you come back to us?'

'No.'

Silence fell between them. The silence of time standing still. No hum of insects, no sound of water, no breath of wind. With what she knew was the last of her energy, she forced her body to move towards him. Very gently she placed a hand on his downturned head. 'I have to leave, Igrat,' she began softly, 'I have to connect with my true body-form again.' The head nodded its assent. 'When I have rested I will return.' Again the silent yes.

For a moment Injya doubted that her soul had the strength for the journey, but she need not have feared. The atoms that she had called together to clothe her spirit-form fell from her as easily as dew from a grass blade. She felt her spirit lighten then soar through the crystal sky. Home. The word was scarce thought, the wish scarce wished, than it was so. Before her sat her body, as she had left it, only the slight swaying in the spine and the total silentness of the form showing that her spirit had been absent. The pain was less this time – the searing tugging in her solar plexus less acute, as her soul reunited with her body. A faint sigh was all that would have been heard had anyone been in the sancar to witness her return – but to that person, there would have been no gap in time between the sigh she had exhaled when she first sat, cross-legged on the floor of the sancar and the sigh she now breathed. Earthly time had not moved.

Stiffly, Injya rose to her feet, but the effort was too great. Like a child she allowed her body to fall to the soft fur-covered floor of the sancar as utterly exhausted, she fell into the arms of a deep, dreamless sleep.

CHAPTER TWENTY-FOUR

Bendula carried the now purple-faced Pentesh round the encampment. Tender words of encouragement were of no use. Pentesh sucked avidly at the tip of Bendula's little finger for a moment then screamed in hungry frustration. Why were babies so hot and heavy? Bendula wondered as she trudged round the back of the circle of sancars, away from the questioning looks of the women and the sudden frowns of the men. And when, she continued the internal questioning, when is Injya going to wake up? She looked up at the high blue sky for an answer but none came.

'Pentesh,' she said aloud, looking into the livid, scarlet face of the screaming baby; 'you will just have to wait – Injya is asleep and even your crying will not wake her!'

Pentesh's green eyes flashed up at her for a second as she caught her breath as if summoning up more air for an even louder scream of starvation, but then she seemed to think better of it and with a tiny sob-staggered sigh, closed her eyes and fell instantly asleep.

'Just as if she had understood every word I had said,' she told Injya later, 'every word!'

The sun was nearly at its highest in the heavens when Injya was gently woken by Halfray's touch. The air inside the sancar was hot as were Halfray's fingers as he passed them lightly over Injya's forehead. She closed her eyes in an effort to cut out her brother's pale face, not wanting to answer his questions, only wanting to sleep endlessly in the hot, dark sancar. But the ray of sun which shone through the smoke hole in the roof of the sancar was as insistent as Halfray's unspoken question and reluctantly Injya finally heaved herself up on an elbow and looked at him.

'I found him,' she said quietly and simply, looking into Halfray's clear blue eyes. 'I found him – but I wish I had not.'

Halfray's hand dropped from her shoulder and he sat back, expectantly.

'I do not know if we can bring him back here, Halfray,' she began, 'I am very confused – as he is – I could not understand what he was showing me, could not read his thoughts – they were all disconnected in his brain. He is in a terrible state,' she added lamely.

'Can you tell me what he *did* say?'

'It is difficult to recall, just words – Xynon's name, Soosha's name but all mixed up with . . . oh, Halfray . . . he kept saying Erlik's name too, but in the same breath he would say love and then death and then Galdr. I did what I could to calm him, healed his spirit-lights and I think he was a little calmer when I left him, but he did not want to come back.'

The picture of the big pink-fleshed man, all smeared in mud, blubbering like a child, suddenly came back to Injya and she burst into tears.

'Halfray, oh Halfray . . . he is in such a dire, demented place, I do not think we can help him any more.'

Halfray comforted Injya, rocking her backwards and forwards as Igrat had rocked himself, not questioning further, just quietly accepting what Injya had told him.

Eventually Injya stopped crying and wiped away the tears. Sniffing loudly she stood up and walked very resolutely towards her bed. Turning round she said briskly: 'We have to go back to him – do we not, Halfray?'

It was a question that required no answer.

'Injya . . .'

'No, Halfray – I know what you are going to say – I know the dangers too – but we cannot leave him there – he has gone to die – you know that as well as I do – we cannot leave him!'

Halfray looked at Injya, knowing what she said to be true, not wanting to admit it. He knew, as everyone knew, that to go naked outside the protection of the encampment meant that one was intent on death. Whatever changes had occurred when the two people of the Skoonjay country had merged, that one had not. It was the chosen manner of death, normally ascribed only to the hunt leaders when they became too old to be useful any more; when they felt themselves to be a burden to the rest of the community – they would, as Askoye had, simply leave their clothes behind and walk naked into the ice, or the snow or the marshlands, never to return. Whatever madness now held Igrat in its grip, had been strong enough to make him choose the death of old men and that, indeed, was a terrifying madness.

'Are you strong enough to take me with you?' He looked doubtfully at Injya's face – she looked very drawn and thin – but then, it had only been four days since Pentesh had been born, he reminded himself.

'I do not know,' she answered calmly. 'But I do know that I have to get back to him – if somehow we can manage to reach him together, then we must try. If not, I will have to go alone again.'

Injya sank down on to the raised platform of her bed and looked at Halfray's squatting figure. She did not know how to begin. She knew herself how to soul-walk, she knew that Halfray knew too, but for both people to arrive at the same place in the same time? Perhaps if she left her body and then waited above the sancar for Halfray's soul to reach hers – but how long would that take? Would not the desire to be with Igrat be so great that she would instantly be with him, leaving Halfray disembodied somewhere, hopefully trying to find her? He had tried to reach Igrat himself and failed – would he fail again? In desperation she searched her memory for anything that Askoye might have said about soul-walking that would help her – nothing but warnings flooded her mind. 'Never exhaust your physical body. Never try more than one journey a day. Never underestimate the power of the evil spirits. Never put your soul in someone else's keeping. Never try to become one with another soul – unless that soul is your heart mate. Never leave your soul unattended. Never wait for another – they have their own paths.' On and on the warnings continued.

'Halfray,' she said at last, 'who taught you to soul-walk?'

The question fell into the dark sancar like a great boulder falling into a bog. When Halfray replied it was through the thick voice of deep emotion.

'The raven-spirit of our father, Vingyar.'

'And what did he tell you of joint soul-walking?'

'Nothing.'

'Do you know what the dangers are?'

'No.'

'Do you trust me?'

'Absolutely!'

Halfray turned his face towards Injya and was startled to see frown lines of worry on her face. 'I trust you implicitly, I trust you as I trusted Mensoon, our mother – I know of no dangers and so, I know no fear. Do not frown so, Injya, I am sure it is as simple as holding hands!'

He smiled at her and was relieved to see the frowns disappear and for the first time today, something like a smile upon Injya's face. Slowly she got up from her bed and sat down in front of him.

'I am sure you are right, Halfray,' she said gently as she arranged her clothes about her crossed knees and straightened her back. 'I am sure you are right.'

It was not quite as simple as holding hands, they tried that and nothing happened. They sat back to back, but Injya materialized over the copse and Halfray near the men's sancar. Eventually, they wrapped their legs around each other's and held each other tightly, their chests and abdomens touching and counted their breathing so that it

278

became synchronized. High above the sancar two souls shone. If anyone in the encampment had been looking, they would have thought that two round mirrors had suddenly reflected the rays of the sun, shimmered for a moment and then quickly disappeared, but no-one was looking in the direction of the birth-sancar. Everyone was far too preoccupied with the preparations for the marriage which would happen as soon as the sun reached its peak, although, as Soosha felt, as she was impatiently waiting for the child to finish braiding her hair, a few people did feel a sudden rush of a hot wind that strangely brought with it a sudden chill.

Igrat seemed not to have moved one iota since Injya had seen him last. He was still sitting, feet in water, head bowed, although at least the terrible colours in his spirit-body had not returned. He seemed totally unsurprised at their sudden reappearance – he looked up for a moment, eyes blank, as Injya and Halfray stood before him, then slowly closed his eyes.

'I think he is near to death,' Halfray's voice whispered in Injya's head.

'I can hear no thoughts coming from him,' Injya nodded and thought back to him. 'We must not talk together – only to Igrat. Igrat,' she began, 'Igrat – we have come back to help you – you must tell us what you know.'

Igrat's head shook from side to side, but no thoughts came from him. Injya looked at Halfray in desperation. Halfray in unspoken, unthought reply, touched the centre of his forehead.

'No!' the thought rang back to him, 'no, Halfray!' But she knew that it was a hollow protestation – it was the only thing that could possibly bring Igrat back to his senses. Dropping her face from his, she motioned that Halfray should stand behind Igrat and hold his head up. Igrat did not resist, nor did the blank look leave his eyes when Injya's hands too circled his temples and her thumbs began to press harder on the place where the spirit keeps its secrets.

Only his body slumped slightly as Injya called for the words to come out, for order to replace madness, for Igrat to see clearly. For a long moment the three were thus locked; Igrat's plump body inert, Injya's hands hurting with the pressure and Halfray's closed-eyed intensity burning through his hands into Igrat's skull. Then the voice began. A deep monotonic singing voice, a voice like a man seeing something a long way away. Hypnotic and trance-like, the voice filled the air like a long, half-forgotten poem. Injya and Halfray dropped their hands as the now swaying Igrat chanted slowly:

> I see Soosha take Xynon to her.
> I see Soosha make Xynon of her.
> I see Soosha take Erlik to her.
> I see Soosha take Erlik into her self.
> I see Soosha open herself to Erlik.
> I see Soosha open herself to Xynon.
> I see Soosha call to Erlik as
> she opens herself to Xynon.
> I see Soosha kill Xynon as
> she takes him into herself.
> I see Soosha and Erlik make
> an infant from Xynon's soul.

The voice faltered for a moment as if the awfulness of the words took the strength away, but it continued a second later, slightly faster but still with the same insistent, bleak calmness:

> I see Xynon taking a knife.
> I see Xynon taking the life.
> I see Xynon over Pentesh.
> I see Xynon over Halfray.
> I see Xynon over Injya.
> I see Xynon over Galdr . . .

280

Again the voice faltered, but this time violent spasms rocked Igrat's body and instinctively Injya replaced her hands on his temple. Whatever he saw, whatever he would see, it *had* to be unlocked. Igrat gasped at the touch as if struggling for air and for a split second a light flickered in his eyes, before the dreadful blankness turned them in on themselves, as they saw once more the horror of the vision. The voice came quicker now, words began to stream from his consciousness, the calm monotonous dirge gone.

'I see Xynon being slain by another at her bidding. I see Xynon, Xynon, my love, die! I see his head severed, his blood spilt, his eyes staring up at me, his mouth twisted and bloody, his body naked and his heart torn out . . . Injya!'

Igrat suddenly screamed, his eyes now alight with the terror, his face and body shaking uncontrollably with the vision and the fear.

'Injya! Save me! . . . '

His voice pleaded as his hands clutched at her arms and his contorted face twisted horribly against the vision in his brain.

'I see the Shining Ones – they have come for me . . . I see old Forek – he is calling for me! . . . Injya! The Shining Ones! . . . They have come for me!'

The words had scarce escaped his lips before the torment fell from Igrat's face. His eyes shone for a brief moment and then the light in them faded. Igrat's body slumped to the wet ground. He was dead.

Injya and Halfray watched as the lights of his spirit-body slowly coalesced into a golden, roseate orb and the thin silver-blue thread connecting the physical to the spiritual, gently fell on to his prone earthly body and disintegrated. They watched helpless, as the orb slowly rose to the heavens and was greeted with the gold and rose and blue sparks of the guardian angels of death. Certain that Igrat had been well received they quickly covered his earth body with reeds and moss. There was nothing else they could do. Neither had the strength. As Injya invoked the name of Hoola, the great Earth Mother, to receive the body of her son, for a second time that day Askoye felt close to her.

'There will come a time, Injya, when you will *not* be so pleased with your gifts. There will come a time when you will wish to weep like any other maiden. There will come a time when you will curse me, Mensoon and the Goddess herself. Do not be too hard on yourself when that time comes. Forgive yourself – no-one else can.'

'Forgive myself? Hah!'

Injya swung round and faced Galdr, hair flying, tears streaming from her eyes.

'How *can* I forgive myself? Igrat would have been—'

'He would have died, with or without your and Halfray's help – you know that, Injya, as well as I do!' Galdr interrupted her sternly. 'And do you know, do you *really* know, that he would have died so peacefully without leaving the vision behind him? Imagine what would have happened to him had he died taking that with him – he would have forever wandered the earth, bound by the knowledge of events yet to come, powerless to stop them – this way, you freed his soul! Injya! Stop walking up and down and listen to me – we have to act now, knowing what we know. We *have* to leave, it is all conspiring against us – first the picture – now this. We cannot wait until the trek – Soosha will not let us!'

Injya stopped her hand-wringing striding and let her hands fall to her side. Defeated, she slowly walked over to Galdr and accepted his outstretched arms. Curling up against him she allowed the real feelings to surface, the real feelings of grief, sorrow and loss. But as quickly as she had started to cry, she stopped and controlling her emotions, she said: 'There will be time enough for mourning. Galdr, we have to stop the marriage!'

Galdr continued stroking her hair, saying nothing. He knew, as Injya knew also, that it would be impossible to stop the marriage – as impossible as telling Xynon what Igrat had told Injya and Halfray. He would simply not believe it. Few people would. Halfray himself was not convinced and *he* was not in love with Soosha as Xynon was. But Galdr and Injya knew it to be true, understood the meaning of the vision, knew that it *was* possible to bring forth a living child who had the soul of Erlik.

'Could we not, at least, prevent them coupling?' Injya asked in the feeble voice of one who knows they are asking the impossible.

'We could prevent it for a few days, but for how long? How long will it be before Soosha decides that the time has come for her to murder Xynon as he is filling her with his life and replace his soul in her with that of Erlik's? A day? A moon's phase? A whole moon's passing? Four, five? A season? Do we have that long? Igrat saw Xynon with a knife, standing over Pentesh, you, me and Halfray – on Soosha's orders he is going to kill us before she takes his life. Injya, we must leave!'

He felt her body crumple at the truth of his words.

'Yes,' she said numbly, 'you are right.'

The hand gently stroking her hair comforted her a little, but it could not dispel the hundreds of thoughts crowding in on her, their vague plans of escaping when the tribe moved to the winter caves in an attempt to escape notice too obviously – gone. Her hope of reconciliation with Soosha dashed, her still cherished belief that somehow she could give an impassioned speech to the people of Skoonjay, telling them of her plans for the future, showing them that they had nothing to fear from either herself or Galdr – that with everyone working together a new realization of self-hood could come about; now, they too were thrown on to the rocks of improbability. Now, all that was left for them was a hurried departure, escaping into the night with the few trusted friends they had. Injya felt suddenly very small and very vulnerable.

A cry from outside the sancar, a twinge of pain in her breasts and the sancar was flooded with sunshine as Bendula, carrying an angry bundle of baby, crept hesitantly through the opening.

'I cannot keep her asleep any longer,' Bendula began as she looked wide-eyed at the tear-stained face of Injya and the gentle, surprised face of Galdr. 'She is hungry,' she concluded guiltily, handing the protesting child into the arms of her mother.

'I know, I know,' Injya crooned to Pentesh and Bendula. 'You have done well, Bendula, thank you for letting me sleep.'

Bendula stood, unsure of what was wanted of her, startled by Galdr's and Injya's soft, yet sorrowful looks.

'You can go now, cherished child,' Injya said softly as she began to nurse her own babe. 'One little and vulnerable soul comforting another, aren't we, Pentesh? Aren't we, Galdr?'

Bendula hesitated for a moment longer, then dashed out into the dazzling sunshine of the day.

Bendula left her perplexity behind her in the dark sancar and skipped over to the largest of the women's sancars. Lifting the entrance flap a little way, she could see many women clustered together. She knew that in the middle of that huddle Soosha would be having the final touches put to her gown. She wanted to slink into the sancar, but was afraid she would be spotted. Instead she ran to another sancar, looking for Sanset.

Life was very confusing, she decided – not for the first time – one moment Injya only had to hear Galdr's name and she would look terribly angry; now, here she was accepting comfort from him. And why had she been crying? Much was confusing about the grown-up world, women were married, against their will, only to seem happy the next moment because they had a child! She remembered her mother telling her about the time when women could choose to make a child happen, indeed,

284

there was a time when the women knew, absolutely, the sex that their unborn child was! But that knowing, like the belief that it was the moonbeams which impregnated them, had died when the true mystery of conception was understood. Sanset had said that it was that knowledge which had finally robbed women of their power. But that fact, like so many other of Sanset's and Injya's sayings, was incomprehensible to her.

Bendula stood in the middle of the encampment, a lithe, somewhat lanky child, scratching her head, shaking her long, thick plait against her back. She still had not found Sanset – perhaps, she too, was taking comfort from some man. She blushed as the thought entered her head and her wide-set brown eyes clouded momentarily – to imagine her mother with a man! In all of Bendula's eleven years, Sanset had known no man. The young warrior called Prenok who had been Bendula's father had been killed by a bear the year she was born and she knew that her mother had taken no man since – but, she mused as she scrambled inelegantly up to the copse which overlooked the summer-land encampment, with everyone being so silly and topsy-turvy – who could tell what the Goddess had in store for either her or her mother?

CHAPTER TWENTY-FIVE

Grimly, Galdr decided that normality, or what passed for it, had to be maintained at all cost. Galdr *had* to be by his father's side for the marriage, they *would* have to endure the marriage feast, nothing could be done, or said, to alert Soosha to their plans; yet so much still needed to be done and he feared that he had very little time left. It would not be long before Igrat's body was discovered – and who could tell what Soosha would make of that? Galdr left Injya's side with a hasty kiss, leaving her to nurse their child with a heavy heart. Injya seemed to have accepted his contrition, seemed to believe him and Halfray when they had spoken of all that had happened during their stay together in Askoye's cave, but she was still unresolved about their life together. He reminded himself that it was not surprising that she had mixed feelings for him – just because he knew he loved her with an all-consuming, overwhelming love, that was no guarantee that she should, or ever could, feel the same for him.

As he stepped outside and saw that the preparations were complete, noticed the five fires burning brightly, the men already settling themselves in a large ring around them, waiting for the entrance of Soosha, Galdr felt the expectancy of the people in the air. Soon Soosha would enter a marriage with Xynon and only he and those closest to him, knew that this coupling would bring about the ruination of his people! He had almost reached his sancar before the idea which had been lurking like an ache in the back of his head finally could no longer be ignored. He *had* to try!

Turning on his heels he marched over to the largest sancar, the sancar in which he knew his sister was waiting.

For a moment no-one noticed him as he slipped quietly in through the skin entrance, but when they did, a great squealing rose from the women. They may have put aside the practices of the Prental Council, but they still held to the belief that no man should see the maiden for marriage on the day of her marriage in case he tried to coerce her from her chosen partner. A beam from the sun can destroy the magic of the moon and though few would admit it, all believed that the marriage maiden was filled with this magic, just for that day, that she belonged to the Goddess of whom none dared speak.

Soosha hushed the women who were clustering round her, trying to hide her from Galdr's view.

'Galdr is Anfjord's son – if he wishes to see me, he may.'

The women fell silent and reluctantly sidled off to sit in the gloom by the sancar walls. Soon their chattering filled the air as Soosha stood, waiting for Galdr to speak. In the dark interior of the sancar he had difficulty in recognizing his sister from the huddle of women, but once they had moved he wondered how he could not have seen her immediately. Her black hair was braided high on her head, each braid interwoven with flowers so that she looked as if she had a tall conical crown; from this fell long garlands of tiny white flowers which cascaded over her shoulders and back, almost down to her knees. She was dressed in a gown of the palest saffron colour he had ever seen, which fell to the ground covering her feet. Around her waist was a slender belt of finely beaten copper, from which fell strands of golden flowers which rustled faintly as she walked very sedately over to him. That something so evil could come from one who looked so divine!

'So, my brother, you have come to wish me well with my marriage?'

Soosha's tone was soft, appealing and totally disconcerting. Flustered for a moment, Galdr was silent, but finally he regained his wits and whispered: 'Soosha – dearest sister – we must talk.'

A faint smile spread over Soosha's lips as she looked at him – yes, we must, she thought, but you would not tell me what I want to know.

'Galdr!' she said in mock astonishment, 'how serious you are – what could you possibly wish to talk about with me?'

She laughed a tinkling, false laugh, but stopped immediately as Galdr put his hand on her elbow.

'Not here – not in front of all these women, I must talk to you alone!'

For an instant she felt afraid, Galdr was looking so intently, so searchingly into her eyes that she felt he could see into her soul. She shivered slightly and tried to twist her arm away from his grasp, she had to break the physical contact between them, she knew that at that moment he was more powerful than she and she became more fearful the longer he held on to her. She was not afraid of his physical strength, but the strength of his purpose, the strength of his spirit, threatening to overcome her.

'We cannot be alone, Galdr, please!' she hissed through clenched teeth. 'You are hurting me!'

His eyes never left hers as he relinquished his grasp and his arm fell to his side.

'Soosha, I *know* what you are planning!'

The words were spoken so quietly that for a second she doubted her ears. Only Galdr's eyes proclaimed the truth. Shut them out! Shut them out! her mind ordered, but her eyelids did not obey the command, her eyes seemed held by his, by the power of his will.

'Soosha – it need not be like this. I was told that I had to heal the breach between us – I do not know what made it – I do not know how to reach you – but I *do* know what you are planning, and I have come to beseech you, do *not* continue on the path you have decided for yourself. Let me help you, let me guide you, please, Soosha!'

It was the word 'please' which was Galdr's undoing and Soosha's escape. His power faltered for the instant that it took to say the word and she was free from him.

'*Please*, brother mine – since when had Galdr ever said please? No, Galdr, I will do nothing to please you, not now or ever. You say you know of my plan – could you tell me what that "plan" is, pray? I *have* no plan save that of my marriage to Xynon – all else is fancy, Galdr, and you *know* it!' A sneering smile spread over her face as she looked at him, hatred no longer hidden. 'You must leave this sancar, Galdr, I am about to meet my husband!'

She stared defiantly at him for a moment and then turned to the women.

'He must go – must he not?' she asked the women in a singing, trilling voice as if nothing of import had passed between them.

'Yes!' they chorused.

'See, Galdr, even the son of Anfjord may not stay! Come, women, he is unwilling to leave his little sister, we will have to shoo him out!'

The women, thinking by her light tone that all that had passed had been good wishes between brother and sister rushed to her side, laughing and whooping. Galdr spoke softly to her above the noise of the clamouring women – few heard the words, fewer still understood their meaning: 'I have failed you, Soosha – forgive me.'

As he left the sancar he knew that Soosha would not understand the words and would not forgive him. He knew also that he had failed more than Soosha, but – he had tried. Everything now lay in the palm of the Goddess – She would forgive, She would understand.

Halfray, Torben, Eabran and Centill, son of Colnyek, sat huddled together in the sancar that Halfray shared with Galdr, their low voices stopping immediately Galdr entered.

'You must join the other men,' Galdr spoke with quiet authority which belied his thundering heart. 'We *all* must leave tonight!'

Only Halfray did not gasp with amazement, the others, open mouthed, began protesting. Not listening to their protestations Galdr spoke in low, unwavering tones.

'Halfray has told you what has happened, and what will happen. We cannot fight Soosha, nor turn her from her evil path. I have just come from her – she knows that *I* know of her plans. It is too dangerous for us to stay any longer. Go now, it is too suspicious for you to remain in this sancar, take your places among the men. During the marriage feast you will be able to steal back here and hide some skins and the weapons we will need. We will leave when the sky is darkest. Go! It is too dangerous for us to be seen together!'

Galdr turned to Halfray as the men rose and silently, one by one, left the sancar.

'Go to Injya, stay with her, tell Sanset to get the women ready. We must all leave separately – I will tell each one to leave when I feel it is safe, we will group on the other side of the copse. Halfray – tell Injya that I did what Askoye asked – but she would not listen. Go!'

Halfray looked at Galdr in stunned silence. Galdr looked back at him with clear eyes.

'All, now, is in the hands of the Goddess – I know we are right.'

Halfray and Injya sat with Bendula and Sanset on the slight rise which marked the beginning of the copse. Pentesh was sleeping peacefully, the sun, dappling through the fair leaves of the slender birch tree that served them as a back-rest and shade in the sunshine of midday, made dancing shadows on the child's untroubled face. Below them, in a great ring, sat all the men, they could just make out Galdr's figure sitting next to Anfjord, through the heat haze and the bright orange sparks of the ring of fires. The silence was as tangible as the heat as Soosha took her place in the centre of the ring. She looked magnificent, ethereal, the flowers of white and gold cascading down her slender form like sunlight glinting on golden water. She stood, completely motionless, facing away from the copse, looking in the direction of the sea. Even the crackling fires seemed stiller as she stood, unwavering, unmoving in the heat. Total silence. Not even bird-song greeted her.

Suddenly the five drums began their low beating and the men started chanting the name of Xynon. The chanted name grew in speed and intensity and in response, from far behind Halfray and Injya, there began a faint thudding sound. Without turning round, Halfray and Injya knew that Xynon was coming to Soosha, on horseback, from the depths of the copse. The leaves above their heads trembled slightly as, unseen, the rider moved slowly through the whispering trees. Suddenly, a little way to their left, he came into view, his back straight, his horse shining with heat. The horse walked slowly towards the lone figure, the circle of men moving almost imperceptibly to let horse and rider through.

Still Soosha looked towards the sea as Xynon rode towards her back. He stopped the animal when its muzzle was a hand's breadth away from her and dismounted. With great solemnity he walked up to her and putting both hands on her shoulders turned her round to him. Instantly, the drumming and calling stopped as in the silence Xynon's words rang out:

'I, Xynon, claim you, Soosha as mine!'

'I, Soosha, hear your claim and accept it as mine.'

'I give you my heart. I give you my thoughts. I give you my body, Soosha, my wife.'

Xynon grasped her hand in his, pulling her towards him slightly.

'I give you my heart. I give you my thoughts. I give you my body, Xynon, my husband.'

'I am yours!' they said together as they pulled each other closer. 'We are one!'

They embraced each other, kissing ardently as the women and children came running helter-skelter from the sancars, whooping with joy, throwing great handfuls of petals at the couple, entwining them with long garlands of flowers so that they were totally entangled with the fruits of the sun and earth. A loud roar from the men joined the rejoicing women and suddenly the whole encampment was alive with men and women embracing, running children being picked up willy-nilly, tossed in the air and kissed wildly as round and round the couple the people began their marriage dance; the men on the outer ring, stamping and strutting to the right like great reindeer stags, the women, on the inner ring, turning moon-wise, bowing almost double, sweeping the ground with their fallen hair as they gracefully swung their bent bodies in the manner of the accepting doe.

Injya and Halfray looked on silently – both too sickened by their hidden knowledge to feel part of the celebrations. No-one had seemed to notice their absence, for which they felt great relief, although they both knew that soon someone, probably Anfjord, would call them hence. They were now as silent as the crowd was noisy – there was nothing to say. Sanset had told the other women Galdr's instructions – whether they had the courage to carry them out was something no-one could foretell.

Injya felt nothing other than a half-hearted loathing for the sham before her eyes. It was as if she had been so numbed by Igrat's death, that nothing could touch her now. She had not felt surprise when Halfray had relayed Galdr's message to her – obviously he had tried to talk Soosha out of her plan and had failed – and she had no feeling, other than expectation, that this very evening she was to leave her people once again. Nothing mattered any more – in the past five days she had escaped death at the hand of Soosha, given birth to Pentesh, soul-walked *twice*

292

and had been instrumental in causing the death of one of her kinsmen; the fact that they were now to set off in the middle of the night, ill equipped and ill prepared to go no-one knew where, was almost inconsequential! Compared to birth and death, what was escape?

She tried to focus on the Goddess, tried to invoke the power of the hidden moon to give her some sustenance, but all she felt was tired. As the smell of the roasting reindeer meat and fish rose from the fires she knew that she should eat, should build up her strength for the journey, but the thought of taking one morsel of the feast of the marriage nauseated her. Finally she succumbed to tiredness as she allowed the warm sun to bathe her exhausted body and the comforting arm of her brother round her shoulders to lull her to sleep.

Halfray was pleased that she could rest. He, himself, felt curiously full of energy. As he watched the dancing, swirling people he had to keep reminding himself that this was no ordinary marriage feast. He caught himself wishing to be with the group of celebrating people. He had no doubts about leaving the encampment, he knew that his spirit-guide would help them, that they had nothing to fear but fear. As the shadows began to steal around the rings of people he saw Galdr move to Torben, clasp him round his shoulders as if sharing a secret and then the two men laugh heartily as if they had shared a great joke. No-one would have thought twice about the fact that Galdr then resumed his seat next to Anfjord and that Torben walked off to a sancar, still clutching his sides in apparent mirth. A few moments later Torben's head could just be seen in the reeds as he skirted round the encampment and then it vanished into the twilight. The move had begun.

Injya jumped awake, startling Pentesh from her sleep who cried angrily.

'Oh, Halfray – I fell asleep!'

Sleepily she rubbed her eyes and offered her breast to Pentesh who suckled half-heartedly for a few moments and then fell back into sleep. Wrapping her child in her carrying sling she asked: 'What has happened . . . look, the sky is getting darker . . . have any left yet?'

'I saw Torben leave a moment ago and – yes, look, Sanset is talking to Djyana – see, over by the horse svarge – yes, Djyana is going – see?'

Injya craned her neck and just caught sight of Djyana apparently innocently wandering off in the direction of the sand-dunes.

'She is going in the wrong direction!'

'Do not panic – she will circuit around – we cannot all go marching off to the copse without it looking a little odd, can we?'

Injya managed a little laugh. They both peered through the growing gloom for more signs of people leaving the encampment for a while, when suddenly Injya announced: 'Soosha's marriage or not – I am *starving*!' and rising, she walked down to the encampment fires, searching for food and Galdr. She had to find out herself what exactly he had said to Soosha but even more importantly, she *had* to eat. Halfray followed her, only stopping to notice a figure slide into the shadows of a sancar and then disappear into the dark violet of the night – another one free.

They found Galdr deep in conversation with Xynon who broke off as he caught sight of Injya.

'Injya! You might know – have you seen Igrat? I have been telling Galdr here – we had an argument yesterday, nothing important, but when I awoke this morning he was not there – tell me what your woman's intuition tells you of that!'

Xynon's jovial voice and slightly florid complexion told Injya instantly that he had drunk too much of the summer-land wine, but she tried to match his light tone as she answered.

'Why – he will be out in the dunes, tupping with a maiden because you have taken a wife – why, Xynon! I

294

am surprised at you! *I* do not know of his movements – perhaps he is looking for a Soosha for himself!'

She moved to Galdr's side as Xynon burst out laughing and clutched at Galdr's shoulder for support.

'Yes, yes,' he laughed, 'of course! Injya, you are right – silly man – silly man!'

Xynon burbled on for a few moments more, laughing at himself and the image Injya had woven of Igrat with a woman and then stumbled off in the general direction of Soosha, little noticing the flush of a liar on the face of Injya. She looked into Galdr's eyes, knowing that he was wondering the same thought – how long did Xynon have before that light tone, that quick smile would be extinguished? How long did any of them have? As she looked into Galdr's face, saw the pity and fear for Xynon, saw too the deep hurt he was feeling, she knew that she could fight with him no more. She turned to Halfray, who, as if he could read her thoughts, put one hand on her shoulder, the other on Galdr's. With his pale blue eyes beginning to fill with tears he said in a low voice: 'Injya, I love you and Galdr with all my heart. Come with us, if not for your own sake, then for the sake of your child, for me, for Galdr. Time *is* running out.'

She turned to Galdr who extended a hand towards her. In the dancing flames his eyes were ablaze with hope and love and as she gazed into them she felt her heart melt. Cautiously she placed her hand in his.

'Is love the only way?' she asked of him, her voice tiny and wavering.

'It is the only thing left, Injya.'

She tore her face away from his and looked at the throngs of people around the fires – some would love, some would know real love, but Soosha and Xynon? Would they murder that as they planned to murder her? She shook away the thoughts of terror – it was time to leave them behind – wherever they were going, whatever would befall them, fear and doubt had no part.

She was decided. In a low whisper she asked: 'How many of us have left?'

Injya's everyday, unemotional tone sang out to Galdr. The innocent question which meant – I have decided to trust you, to love you – made his heart feel as if it would burst with joy. Desperately trying to restrain himself from picking her up there and then and showering her with the kisses his heart willed, he replied as evenly as his thundering heart would allow.

'Toonjya is coming. She has taken little Potyami and Wa-Oagist to "watch for spirit-lights in the sky". Ullu, Aywe and Tyanka have gone off to the copse apparently looking for young men, and Torben went looking for more fish quite some time ago. Djyana went to quiet the horses and has not returned yet and Centill and Oanti went off to look at the sunset. You and Halfray must go next and then Sanset and Bendula. Djyana and I will bring the horses.'

'Horses? We cannot take horses – Galdr, what *are* you thinking of?'

'Beloved – if we do *not* take horses we will be found and brought back.'

Galdr could not control himself any longer – he put his arms around Injya and drew her close to him.

'Injya, my beloved, trust me – all will be well. Eabran has already secreted the most precious of our possessions under a shrub by the horse svarge and has led two horses away laden. I will bring as many as I can without being noticed – the rest I will free – it is the only way!'

'But . . .'

'There is no room for "buts", beloved. Go – feed yourself and Halfray and then slip away. I will be with you before you know it.'

He brushed her cheek gently with his fingertips and kissed the just visible head of his sleeping child. 'Halfray – make her eat and then take her away – time is running short.' Without another word he turned and walked back to the now prone figure of Anfjord.

Anfjord had watched the tender scene through drink-sodden eyes; Injya seemed to have developed a true liking for his son, more than she had done for him. For a moment his fuddled brain tried to work out how, when she had only known him for five days, they could have become so attached to each other, but it gave him no answers. Tired of the effort of thinking he called loudly for more wine, perhaps that would set his mind straight – and if it did not, he would sleep sounder and probably wake wiser. He tried to focus his eyes enough to pick out Soosha and Xynon in the crowds of people, but the red fire-light turned the pale sky black in relief and everyone seemed made up of grotesque masks of red, violet and black.

Later, when the stars twinkled high in the deep purple night sky Anfjord thought he saw two women and a child run into the copse together but he could not be sure. He asked the girl whose breast he was idly fondling if she had noticed them, but he could not remember what she said. Time passed and when he looked again some people had started slow, swirling dancing again, rings of people round the five rings of fire. As the whirling figures spun round in front of his dazed eyes he fancied that they had been joined by a long line of horses, but when he shook his head, the horses were no longer there. Only the red, purple and black dancing shadows.

Dark violet turned purple, then black, as overhead heavy rain clouds obliterated the faint twinkling stars. The hot air oppressed the gathered group into a whispering, tremulous huddle. Galdr and Djyana brought only six more horses. In the dense, sticky night the group fell silent as they approached. Galdr motioned towards Djyana who understood without words and gently led the wide-eyed horses to trees where she tethered them and stayed, patting their gentle muzzles, stroking their sweat-drenched flanks.

'Are all the water-sacks full?' were his first words to the expectant, frightened people. In answer Aywe pointed to the two horses that Eabran had brought with him, their backs laden with skin water-sacks.

'Fill your own pouches, drink what you need and drain the rest. We cannot carry water – there are too many of us.'

The stunned group looked around them – thirteen adults, Bendula who was almost fully grown, Potyami who was already four summers old and two babes in arms and only eight horses to carry them! Faces turned towards Galdr once more – they could not escape! Injya, sensing their fear, spoke out.

'We must do as Galdr says – we cannot waste horses for carrying water – no matter how precious it is!'

Solemnly the group did as they were bid and eventually, coupling smallest woman with largest man they mounted the patient horses.

It was the faithful willingness of the horses which momentarily stopped Injya in her business – the total trust they displayed – if only she could feel the same. Suddenly the enormity of their actions hit her and with the realization that they were leaving their world for ever, Askoye's words rang in her head: 'Always give thanks to the earth – never leave it in sorrow.'

She dismounted and faced the riders.

'We cannot go like this – if our way means anything – we have to stop and give thanks – yes, Centill' – she looked at his astonished, eager-to-be-off, face – 'yes, thanks even for the hardships and cruelties – all of them have brought us to here and all of them must be left here – to take them with us would mean we are taking the old with us, which will, in time, taint the new.'

'Injya—' Galdr began, but was silenced by her determined look.

'Now, all of us, take a look at the copse, the trees, the leaves, the good ground. Surround all you see in light. Trust that our light will safeguard those who walk here. Do not leave this place with sorrow.'

She raised her arms to the black sky, turned her face towards the threatening clouds and then back to the people who stood silently before her.

'Beloved Goddess, I leave this place with love. I leave this place with trust. Cleanse this earth of our sorrow and doubt. I give it back to you as if untouched by my fear, sorrow and anger. Beloved Hoola, Mother of the Earth – take away all evil from this place, release it from darkness and let us go free into your good world.'

For a moment there was total stillness as if the earth had breathed in the words and was contemplating them; neither human nor animal moved when suddenly a great streak of lightning ripped the sky in two and a deafening thunderclap broke into the peoples' ears, shattering the stillness and the earnest prayer. The horses reared in fright and in the milling, churning panic they heard on the thunder-laden air a voice scream out: 'Xynon! Xynon! I have found Igrat!'

As clearly as the lightning had torn through the sky they heard the words they all feared. In panic they galloped away from the copse, away from the voice. As the first hot, heavy drops of rain fell upon the people, each knew that now they would need all the power the Goddess could give to aid their escape.

CHAPTER TWENTY-SIX

Soosha had managed to watch Galdr's every move throughout that long, hot day. It was as if she were two people; the Soosha who was married to Xynon, the Soosha resplendent in gold and white who willingly gave herself to her chosen man; and Soosha the Watcher, Soosha the secret-searcher. Galdr had frightened her. If what he had said was true – somehow he had found out her innermost thoughts and desires. Now, even more than before, she *had* to find out the secret of his power. She had watched him closely – he behaved as he always behaved – on the outside he seemed unchanged – he drank much of the summer-land wine – he petted maidens as they passed, he ate heartily and he seemed never to leave Anfjord's side, keeping him constantly amused. But the light behind his eyes was not the light of the old Galdr, he had the look of a man sure and strong, full of something which she could not fathom. She, too, had noticed the gentle scene between him and Injya and although her head was telling her that it was all fancy, she knew that the secret to his strength was linked to Injya, and, to a lesser extent, Halfray. If only she could find out what it was!

Soosha, the maiden for marriage, was joysome and light. Laughingly she had accepted the flowers and the gifts, the songs and the dances in her honour. As the flames of the five fires died down, the flame of desire grew in her, quieting Soosha the Watcher until the mantle of Soosha the Watcher fell from her as easily as her marriage gown fell from her body in the dark hush of their marriage sancar.

Xynon had stared at her naked body in the light of the solitary taper, suddenly unsure. He swayed slightly and shook his head – how he wished he had not drunk the wine. Soosha touched his head, cupped it in her hands and brought his face close to hers. He could feel her sweet breath upon his cheeks as her lips closed over his and his head began to clear. Soon she was holding him, her arms enfolding him as they fell upon the furs of the bed. Again the hands were holding his head as she drew her body upwards and he found her secret place with his mouth. He felt as if he could stay there, hidden from the world, safe in her womanhood forever, when again the hands searched for him, bringing his body upon hers, thrusting her moist darkness towards his manhood.

The moments were exquisite, each time he strove deeper and deeper inside her body he felt as if any moment they would fuse together and become one being in the heat and the passion of the moment. A thunderclap rang out, the heavens were with them too – their passion was crashing round the very clouds – and then the voice – the scream – the words: 'Xynon, Xynon, I have found Igrat!'

The pounding urgency in his loins stopped. Only the pounding of fear grew in his heart. Igrat. Soosha, still gripped by passion would not release her hold. She clawed at his back, moaning and writhing: 'Xynon! Xynon! Beloved!'

But the beloved had fallen to fear. Xynon stared at his wife: her sweat-drenched hair and breasts, her bruised lips still desperately seeking his, then he felt her body suddenly go limp as she realized that he was incapable of continuing. With eyes still closed she had said in an icy tone: 'So, Igrat's return robs Soosha of her husband!'

Xynon stared at her impassive face, not believing her contempt of him.

'I have to see, I *have* to, Soosha!'

In silence he withdrew his shrunken sex from her and rose swiftly. Through closed lids Soosha watched the shadow of his form cross the sancar and stoop low

301

through the flap. So, she thought to herself, the stories are true, Xynon has more than one love.

She dressed carefully, trying to smooth away her unfulfilled desires with the folds of the gown. Outside she heard urgent voices and quickly she joined the young girl and man who had brought the news to Xynon. The girl was weeping, her damp, mud-stained clothes clinging to her as she clung to her man. He, for his part, was looking at Xynon, horror writ upon his face. They fell silent as Soosha came out of the sancar. Rain began to fall as Soosha saw people coming towards them, running to hear the news.

'Get inside – both of you!'

Holding the entrance flap open she spoke to the advancing people: 'Go back to your sancars – the night is not fit for news!' A howl of anguish came from inside the sancar, making the people hesitate.

'Go!' she shouted, 'I will tell you all – soon – GO!'

In a swirl of skins she swept back inside the sancar, leaving the open-mouthed people behind her to run back through the torrential rain, their curiosity as unsatisfied as her passion.

Xynon was lying on the furs, huddled up in a ball like a baby, crying and rocking himself. The young couple now looked up at her, unsure of what to do, or say.

'Tell me' – she ordered sternly – 'Quickly and quietly – I have a grieving husband I must attend to!' They told her what they had found, how they had wandered off far into the marshes, until they had found somewhere which they felt was right for them.

'Go on, go on, I am not interested in your sordid embarrassment – what did you find?' With his head bowed low, the man continued, stumbling over his words until the story was told.

'So!' Soosha said at last, 'Igrat is dead – and not by his own hand – covered with moss and earth – buried. Tell no-one – go to Galdr's sancar and bring him here – tell no-one until sunrise – go!'

The couple hastily left the sancar, glad to escape the searching eyes of Soosha and the keening Xynon. Soosha turned her attention to Xynon – what a fool she had been to think that a man who cries like a child could be for her! Roughly she shook him by the shoulder.

'Xynon – you have to stop crying – tears will not bring Igrat back – we have to find out who did this. Xynon!'

Xynon took no heed of her hand upon his shoulder, took no notice of her harsh words – he knew what had happened, he knew that Igrat could not bear to see him lose himself with Soosha, he knew that as surely as if he had done it with his own hands, he had killed Igrat. The entrance flap opened again as the man returned.

'Soosha – his sancar is empty – neither Galdr nor Halfray are there.'

'Go to Injya's sancar.' The man hesitated, eyes wide, staring at the sobbing Xynon. 'Now!'

Instantly the man left and Soosha stood up – not wanting to hear the news, thoughts in turmoil – she paced the sancar. A few moments later the man was back. He stood dripping in front of her, head bowed.

'Injya's sancar is empty, Soosha,' he said quietly. 'Neither Injya, the baby or Sanset and Bendula are there. They have gone.'

The words ran through her mind like rivulets of water which were running down the nape of the man's neck. As the droplets formed a small patch of water on the floor, her thoughts formed themselves into action.

'You have done well, Vronjyi.'

The man looked up at her, his dark eyes framed by black wet lashes, his supple, slender body glistening with the rain.

'We must raise the alarm – now go to my father – he will know what to do.'

Vronjyi backed out of the sancar and she heard him shouting outside as he ran to Anfjord's sancar: 'Awake! Awake! Igrat has been murdered!'

Quickly Soosha took her hooded cape and wrapped herself in it. As the noise outside grew she spoke harshly to Xynon.

'Get up, put on your clothes and take this.' She handed him a small dagger, 'Your beloved Igrat has been murdered by Injya and Galdr – take it!' She shook the dagger in front of his face: 'We have to find them and bring them back – Galdr has done this to harm us – we *must* bring him back!'

As if in a dream Xynon slowly got up off the bed and looked at her – all he could think of was Igrat, lying naked, covered in mud by some wretched stream. Hot tears sprang to his eyes once more as he looked at the dagger. Galdr and Injya would not have killed him – he had. Slowly he shook his head at her.

'No, Soosha, you are wrong. But I will dress. Galdr and Injya *should* be found if only to clear their names – we will organize the hunters but I will not be one of them.'

Knowing that it was useless to argue with him, she left him to dress in darkness as she took the taper from the sancar and went outside.

People were darting to and from the sancars, their flickering tapers hissing and spluttering in the rain. Smoke billowed from the embers of the fires and all around her the scene of confusion and panic grew. A breathless Vronjyi caught up with her as she made her way to Anfjord's sancar.

'I cannot rouse him, Soosha – he is deeply asleep!'

She stared at him for a moment, as if she could not understand the panting rain-sodden man, then continued towards the sancar again, Xynon trailing behind her, stumbling in the rain and the blackness. It was as Vronjyi had said: Anfjord, flanked by two frightened women, snored on loudly, oblivious of all.

'Get back to your sancar!' she ordered the two girls as she swept outside again. 'Xynon – organize the men!' Xynon looked at her blankly. She clicked her tongue in annoyance

304

and turned to Vronjyi: 'Vronjyi – fetch the horses here. Xynon – *call the men*!'

Xynon still looked uncomprehending.

'Ach!' she uttered in frustrated rage: 'Vronjyi – *you* call the men here – Xynon, can you go to the horses, or do I have to do that too?'

Without answering, Xynon walked off in the direction of the horse svarge.

Within a few moments fifty men stood in front of her, their hissing tapers smoking, their dark, worried faces strained and anxious.

'I want six of the best hunters we have. Galdr and Injya have murdered Igrat – they must be found and brought back. Who will go?' A clamour arose, hands thrust into the air, suddenly the air was filled with purpose. 'We must act quickly – they cannot be far away – I want only the fleetest, quickest hunters – Vronjyi – you know the men – choose only the best – I want Galdr back!' She turned from the crowd and saw Xynon bringing one horse only towards them.

'The horses, Xynon, the horses!' she shouted at him.

'They have gone, Soosha – only this remains!' He led the horse right up to her – it had been the horse upon which he had rode to his marriage.

'The horses have gone,' he repeated dully to the silenced crowd. 'All gone.'

For a moment Soosha was stunned into silence and even caught herself wishing that Crenjal was standing by her side – he would have known what to do! Instead she was faced with a pale, frightened Xynon and an unsure Vronjyi. How long must they delay in their search? Hopeful of an answer, she looked at the sky. The near-full moon was hidden by the purple-black clouds, but the sudden glimpse of silver showed that they were being moved by a wind from the sea – slowly, but they *were* moving eastwards, soon it would be dawn, then daylight. By day they could round up the horses – they would not have strayed far. Heartened by the scudding clouds, she turned to the crowd and said: 'There is nothing more we can do tonight – find out if anyone else apart from the snakes, Sanset and Bendula, have gone with them. As soon as it is light, we will round up the horses – they will not have gone far. At first light we will go!'

A low mumble of assent rose from the sodden men who, hunched against the rain and the night, trouped back to their various sancars. Soosha watched them go with mounting contempt and anger – would these cowed men ever turn into brave warriors? Oblivious to the rain which, although less ferocious now, was still blustering down in great sheets, Soosha stormed back to her sancar, her anger burning inside her, keeping the cold rain at bay. She was shaking, not with cold, but with pure rage. How dare Galdr thwart her! And why would he kill Igrat? She swept into the sancar, nearly tearing the skin entrance flap clean off, seething with fury.

Throwing herself on to the bed, she kicked viciously at the crumpled wedding gown still lying where she had abandoned it, now all smeared with green from the crushed, wilting flowers. Hate exuded from her every pore, soiling her skin and her soul. She hated Galdr, Injya, her father, Sanset and her brat, but more than these she hated Xynon. How could she have been so blind as to think that he could be of any use to her whatsoever? With head buried in folded arms, she angrily kicked away the last shreds of her wedding gown which still clung to her heels.

What had made her so blind? What was it that made her not heed the talk, the whispers, the smiled innuendoes about Xynon and that fat idiot, Igrat? She must have been dreaming, caught up in a fantasy world which had blinded her. She relived all that had happened since she had first formulated her plan and with a feeling akin to sickness she realized that her rage was born not of hatred but from love. She had somehow allowed herself to feel for Xynon something she had never felt for any person before

– and that feeling had produced a dream; a dream which had stopped her seeing him clearly. She had produced the dream state of love out of wanting it to be true. Her heart lurched as she realized that her anger was not about being thwarted in her plans, but about feeling rejected by Xynon. Her rage grew in her, gnawing at her innards and gripping her throat. Rage against the dream state of love, rage against the dream dying, rage against the dream which now was shattered into a thousand pieces.

But the rage would not let her cry. In the midst of her inner turmoil, Soosha the Watcher returned. She lay, perfectly still, feeling the tension in her shoulders and back, mindful of her clenched fists and teeth, not changing them, just watching the emotions ride over her as if she were a rock being washed by an angry tide. She remembered the last time she had felt this angry. Then, she *had* been the rock washed by the turbulent sea. She had sat on the rock and from her anger had come her strength, which ultimately led her to harnessing the power of Erlik. It was Erlik who was her true power, not love of Xynon. She steeled herself further, made her body harder. 'Like a rock!' she thought, 'I shall be like a rock and this is how I shall be for ever – *this* is the real me!'

She did not hear Xynon as he crept into the sancar. Suddenly she was jolted by him sitting heavily on the bed beside her. She watched her reactions: more tension in her calves, a tightening in her stomach, no more. He touched the small of her back. Shock waves rippled up and down her spine. His hand moved firmly up to her neck, then back down again to the base of her spine. Pin-pricks of sensation, nothing more. His hand moved once more, coming to rest on her waist – the touch of a mother to a child – the touch of a father to a daughter. As the palm rested, warm and assuring, in the curve of her back, Soosha the Watcher suddenly disintegrated, as her dreams of love had done, into a thousand tears of sorrow.

Xynon stole from the sancar as quietly as he had entered. He had stayed while Soosha's rattling sobs had heaved their way out of her heart, feeling strangely distanced by the spectacle, relieved almost that she was capable of tears. Eventually the racking sobs had changed and she had allowed him to cradle her in his arms; slowly they too had ended and exhausted she had fallen asleep. Gently he had disentangled himself and had laid her down on the bed, covered her with a skin, like a mother would a child, stroking her tear-drenched hair and cheeks and leaving her with an anxious backward glance.

Outside, a light grey drizzle fell from a light grey sky. To the east the black clouds hid the rising sun from view and in the yellowish dawn, shadows of men moved. In front of him he could see two women, struggling with armfuls of wood as they set about starting the first fire of the day. Soon, he knew, the whole encampment would be alive with people, but at this moment all was hushed and muted, as if the soft rain was wrapping everything in a miasma of uncertainty.

Frail. The word kept resounding around his head. A word that never before had he connected with Soosha. That Soosha could ever be described as frail was as ridiculous as describing the sun as ice. But the word would not leave him. She *was* frail – as fragile as birch leaves in autumn – as fragile as Igrat had been, despite his size and slow, lumbering ways. He walked carefully through the puddles to one of the men's sancars, pausing only to register their muffled and concerned voices. They fell instantly silent as he entered; dark faces upturned towards him, cold looks and distrust.

'It is light – we can round up the horses now.' Not a soul moved. All sat, staring at him, waiting for something more. He gave them nothing. Eventually he said, scarce keeping the contempt from his voice: 'Do I have to find them all myself?'

Slowly, one by one, the men got up and shambled outside. The drizzle had nearly stopped and the sickly yellow had turned grey-white. As Xynon was directing the men towards the sea, other men came from their sancar led by Vronjyi, and gradually more men emerged from sancars they were sharing with women. Almost silently they formed themselves into a wide circle and moved out from the encampment. When the last man had gone, Xynon went to the horse svarge, mounted his horse and rode off in the direction Vronjyi and Kanshay had indicated – he would say his farewells to the body of Igrat in solitude.

Soosha had been right. Long before the sun reached its full power the men had found and secured fourteen horses, ten were still missing, presumed all gone with Galdr. Even with the brilliant sun shining from a clear wind-swept sky, no-one dared wake Soosha or Anfjord – to lose almost half of their stock of horses was a catastrophe, the news of which no-one wanted to break. All the people who had left with Injya were now accounted for and long discussions entered into about why, who, how and where. Rumours spread like scrub fires – the women had all been spell-bound by Injya's Goddess-inspired magic, the men forced into submission by Galdr – the horses had all magically grown wings and flown away. Some said that the avenging spirits of Vingyar or Crenjal had simply wiped them all out and that sooner or later their grisly remains would be found, frozen into the tundra, on some wind-swept hillside.

Only Vronjyi seemed untouched by their scaremongering; even Kanshay, whom he loved for her clear single-mindedness, had been infected by the wild talk. But *she* had not been the one to see the face of Igrat as he had done. He knew, as he looked into the waxy, luminous face, that it was not the face of someone who died in fear. Igrat's face was clear and serene, his face was at peace. And as clearly as he knew that Igrat, whatever the manner of his death had been, had somehow connived in it and was happy

309

with it, he knew too, that all the wild speculation was the outward manifestation of a deeper fear that everyone felt. It was as if, without the figures of Injya and Galdr to bear the brunt of Anfjord's wrath or love, the people were now mindful that their places would have to be filled by someone. Vronjyi shook his head as if to shake away the thoughts which gnawed at him. Now that the people had all been told that Injya and Galdr had murdered Igrat, he would be surrounded by men held in the grip of revenge, men who would take unnecessary risks. This would be no ordinary hunting party, it would be a party of hate.

Still shaking his head he left the group he had been listening to and walked quickly towards Soosha's sancar. He wanted no part of the search party, of that he was clear; what Soosha now chose to do was up to her, but he would have no part in it. Standing in front of the entrance flap he quietly called her name. There was no response. Unsure of how to proceed he turned and looked at the crowd of people he had just left. They were silent now, looking at him expectantly. A woman raised her hand and flicked it in the direction of the sancar, as if shooing him inside. 'Bai Ulgan!' he muttered to himself, 'I have put myself in the position of spokesman! What a fool!' There was no going back. Frowning, he turned from the crowd, coughed loudly and entered the sancar.

Soosha was not sleeping as he had imagined her to be, but was sitting naked, cross-legged on her bed. Her staring eyes did not flicker at his entrance, neither did her body move. Stumbling in the sudden darkness of the interior, Vronjyi hesitated and stared at the motionless figure. Taking a step backwards he averted his eyes and confusion robbed him of his words.

'Yes?' Soosha's voice seemed far away, as if not coming from her body. 'You have come to tell me that you have the horses and that you do not wish to be a member of the search party – yes?'

310

How does she know who she's talking to? Vronjyi's confused mind reeled – she had not moved, has not looked at me – it is as if she knows all the answers anyway!

'I . . . ' he stammered out at length and then stopped, overcome with embarrassment, confusion and anxiety.

'Vronjyi,' the impassive figure spoke again, 'you, among all of our men, are the only one who can lead this party. You, among all our people, are the most skilled hunter and knowing scout. I have been told, I have been instructed, to tell you that what you will be doing is the wish of one who is greater than you, or I, or even Anfjord himself. Come here!'

At the final words her head moved slowly round, her eyes blazing out at him, compelling him to move. Robbed of words, free will and thoughts, he stumbled forward to stand, eyes downcast, as awkwardly as a naughty child, confronted by a wrathful mother. When she next spoke, Soosha's voice had lost the faraway sound, but something in the tone which she used chilled him to his very core.

'Vronjyi, do you believe in the power of good?'

He let his eyes rise for a moment, taking in her long, naked body and finally coming to rest in her deep, unfathomable eyes.

'Yes.' The answer was scarcely audible as fear clutched at his voice.

'And, if you believe in the power of good, you must also believe in the power of evil – yes?'

Vronjyi could do no more than nod his head. He heard the soft furs moving, the swish of cloth and suddenly Soosha was standing before him, a cloak wrapped round her body, her eyes blazing into his.

'I have just had a dream, Vronjyi, a dream which showed me my brother, my own brother, stealing the spirit of Igrat. He did this as he killed him. He caught his spirit in his hands and swallowed it. I tell you, Vronjyi – the power of evil is very strong – if we do not find Galdr and Injya – all of us are in the gravest danger. Do you understand what I

311

am saying? If Galdr can steal the spirit of one he has just slain, then he is stronger by that spirit. Soon, they will all come, they will all want to take our spirits for themselves. They will try to steal our spirits while we sleep, and if they cannot do that, they will bring sickness and death to our people instead. Vronjyi, we are fighting the very power of Erlik himself – they *must* be found – and only you are strong enough to find them!'

Soosha stopped speaking, the silence falling between them as deep and profound as the words she had just said. To his disgust, he found himself trembling as if cold, shaking not from fear but from the very nearness of her physical presence.

'You are trembling with the light, Vronjyi,' she whispered, 'you are shaking with divine power – use it, Vronjyi – take the men, lead them, find Galdr and Injya and bring them back here – it is the only way we will ever be safe – believe me!'

Vronjyi was not aware of leaving Soosha, it seemed to him that one moment he was with her, the next he was standing in the sunshine, facing a mass of expectant faces. Stunned for a moment, he looked blankly at the people in front of him. If what Soosha had said was true – they were, all, in the most terrible danger. Suddenly a hand touched his shoulder and a thrill of fear trembled through his body. Soosha stood behind him.

'Go to Anfjord – tell him all,' she whispered, 'I will talk to the people.'

He staggered forward, the crowd parting silently to let him pass, his thoughts in turmoil, his heart pounding. As he walked blindly towards Anfjord's sancar, he could hear Soosha's voice ring out and the fearful gasps of the people as she told them what she had just told him. As he reached the sancar entrance, he heard children begin to cry with fear and mothers, afraid themselves, making feeble attempts to quiet them as Soosha's voice rose.

'They are filled with the power of Erlik!' he heard her shout at the people. 'They will come in the night and steal the souls of your children, they will rob you of your life-force while you sleep, believe me, once they have found the power of taking another's spirit, they will want more!'

The crowd broke into a spontaneous roar and the women started weeping with the children. It was too late to go back now – it had to be him to tell Anfjord that once more, his son was an outcast.

CHAPTER TWENTY-SEVEN

The horses had already been loaded, the men already fed, the outcry already died down into a simmering, scarce-spoken fear, when Xynon returned to the encampment. The shadows had only just begun to lengthen when he was seen, walking his horse, coming to the encampment from the direction of the marshes. For a second time that day a crowd had parted in silence to let another through. They stared dumbfounded at the dull-eyed Xynon, the wet-flanked horse and the crudely covered bundle strapped on its back. And for a second time that day they dispersed silently as Xynon walked with his horse and its gruesome cargo through the encampment and up the rise to where, far above the smoking fires and the safety of the encampment, the death stones lay. No-one turned to watch as he struggled to take the body of his friend from the beast's back and none offered to give him help. It was as if, overwhelmed by the events of the day, none had the heart left for this last effort of will.

But Soosha watched. Soosha, standing with a broken Anfjord, supporting him as she had done since his raging tears, had reduced him to little more than a babe; she watched. She saw the first bird circle in the air, long before she heard the sickening crack of Igrat's skull being cleaved in two. Soosha the Watcher saw the tattered, dusty-winged raven circling high over the death stones, almost before Xynon had reached them. And she watched, with a dead-eyed smile, as it circled twice after the skull had been broken and then flew away, cawing loudly; giving way in the sky to the bare-necked birds of death who suddenly darkened the sky above the death stones as they silently glided round, waiting for Xynon to leave his beloved to their cruel beaks.

'The men' – Anfjord's croaking voice rasped in the silence – 'I must see the men!'

Together they turned away from the sight and towards the horse svarge, where, out of deference for the moment, the men were standing silently holding the muzzles of their horses. 'You must bring him back,' Anfjord managed to say before the tears claimed his voice once more. Soosha smiled at the six young men before her: Vronjyi had done well, they were all strong, capable hunters. They would find what they were looking for.

'Take care, Vronjyi, and return soon to us – we will all pray to Bai Ulgan for your success – will we not, Father?'

Anfjord nodded his greying head slowly, his eyes full of tears. Of course he wished them success, but their success meant Galdr's downfall. He felt that his heart would break with the pain – to find a wife, to lose a wife – to find a son, to lose a son – all for what? Suddenly a thought flashed into his mind, so simple in itself that he wondered he had never seen it before. It was Injya – it was all Injya's fault! Ever since she had returned, life had been terrible – first Crenjal, then him, now his son, had fallen under her spell. Galdr was innocent, Galdr had nothing to do with the death of Igrat – of course not, it was Injya! Injya was to blame!

'Men!' he suddenly shouted, 'bring back my son to me – never mind all the rest – kill them if you like – but bring Galdr back to me. Soosha has got it wrong, it was only a dream! It was *Injya* who stole Igrat's soul, Injya, not Galdr. All along she has brought trouble in her wake – look what Crenjal did to himself under her spell – even I, Anfjord, strongest chief of the Branfjord people, even I fell under her spell. She is the one with the power of Erlik in her! What fools we have been – she was telling the truth when she said that she was not practising the ways of the Goddess – she was not, she was practising the ways of one more evil than the Goddess – she has the power of Erlik in her heart – she *is* Erlik in form of a woman! Go, my men, kill her and all her women. Kill all the men too, but bring back my son. Galdr is innocent!'

He looked at the amazed men. 'Well, what are you waiting for? I have spoken – go – and bring my son back unharmed to me. I need him here!' Without a backward glance he turned smartly on his heels and strutted back to his sancar.

Soosha watched him go, seeing the man who, only a short while ago, seemed broken and cowed, and she vowed silently to herself that before winter sent her chill winds upon her people, Anfjord too would follow in the footsteps of his beloved son to exile and certain death.

Halfray became increasingly alarmed. It seemed as if the dawn would never come. When it did, it did nothing to allay his fears. A quick glimpse of putrid yellow and then more blackness, as the rain obliterated the sun. The party which had set off at a mud-spattering gallop now were reduced to a plodding pace as they slowly walked towards the sun, the horses shivering with cold and steaming in the rain. In a brief, glorious moment of light, he could see a vast expanse of earth laying before them like a gently undulating sea of brilliant greens and purples, but then the vision passed as once more the clouds and torrential rain obliterated the vista.

The party stopped in a thin copse of lank-looking willow trees which afforded them little or no shelter. Afraid of showing their position, they did not make a fire and remounted their horses still as sodden as before, after a desultory meal of cold meat and berries. The rain continued unabated as they galloped, then trotted, then once more walked onwards, the howling wind distorting what few words they uttered, until speech was reduced to shouted warnings. Night fell upon the riders who found themselves in a vast marshy plain which was devoid of any shelter. Drenched to the skin, cold and exhausted, they could do no more than cover themselves with damp skins and furs and huddling together for warmth, fall into dream-riven sleep from which none woke refreshed save the lusty Wa-Oagist and a clear-eyed, wide-awake Pentesh.

The rain was as unrelenting on the second day. It was as if the elements were mirroring the group's own determination and had decided to stay as unmoving and solid as Injya's resolve. When the sun should have been shining at its peak, they came upon a solid black wall of forest. It took them till the near-full moon came to walk through. With the forest behind them Galdr felt safe enough to light a fire. It was the first warmth, the first chance they had had of getting dry, for two days and nights of unremitting rain. He had hoped that the fire would warm the spirit of his horse-mate, Tyanka, who had been shivering constantly ever since they had first set off, but the chill only seemed to grow worse, the heat only increasing her feverish ague. Injya gave her some of the precious essence of ento which sent the girl into a deep sleep, but which did nothing to abate the shaking. As the lightening purple heralded the dawning of another rain-lashed day, Tyanka continued her shivering, coughing journey, unable at times even to hold on to consciousness.

Centill was at the head of the thin line of horses when he heard the sound which he had only ever been told about, the sound which marked the end of the earth for the Branfjord people. With a motion of his arm, he halted the group, straining forward on his horse to catch the noise again. Unmistakable. The sound of thundering water. They had come to the great river, the river which they called Pchektora – river of boundless pchekts. As if unable to compete with the rushing waters, the rain stopped and as they zig-zagged across the marsh which brought them ever closer to the sound, he knew that each of them had the same fear, the same terror. They were going to cross the boundary between one known world and another – the land of mountains, bears and beasts twice the size of the biggest reindeers – the land where the white tears of winter could take away the land in a trice – the land beyond the known.

As if waiting for this moment, the sun made a molten-red explosion of colour behind them, then sank from view. In front of them ran the river, swift running, more than a hundred pchekts wide. On the other side, a steep wall of rock and beyond, mountains. As they drew nearer, the mountains disappeared from view, hidden by the rock face. It was as if the river did indeed cut the world in two. On the side which the party, now dismounted and looking in astonishment, were standing, the earth was marshy, flat, green-brown with lichens, mosses and delicate-headed flowers adding rare colour; on the other side, where the river turned, it had cut into the bare rock, eating away at the russett coloured stone, creating overhanging ledges atop of which brackens and bright green ferns dripped deliriously. The rock face rose ten, perhaps fifteen pchekts high and as the darkness of the half-night drew on, they felt darkness descend on their spirits. To cross such a river – to scale such a face!

The sound of the torrential water was deafening as the rain-swollen river rushed violently over its rock-strewn bed, seeking its release into the ice-cold waters of the frozen lands to the north. Shaking his head in wonderment and in a vain effort to rid himself of the thunderous noise, Galdr shouted: 'We must find a place to rest for the night – tomorrow we can find somewhere to cross the river!'

Leading his horse by its halter he turned away from the river, walking slowly southwards, the long train of people and horses following his footsteps silently. But his brave words had a hollow ring to him, it would be impossible to cross the river. In the dim violet light he scoured the ground for an answer – perhaps further up-stream it would be less hazardous, perhaps they could make umiaks to carry their furs and themselves across, while the horses could swim. But the booming sound in his ears seemed not to decrease, seemed only to menace and crush his hopes. Perhaps his father had been right – perhaps there was no land of giant trees and soft yellow metal. A cry from Halfray pierced the thundering roaring of the river: 'Here! Come, see this! Here!'

Halfray and Ullu had led their horse in a wide arc from the main group and were now quite some distance to the right of Galdr. Even in the gloom, Galdr could see excitement shining on Ullu's open face as she jumped up and down, waving to the others to join her. He thought about mounting again, but Tyanka was, for once, looking as if she were sitting comfortably on the beast's back, so he shouted up to her: 'I am going to run over – here, take the bridle.'

With hope rising in him for the first time that day, he ran towards them but suddenly stopped dead as he saw Halfray disappear into the ground before his eyes. Panic took the place of hope as he dashed through the muddy marsh to where Ullu was standing, gently patting her horse's muzzle and whispering to him.

'What the . . . ?'

'It is some sort of chamber, cut into the earth, see – there are steps down!'

Ullu was standing above a square hole which had been lined with red stones, the same stones as the cliff-face. In the gloom he could just make out dark steps leading into the earth. Dropping on to his knees he stared into the hole. Halfray's echoing voice floated up to him from the depths.

'From what I can feel, it is all made of rock – even – yes, even the roof. It is low, I am bending quite low – ouch! There is a ledge made of rock too. I am coming up – it is huge – huge down here!'

The fire seemed even more reluctant than the previous day's to get going, but eventually they had it lit. One by one they all descended into the chamber with tapers and each came out with the same startled eyes. It was, as

Halfray had said, a huge, stone-walled chamber, easily nine pchekts long by three wide. Along one side ran a low ledge, and along the other side niches had been carved out of the rock face. Each of these niches contained the skull of a bear. The wall opposite the opening was covered in black charcoal drawings, showing stick-like men with spears killing bears and what looked like enormous bulls with very long noses, huge ears and enormous tusks. Even more startling than this was the fact that the chamber had not been roughly hewn out of the earth, but had been made up of blocks of stone resting, one upon the other, the roof containing gigantic slabs supported by the walls. This was no accident of nature – this was a man-made room – for what purpose, they could only guess at.

It was Tyanka who finally ended the argument about whether or not they should shelter in the chamber by managing to stutter: 'I am sure that if I once get dry and warm, I will be well again – please, Galdr, even if you all decide not to rest in it, please let me – I shall die if I sleep another night on wet furs!'

As if to add weight to her plea, the rain started again.

'That settles it!' Injya said, 'We shelter inside.'

Stoically the hobbled horses looked on as their masters descended from view into the earth. Flicking their hides and sending plumes of breath into the night, they stood round the opening, ears pricking at the unearthly sounds, eyes blinking slowly in the gloom until one by one they gracefully allowed themselves to lie down and sleep, confused, but as accepting as ever.

'But, why is it not wet?'

Thirteen pairs of eyes instantly looked at the stone-clad floor. There were no gaps in between the slabs.

'And why,' Centill continued, 'is the room not filling with smoke from the tapers?'

Potyami joined in the guessing game and fourteen pairs of eyes now looked up at the roof. There seemed to be no gaps there either.

'And why does it not smell?' Djyana ventured. In answer Oanti pointed to a taper they had pushed into one of the niches. The flame was wafting, gently, but definitely wafting in the direction of the wall with the drawings on it – as were, they suddenly realized, the flames of all the tapers. But close examination of the other far wall showed no visible cracks either.

'The wind must come from the entrance.'

'But there is no draught from the entrance at all!' Oanti insisted – outside the entrance had been banked all round with earth to stop such an occurrence.

'Somehow it reminds me of our cave, Galdr – does it you?'

Galdr shook his head in answer to Halfray's question – it felt quite different to him. Although it was clean and sweet-smelling, there was something disquieting about it, something indefinable and intangible, but there *was* something present in the very stones themselves which made him uneasy. Injya too was shaking her head, but she was not shaking it over a vague feeling of unease, she was shaking it to try to clear her head – she had a faraway memory of something Askoye had once said about her own people, but, like Galdr, she could not quite grasp it – something in the chamber itself was stopping the memory from freeing itself.

Eventually, the questions became fewer, the chat slowly dying down as one by one the people found themselves somewhere to lie and sleep claimed them. Soon, Galdr with Injya cradled close to him fell asleep and, after a long time, Injya also succumbed to the gentle arms of the mistress of the night. Outside, the horses, vigilant even in their sleep, could hear no more than the sounds of gentle snoring coming from the ground. If the wind had not been so high, if the snoring had not been so soporific, perhaps they would have picked up the vibrations on the air which would warn them that they were not the only horses abroad that night. But as the moon played with the clouds and the wind tossed soft breaths to the heavens, men and beast alike slept blissfully unaware of danger.

Injya knew that they could not see her. She knew she was invisible to them – but that did not stop her thundering heart beating so quickly with terror that she thought it would burst out of her body. In front of her the people danced round the great fire. Naked, save for hideous white body paint outlining their skeletons, the people danced round to the sound of the drum. Far away, at the back of the cave sat an old woman, older even than Askoye, her wrinkled skin hanging in great scraggy folds round her shrunken frame, dried dugs shaking with the drumming. Over her head rested the skull of a great brown bear, his flayed skin flapping round her shrunken shoulders as relentlessly she beat the drum. Bright eyes lit by the brilliant orange fire flickered over the grotesque dancing people as they swirled, faster and faster, to the beat of the drum. One by one, the dancers fell to the floor, squirming and writhing, screaming in agony, but the drum continued its ceaseless beating until only one person was left, standing stock still, scarce breathing, staring hard into the eyes of the bear-woman.

The drumming stopped. The people on the floor shook themselves and crawled away to sit huddled against the walls of the cave, staring numbly at the one who was still standing. He, for his part, stared glassy-eyed at the old woman. A thin smile parted her puckered mouth as silently she moved the drum away from her lap and stood up, facing the one who was still standing. He did not flinch as the old woman muttered her words as she stalked round his fine, straight body. She shook her arms at him and mumbled low words as round she walked. Quite suddenly she stopped, clapped her

322

hands over her head, spat twice on the floor and ran to join the others.

As if drawn by an invisible thread, the bear entered the cave. Injya screamed at he who was still standing: 'A bear! A bear! Behind you – A bear!!!'

But he did not hear her. Slowly the bear lumbered forward then, as if seeing its quarry for the first time, he raised himself on his hind legs and struck the man. With a single movement of its massive arm it felled the one who had been standing. Without a sound the man dropped to the floor of the cave and in utter silence the bear ripped at the flesh with his fearsome claws. He who had been standing was no more than a bloody mess of tattered skin, muscle and bone and the bear, as if no longer interested in the game, gorged himself in a desultory manner for a few moments, then quite suddenly turned around and padded softly from the cave.

Injya, high up in the roof of the cave felt sick with the loathsome smell of the exposed entrails but was unable to move, or to close her eyes against the sight – as if she had been rendered senseless by the evil old woman. Again the woman clapped her hands and the other people in the cave rushed forward and hacked at what was left of the one who had so bravely stood alone. The old woman raised her arms and began chanting once more, her glinting eyes growing bigger, her voice more evilly insistent as she watched the people who now were holding parts of he who had stood in their blood-encrusted hands. The old woman dropped her arms suddenly and fell silent and as if this had been the signal they had each been waiting for, the people began to devour he who had once stood.

Injya tried to force the words from her mouth which had fallen open with shock, but none came.

'NO!' She tried to shout, but her mouth was dry, no sound came out. 'NO!' She willed again as she watched the bloody fragments go again to the mouths of the people; but nothing, no sound, only a dry tearing terror filled her throat. Suddenly she found she could move. Released from her prison of immobility she ran round the people, slapping them, punching them, trying to tear the livid flesh away from their fingers, but they flicked her away as if she were no more than a troublesome insect as they continued their loathsome meal.

'Help me someone!' she at last screamed. 'Someone help me!' But none seemed to hear the voice which finally escaped from her fear-filled throat. 'Galdr! Help me!' she screamed as she began to weep with frustration. As the tears took hold of her body, the dream faded and she woke, sobbing, hearing sleepy, anxious voices calling her name, feeling Galdr's strong arms rocking and holding her.

The awfulness of the dream subsided and eventually she stopped sobbing enough to feebly apologize. She assured her worried friends gathered around her, that it had 'only been a dream'. After a long time, she felt Galdr relax his arm and fall asleep. But for her, sleep was no longer a possibility. She had found the memory she was searching for, had found the secret of the cave. Clearly she remembered Askoye's veiled hints about what had happened to her people – but here, sleeping in the very heart of their land, Injya had discovered the true answer. They had taken their reverence of the bear to its ultimate conclusion – if caring for a bear nearly all its life then eating it gave them the strength of the bear and freed his soul for a better life, so too, the same must be true of humans. The very chamber that they were sleeping in now was their most sacred shrine. It was the shrine to all the bears over the millennia who had 'chosen' the person to be 'honoured' by giving his life for the enrichment of the tribe's strength. Injya shivered again at the recollection of the dream and waited for the dawn. Tomorrow they must cross the river. She would not spend another night on this land.

Pentesh was again the first to herald the dawn. As the first muted bird-song fell upon the sleep-filled ears of those in the chamber, Pentesh was noisily letting her hunger be known to all. As Injya struggled to calm the insistent child and sit up comfortably to nurse her, Galdr too awoke and as the milk calmed the child they talked in whispers of her dream. Soon Wa-Oagist awoke, demanding the same treatment and by the time that the first pink tints of dawn showed on the horizon everyone was awake. Tyanka did seem to be feeling better for her rest and even offered to assemble the umiaks, but as the day wore on, she again became sick and begged to be allowed to rest once more in the chamber.

The sun was beginning to set before the umiaks were finished and Centill and Halfray had returned from their reconnoitre.

'We have found it!' Centill said somewhat breathlessly, 'by the time it took our shadows to reach full height – and that was not riding fast either! There is a place upstream where the river is not so fast – it is wide, but on the other side is flat ground too. You can see the mountains quite clearly Galdr – they are – they are . . . ' he trailed to a stop.

'Very big!' Halfray finished the sentence for him. 'But I am sure we can find a pass through them. Tomorrow we can ford the river – yes?'

'No!' Injya's voice was hard and utterly resolute. 'No – not tomorrow – we go tonight!'

Halfray and Centill had been right. It took them almost no time at all to reach the place they had described. They lit their fire and by the light of the fire and the rising full moon they packed their boats. In the flat meandering plain the river looked less menacing. Although it still burbled, it looked considerably shallower than when they first saw it. It was elected that Torben and Eabran, being the two men most adept at sea, should cross first. Eabran led and it was his umiak that hit the fast-flowing water in the middle of the river first. Paddling furiously, first on one side then another, he shouted directions to Torben. In the silver and black of the moonlit night all that could be seen was spray and wildly-flailing oars. Everyone held their breath as the two tiny boats floundered, circling in the water, but then, miraculously reached calmer water. Eventually the two tiny boats went out of sight and it seemed a very long time before they heard a loud, triumphant whoop and the words: 'We have made it! We are coming back!'

An age seemed to pass before the ghostly figures were visible, cutting their way through the silver ribbon of water. This time they took Ullu and Aywe over and Centill put Injya and Pentesh in the other boat and following them closely, they too reached the other side. Back again the two boats went, this time depositing Bendula clutching an excitedly shouting Potyami close to her, Toonjya with Wa-Oagist sleeping miraculously in her arms and a very shaken Tyanka, on the shore. Another crossing, and this brought Sanset to safety with Centill. Djyana with Eabran and Galdr with Torben were left leading the horses across.

Their two boats were not visible for a long time and when eventually the four people clambered ashore, Djyana was weeping profusely. Two of the horses had floundered. A massive tree trunk had hit the leader of one of the long lines of terrified horses, broken the rope and carried him and one other away downstream. She was inconsolable with grief; it mattered little that everyone thought she had acted with amazing bravery, jumping into the fast-flowing icy water, catching the broken rein of the rest of the line and somehow managing to half swim, half ride with them back to the shore, but as her tears fell, so too did the spirits of the people. With two horses less, progress would be very slow. Galdr had a lot of difficulty restraining Djyana who wanted to run off into the night, down the banks of the river, in an effort to find the horses, but finally, overcome with tiredness and sorrow she fell asleep, curled up in the lap of Centill like a big child, still catching her breath in her sleep with dreaming sobs.

All had been drenched through once more by the spray in the river and wet, cold, and without having the heart to travel further that night, they made a fire out of the wood of one of the umiaks and huddling close together for warmth they watched the moon and the stars and the scudding clouds until all but Injya fell asleep.

CHAPTER TWENTY-EIGHT

Vronjyi, the hunter, stared hard into the cascading water
– there it was again – he was sure.

'Bring that taper over here – there is something in the
water!' he shouted. Kendosh came running over from
where the men were examining the hoof-prints.

'Give it here – look – over there!'

Kendosh peered in the direction of Vronjyi's pointing
arm. Boulders covered with foaming water – that was all.

'Look – there!' Vronjyi shouted in exasperation at
him. 'There!'

Straining his eyes in the darkness Kendosh could just
make out what Vronjyi was so excited about. The carcass
of a horse, wedged between two boulders, its broken legs
waving sickeningly in the rush of water.

'Vronjyi!'

It was Moodolk's turn to shout against the roaring of the
water: 'Sopak has found fire ashes!' As if mesmerized by
the sight of the horse, Vronjyi found difficulty in tearing
his eyes from it. They were near, of that he was sure.
Galdr and the rest of them would have tried crossing
the river further upstream and lost their horses – or –
certainly this one!

'Vronjyi!' The insistent voice behind him nagged at
him. 'Come, Kendosh,' he said eventually, tearing himself away from the river. 'Let us see what has been
found.'

The men stared for a long time at the cold wet patch
of ashes, the flattened grass where the horses had slept,
the earth turned to mud round the hole in the ground,
before any dared to enter the chamber. Moodolk was all

for carrying on, tired and wet as he was, he felt sure that they could not be far.

'They hid in here during the day – that was why we could not see them – they have only just left, I am convinced.'

'And what of the cut trees we saw? They were already dry by midday – that had been done this morning, no – they would have sheltered here last night, cut the trees to make a fire this morning, and be safely on the other side by now. We are already a day behind them,' Vronjyi argued with him sensibly.

'That is what they did, they rested in here last night while we were still trying to find their trail through the forest.' Rudju looked at Moodolk earnestly and continued, 'If they had lit the fire this morning, it would not be wet, it has not rained today.'

'All the more reason for carrying on!' Moodolk answered hotly. Vronjyi stood up and winced as he banged his head on the roof of the chamber.

'Moodolk, *you* may feel like carrying on tonight, but the horses are tired out – and so am I!' Sopak and Tronüg laughed at his honesty. 'This might not be the most comfortable of resting places, but it is out of the elements and dry! We will sleep here and at first light find their trail. They cannot be far ahead – and, do not forget, they have lost one, maybe more of their horses. We are six with our own horses, they are thirteen with only nine – maybe less – and they have two babes in arms and that wolf-cub Potyami – do not fear, we will catch up with them in our own time.'

The men, apart from Moodolk who still looked furiously thwarted, all murmured their assent.

'Well, I, for one, am not sleeping in here – this place is evil!' So saying, he stood up, banged his head on the roof and cursing loudly, stumbled up the steps and out into the cold night air.

'I will sleep with the horses' – he shouted after him – 'I am not one for sleeping with bear skulls!'

The men arranged themselves variously on the ledge and floor and wrapping themselves in their skins lay talking in whispers about the chamber in which they were now resting. They too could come to no conclusion about the engineering of the chamber – it was completely outside their knowledge. No-one had ever heard of a people who cut stone out of rock and built underground shelters with it. And the pictures! Baffled by the enormity of their find, they gave up their questioning and peace descended as snoring slowly took the place of conjecture.

Outside the chamber Moodolk was having a more difficult time getting to sleep. He was tired, but sleep seemed to elude him. He could not get the idea that Galdr and his people were very near out of his head and it was only the thought of how hard the travelling had been so far, that finally stopped him from disobeying Vronjyi completely and setting off on his own. It had been much harder travelling than anyone had expected: the rain had washed away tracks made by the animals and often during the two-day trek the men had found themselves following one track, only to find that it led innocently to a group of reindeer or a lone, startled bear. Moodolk chuckled as he remembered the bear – he did not know who was the most surprised, he or the animal: the animal because Moodolk did not immediately try to kill it, Moodolk himself because the bear did not attempt to kill him.

He tried making patterns out of the stars but their twinkling brightness only served to wake him further. Soon it would be daylight, surely. He lay, head resting on a horse's warm flank and slowly, sleep crept up on him. Moodolk felt that he had no sooner closed his eyes than he was awoken by a blood-curdling scream from inside the chamber. Heart throbbing, he lurched down into the bunker, banging his head once again as he tried to take in the scene in the dancing shadows of the taper-light. It looked as if Sopak and Tronüg were fighting with Rudju, who was still screaming and thrashing his arms and legs

330

around on the floor. Vronjyi was fighting a losing battle trying to catch hold of Rudju's flailing legs as Sopak and Tronüg tried to wrestle with his body. Kendosh was holding Rudju's head as he tossed it to and fro on the stone floor, trying to stop him banging himself into insensibility. Rudju's eyes were wide with terror, as if he had just seen the most hideous horror of his life and from his mouth, twisted and contorted, foaming spittle poured forth.

'Stop his screaming!' Vronjyi himself shouted as he caught sight of the startled Moodolk. 'For pity's sake – stop his screaming!'

Moodolk ran round the struggling heap of men and put his wrist into Rudju's mouth. For an instant Rudju's eyes met those of Moodolk and a look of recognition flashed through them, but as quickly as the look had come, it went and an instant later his eyes glazed over and his body went limp.

Sleep was an impossibility. Without further discussion they strapped the insensible Rudju on to his horse and left the chamber. In the bright moonlight the hoofs' imprints left by Injya's horses were quite distinct. At a walking pace, they followed the tracks upstream and at dawn came to where the fire had been made. In the pink-grey light of early morning, they could see quite clearly the plume of smoke on the other side of the river lazily licking away at the sky. There were no signs of people, no tall shadows of men on the opposite bank, just the fire left for all the world to see.

Injya had not been able to sleep either that full-moon night. Tyanka worried her. The poor girl seemed to be getting weaker by the moment. Injya had administered more essence of ento and once again Tyanka had fallen into a deep sleep. When she slept her shaking stopped, but she became burning hot and her body smelt – a sweet, sickly honey-like smell, with a tinge of burning autumnal leaves. She had sat with Tyanka's hot head in her lap, talking quietly with Galdr and Halfray, the rest of the people lying together round the fire, half listening, half sleeping.

'No' – Injya was saying to Halfray – 'I think that the sweetness is her own sweetness of spirit. Her childlike innocence was abused by Anfjord and is now being transformed into an inner rage – hence the smell of burning with it – she is burning up her innocence.' Halfray shook his head as he touched Tyanka's feverish brow.

'No, it is the smell of the earth – her true womanhood is coming to the fore and battling to get out!'

'That, if I might say, Halfray, is a typically male remark! Tyanka has not even had her first course yet! She is nearly fifteen summers old, but her courses have not come – she is still a child inside, a child burning with anger and hatred. Oh, I had hoped that once she was away from Anfjord she would be well, but she has got steadily worse, it is as if . . . '

'As if Anfjord still has some part of her spirit.' Galdr finished Injya's sentence for her, his voice low with worry.

'It is as I said,' Halfray joined in once more. 'We must use the drum for her – whichever it is, the spirit or the rage, it has to be released – it is her only hope!'

'But not tonight, Halfray, not tonight, let the ento have one more chance – she is sleeping and we are all exhausted. And this place – it does not feel good for drumming – tomorrow we will find somewhere that is right and then, if she is no better, we will try the new way.'

As Injya lay awake, staring at the stars and the moon, she wondered what Askoye would have thought of the way Galdr and Halfray used the drum. Perhaps that was its proper use all along, as an instrument for summoning out the spirits of sickness. All she could remember of what Askoye had told her of the drum and her using the drum herself, was that through it she would become aware of the spirits of the animals which guided her own spirit. She had said nothing about sickness being brought on by evil spirits

– to attribute sickness solely to evil spirits entering one's being was to deny the efficacy of all the herbal remedies she had so painstakingly learnt. Surely, if everything could be done by the use of the drum, Askoye would not have bothered teaching her all about the healing properties of herbs and roots! No, the answer had to be a fusion of the two! She wriggled about uncomfortably in her skins, trying to make sense out of chaos. Halfray had brought forth two spirits from her – one of a horse, one of a mountain leopard – were they her enemies? The enemies of her then, unborn child? When she had used the drum, she had felt as if she *was* the animals, but that each animal was *giving* something to her, *showing* something to her, helping her understand part of her human nature. Why then would the animal spirits hinder her *and* her child? She could find no answer and finally, in desperation, she left the group of sleeping people and, finding a small hillock, climbed to the top and stared hard at the moon.

Its full opalescent face was its usual enigmatic self. Closing her eyes she drank in its power. Feet on the earth, head in the stars, just like her mother had been. 'Beloved Ahni Amwe, help me to understand, help me to see more clearly,' she prayed; but the moon simply shone down her cold white light upon her daughter, as she shone upon all – evil and good. Injya dropped her raised arms and felt dejected for the first time since they had left the encampment. Would even the power of the Goddess leave her now? She turned and was just about to rejoin the group when she thought she caught sight of a movement on the opposite bank. She froze. Every hair on her body, every sense alert. There, on the opposite bank a long way off – tiny, but unmistakable – shadows of riders. The wind brought the faint sound of distant hoofs on earth and then whisked it away almost before it could be interpreted by her brain. Injya did not need time to understand what each atom of her senses was telling her. Soosha had sent a search party – and they had been found!

Quicker than the mighty river Pchektora itself she ran silently back to the group. Putting a hand over each mouth, she shook the sleepers awake.

'No words!' she whispered in warning to each as she woke them: 'Hunters are coming – we must flee!'

As silently as moonshine each rose, gathered their furs and skins and loaded the horses with them. Djyana whispered in each of the horses' ears the need for silence and, as if understanding every word, not one whinny came from them. Both Wa-Oagist and Pentesh were picked up and immediately given the breast to hush any protestations, as almost without any sound whatsoever, the group walked their horses onwards, to where the sun would rise.

The sky was already lightening when they saw the foothills of the mountain range and they realized now that they had looked so dark and foreboding from the other side, because they were deeply forested for at least a third of the way up. Daring now to mount the horses, they galloped and ran through the rest of the brief night until breathless and exhausted through lack of sleep, they gained the first of the trees. Not daring to stop, they walked with difficulty up through the pine forest. The massive swaying black-green branches blotted out the sunrise and the warmth of the risen sun. Onwards and upwards they clambered, slower and slower until they could go no further. Horses and people utterly exhausted, they finally were stopped by a massive black boulder, positioned in the middle of the forest, as if a gigantic hand had dropped it from the sky. Here, they sank gratefully to their knees and gasping for breath looked at each other in bewilderment and astonishment at their flight.

'We are safe!' Halfray gasped at length, 'They will never find us here!'

But each knew that the words were wishful thinking. If *they* could reach here – wherever *here* was – so could the hunters!

'I am hungry!' Potyami stated in the silence, echoing the unheeded messages from everyone's stomachs.

It was Oanti who found Tyanka's body. She had gone to unpack the dried meat from one of the horses. She saw her lying, face down, among the pine needles. Too late for drums now, Oanti thought, as she bent her short body double to pick up the tiny frame of the child-woman. Too late for the child who would never be woman. With her heart breaking she carried the body of Tyanka slowly back to the horrified group.

'I no longer feel hungry,' she said quietly, as if her burden needed no explanation, 'not at all.'

Vronjyi had stared at the fire on the opposite bank for such a long time that Moodolk was tempted to prod him to see if he had suddenly and mysteriously fallen into a trance – after last night – anything was possible! With a start Vronjyi came to his senses and whirling round upon the mounted men who were eagerly craning forwards, staring, as he had done, at the fire left enticingly unattended, he ordered: 'Umiaks!'

Everyone, except Rudju, leapt from their horses and started unpacking the pre-cut poles. Vronjyi marched over to Rudju, pulled his head back roughly and stared into his unseeing eyes. No response. Dropping his head again which swung for a moment or two over the belly of his horse, he turned to the men who were now quickly and expertly lashing together the poles while Sopak spread out the two pre-sewn skins which would make up the boats.

'Sopak – you are to stay here with Rudju. If he does not regain his senses by this time tomorrow, you are to leave him and follow the best you can. We cannot delay for a man still possessed by a stupid dream!'

Without waiting for any reply, he began unstrapping Rudju's senseless body and with a gentleness belying his earlier roughness and harsh words, he lifted him from his horse and laid him carefully on the ground. Rudju's eyes were still wide open but unseeing, his breath coming evenly and deeply, his face pale; he looked for all the world as if he were simply asleep with his eyes open.

Vronjyi had no more idea than the others had as to the cause of this catatonic state. He had woken to hear Rudju scream something about bears and then just scream. He looked at his high cheek-boned face, his shining black hair, his athletic, bronze body – he could have been looking at a slightly shorter and younger version of himself! Why Rudju? Why a dream so horrific that it robbed him of his senses? He thought again of Igrat's face – all pink and bloated but as serene as the moon. There was no comparison: Rudju's normally sun-tanned face was lineless as Igrat's had been, but there the similarity ended, for behind Rudju's unseeing eyes lay a deep horror. Vronjyi shut his eyes against the memory and the sight of Rudju, feeling afraid that by looking further, he was putting himself in danger of the very thing that had so robbed Rudju of his senses, afraid almost that whatever it was, could leap out of him and take over Vronjyi himself. Quickly he turned and watched as Kendosh and Sopak were struggling to pull the stiff skins over the frame which Tronüg was holding.

'Wet them first!' he barked at them. The three men clicked their tongues in self-annoyance – how could they forget? Moodolk, dropping the frame he had just completed, said: 'Vronjyi, there is no point trying to cross here. Why do I not go further upstream to see if there is a safer place to cross?'

'Time?' Vronjyi snapped sarcastically.

'They are no more than half a day away from us now – a small delay will make little or no difference – you said as much yourself last night – and perhaps poor Rudju here will have come to his senses by the time I get back!'

Vronjyi considered for a moment then, seeing the sense in Moodolk's statement, said in less acid tones: 'All right

– go, quickly – you seem to have boundless energy, Moodolk – the sooner you go, the sooner you will be back!'

Moodolk grinned at him, his broad freckled face creasing into tiny lines. Vronjyi knew that he was one of the swiftest riders of their people – he might not be the most cunning of hunters, but by Bai Ulgan, he could ride well. Without another word Moodolk leapt on to his horse's back, dug his heels into her flanks and galloped off upstream. Vronjyi watched him go for a moment or two then turned back to the men.

'We may as well eat here – who knows when we will have another chance to eat in the sunshine of our own country.'

Moodolk slowed his horse down to a walking pace after his initial triumphant gallop – Vronjyi was quite senseless sometimes! he muttered to himself – what was the point of crossing a river at a place which had already taken one horse's life without at least looking for another crossing point? He scoured the river bank to his left as his horse delicately wove her way round the clumps of tall marshgrass – still it looked fast flowing and dangerous. He gained a small rise round which the river curled in a lazy arc and saw, to his delight, that although at this point the river was, if anything, wider than before – he could clearly see the bed of the river, virtually to the other side! He cantered down and urged his horse into the water. Yes! He could have jumped for joy!

He was two-thirds of the way across and could now see clearly to the other bank – it was shallow and gently dappling all the way to the other side. The riverbed itself was made up of tiny stones and good solid rocks, not mud, and the water was clear as daylight, reflecting the cloudless blue sky and the bright sunshine of the early morning. The further bank rose quite steeply here, but the horses would gain the rise without difficulty. Feeling enormously pleased with himself he wheeled his horse round in the sparkling water and just had time to see the long blade flash in the sunlight, the bearded low-browed face, before the axe struck home and his head fell from his neck in a screaming rush of gore.

The men had held Moodolk's body in the water until the bright blood ceased flowing and the water ran clear again. It had taken all six of them to carry and drag Moodolk's headless body back to their underground home. The horse had dashed free, cantering down the riverbed before they had a chance to spear it. They watched it go, their dark brown eyes registering nothing – horses they could hunt easily – man, on the other hand, was a rare delicacy. The women would be pleased – another year when one of their own number would be saved.

The women pored over Moodolk's virtually hairless body, touching the pale, damp flesh, stroking his long straight back and legs – so different to their own short, hirsute forms. As they silently dismembered his body they shared a single thought: this one man would give them the strength of many. One woman, heavy with child, hoped perhaps more than the rest, that by eating flesh from his straight legs, her child might take on this strength of limb; that her child would perhaps be the one born in their fast-dwindling tribe who could grow to be strong, straight-backed and braver than them all.

Vronjyi swore as he stared angrily into the white foaming river. Impatiently he stamped his foot on the bank. How much longer was he going to have to wait for Moodolk's return? He twisted his head this way and that, screwing up his bright black eyes as he peered into the sunshine. He crossed his browned arms over his muscle-bound chest, heaved a sigh and was about to leave the riverbank when the sparkling foam before him was suddenly and momentarily, tinged with red. Almost before he had time to recognize the colour even, the ghastly severed head of Moodolk tumbled by in the rushing water, innocent as a stone, and was gone from sight. Before he could collect his senses, Sopak shouted behind him: 'Vronjyi! . . . Moodolk's horse!'

Numbed with shock, not wanting to believe his eyes, Vronjyi eventually turned away from the river to see the animal canter up to the other horses, her coat stained with blood, her huge brown eyes showing white with terror. Sopak and Kendosh ran to her first.

'She is covered in blood!' Kendosh shouted to Vronjyi, who was still rigid with the onslaught to his feelings.

'I know!' His hoarse voice was quiet, the words echoing around the men. 'I know!' he said again as he stumbled over the tufts of grass and lurched towards the startled men. 'I have just seen his head floating down the river.'

Moodolk's horse was led to the river and washed free of his blood. In shocked silence the umiaks were tied on to her back. The five men and six horses followed the tracks left by Moodolk's horse until they reached the place where they stopped and entered the river. As far as their eyes could see to the south, there was nothing but softly undulating landscape and away in the distance, a dark outline of a forest. There were no marks in the grass save those made by Moodolk's horse, no sign of blood, no broken clods of earth, nothing. Across the river, up the rise of red rock, the land looked flat for some way, but then rose forebodingly up darkly wooded mountains.

Eventually Vronjyi said: 'He has been killed by Galdr. They saw him and killed him and have taken his body to the other side! Come – onward – we will catch them tonight!'

'*NO!*'

From behind him Rudju's shout rang clear. He wheeled round to see Rudju struggling in a vain attempt to right himself from his ungainly position, straddled across the back of his horse. Kendosh was by his side in an instant.

'Rudju! Rudju! You are back with us!' He hurriedly dismounted and tore at the ropes which secured him.

'No, Vronjyi,' Rudju repeated when he finally found his feet, 'Galdr did not kill him – the Bear People did!'

'What bear people? What are you talking about?'

'The Bear People, the people in my dream. I saw them last night – that chamber, it is the chamber of their sacred bears. It was they who took Moodolk away, I know it!' Rudju began shaking and wringing his hands, as his flickering eyes darted from one to another in a desperate attempt to make them understand.

'Rudju, you are not making sense,' Vronjyi held him by the shoulders, staring into his eyes. 'What did you see? How?'

'Do not ask me to tell you – I could not – it was too terrible. Just believe me, Vronjyi – I know, I know!'

Vronjyi stared in disbelief as he struggled to hold on to Rudju as he twisted and struggled to be free of the hands on his shoulders.

'Vronjyi, you do not know how terrible it was – how horrifying, how full of blood, and the eyes and the hearts, still beating hearts. Do not ask me to go back there, I beg you, Vronjyi, please!'

'Rudju – listen to me, I am not going to send you back there – Rudju!' he shouted as he shook the young man, trying to make him understand that no-one could send him back; but Rudju could not see his intense eyes, could not sense the urgency of his strong hands holding him as once more, as if in a desperate attempt to blot out the memory, his eyes glazed over, rolled up in his head and his body slumped unconscious against Vronjyi's chest.

Vronjyi struggled to hold on to Rudju's limp body as he struggled to hold on to his own sanity.

'What magic is this?' he hissed to the terrified men, 'what magic has Galdr woven now?'

For a moment all were still, as if frozen in an instant of time, a frozen tableau of fear, then, as if suddenly waking from a nightmare, Vronjyi shook his head violently and barked: 'Kendosh, fill the water-sacks, Sopak, dismantle the umiaks. Kendosh, you will ride Moodolk's horse – let yours rest, we must not exhaust the horses. Tronüg, tie Rudju upright on his horse! We must see their fire tonight!'

He looked anxiously at Rudju's crumpled body as Tronüg took his weight and added grimly: 'With Moodolk gone, we cannot leave him here!'

It took the men until sunset to pick up the tracks of Galdr and the rest; the ground on the other side of the river was less sodden, springy turf leaving few traces. They stopped often, listening intently for any human sound. Rudju became conscious only twice on the journey, both times shouting about bears and begging not to be sent back. Vronjyi vowed silently to himself that if he was no better upon the morrow, he would have to put Rudju out of his mental agony; he could not allow the whole safety of the party to be put at risk by the actions of one man.

As they silently travelled onward, Vronjyi had the distinct impression that he was being watched. Two or three times the feeling was so strong that he was compelled to turn round abruptly and stare into the gloom behind him. Each time he saw nothing, heard nothing and each time he berated himself for being such a baby. As night fell, great black clouds obscured the moon and any trace of footprints. They could not continue. They could not light a fire for fear of being seen. Six horses, five men, each in their differing natures fearful in the enormity of the still, black world. Wearily they dismounted, silently hobbling the horses and wrapping themselves around with furs, desperate to rid themselves of their anxiety, they tried to sleep away the horrors of that day.

CHAPTER TWENTY-NINE

Darkness. Humid, insect-humming darkness. All around Soosha brown, sweat-glistening faces were upturned towards her, their bright eyes wide with amazement. Sweat ran down her throat and trickled slowly down the valley between her breasts. Outside the packed sancar the huge red sun still wobbled on the horizon and the sky, turned magenta by its rays, refused to darken; but inside the sancar the shadows were dense, the air thick with smoke and musky with the smell of so many. Sure of her audience Soosha very quietly spoke.

'It took Nihay three days for her waters to cover her mother Hoola, as so it took three days for Bai Ulgan to weave the cloak of night around him. So it is tokened and so it is, that it will take three days for Vronjyi to find Galdr.'

Glittering eyes watched Soosha's every move as she sat with the sacred bark sheets spread out on her knees. She paused, aware of the silence, aware of the intensity of concentration around her. She dropped her head and looked again at the fragile beaten bark strips that held the secret symbols of her people.

'It is all here, all quite clear.' Anfjord leant over and touched her on her shoulder.

'Tell us, tell us again – it has been a long time.' His voice trailed off as he remembered with sadness the passing of Colnyek the Tokener. Even Colnyek had not wanted to speak the words often, insisting that each time the symbols were exposed, they lost some of their power.

'I do not know if I should, Father,' Soosha began, head still bowed, 'Colnyek always . . . '

342

'Never mind what Colnyek always did or did not do. You have found the answer in the tokens. Who knows what other answers we will find in it. Tell it from the beginning, I want to hear it.'

He sat back and closed his eyes. The matter was closed.

Pleased that her demurring brought the response she wanted, she glanced at the assembled crowd. Dark, eager faces met her gaze, all were still, each hushed by the importance of the occasion. Babes in arms no longer struggled, lulled into sleep by the cloying air and the insistent urgent concentration of their mothers' need to hear. As if suddenly embarrassed by the honour of being allowed to divulge the age-old symbols of her people, Soosha cleared her throat and began talking as if she had not seen the tokens before, often stumbling over the symbols and hieroglyphs and peering at them as if the frail bark sheets were difficult to see. Only Soosha knew the subtle changes she had made to the story, the alterations which would finally give authority to her plans.

'In the beginning of time there was only Hoola, our Great Mother Earth. All around her was darkness and silence. Hoola lay and waited in the darkness for life to quicken inside her. After a long, long time she sighed a great sigh and the darkness took pity on her. Her sigh turned into Oagist.

'Thus it was that Oagist became the God of the Winds.

'Oagist, the God of the Winds, caressed the body of Hoola and surrounded her with love for being created. From that caressing love they breathed life into five children whom she called Por, Erlik, Bai Ulgan, Nihay and Ahni Amwe. The first three children were boy-children who pleased her because they were different from her. Nihay and Ahni Amwe she made into girls which pleased her also. As they grew up Por fell in love with Ahni Amwe and took her to be his wife. They lived on the Great Mother Hoola in great happiness. Bai Ulgan and Erlik too wanted a mate and they quarrelled bitterly over who should have Nihay. They

eventually fought and Erlik killed his brother and tried to bury him in his mother's body.

'Hoola was not happy with her son being in her body and kept breathing life back into him. Eventually, Erlik cut up Bai Ulgan's body into a thousand pieces and scattered them all over Hoola's form. Hoola could not now breathe life back into Bai Ulgan, but she shook the pieces off her and they fell into the sky and became the stars.

'Thus it was that Bai Ulgan became the God of the Heavens.

'Bai Ulgan, God of the Heavens, looked down on his brother, Erlik, who was still happily living on his mother, and vowed to avenge himself. He called to Nihay to join him in the sky, but she said that she could not because she was still bound to Hoola, her mother. Bai Ulgan was very sad, as was Nihay, who started to cry. Oagist saw her great sorrow and took compassion on her. As she cried she became wetter and wetter and eventually she herself turned into countless tiny drops of water. Oagist then blew the drops of water into the heavens to join Bai Ulgan.

'Thus it was that Nihay became the Goddess of Rain.

'Nihay, the Goddess of Rain, poured down upon her mother and Hoola became so displeased that she was being made wet that she tried to shrug off the water, thus creating many folds in her soft skin which are today the great mountains which cover her. But still Nihay rained upon her and so Hoola made her skin thicker and thicker, but no matter how thick she made her skin she still felt very wet. And still Nihay rained upon her and now the folds in her thick skin filled with the waters and became the seas and the rivers. Oagist felt compassion for his wife, Hoola, and tried to blow the tears of Nihay from Hoola's body, but the harder he blew, the more Nihay cried. Eventually Hoola called on her one remaining daughter, Ahni Amwe, to reason with her sister, Nihay.

'Por heard his mother's words, carried as they were by mighty Oagist, his father, and felt very angry. As first-born boy-child it was his duty to speak to Nihay. Por told Ahni Amwe to obey him at which she became very angry also. Por then beat

344

his wife saying that she must not go against the wishes of her husband or her brother, Bai Ulgan. She took no notice of these words and he beat her more. That is why today you can still see the bruises on Ahni Amwe's face. Furious that her husband and brother beat her, Ahni Amwe called on her brother, Erlik, to help her.'

Soosha stopped suddenly and her eyes darted round the sancar. Not a single face registered alarm, no voice exclaimed, 'That is a lie!'; all seemed fascinated and mesmerized by the words, not the content. Not daring to delay further she continued her halting, yet sonorous, hushed reading.

'Erlik had just found one tiny piece of Bai Ulgan which Hoola had not noticed, when he heard his little sister calling to him. Angered that Por had so mistreated his wife, he breathed his hot hatred on to the last piece of the body of Bai Ulgan. The flesh turned into a man of fire, and Erlik named him Ipirün.

'Thus it was that Ipirün became the God of Fire.

'Ipirün, the God of Fire, burnt a great hole in Hoola's side and crept inside to keep himself safe from Bai Ulgan, but Erlik commanded him to come forth. Hoola tried to stop Ipirün from leaving her as he made her warm, but he broke through her tough skin at the very spot where Por was standing. Por became a ball of fire so hot that Hoola could not bear it and she threw him into the heavens.

'Thus it was that Por became the God of the Sun.

'Por, the God of the Sun, shone his light down upon his mother. From this light came all the people and animals that live upon the earth. Thus it is that the God of the Sun is the Father of Man. Bai Ulgan wove a black cloak to hide himself from Por. It took him three days and when he had finished Por could not see him because of the black cloak which from that time on has been called the cloak of night. Frightened that Por would now see her and beat her again, Ahni Amwe ran away from the light of Por and tried to hide in a big hole underneath Hoola.

'Nihay, angered that Bai Ulgan had been forced to hide himself behind the cloak of darkness poured forth her rage once more upon her mother. In three days her waters reached even where Ahni Amwe was hiding and, unable to protect her daughter any longer, Hoola turned her into a huge white star, bigger even than all the stars of Bai Ulgan put together. This big round star she kicked into the blackness under her feet.

'Thus it was that Ahni Amwe became the Goddess of the Moon.

'As Ahni Amwe, Goddess of the Moon, left the big hole underneath Hoola, she left behind a part of her flesh. Nihay turned the flesh into seals and fathers of the waters and from them came all the sea creatures.

'Thus it is that Nihay, Goddess of Rain, is also the mother of all the sea.

'Ahni Amwe sought the protection of Bai Ulgan, but He, in His wisdom, knew that it was wrong for any woman to disagree with her husband but felt compassion for her and covered her with his cloak of night. He then called upon his beloved, Nihay, to seek out and kill Erlik and Ipirün. It took the Goddess of the Rains three days to cover Hoola completely with her waters. Erlik was drowning in the waters which now covered all of Hoola and she, wanting to protect her only remaining son, forgave him for chasing Bai Ulgan away, and she opened her mouth and let Erlik climb down into her.

'Thus it was that Erlik became God of the Underworld.

'Erlik, God of the Underworld, called Ipirün into the womb of his mother and between them they so warmed their mother that Nihay's waters slowly receded. Por still looked for Ahni Amwe during the day, rising over his mother's head, shining all over her and then falling under her feet at night. At night Ahni Amwe rises, still protected by the thick blackness of Bai Ulgan's cloak, still always trying to pull her sister Nihay's waters from her mother's body.

'Thus it is that the world lives and breathes.

Thus it is that blackness follows sunlight.

Thus it is that goodness follows evil.

346

Thus it is tokened that this is the natural order of the world.

'As Ahni Amwe is forever held by the power of Por, thus women are ever held by men.

'As Erlik is ever held by the power of Bai Ulgan, thus the rage of the mother is held in check by men.

'As Nihay is ever held by the power of Ipirün, thus women's tears are ever taken by the fire of men.

'As Hoola is ever held by the power of Oagist, thus the earth is ever owned by men.

'These are the sacred truths of the people of our land. As they are truths, no-one who hears them cannot say that he does not know the truth. These truths are the truths of the world – break them and you break the natural order of the world and the wrath of the Gods will be upon you. Hoola will release Ipirün from her womb and fire will rage over the earth. Mighty Oagist will blow his winds and tear the cloak of night from Bai Ulgan. Bai Ulgan will be burnt into a thousand, thousand ashes and Nihay, in her rage, will rain down upon you and cover Hoola once more with her waters. Por, Father of Man, will be put out by the rains and darkness will come upon the face of Hoola once more. Erlik, God of the Underworld, will rise and bring with him all the spirits of the dead. Thus, great Hoola and all her people will die, covered by the spirits of the dead and the darkness of the void. These truths are the truths of the world – break them not!'

Soosha closed her eyes and shivered. The sancar felt very cold. Her sweat felt cold and clammy on her body. She waited, silent, for the first sound, the first voice. None came. Cold rivulets of water ran down her spine. She dared to take a deeper breath and then, without moving her head, she opened her eyes. The people sat in front of her, eyes closed, tranquil faces; they too scarce breathing as if each was in a light sleep. A sound, a light snore from her left – Anfjord had fallen asleep! The soft sound so ordinary and mundane released her from the spell her words had cast and she raised her head and stared at the faces in front of her. Slowly, first one, then another, opened their eyes and returned her stare. She saw nothing but love shining from them. The story, the words, the poetry of the sacred symbols had worked their magic. The people loved her for her words – they trusted, admired and venerated one who could read poetry to them – Soosha had got what she wanted – power!

She smiled at the sea of faces and they smiled back at her. She felt the growing warmth of power rise from her belly, making her head swim as she realized what she had accomplished. Her people had accepted the words she had spoken, they knew now that Por was the Father of Man, it was to Him that all homage must be paid. She had accomplished in the space of time it took to tell the tokens something which Anfjord and his father before him had been trying unsuccessfully for two generations to accomplish – the total demolition of the cult of the Moon and the awakening of Man as the power on earth.

A baby cried and with the cry the atmosphere changed totally. Again the sancar became hot and filled with the whine of insects who, too, had been as still and silent as the people had been. Someone coughed and children began to squirm.

'Father' – Soosha began quietly as she gently tugged at his sleeve – 'Father, it is over.'

Anfjord jumped violently awake and stared at the people who were waiting for him to dismiss them.

'Yes,' he said after a long pause. 'Yes, it is over.' He fell silent once more, searching the faces for the answer to a question he had not voiced.

'Three days – and then three days back. Well! We shall see!' He struggled to his feet and looked down on his daughter. 'Good,' was all he said before he turned away from her and stumbled from the sancar. The people rose in twos and threes and left the sancar without speaking to each other; soon there was only Soosha and Xynon left. They too sat in silence, each wrapped in their own thoughts. Eventually Xynon broke the silence.

348

' "As Ahni Amwe is for ever held by the power of Por, thus women are held by men," ' he quoted without looking at her. 'Are you ever held by me? Is *that* what you are saying – or is that just for the people – does it apply to a chief's daughter too?'

Soosha sensed his mocking injured tones, knew that he, perhaps only he alone, did not believe the words she had spoken. But she checked her instant response of ridicule, choosing instead to reply meekly.

'I am your wife, Xynon. It is tokened: "These are the truths of our land – break them not." I cannot break them, no matter who my father is.'

'And when Galdr returns – who will you obey then?'

'Galdr will not return, Xynon. You will be the next chief of the Skoonjay people and I, as your wife, will obey only you.'

Xynon snorted and stared at the ground. He had not heard the words of the Skoonjay people before. He only had a dim memory of hearing the truths of his own people, the Gyaretz, once before and although some of the phrases sounded the same, some of the truths, some of the stories of the Gods, there did not feel right to him – something had been added or taken away – what it was he was unsure, but he knew that, before, the words were telling him that everyone was equal – man and woman together, inexorably linked, each sharing the earth – but her words, Soosha's words, meant something else. He shook his head with exasperation – so much had happened – so much had changed – even Soosha herself was almost unrecognizable. Two days ago she had been furious and contemptuous – yet here, now, she was the sweet girl who had taken him in her mouth, who had lain with him in the copse, who had become his bride. He turned to face her, his eyes searching her face for an answer to his confusion. In response she smiled at him and lowered her eyelids slightly. When she looked up at him again, he saw shining love in her eyes, the warmth of desire in the curve of her lips and he felt the confusion melt within him. She surely *was* that sweet girl who had so captured his heart only a few days before, but a lifetime of change ago.

'Soosha . . . '

'Hush—' She put her fingers up to his mouth to silence him, 'let us go to our sancar, beloved.' He held her hand to his mouth and kissed her fingers lightly. 'Come,' she said quietly as she withdrew her hand, 'this night we make a son together.'

Hand in hand they walked from the sancar out into the violet half-night of the summer-lands. All around them came the gentle sounds of people sleeping as they stole into their sancar to make secret love. But secrets are not secrets as long as ravens fly – or so a saying of their people went – and it was a raven who saw and heard their words, a very weary black raven who had perched on the women's sancar roof and heard the words Soosha had so beautifully intoned. The same raven now flew away to the land of the rising sun to whisper the secrets of the night into the dreams of the sleeping Halfray.

'There is no return,' he said, over and over again. 'There is no return to the land of your forefathers – that land is changing and will have no place for you, no time for the real truths, that land is already dying.'

CHAPTER THIRTY

Halfray awoke with the words of Vingyar's spirit-raven ringing in his ears. He knew that there was no return – as there was no return for Tyanka – she had been the first victim – how many more would succumb? He gazed upwards through the dark branches overhead and glimpsed tiny snatches of pale pink sky. The third day of their new life had dawned. He shivered slightly, realizing that he was chilled. Cold dew lay glistening on top of the fur which was covering him. Soon autumn would be here, all too soon the brief summer would be over – who knew what the new land would bring? He listened to the sounds of the sleeping people around him, their rhythmic breathing making a soft cushion of sound for his worries to fall on. He closed his eyes, trying to push to the back of his mind the thought of the hunters – had they travelled all night? Were they, right at this moment, watching the sleeping group, waiting to pounce on them?

A rustle in the undergrowth to his right stopped his heart. It began beating wildly as he heard the crack of a twig and sweat broke out all over his body.

'Halfray! Halfray! Are you awake?'

He thought he would die with relief as he heard Sanset's hushed voice. Trying to keep his voice level, he whispered back into the darkness of the trees: 'Yes!'

'Put your arm up – I cannot see where you are yet.'

'Over here!' he whispered louder. Propping himself up on his elbows he looked through the gloom and finally made out her crouching figure tiptoeing between the still sleeping people.

'I am cold – can I join you?'

In answer Halfray lifted up his fur covering and Sanset crept under it, pulling her own skin round her, shivering with cold.

'It will soon be fully light,' she murmured. Halfray silently agreed with her.

'Halfray . . . ' she began, twisting her face upwards towards his. 'Halfray . . . ' she began again. 'I do not know how to say it – oh, never mind!' she ended lamely. Halfray found his voice again and said in what he hoped were reassuring tones: 'Go on, Sanset, you can tell me – what is it?'

Sanset was obviously having difficulty finding the words but eventually she blurted out: 'I am frightened!'

Halfray fought to control his laughter – me too – he thought – me too. But that Sanset could ever be afraid seemed almost impossible to him; she was always so capable it had never occurred to him that she could be frightened. Feeling comforted that even sensible Sanset could be afraid, he gently put his arm round her shoulder and pulled her nearer to him.

'You will never get warm if you keep your body all over there, Sanset, here, snuggle closer.'

Even through the thick fur skins he could feel her shoulders cold against his arm.

'That is better,' he said when she had wriggled close to him and rested her head on his shoulder. 'Now – tell me why you are afraid.'

He felt very strange speaking to Sanset thus – it had always been her that had comforted him – Cousin Sanset had always seemed more like a favourite aunt and yet she was only one summer older than he. At length she answered his question.

'I am frightened because I do not understand. You and Galdr and even Injya, seemed so – oh, I do not know – so detached, yes, that is the word, detached. It was as if you did not care one iota that Tyanka had died. All three of you just doing those strange things around her body – it

352

looked like you were combing her body with your fingers – and then when you had done all that, you did not seem concerned at all. Why – you did not even help Centill cover her body and you did not say anything about why it was suddenly all right to bury her in the ground, when I have always thought that burial was the worst thing that could happen to someone who had just died. But worse than that – none of you would tell us what was going on – what you were doing or why. I feel very alone, Halfray – you always shared everything with me before you went away – now you are back you no longer talk the way you used to and I am afraid, afraid that you . . . ' Her voice, which had risen to a thin whine finally stopped.

'Afraid that I what?' Halfray prompted gently.

'Ooooh, afraid that you do not love me any more.'

Halfray could not have been more shocked if she had said the sun and the moon had suddenly joined forces or the goat had laid down with the bear. He did not know that he *did* love Sanset, but that she loved him was obvious. When he could marshal his thoughts a little he said quietly: 'Which are you most afraid of – what we did to Tyanka or my feelings for you?'

'*My* feelings for *you!*' she mumbled glumly. She was lying very stiffly in his arms as if afraid to move. Slowly the realization dawned upon him – this was Sanset's declaration of love – she was afraid of her feelings for him. Very tenderly he stroked her hair as, trying to keep the surprise from his voice he asked: 'Do you *want* me, Sanset?'

Her body became even more rigid and her whispered reply was so low that he had difficulty catching it as she mumbled the word 'Yes' into his shoulder. Now what to do? His heart and thoughts raced – Sanset loves *me*! How strange – Sanset *loves* me! I do not know if I love her, I do not know if I love anyone. What to do about Tyanka, how to explain everything? Would she still love me if I told her what I wanted to do? Do *I* know what I want to do? Round and round the thoughts raced until they were stopped by the sudden cry of an infant. Pentesh had woken. As if the baby's crying cleared his brain, he suddenly said: 'Sanset, you have taken me by surprise – I will do anything to stop you being afraid. First, I must tell everyone what happened with Tyanka, then we must talk. Sanset, you do understand that I had never thought, never dreamt, that you felt this way about me? I am all confused! Oh dear, now it is my turn not to know what to say – dear Sanset – how can you love such a fool as I?'

In answer, she struggled out of the heavy furs, kissed him quite hard on his temples and jumped up. Throwing her arms to the heavens she shouted: 'He loves me! Halfray loves me!'

Everyone woke. Wa-Oagist, thwarted that it had not been his early morning shout that had woken everyone, wailed the loudest as confusion reigned. Bendula who had sobbed herself to sleep the previous night now felt the confusion the strongest. She was pleased that her mother felt loved, but angry that this detracted from the loss of Tyanka. It was Injya who helped her voice these two conflicting emotions and by so doing, released the same feelings in Ullu, Tyanka's special friend. Through her tears Ullu managed to say that she had seen, 'A thin blue line rising to the sky and lots of lights all in the trees, shimmering and shining', but then had collapsed in a fresh bout of sobbing. It was as Injya had suspected. Ullu too had the sight. She looked to Galdr for help – the people must be made to completely understand what was happening – even if it meant staying on the edge of the forest all day – no-one must be allowed to feel separate, alone and confused. That was the old way and if their tiny group was to survive, the new path of truth and openness must be understood by all.

They listened in silence as first Galdr, then Halfray spoke. They explained exactly what had happened with Igrat and with Tyanka; how, with their help, the soul

354

was already free so it was of no matter that the body was interred. Even Toonjya, who had been the most sceptical, asked no questions and in a very short time they found themselves comforted and strangely enlivened. Fear and doubt drive hunger away and with these gone, everyone suddenly felt immensely hungry.

As Eabran made the fire, Torben managed to scale the big black boulder that marked the uppermost boundary to their overnight encampment. From the top of the rock he could see over the trees. Far below him he could see the vast expanse of plain they had crossed, and in the far distance a glinting, silver thread was all he could see of the wide river. A warm wind blew from the valley and for a second Torben fancied he could smell the sweet salty tang of the sea, but he knew that they were too far away. He took another deep breath, wondering how long it would be before he saw his beloved sea again and smelt the strange smell once more. Wood-smoke? No, not wood-smoke, pine needles? – certainly the aroma from the trees was almost overpowering but no, it was something else.

He had missed them. So far away that he had mistaken them for a dark boulder. But now he could see their smoke clearly and identify the smell. Their hunters were cooking fish! They were no bigger than flies on the gentle skin of the earth, but he knew that they would have a horse each, knew that they would have been chosen as the fastest riders, the most skilled hunters of their people. And here they were, half a day's riding below him, already eating, soon to be ready to ride once more. His stomach lurched, not with fear but with disappointment – no grilled fish for him and his kind today – perhaps not tomorrow either. Almost as angry about being robbed of a meal as being followed, he slid down the boulder and said in a voice that was desperately trying to be cheerful: 'Do not bother with that flint, Eabran – the hunters are in the valley, I do not think we should light a fire!'

355

Injya watched her people. A feeling of warmth towards them spread throughout her body. Torben's news had not thrown them into disarray, they had not panicked. With hardly a sigh they patiently repacked their furs, stopping only to thank Aywe as she quietly went around each of them, handing out the precious nuts and few berries they had. Injya looked for and found Halfray and Sanset, deep in conversation. Sanset looked radiant as if some great weight had just been lifted from her shoulders; Halfray was frowning and gesticulating, talking in a very animated fashion. Why had she not seen this before, she wondered – now that Sanset had told everyone of her feelings for Halfray, no-one expressed surprise, everyone had said the same thing – naturally, of course, they were a perfect match! Her gaze wandered to Galdr who was talking with Eabran and Centill, and wondered if the same had been said of her and Galdr – a perfect match. She felt a sudden sadness pull at her heart. Of course they would not say that – she had taken to her side her parent's murderer – how *could* she ever forget that? She looked down at the sleeping Pentesh and saw Galdr's features merging with hers in perfect symmetry. She looked up again as Galdr walked towards her, face shining, lips parted in a smile. He stretched out his arms to take Pentesh from her saying: 'Come, we must go. Let me help you strap this pretty bundle on your back.'

He kissed the sleeping baby on her downy cheek and smiled as Injya got to her feet.

'You must ride as high as the horse can carry you, Injya – every one else is walking the horses – oh Injya, you look so tired.'

His brow creased as he looked with concern at her face. Injya knew that he was looking at the dark rings under her eyes and her pale skin – yes, she admitted to herself, she was tired, but in a curious way, she was also happy. She knew that somehow a great change had come over her – it was more than an unwilling acceptance of this man – she

356

was not sure that she *did* accept him totally even now – but something inside her had changed. It was no longer a belief, it was a knowledge.

As she looked into his eyes, she suddenly remembered a long-ago conversation her mother had had with a younger woman of their tribe. The girl had said that *she* did not need any belief to help her through her life and Mensoon had replied, quite calmly, that she, herself, had no beliefs, only knowledge. 'When you know something, like you know the trees and the streams – you do not have to believe in them, they simply are – that is all. *That* is what I am talking about, dear, I do not believe, I *know*!' She stared at Galdr's face for a moment longer – was this too, her truth?

A shout from Eabran broke her thoughts: 'They are moving . . . They are coming!'

When the sun was at its highest point in the heavens they left the cover of the trees. A little further upward and Injya had to dismount. The horses, sure footed as they were, began to slide on the shaly surface of the mountain. They travelled silently, heads down, only occasionally looking upwards to Eabran who was ahead of them, desperately trying to find the easiest way over the mountain. Galdr's hope was that the hunters, once inside the forest beneath them, would not be able to see them on the bare mountainside. The sun was shining mercilessly down on their backs, turning the grey mountain into a shimmering mirror of heat. Sweat poured down his face, stinging his eyes and more than once he feared that his hands would lose the rope that was pulling his very reluctant horse upwards. He was at the head of the party, trying to follow every direction Eabran gave him and relaying that down the line. His head swam in the heat. His body had long since forgotten food, but his mouth was demanding water. He had not known that it would be so hot and began to regret not bringing more water with him. Silently he vowed to himself that next time he would leave nothing to chance! Next time? He almost laughed out loud – if they did not find water soon, there would be no tomorrow.

Galdr stopped again and putting his hand up to shield his eyes from the glare of the mountain, scoured its bleak, soilless face. Eabran was nowhere to be seen. He could not see the mountain top without putting his head quite a long way back and although his reason told him that there was no use looking more than fifty pchekts ahead he stared at the top of the ridge. Not a sign. The mountain looked steeper, drier, and more menacing as it rose towards its summit and Galdr's heart dropped. Unless Eabran could find a pass, they would never cross the mountain.

A cascade of pebbles came crashing down to his right as Eabran suddenly appeared standing on a rock which jutted out of the mountainside like a finger. He waved his arm, directing Galdr to look to his right. For a few moments Galdr could not see among the splintered rock the course that Eabran had taken but suddenly he had it – a dried-up riverbed, narrow and steep, but it led behind the rock upon which Eabran was standing.

'I can see the other side!' Eabran's voice, though hushed and distorted by his cupped hands, was audible. 'We can get through!'

Galdr wished that he could run up the mountain like a goat and kiss Eabran for his news – instead he waved madly, grinned broadly and turned to Centill who was quite a way behind him. Galdr slipped and almost tumbled down the slope, coming breathlessly upon Centill.

'Eabran has found a pass,' he gasped. 'We will wait and then all go together.'

The two men turned round, hands shading eyes, staring into the high red sun, as Djyana came into view. Djyana was a woman of few words and the news did not alter that, but she smiled warmly at Galdr and then flung her arms round Centill, kissed him hotly on the cheek and burst into tears with relief.

358

The sun was sinking by the time everyone was through the pass. In the deep shade which hugged the other side of the mountain any path was almost invisible. Way below them they saw a land of few trees, much water and vast areas which looked like dark yellow-green marshlands. But it was not the undulating ground which held their attention, nor the sight of so much water, but the vast herds of grazing animals, which, even at this height, looked far bigger than any they had previously seen.

As the light faded, the seemingly inexhaustible Eabran found a small cave – so small it was no more than a depression in the rock-face, but no-one wanted to deflate his triumphantly delivered: 'I have found a cave!' and as night fell, coldness and tiredness overtook them all. What was left of the water was drunk, most given to the horses, then the children and nursing mothers, then the rest. Huddled together, too exhausted to bother eating, too worn out to talk they all soon fell asleep, warmed by each other and the certainty that they were surely in a new land.

It had been Bendula who had suggested that they collected any dung the horses might drop and throw it far to the side of their path. So, had he but known it, it would have been her name, not Injya's that Vronjyi would have cursed as they struggled out of the woods and started to ascend the mountain. As the light faded Vronjyi gave up particularizing his curses and simply cursed. He knew in his bones that they could not be far ahead and as he pulled his sweating, stubborn horse behind him and watched with growing exasperation the gap between him and Sopak widen, he cursed even more. They would *not* see their fire tonight, any more than they had seen it last night. Damn them and damn the horse and damn Soosha and damn the men! As the first stars flickered at him he felt that they were mocking him and his useless rage.

'And damn you too!' he shouted at the heavens. 'Damn you!'

CHAPTER THIRTY-ONE

Galdr alone did not sleep. Although every muscle in his lean body ached, although every thought told him to relax – his senses were too alert to danger to let him indulge in the luxury of sleeping. He watched the stars glitter and then fade behind a bank of cloud and when he was sure that Injya and Pentesh were deeply asleep, he silently removed himself from their side and walked barefoot over the sharp flints and returned to the top of the pass. The low clouds obscured the moon and though the lack of light made his progress slow, it comforted him to know that it would have completely stopped the tracking hunters. Several times he doubted his senses as his eyes, though accustomed to the gloom, deceived him, but eventually he found the narrow gap, less than a pchekt wide, through which they had squeezed.

From Galdr's side of the mountain, the gap was just visible but he knew that from the other side the pass was concealed by overhanging crags. He felt a brief rush of exhilaration on gaining the pass, a feeling which turned a second later into anxiety as his toes touched something soft. A skin! He bent down and picked up the fur which his fingers and nose told him was a small pelt of seal skin. He recognized it as belonging to Toonjya – she had made it into a tiny jacket for Wa-Oagist, he could smell the child all over the jacket and as his hands turned the supple pelt over and his fingers ran along the tiny seams, he became gripped with fear.

His rational mind argued that in the scramble through the pass, in the hasty unpacking of the horses to get them through, it was not surprising that something had been dropped. But his hunter's mind would not listen to the rational – how many more signs had they left of their escape? Underlying this fear was an even deeper one – had Toonjya dropped this little jacket on purpose? No sooner had the thought crossed his mind than he tried to censure it with a 'That is unfair!' but, like a seed, once planted the thought began to grow. He leant against a rock and examined his feelings as minutely as a moment before he had examined the fallen garment. Finally he allowed himself to admit that he did not like Toonjya – he did not like her never-voiced but often felt resentment. It was as if she had never come to terms with her grief over losing two of her children, never really opened her heart to love her foster-child, Wa-Oagist, as if she was always keeping something in reserve, something hidden from the group.

Galdr felt very uneasy and angry with himself. He had clambered up to the pass to look for the hunters, and yet here he was, thrown completely by a dropped jacket! A feeling of tiredness suddenly overcame him and he sank down, resting on his haunches.

The rock upon which he leant his back pricked him as uncomfortably as his thoughts. He *had* to find out what was behind his feelings for Toonjya. He knew that every person was a part of himself, every person was a mirror for an aspect of himself which he either liked or disliked – what was it about Toonjya that mirrored something in himself that he was unwilling to admit? As reluctant as the horses had been to cross the pass, his brain fought against the answer which felt as if it were being dragged out of him. Eventually it fell into the small space of clarity which is kept open to receive such gifts. He, like Toonjya, was guilty of not sharing, of keeping something hidden – not only from the group, but from himself; with a sigh he allowed the truth to focus clearly. Not since his intervention in the birth of his daughter had Galdr allowed the power of the divine to enter him. Even when Tyanka had died, he had been aware that he had shut off his sight, had shut out the knowledge from himself that he was shamming the power to cleanse her body of earth-binding pain and help release her soul to the shining ones.

A stab of pain pierced his heart as he realized that he was afraid, afraid to allow the animal spirits to enter him again, frightened to open himself for divine direction. He struggled against the tears of self-pity which pricked at his eyes, and forced himself to breathe deeply, to untie the knot of apprehension in his stomach. He was afraid and a warrior had no use for cowardice.

'Oh, give me something to take my fear from me!' he prayed urgently to the dark scudding clouds: 'Take my fear away on the wings of your winds, Great Oagist, bring me a sign!'

The more urgently he prayed, the greater the pain became. Suddenly he had a split-second of remembrance; the pain was the same as he had experienced when he had tied himself to his death-tree and in that instant of recognition he felt his spirit soar. His spirit rose to the heavens as if on the wings of a great eagle. *This* was the power of which he was so afraid, his own spirit-power, his eagle-self. Instantaneously he knew, without fear, that he was inhabiting his eagle-self. His spirit had left his body and now inhabited his other self. Feeling tremendous certitude he willed his spirit to clothe itself.

. . . Silver-white eagle Galdr feels the warmth of blood coursing through his body of sinews and muscles and feathers. Effortlessly he rises and hovers for a moment over the sight of his earthly body and then, with an almost imperceptible movement of his wings he flies down the scree slope of the mountain, over the tops of the trees and back up the slope. A third of the way up the mountain all-seeing eagle-eyes picks out the group of hobbled horses and the tiny figures of the sleeping men. He soars again to the peak of the mountain, bright yellow eagle-eyes noting every boulder, every stone, on the face of the mountain. With the instinct of the ultimate hunter he drops down and picks up a rock with his fierce talons. Up again he flies with his stone, up until the sleeping men are no more than tiny black dots upon a mountain which looks no more than a hillock. With the precision of a bird able to catch a swimming fish in the fastest flowing river, he lets the stone drop exactly at the point he wants. The stone whines through the air for many seconds until it crashes to the ground. The sharp crack of stone on stone rings through the soft night with a loud report, but soon that sound is lost as first one, then ten, then a hundred stones begin to move. In an instant the whole of the mountainside looks as if it is becoming liquid as the shock-waves run down its face. Boulders begin to roll, dust rises thickly as the sound of the landslide becomes deafening. Far above the mountain Galdr the Eagle hears the cry of terror from the men far below him, the wild snortings and whinnyings of the hobbled horses, the smell of their fear, but he feels no pity for his quarry. The spirit of the eagle is too old and too wild for compassion.

Silver-white eagle soars over the mountain pass. His bright eagle-eye notices the slumped body of a man. His cruel down-turned beak opens in silent homage as out over the vast marshy plain he swoops. Almost skimming the surface, his darting eyes see the giant beasts, their dark fur trailing the ground, their tusks, longer than his wing-span is wide, shining bright and white in the blackness of the night. A river, sluggish and black, lurches northwards but silver-white eagle flies onwards over the vast treeless tracts of land. Suddenly a copse, silver birches showing their bark bright to the stars. Yellow darting eyes of brother wolf still hoping for cover. Away, over the trees, southward, rising land, low hills black with fir trees, alive with cats of the forest. More huge black shapes, sleeping in the secret night, their brown-bear smells rank in the pure night air. A long flight, over the hills, each wing beat making him warmer, giving him new strength. Below his beating wings stretches thousands of pchekts of flat ground, covered in warm, sweet-smelling black trees. Another river, wildly rushing, cutting the trees in two, making a wide band of steely grey in the denseness. Twist, once, twice, turn the head, see the river, feel the warmth of the south, along the route of the mighty rushing river. Ahead, the river's source, a wide lake resting among the high mountains, nestling among them, the breasts of Hoola herself. Far higher than any mountain silver-eagle has crossed yet, far higher than even the old soul of the silver-white eagle could remember in all his lives. The peaks still covered in the white rains of winter, but between them nestles the lake, and beyond – shelter from the winter's white rains, more mountains, more giant beasts, but also deep, verdant valleys, peaceful and warm.

Yellow eagle-eyes knows of the yellow light before it bursts forth far to the east of him. The head tilts, the wings flicker and one lowers and silver-white eagle heads back along the invisible path in the sky, back across the vast lake and the river, the wide black band of trees and the beasts. Flies back over the bog-bursting banks of the lazy river; blinking yellow eyes wide, as the sound of his feathered brothers waking to the day, reaches his ears. Silver-white eagle flies down to the body left on the pass, sensing it feeling the cold of the early dawning day. Fluttering his wings he settles on the rock above his body. The head darts backwards and forwards, open beak pulling along each feather, straightening the flight feathers, puffing out the down under his breast. Beak pecking at his claws, cleaning his talons. Light coming from the east, sounds of brother ptarmigan and grouse, brother kestrel and hawk, calling to him, willing him to return. Galdr the Powerful releases his will and silver-white eagle soars away . . .

Galdr, son of Anfjord of the Skoonjay people, becomes aware once more of his body. Rubbing his aching arms he stiffly rises and without a sound returns to the sleepy warmth of Injya's side and watches, wide eyed, as the yellow streak of sun shatters the dark horizon.

*   *   *

It was mid-morning and they had come to rest by a tiny stream which cascaded down the mountainside. Perched somewhat precariously on ledges and gratefully eating smoke-dried fish washed down with the icy water of the stream, they listened in profound silence and awe as Galdr explained what had happened while they had been sleeping. So sure was he of their path now that none questioned him for a long time after he had finished his story. When the first one came, however, Galdr felt surprised.

'How?' Oanti's monosyllabic question was greeted with quizzical looks by everyone, but Galdr knew what the 'how' alluded to.

'I willed it to be so,' Galdr replied with a smile.

'Yes, but how?' Oanti's fine delicate face seemed to crinkle all over with frowns as she tried to understand what Galdr had told them. She drew her hand through her short black curly hair and laughed suddenly.

'*I* might wish all sorts of things – but they do not happen for me – how did you do it?'

'*I* did not.'

'But you just said . . . ' Oanti stammered in confusion.

'I prayed and it happened. *I*, Galdr, did not will it, me, the me I call I, was, briefly, not present any more. If you like, I dropped my will and was open to the will of the great spirit. It was the great spirit of the universe who allowed me to inhabit the form of the eagle – that is all!' Galdr laughed suddenly at the total incomprehension on Oanti's face. Instantly he saw that she was hurt by his laughter and he stopped.

'Dear Oanti – the truth is, I do not know. I know that I have been an eagle before, I know that when I was close to death, before I understood how to be, I became an eagle and I remember that the crone I saw in my vision told me that my spirit was an eagle – but that is all. I do not know how precisely, but I know why.'

'Why then?'

365

'Why? So that I could see the hunters behind us, do something about them and then find the path that we must follow before winter settles in – that is why!'

He grinned broadly at her, then at Injya who still sat silently by his side nursing Pentesh. Oanti stared at Galdr again, then asked: 'Do we all have animal spirits? Do I?'

Her normally big brown eyes opened even wider as her imagination took hold of the concept. This time it was Djyana who laughed.

'If you open your eyes any wider, Oanti, they will pop out of your head!'

'What do *you* think, Djyana?' Injya asked before Galdr could reply to Oanti's question. All eyes turned to Djyana now as she looked first at Injya, then at Galdr.

'I think,' she said slowly, 'I think that we do, or at least part of our spirit is an animal.' She dropped her head and added in a low voice after a short pause: 'I sometimes think I am a horse inside.' She said this so quietly that several people murmured: 'What did she say?' but Injya, Galdr and Oanti had heard.

Oanti covered her mouth to hide her giggles, there was something very absurd in Djyana thinking she was a horse inside. She was an enormous woman, taller even than Injya; heavy legged and bovine faced, with lank thick hair which she insisted on wearing short instead of braiding like all the other women; her shoulders were as broad as any man's and the tops of her arms were almost as thick as her own thighs! To imagine this slow-speaking, slow-walking, hefty woman as a horse was too ridiculous! But Injya and Galdr sensed what she said to be true. Galdr smiled at her, then realizing that she had spoken something of her deepest heart, went over and sat down in front of her.

Very quietly he said: 'Djyana, do not be afraid of what you have just spoken. Your feelings are right. Do you think any one of us could have calmed the horses when it has been necessary the way you have? Do you think any of us could have rescued the horses from the water the way you did?

It is no coincidence that horses respond to you, Djyana. What you have said is true. Inside you *is* the spirit of a horse. A fine, swift running, faithful horse.'

Everyone was silent, watching Djyana who kept her head bowed to the earth and Galdr who sat before her, eyes shining, love pouring forth from every muscle in his body. Slowly at first, Djyana's shoulders began to shake and then as the emotions moved more strongly inside her, her back curved, her head lowered further towards the ground and she broke into convulsive sobbing.

'I am not!' she was blubbering through the tears. 'I am not – look at me! I am fat and slow and ugly!'

More tears stopped the words and Ullu and Aywe, unable to restrain themselves from her sadness, rushed forward to comfort her. They were stopped by Galdr raising his hand and shaking his head. Bewildered they sat down again, staring at Djyana's shaking shoulders, frowning as her sobbing seemed to reach an even deeper level.

'I . . . am . . . not fit . . . to be likened . . . to a horse!' she managed to sob, suddenly raising her face and glaring at the impassive features of Galdr before her. 'How . . . how can you say . . . that I am?'

Only then did Galdr touch her. He leant forward and with his index finger touched the place between her breasts where he knew the pain was hurting most. It was as if he had sent a bolt of lightning through her body. It shook violently, then the whole of her body seemed to disintegrate. She fell forward, face down in Galdr's lap and cried like a new-born child. Only then did Galdr look up at the silent, shocked faces around him. As he gently stroked Djyana's back and rocked her slowly backwards and forwards he said quietly: 'Djyana, the mare mother has just been born – love her if you will.'

Ullu and Aywe were the first to rush forward and stroke the still-crying Djyana, but soon everyone was crowded round Galdr and Djyana; after a short while her crying stopped. Struggling to get up she was finally able to sit back on her haunches and wiping away the tears from her face, she sighed deeply and looked straight into Galdr's eyes as if she were seeing him for the first time.

'What did you do to me?' she asked simply, her brown eyes shining, reflecting the new-found feeling of calm acceptance in herself.

'Nothing, I simply helped the spirit to come through the barrier you had constructed in your heart. That is all.'

He smiled at her, seeing her trusting self open to him, seeing the strength flow through her, the strength of her guiding spirit, the mother mare coming home to rest in her capable body. For a brief moment Galdr had the vision of Djyana the mare; strong, sure-footed, swifter than the fastest stallion, and he knew that very soon Djyana herself would recognize and feel that part of herself.

No-one wanted to move. The warmth and tenderness of Djyana's 'home-coming' had touched each deeply and for a long time afterwards they sprawled about somewhat uncomfortably on the gentle slopes of the mountain. But eventually Potyami's constant: 'Come on, come on!' made them reluctantly get to their feet and resume their journey down the mountain.

The descent was much less steep than the ascent and although it was still too steep to ride, everyone felt that this gentle slope was a very good omen. Ahead of them they could see the vast plain stretching as far as their eyes could see. Although the great hair-covered creatures which they had dimly glimpsed the previous evening were still a long way off, these curious tusked animals seemed even more enormous than they had first anticipated. They had been able to see in daylight all the game which wandered over the green marshland below and although they had a large deep forest to ride through before they came to the plain, nothing could lower their raised spirits. Very soon they came to some trees and then the ground began to level out; once through this they would be on the pastures of a future.

By nightfall Galdr estimated that they had covered nearly half of the forested expanse and wanting to rest the horses as much as himself, he ordered the party to make camp for the night. Jubilant at the thought of safety, Eabran, Torben and Centill cut thin boughs from trees and intertwined them roughly with bent saplings to make make-shift sancars. All the women helped to cover the frames with skins and by the time Halfray had found heathers, dried branches and twigs for the fire, the sancars were finished.

'Our first free fire of our free life!' Centill announced gleefully as he watched the flint spark catch the brushwood and the blaze take hold.

'Our first decent meal!' Eabran exclaimed as Torben dropped the third rabbit he had caught that day into his lap. Sanset and Bendula prepared the rabbits skilfully and soon they were cooking over the fire. As Bai Ulgan drew his cloak of night over the heavens and the stars began their dancing, everyone became sleepy and soon there was only Sanset and Halfray, Galdr and Injya left awake. They talked together in hushed voices, sharing their innermost thoughts until they too could resist sleep no more.

The full moon shone down on the four tiny sancars among the tall fir trees and reflected the serenity of the hearts of those sleeping inside. For once she did not call to her sister the rain, or her father the wind and, as if infected by her liquid silver light, the beasts of the night did not venture near the fragile homes and all slept safe and secure for the first time for almost a moon's whole passing.

Ahni Amwe shone down also on the men who would bring savagery to this silvan scene. She shone her cold white light upon their bloody arms and legs, the carcasses of two of their horses. Unmoved she shone down on the pain-distorted faces of the men who, not finding the pass through which Injya and her people had squeezed, were sheltering, shivering, on a ledge on the far side of the mountain. Frightened, cold and injured, they too slept, the words of their chief riddling their dreams with raw anger: 'Kill her and all her women, kill all the men too, but bring back my son!' Serenely, she continued her journey through the heavens, untouched and unfeeling, reflecting only the spirits of those below her, shining back to them their most deeply-felt loves, their most hidden longings and their most secret desires.

CHAPTER THIRTY-TWO

Pentesh hiccuped and looked into Injya's eyes in a startled manner. The sudden movement in her baby's body brought Injya back from her reverie. In the darkness she could hardly see Pentesh's upturned face but she knew what her look would be: wide-eyed amazement.

'Bones in it, are there?' she asked her now contentedly suckling child. 'You are going too fast, that is all, my pet.'

Carefully rearranging her cradling arms, she gently rubbed Pentesh's back. A second later the tiny child stopped sucking, burped faintly, cried for a second, then resumed the task in hand. A few moments later Pentesh sighed, sucked once or twice more in a half-hearted fashion, then fell heavily asleep. Injya gently laid her child down on the fur-covered floor and wrapped her first in the woven cloth, then the kid, then the baby seal-skin. Picking up the soiled cloth of night she crept out of the sancar, secure in the knowledge that should Pentesh so much as whimper Sanset, Bendula or Aywe would be instantly at her side.

Outside Injya stretched her hands up to the leaf-covered heavens, twisted her aching body and yawned widely. The air was shockingly cold and her yawn shone white against the still grey of the early dawn. Picking up the night-cloth once more, Injya hurried over to the tiny stream by which they had camped. Here the trees were less dense and the rivulet seemed to sparkle as if dancing with a million tiny gems as the first rays of the rising sun filtered through the leaves. The water was icy cold, but after washing the soiled garment Injya could not resist the need to bathe any longer.

371

Shivering wildly she threw off her layers of clothing and waded into the stream. Catching her breath and swallowing back the urge to scream like an excited child she splashed herself all over then, taking a deep breath to brace herself, she sat down on the stone bed and let the icy water wash away the last few traces of birth. Only ten days had elapsed since Pentesh had been born. Ten days of terror, travelling and little sleep, but as Injya watched the clear water ripple down over her thighs she felt enervated, not only physically clean, but spiritually cleansed, as if the water, by taking away the last traces of birth-blood was also obliterating the memory of their fright-filled journey.

She got out of the water quickly and dashed over to the fire. Wrapping herself in the largest fur, she turned over the night-log and discovered its bright red underbelly. A few scraps of dried leaves, a few twigs and the fire caught again. Soon the twigs were crackling, while red and blue flames leapt into the frosty air. Several slender branches were added and the fire responded, settling down to eat its way steadily through the offered fuel. Injya wanted to sit on her haunches and shiver herself dry, but she gave way to commonsense, ran and fetched her woven under-shift and quickly got into her layers of skins and furs which would keep her warm until the sun gave some of his strength to the day. She stood by the fire for a few seconds, staring eastwards.

Through the massive dark trunks of the pine forest shot bright amber arrows of the new day's sun. High above the black canopy, tiny speckles of indigo sky were visible, they too streaked with the orange needles of the dawn. The frost-crisped air smelt so strongly of pine-needles that it almost took her breath away; Injya wished that all their journey should be so scented. Noiselessly, she seated herself by the fire and listened intently to the sounds of the forest: the first few birds sang almost cautiously, as if they, too, were listening; while all the time the trees whispered and swayed their song of the boughs in the gentle breeze;

372

a faint rustle to her right and turning quickly, Injya saw the darting shadow of a squirrel or perhaps it had been a pine martin. Before her mind could play its guessing game, the sound and the shadow disappeared. The crackle of the fire, the bird- and tree-song – a perfect moment of rare aloneness and peace.

Hugging her knees and rocking slightly with pleasure, she stared into the dancing heart of the fire. As if to remind her that such moments are very rare, a picture of Tyanka suddenly leapt out of the fire at her. She shook her head sorrowfully as she thought of Tyanka's death. It gave her no pleasure to know that she had been right all that time ago. Tyanka had been doomed to die – her soul had been crushed by Anfjord as her slender, childlike body had been and her spirit robbed of the will to live. She shivered at the thought that perhaps the hunters had come across her shallow grave and then remembered Galdr's eagle-flight. He would have seen, he would have been drawn down to the earth if Tyanka's mortal remains had been disturbed – but he had not, he had caused an avalanche which had killed the hunters – they, and Tyanka, were safe. And as her memory retold the strange tale of Galdr's eagle-flight, she realized with a shock that up to this moment she had accepted everything that had happened to them, everything that she had been told. She had not really questioned anything.

As if suddenly shifting a giant tree, behind which lay a swollen river, her brain was awash with questions, each tumbling and rushing upon another in its urgency to be answered. So quick was the torrent, that before she had finished one, another would come bubbling to the top of the rapid river of doubt. But each bubbling question was dashed upon the solid, immovable boulder of one – the biggest of all – why? Her face flushed as if she had been caught stealing, as the boulder of why became larger and more impenetrable. Injya heard the croaking, thin voice of Askoye saying, 'Not why – but how?' but her voice was being drowned out by the voices of the questions, with the voice of 'why?' shouting louder than any other.

Why did she accept Galdr into her heart when her head was screaming no? What had really happened when Galdr delivered her baby? Why did he seem to change into an animal? Why did he change into an eagle? Why did *he* undergo that terrible ordeal into the underworld and not her? What was so special about him – why did Askoye not show the same to her? What were they doing – searching for a new homeland or a new identity? And why the years of training with Askoye if now all seemed to be of no use? What was this new power that Galdr had and where did it come from? She felt tears welling up in her eyes as her confusion grew. Now, instead of feeling at one with the universe, she felt unutterably alone – her frantic questioning robbing her of her power. She felt like a cheated child, surrounded by adults who knew the answers and who were enjoying her perplexity. She jumped up, trembling with rage – how dare he keep secrets from her – how dare this man come into her life again, taking away her power? She stared at the sancar in which the men were sleeping – willing Galdr to come out and confront her, willing him to answer the questions still raging inside her head.

She took a step towards the sancar, muttering through trembling lips when, staggering in its simplicity, came the answer – because it is my will! It was not Askoye's voice which rang in her head, nor that of her mother or her grandmother. It was not the voice of the wind-caressed Ahni Amwe or even the deeper voice of Hoola, the great Earth Mother, it was a voice which came from the trees, the sky, the earth and the tiny stream. It was the voice she had not dared to question before – the voice of the universe.

She sank to her knees as unbidden, her memory unlocked the doors to the vision she had seen when she had ascended the tree of life – the vision of Bai Ulgan's universe – pure love. Below her had been the shining orbs

of those about to incarnate – above her divine radiance –
in her, a longing to be nearer to this power so strong that
it tore at her tiny bird-fluttering heart. She remembered
the overpowering feeling of wanting to be part of this
great love. Again, another memory flooded forth – Injya,
standing in front of her cave, arms raised to the heavens,
begging Ahni Amwe to come to her, begging her to breathe
Her life and light into her – and after she had done that?
Did she not know, wholeheartedly, that everything that
had happened to her and would happen to her in the
future was because she was acting out the Divine Plan?
As she remembered, a small part of that great love she had
felt filled her heart and gave her wisdom. The knowledge
told her to rid herself of questions, be done with jealousy
(for that, she realized with a sickening jolt, was what lay
at the root of her questions about Galdr) and to open
her heart completely to the new manifestation of power.
Slowly she became aware once more of the bird-song and
the whispering trees and she heard the answers she was
seeking in the gentle murmuring sounds of the world
around her.

The power of Ahni Amwe she had clung to had diminished
– that was right. When mankind had understood that
though She ruled the courses of women, She did not
create life in their secret places, but man and woman
together created the new lives – it was right that Her
adoration should decline. As that deeper understanding of
the mystery of birth had come so recently to their people,
so too, was it right for a deeper understanding of the world
to manifest. Their world was made up of total mysteries,
rivers, floods, ice, the fishes in the seas, the animals of the
lowlands – all had their part to play – all were connected
and each could teach the other. Galdr, a soul once so evil,
had been chosen, perhaps because of his very flaws of
nature, to act as an intermediary between mankind and
the world of spirits. It was not anything he had *learnt*, but
was something given by Bai Ulgan himself – the ability to

transcend his form, to take on the spirit-form of the very animals and birds with whom they shared this universe. Great lessons would be learnt – truths, as earth-shattering as the truth about birth, would be shown to them, a new age of understanding was dawning and Injya had been allowed to be part of it.

She felt again a warm sense of belonging and wandered off into the trees: she found herself saying that if it was in the divine plan – she would find something good to eat – as if by a miracle food would suddenly present itself to her. As she ambled along the streamside she found her thoughts wandering to Halfray and Sanset. They had been inseparable since Sanset had declared her love for him. She smiled as she thought of Halfray – she had never thought of her brother as a man, a man who could have strong desires. Certainly he had never known a woman before, of that she was sure and she could not wish for a better partner for him. Strong, sensible Sanset, *she* had her feet on the ground, she would keep Halfray safe. She wondered why safety seemed to loom so large whenever she thought of Halfray – it was as if she still thought of him as he had been before she had lived with Askoye and not the man he had grown into, as if she were his elder brother, not the other way round. She thought then of the other men in the group: Centill, as soft as his name sounded, silent Centill, a man of few words but his tall, wiry frame charged with a driving energy which shone from his clear, grey eyes; and there was Torben and Eabran, childhood friends, scarce out of childhood themselves, both strong, short statured, dark haired and dark eyed, but Torben very much the leader of the two, the innovator, Eabran the one who carried out Torben's ideas – they would grow into strong men.

She could not help wonder whom they would each choose for partners, Oanti or Aywe. Injya suddenly remembered Torben's flushed face when she told him to ride with

Aywe when they first escaped. So, she said to herself, that leaves Eabran with Oanti then! The two girls were the natural choices as all four of them were roughly the same age. She let her mind happily wander on until she realized that she was matchmaking as if she were an old woman already – not one who was herself only a summer or two older than they! Who knows what would happen? Ullu was fourteen summers old and would shortly become a woman and then, of course, there was Bendula, who, although only eleven summers old, was displaying all the signs of early maturity.

As she thought of Ullu and Bendula, she realized that she had never thought of Ullu with a man. Not simply because she was not yet ready for a man, but because she felt sure that the Goddess had other work for Ullu to do. She pictured the slender girl, her open, freckled face always smiling and remembered the embarrassment she had displayed when she admitted that she could see Tyanka's spirit-lights leave her body. Injya knew not whether to pity or celebrate her gifts – she was obviously a natural seer – would she be called upon to teach her, or would some other initiation happen for the girl? Only the Goddess knew.

Behind her a horse whinnied and stamped its foot. The sound of the horse moving made her think of Djyana – Djyana, the horse soul. Would Centill want to take her for his mate? If Djyana allowed her mother mare to come out, she would surely lose some of her heaviness and seriousness. Would that attract Centill? Suddenly she laughed out loud. Enough – the Goddess – or the animal-spirits – would decide these matters – not her!

She left the side of the stream and walked deeper into the trees. Denser here, the blue sky obliterated by the canopy, her thoughts turned dark too. What of Toonjya? Poor Toonjya, always the first to moan, the first to want to rest, the one least willing to try. She thought of the first time she had really noticed Toonjya, just after Ucatt had died and the other women had elected her to be Wa-Oagist's foster-mother. Toonjya had not complained, had accepted the sense in not wasting all her milk, but the defeated way in which she accepted their decision had worried her. It was if she, like Tyanka, did not have a will strong enough to either fully accept or reject. As the oldest woman by some five summers, it should be Toonjya to whom everyone turned and yet, no-one ever did. She was almost ignored by everyone, herself included.

She stopped, suddenly realizing where her idle thoughts had led her – she thought she had been indulging in idle matchmaking, but in fact she had come to understand something of great import. If *she* felt like this about Toonjya, perhaps everyone felt the same. Small wonder that Toonjya was the whining, reluctant one, she had good reason to feel rejected, she had good reason to moan! Injya suddenly felt very small inside as she realized she was as guilty as the rest of them in excluding Toonjya. She knew that for the group to survive, they had to be a cohesive force; small but linked with each other to create a powerful channel. She turned and ran away from her dark thoughts and the dark trees. All the clarity and understanding of the past few minutes were for nought if one of their number was excluded.

As she got back to the fire, she heard Galdr's voice mumble from inside the sancar.

' . . . the kind of dream that leaves you with no doubt in your mind that what you dreamt was true.'

'And you are *sure*?' Halfray's response was softly spoken, but quite audible. Injya stopped – unsure what to do – everyone else was asleep. She walked towards their sancar, but the words which Galdr spoke stopped her in her tracks.

'I am afraid that our hunters are not dead. As clearly as I can see you now, I saw five men, bathed in the moonlight, shivering with cold, huddled against the mountainside. I saw one raise his blood-smeared arms and shout his rage into the heavens – I heard him shout my name. Halfray, the hunters have only been delayed, not stopped.'

And Injya felt her heart sink – there would be precious little time to share her insights with everyone *this* day!

CHAPTER THIRTY-THREE

On the eastern slope of the low black hills, a small group of people slowly descended, their horses picking their way through the thinning trees, taking in the unfamiliar sights and smells of this new southerly land. On the western slope of the hills, two days' ride behind them, five men and four horses, thankful for the trees' shade after the burning heat of the plain, painstakingly followed the people's tracks, grim determination scarring their faces. And far away to the west of these mountains, over the plain, over the high mountain range, over the mighty river Pchektora, on the flat marshlands which bordered the turbulent autumn-icy seas, the people of the Skoonjay land, the two tribes of the Gyaretz and Branfjord, made fast their homes. For the first time in their histories, they were not going to the winter cave-lands; the cave-lands which had always protected them from the winter's harsh white rains and fierce bone-chilling winds.

Only the fear of the white rains was common to each three groups. The white rains which brought in their wake such an intense cold, that the breath froze on their lips and nostrils. The cold, so bitter that their fingers and toes became so chilled that they longed for the numbness which would eventually follow, even though they knew that beyond that came the burning heat, the cracking skin, the wounds that would not heal; the cold which would freeze a freshly-caught fish so quickly, that when re-heated, it would seem to come alive again briefly; the cold that would freeze even the foaming seas and turbulent rivers into corrugated ice-sheets which tore at the soles of their skin shoes and creaked in the howling black nights.

Three moons had passed since Injya, Galdr and their people had escaped, and the weather was on the turn. At first, a light whispering wind played with the grasses and the fragile aspen and birch leaves, seeming to mock the fear of the people, who knew that before long, it would no longer be toying. In one awful deep-throated cursing night, the trees were stripped bare and the grasses no longer danced, but rippled in the wind like waves on the oceans. This was the beginning of the fear, for as surely as each knew that soon the white rains would fall, each feared mighty Oagist who would seek out the weakest among them, find the cracks in the sancars, tear out the very trees from their mother earth and wind, relentlessly, round their bodies and homes, seeking entrance to their souls.

Anfjord knew this to be true. He knew that the winds, no matter that they had come early that year, meant the onset of winter – he knew the elements as well as he knew his people. He had lived for over forty summers on this land and he knew, as he knew his own hand, that to attempt to stay in the summer-lands over winter was not just folly – it was insanity. But something was stopping him from going against the wishes of Soosha; his daughter had changed – he feared her even more than he feared the white rains, the darkness, or even mighty Oagist himself. No matter how much they argued, Soosha was immovable and he understood, as clearly as he understood the weather, that he was now totally powerless against her wishes.

He felt like an outcast among his own people. Even his own brother, Bran, had sided with Soosha saying in his womanish way that perhaps it would be safe – no-one had ever tried before – was he so sure that they would all perish? Anfjord shook his grey head in disbelief. And all his people, they too had agreed with her – sided with Soosha, not him!

In the distance he could hear the dull thudding of men felling trees. Nearer to his ears came the sharp reports of flint on flint as axe-heads were being prepared and mixing with the whispering wind came the slow swishes of the reeds being cut. It would take more than reed padding between two skins to save them from the ice of winter! It was hearing that this last ridiculous suggestion of Soosha's was actually being carried out which made Anfjord suddenly decide to leave his people. Come what may – *he* was not about to let himself freeze to death on the mere whim of a woman!

'Soosha!' he roared over the clanging stones as he stood, arms crossed in anger over his chest. 'Daughter – come out!'

Instantly the axe-makers stopped their chopping, the children their laughing games, the women their incessant chattering. Only the wind disregarded his furious barked instructions. A long moment passed, then slowly Soosha drew back the entrance flap on her sancar and came out to face him. Her face was flushed, cheeks scarlet, eyes blazing. She too crossed her arms on her breast and with long black hair tossing round her shoulders, she returned the look of anger her father gave her.

'Daughter – you are wrong!' Anfjord shouted at her. Her defiant look, her wildly tossing hair further infuriating him. 'You will not see it – you will not listen! You are too full of your love for this Xynon creature – it has addled your brain! I will not allow this folly – I will not allow you to put all our people in danger! I say that we go to our winter homelands – and – we go now! It is already late – we are going – NOW!'

Soosha stood her ground and continued staring silently at her father. Her defiance turned his anger into blind rage. He took a step towards her, hand raised as if to strike her, then seemingly thinking better of it, suddenly whirled round and shouted to the group of people who were standing, open mouthed, behind him.

'Well, you have heard what I have spoken. I, Anfjord, chief, *only* chief of the Branfjord people, command you to

382

obey me. We are going to the winter homelands. Make the preparations!'

Not a soul moved. Eyes left his and lowered to the ground. He turned round and stared at Soosha, then back at the crowd. She had them all under her spell – none would obey him. Suddenly he saw the enormity of her power. It was not simply a matter of moving to the winter homelands or not – it was more than that. Never again would he be welcomed by his own people, never again could he command respect. He was now as much of an outcast as his son. There was no longer any place for him with his own people. He lowered his arms from his chest and stared at the bowed heads before him.

'Is there not one among you who will come?' Out of the crowd, only two men shifted their feet uneasily, only two whose bowed heads seemed to drop further on to their chests with discomfort. 'Am I to go off into the winter with no-one? Am I to end my days in exile?' Two more heads bobbed as their owners squirmed with uncertainty. Anfjord's thoughts were racing – that made four, four men, not many, but four men – perhaps their wives too – I could make a new tribe with that number! *I* could find new lands, *I* could make a new life – me – Anfjord! Chief of the Branfjord people! I will not stay in the caves like a sulking, sleeping animal, I will go beyond the caves, beyond the mountains, I will find a new home, new lands, better lands. As the idea grew in his head, it was all he could do not to shake with excitement – it was not exile that faced him, it was adventure!

'You men – yes – you, and you. Come with me. I will lead you to a new life – not a life here, waiting for the winter to kill you off one by one, but a new life in a new land, far above the white rains, far above the winter caves – I will find the land for a new home – a home in high mountains and deep green valleys. I will take you to the land which is always bathed in the spirit-lights of our ancestors, the land of our manhood where women, daughters, wives, will never again dare to raise their voices against us. You – Amjund – you will come with me, yes?' He looked eagerly at the man whose scarlet face lifted as his name was called; 'And you – Törhilde – yes?' Without waiting for any reply he wheeled round on the still silent Soosha. 'See, my dearest daughter – you do not own the will of *all* of my people yet!'

Turning round again, flushed with success, he once more exhorted the men to follow him, to listen to the voice of wisdom. The other two men who had shuffled were named: Hunvor and Tjorsen. They too agreed with a silent nod of the head, the crowd making spaces around them, as if already dead to them.

'And what of Galdr?' Soosha's voice was low and threatening behind him. 'What of your precious son – you will never see him if you go off to new lands – what of your son, Anfjord?'

'Erlik take my son!' he spat out at her. 'Your brave Vronjyi did *not* find him in three days. It is three *moons* now – he has not returned! He is now dead to me! I have lost everything I ever owned, Soosha – my brother, my babies, my people. Galdr stole my favourite wife and you have stolen my people and my land. If Galdr ever comes back – you may do with him as you want. I cursed him once, I curse him again – and I curse you, my daughter!'

The crowd, which, up till that moment had been silent, gasped as if with one breath; only the four named men did not stir or shuffle with fear as Anfjord turned away from Soosha's anger-darkened face.

'Do I have any more who want to join me? Or are you all happy to stay with a cursed daughter of mine – a cursed daughter in a cursed land?' Another head bobbed but this time Anfjord only smiled and said sardonically: 'Oh no, not you, Bran – your place is here – with the women!' and tossing back his head he began laughing, laughing at the wind-torn clouds, the foaming seas, the faces now fearful once more in front of him. As abruptly as he had started, he stopped and strode through the crowd calling the names of Tjorsen, Amjund, Törhilde, and Hunvor as he went, not heeding Soosha's screaming voice behind him:

'You will have no horses, Father. No horses! You will go on foot!'

Soosha's only feeling as she watched the figures walk off into the wilderness, was one of relief. At least she was free from the crime of patricide which she had convinced herself was the next step. She could leave that to the elements. Five men, four women, two children – they would not survive the first moon's passing – the wind, the white rains, the cold – they would rid her of her troublesome father and his outdated ideas.

She turned to Xynon and smiled up into his sombre face – how little faith he had! Wrapping herself more tightly in her furs she walked away from him towards a group of men who too had watched the figures until they were small insignificant shadows on the landscape. At her approach they resumed their former task – that of hacking off the branches from the sturdy trees they had felled. Soosha smiled at them, a distant, vague smile of an indulgent, but otherwise occupied parent to a child, and walked on to one of the women's sancars. Inside, skilled fingers were twisting and winding, pulling and plaiting the fibrous threads of the bark of the fir trees. Great coils of rope already prepared lay in twisted piles all over the floor. The sancar fell silent as she entered, the chatter resuming only hesitantly after she left.

Soosha turned her attention next to the smoke-house, preferring to stand outside the great conical construction and watch the smoke as it was pulled out of the hole in the roof by the greedy wind. This, at least, was a triumph, she thought as she looked up at the skin-covered building which rose majestically almost twenty pchekts into the sky. Her preoccupied smile turned into a broad grin –

385

how everyone had argued with her – how everyone had thought it was a stupid idea, one large smoke-house where the freshly-caught meat could be slowly dried and smoked instead of the tiny little ones which they had always used before, where, because of the size, the fires were always going out, or the meat catching alight. In such a building, they could smoke food enough for everyone for the whole winter!

She marched away from the smoke-house, away from the circle of sancars and up to the dunes. Here, the wind seemed to rip at her face as the silver-white sand turned each gust into an instrument of torture. Below her, the sea was a menacing dark green, white foam rode on the crests of the breakers as they dashed on to the shore. The sound of the wind and the sea was almost deafening, a thrashing, angry sound. High in the air gulls and guillemots cried and shrieked as they wheeled their effortless flight. Between her and the rock upon which she had sat and cursed her brother, two small umiaks crashed up and down on the waves. Tiny, stick-like men hung over the sides, thin spears in hands as they jabbed into the turbulent water at unseen quarry. She wanted to shout at them: 'Go to the rock – fools – go to the rock!' but she knew that words were useless, the hunters would not hear over the sea's angry song and the wind's bitter howling. Turning back to the encampment, she made a mental note to tell the fishermen to be brave, go to the rock, there they would find seals a-plenty.

In the lee of the small rise of ground upon which the death stone lay, she found her youths and women, hacking at the ground, tearing up and discarding the spiky marsh grass and clumps of lichen. Under the foliage, watery black earth glistened in the feeble sunlight. She looked into the watery mess they were creating and doubt overcame her for the first time since she had spawned the idea. Perhaps even the ferocious wind of autumn would not dry out the soil – perhaps they had all been right.

Suddenly feeling angry by being thwarted by mere soil she strode onwards, gaining the rise of the copse which now looked thin and meagre after the felling of the trees. Underfoot the dried leaves crunched and whirled round her ankles. Angrily she stared at the innocent leaves, wanting to kick at them viciously, wanting to kick at anything viciously. She would not be thwarted! They *would* plant the ground with nut trees and berry bushes, they *would* grow the sweet white tubers from which they could make wine and which tasted so good when roasted – and, her angry brain went on, she would eat freshly gathered fungi – if it could grow in the forest, then it could grow where *she* wanted it to!

She picked up a handful of leaves and hurled them into the wind. They blew back in her face. Furious, she picked up another handful, scraping the soft brown earth away with her fingernails as she did so. As she was about to hurl another handful at the wind, the feeling of the soft earth reached her senses. Not caring that the wind almost pulled her cloak from her shoulders, she ran down to the encampment and straight into the men's sancar.

'I want all of you – right now!' she commanded the astonished looking group of men who had been discussing the departure of Anfjord. 'Bring skins, and follow me!'

By the time the sun fell from view and the winds turned bitter, Soosha and her men had removed a great mound of leaf-mould from the copse and had dug it into the boggy soil by the death stone. They did not believe her when she insisted that when the winter was over, they would plant crops which would grow, quickly and easily. They did not believe her when she said that soon, having to trek for days on end to find food would be a thing of the past, they only obediently obeyed the one who, for reasons they could not understand, commanded their total compliance and trust.

Soosha's earlier feelings of anger had gone completely as she had watched the men scrape and dig. By nightfall she felt exhilarated by her day: the fishermen had caught four good-sized seals and two hunters had returned with a buck which they had killed and a doe and a foal, which they had spared. Soon, as the animals moved to their winter quarters, they would catch and pen many more. Then, all winter they would have fresh meat! Her happiness made her oblivious to the problem of food for the animals in the winter and as she lay in Xynon's arms, listening to the wind outside and the strong thudding of his heart she felt completely confident. Her plan for a new way of life would work, *was* working. She stroked his chest and snuggled closer into his arms. Xynon mumbled something she did not catch and snored lightly. With a moment's annoyance she realized he had fallen asleep while she had been recounting the triumphs of her day to him.

Irritated, Soosha listened to Xynon's rhythmic breathing. Her marriage had not been as easy as she had initially thought. Before her marriage she knew that Xynon had been enraptured by her, but since Igrat's death her power over him seemed to have waned. She wished she did not feel so muddled about him. When she felt clear and strong, she saw him for what he was, a useful man who, once he had served his purpose, she would be rid of. But increasingly she was unsure. Xynon seemed to know her, seemed to regard her in a new light, as if that awful day, when they had discovered Galdr and the rest gone, and he had brought back Igrat's body, had changed him. She too had changed, she knew that. As the moon's phases waxed and waned, as Xynon's love-making became less urgent, more tender, she discovered a new tenderness inside her. But now, all would change, she vowed. Now that Anfjord had gone, the last of the obstacles in her way had fallen. Now, she could realize her true power. Now was the time to summon Erlik.

With rock crystals in her heart, she moved her hand down Xynon's chest to his soft manhood. Gently she caressed him, murmuring to him, feeling his body respond, sensing him awakening to her desire. Without words she continued the stroking, hearing him moaning, feeling his desire grow. When she could restrain him no longer, she took him into her, grasping his sex firmly, as she recanted in her mind the name of her master. The picture began forming behind her eyes, the vision of Erlik growing larger as she fought with Xynon's urgent need. The picture was complete behind her eyes, she could see Erlik clearly, his fish-scale body, his hideous glistening eyes, his licentious drooling mouth. The crystals coalesced, power was hers, the moment was right. She let go of Xynon's manhood and felt him thrust into her. His hot body pounded into hers as slowly she moved her hand to grasp the knife. His body became rigid as deeper into hers his sex strove. Soosha opened her eyes, knife poised between Xynon's shoulder-blades to deal the blow that would end his life as he gave her his.

The sancar was black. There was no vision of Erlik.

Xynon wept with passion spent. Soosha lay inert. A single tear escaped through clenched lids. The knife lay, unseen, unused where it had fallen.

Erlik had betrayed his daughter.

Soosha lay in the velvet blackness, conscious only of the sound of her blood pulsing through her body. Her head ached as the rhythmic flow filled her ears. Without opening her eyes she felt her brow; it was damp, though inside she felt as if she was on fire. Slowly, visions of the previous night came back to her and she shivered, not from the heat of her body or the cold of the air, but from a deep sense of revulsion. Erlik had betrayed her. He had not come as bidden and she knew that she would have to repeat the act of coupling, over and over again until he did materialize.

Her stomach lurched at the thought. She thought of Xynon lying sleeping peacefully beside her and her stomach turned again. She had enjoyed him once, but that was then – now she had only one desire: to receive his seed, to take his soul and from that create one who could enact her wishes, unencumbered by the cloying need for tenderness or the frailties of her sex. Once she had the power of Erlik growing inside her, once the power of Erlik had been given life, she would have no further use for any man. She mouthed the word again: power. Power – the very word seemed to change her body, her being charging it with ice-sharp clarity and energy. She opened her eyes and lay, blinking in the darkness, as thoughts raced through her head. Anfjord – she had hated him as long as she could remember: Galdr, favoured Galdr, whose arrogance had turned the most minor feat into something of wonder and daring in the eyes of her father; the boys with whom she had grown up, the swaggering, self-important youths who had become rutting animals and finally, subdued by women, reluctant, inconsequential fathers – how powerless they really were! And then there was Xynon, foolish, blind Xynon! She wanted to feel sorry for him, but he was not worthy of her pity – he was a fool. He was as blind to her real ambition as he was his own fate.

She rose giddily from her low bed and instantly felt nauseous. Holding on to the central pole of the sancar for support, she felt her body sway as the room reeled. Her knees felt as if they had suddenly turned to jelly as she stumbled over to the pitcher, broke the film of ice on the top and splashed freezing water on to her face and neck. Gasping from the shock she forced herself to stand upright. A sticky warmth ran down between her thighs. Her courses had come again.

Cursing nature she furiously tore at her clothing and dowsed herself mercilessly with the ice-cold water. A grim, tight-lipped smile was the only expression on her face as she understood why Erlik had not come to her. Now, she would have to wait for half a moon's passing before she could summon him again. Xynon had been spared for another half-moon and she would have to suffer him for perhaps even longer.

Little served to change the grim, determined smile she wore that morning. Outside the wind had died and in its place the earth had covered herself in a crisp layer of frost. Each hardened blade of rime-encrusted grass seemed to mock her certitude, each sparkling spider's web glinting in the early morning red sky, laughed at her insistence that life in the summer-lands over winter would be better than the safety of the caves. At the morning meeting of the tribe, some of the men cast aspersions on her planting plan and a woman brought up the subject of animal feed.

She felt inwardly furious at having been doubted, but she swallowed her anger as she once again spoke of her vision of a settled family community, each sharing but each separate. As she talked she felt the tribe warm to her and before long each was fired with enthusiasm once more. As she rose, she delivered the *coup de grâce* – that of reminding them of the danger they were under from Galdr and Injya. It was the catalyst that galvanized them all into action and throughout the rest of the day which she spent resting in her sancar, she could hear the sounds of building all around her. Her grim smile changed at last into a rueful one as she wished that Erlik also would be as amenable to her wishes.

Seven rain-sodden, gale-lashing days turned every job into a freezing chore as the earth turned to mud, the fires guttered, and smoke and grime turned everyone's fingers and faces black, but within seven days the cluster of twenty-five sancars had been replaced by four enormous ones, each longer, lower and more solid than they had ever built before. Every available skin had been used to make the double walls, the cavities packed solid with damp reeds for insulation. Each sancar had four hearths, and, therefore, four smoke holes and the long oval buildings had been placed, not in a circle as previous encampments, but side by side, their slender ends facing the prevailing winds. Between each sancar a low tunnel had been constructed, linking one with another. On the wind side of these tunnels, palisades had been constructed to deflect the wind and on the lee side, two flaps half a pchekt apart served as entrance and exit.

Xynon, standing on the denuded hillside, stared down on the curious buildings. The encampment looked like a curious thin-bodied, fat-legged animal, tethered by hundreds of ropes to the black glistening earth with its head, the conical smoke-house, severed from its body. Ice was in the rain which was gusting horizontally against his back. He did not know which way to face. Both sights, the flat wind-bleached marshlands behind him and the encampment before him, filled him with foreboding, and despite his love for Soosha, despite the preparations they had all made, despite the planning, arguing, reasoning that each had exerted so much energy on, a small frightened voice inside him still kept gnawing away, telling him that this was madness, whispering that nature would take her revenge. He had climbed the hillock to rid himself of this foreboding, only to feel it more keenly. As the short grey day died and the wind blew harder, his feeble hope died too. They would never survive.

At first, the white rains fell slowly and softly. As if intent on simply covering the ugly-turned earth in a gentle blanket of glistening white. Children played, screaming and rolling in the sparkling soft snow, rushing into the sancars to drip copiously round the fires only to rush outside again, oblivious to their mothers' scolds. For two days, nature played her winter game with them seeming to say: 'Look, see, it's only a trifle colder than yesterday.' On the third day, she became bored with the game, or, perhaps she was only joining in with it, as she began blowing the crystals around on the ground, and, sensing that there would not be enough to last the winter, decided to send some more. The children no longer played with her. Perhaps it was anger at their departure that made her turn her playful breezes into the ferocious, ice-knived claws of death. For three days she raged, turning the whole world white; it was impossible to see outside the sancars, searing white winds obliterated the sky, wiping out the horizon as the temperature dropped even further, until even to think of putting one's face outside was untenable. Whatever was touched would freeze instantly to already cold-reddened fingers and even inside the sancars, icicles formed on the roofs. Soon the sancars glistened inside as the walls iced over and terror filled the hearts of the inhabitants as the sancars groaned and swayed under the weight of the white rain. Every day the young men fought against the banks of snow, desperate to keep the entrance flaps clear, but by the time the earth had been covered for five days, they had been forced to give up and the smoke-house fire was left to go out. The animals, in their svarge, died as the fire had, slowly and coldly.

Five days became five weeks and then five moons passing. The people of Skoonjay country lived in white silence, eating little, sleeping, fearful of ever waking, frozen in a daily battle for simple survival. There was no dissent as there was nothing to do – they were alive, just, and the summer would come again. Miraculously no child died, perhaps even more miraculously, the two oldest men survived also and as the days began to lengthen a tiny spirit approaching joy began to grow inside each heart. They had survived the winter. This was no longer the summer-lands, this was their home.

Anfjord had walked through the rain for only five days before he and his party experienced nature's playful first flakes of snow. On the seventh day of their journey north, the wind which caused such misery to his daughter and people was already gnawing at his fingers and toes, biting into his weather-toughened cheeks, bringing tears to his old eyes. But luck, always on the side of the unworthy, brought them in the path of a herd of migrating reindeer. As if guided by an unseen hand they were able to slaughter five animals before the herd outwitted them and fled with wide, wild-eyed terror.

That night, they slept in the shelter of the piled up carcasses of the animals and in the morning woke, snow covered, but alive. Törhilde was sent off into the whirling whiteness and while the brief daylight stayed, the animals were skinned, gutted and jointed. It was not until Anfjord (and Törhilde's wife, Bortar) were both beginning to despair that Törhilde returned, stumbling upon the gore-smeared party with snow-blinded eyes.

'Half a day!' he gasped. 'Half a day towards the moon-star – caves!' As if speaking had finally sapped the last of his energy, he collapsed into the ring of surprised and silent people.

At first light the group, tied together for safety, battled through the snow in the direction Törhilde had intimated. Törhilde himself was too weak to travel and had been left behind in a shelter made out of the frozen animals and snow. By nightfall they had found the caves which were no more than shallow depressions cut from the rock by the prevailing winds; a fire was lit, skins were pushed into crevices in the rock-face and secured by stones at the bottom edge and the men and women and children slept. The following day the snow had increased so much it was impossible to move. Each, in his or her own way, prayed that the storm would pass quickly enough for Torhilde to rejoin them.

By the end of the seventh day, they were reduced to gnawing at the skins for scraps of meat or fat. On the eighth day, Charek, the boy-child of Hunvor and Matild, did not wake. On the eleventh day Matild walked out into the storm to die. She could not eat her own child.

CHAPTER THIRTY-FOUR

Far, far away from the ice-bound cave of Anfjord and the snow-covered homes of the Branfjord tribe, Vronjyi found himself wishing for the winter that his people feared so greatly. He hoped, prayed, that when the white rains came, Rudju would finally see sense and his sickness would leave him. Vronjyi drew his knees up closer under his chin and stared into the embers of his fire. Away to the south – half a day's ride – no more – he could smell the smoke of Galdr's fire. He knew that if he could smell Galdr's fire, the same was true for him, but it no longer mattered. Not for the first time he found himself wondering what did matter. He sat on in the darkness, thinking of the times during these past three moons when he had actually caught sight of the band of murderers as they picked their way across the plain, but each time he thought that they had them within their grasp something would delay them. Now he knew that on the morrow hunter and hunted would finally meet. But did it matter?

When the avalanche had taken the lives of two of their horses, when the great crashing boulders had broken Kendosh's leg, when Sopak had lain, half dead, feverish and shaking for three nights, then he had known, beyond any shadow of a doubt, what mattered. But as his own wounds healed, as they had overcome one difficulty after another, doubts had replaced the certitude born of anger.

When they had first set off, he had felt unease at leading men who were motivated by anger. When Moodolk was murdered, anger had consumed him also, robbing him of the clarity a good hunter needs and when the avalanche had left Kendosh limping, and Sopak's big face scarred with

395

pain, rage filled his soul, but as the journeying continued his anger had left him. Now it was replaced only with a dogged determination. He had to reach Galdr – no matter what Anfjord had said, he had to kill him – if not for vengeance for Moodolk, then for Rudju's sake.

That damned chamber! Galdr had conjured up a spirit and left it in the chamber! That was why Rudju was still haunted. He felt sickened and disgusted every time he thought of Rudju – yes, that, if nothing else, was what mattered – returning Rudju to his senses. True, Rudju had regained some of his sense – the avalanche had, if nothing else, stopped the screaming nightmares that Rudju had suffered from, but if his doubts had any cause, it was the constant insistence by Rudju that they had got everything wrong. Rudju's young mind was convinced that it was Soosha who had, possibly indirectly, caused the death of Igrat, not Galdr. Of Moodolk's murder Rudju was equally intransigent: Moodolk had been murdered by the 'bear-people' and Rudju insisted, over and over again, that Galdr and Injya had no part in his death. Often Vronjyi had been so annoyed with Rudju that he had found himself wishing that he had left him behind to suffer the same fate as Moodolk, or at least abandoned him when they were reduced to only four horses.

'Why—' he had screamed at him one night, 'why – if you are so convinced that Galdr is innocent are you still with us, Rudju? Why do you not go back?'

Kendosh had laughed and rubbing his leg, stammered out: 'Bbbbecause he's more fffrightened of Sssosha than Galdr and wwwe will not give him a horse! That's why!'

'Damn it – we have not got a horse to give him!' Tronüg had interjected. 'The whole thing is ridiculous – none of us can go back – we have come too far!'

'I am not afraid to go back,' Rudju said quietly. 'I do not *want* to go back – I want to find Galdr and Injya, I want to talk with them, I want to . . .'

'There will be no time for talking – fool!' Vronjyi shouted at him, his square chin jutting out in anger, his black eyes blazing. 'I would rather die than talk with Galdr and Injya – what Anfjord said was true – Injya is evil – she and her people must die!'

Sighing deeply he wished that now, two moons on from that evening spent arguing, he felt the same unswerving resolve. Now, the hunt had turned into a battle of wills – not only with the unseen Galdr but with the doubts he felt inside himself. Perhaps Rudju was right – he no longer knew and, almost, no longer cared. He got up from the fire, stretched his sinuous body and heard the men stirring. Kendosh muttered something in his sleep and Tronüg swore sleepily. Vronjyi rubbed his smoked-filled eyes wearily, another day of silent, stealthy searching had begun. Merciful Bai Ulgan, he thought, make it the last.

Galdr had known, even before he saw them or smelt the fear carried on the wind, that the hunters were nearing. They were tenacious – that much he had to own. For three moons' passing Galdr had felt the hunters' eyes on him and his people; sometimes less urgently, sometimes more so. Every time he had turned around, every time Eabran or Centill had delayed, hidden, looked for traces, the hunters were invisible, but as he stood with his back to the fire, watching the swaying trees for shadows, calming his alarm at the sight of the yellow eyes of the night-animals that darted through the thicket, silent and stealthy – he knew that this time they were very near. The hunters were finally moving in for the kill. One hand grasped his spear which was stuck firmly into the soft ground, the other he tucked into his furs. The night was coldly brilliant. Overhead the stars vied with each other for attention, in front of him trees, behind him the fire and the huddled, sleeping people. He had known since they left the plain that hiding their presence was pointless – if they were to die, better die well-fed and warm.

It had taken all that time to cross the plain, ford the river and gain the low uplands which he had seen on his eagle flight – the uplands of the silver-birch trees. He thought of their journey and felt a thrill of excitement as he remembered the huge beasts of the plain. These gargantuan, long-haired animals, three times the size of a fully grown bear, with huge curled tusks and strange elongated noses which they used as humans would an arm, inspired awe and respect in the people as they realized that they were, perhaps, the first people since the chamber-makers to witness these majestic animals. For here, living on this plain were the creatures which had been so lovingly drawn on the walls of that chamber. Here, mingling freely with the bears, the reindeer, the boars and the two-tusked oxen, these creatures lived in harmony and peace, gentle giants upon the good body of Hoola.

Tomorrow they would leave the safety of the wood and start out across forested flat lands to the river which would lead them to their winter safety, the mountains of the Lake. Galdr pictured them over-wintering in the safety of the mountains and then he let his imagination run riot – after the mountains – what then? Would they reach the land his mother had spoken of in another one – two – winters? He drew for himself this land – the new land of their people, tall red-barked trees she had said, taller than any tree yet seen, and sun-metal – soft metal, the colour of the sun which would hold the key to their future. He thought of the people – they were travelling with him without that vision, relying on him and Injya alone – an awesome responsibility; but then his spirits lightened, as he thought of the morning when he had found the name for the tribe. The name which had come, like bird-song at dawn, an inevitability which did not lose its surprise. Samoyja – people of the sun and moon. Once spoken, the word seemed to unite the people even more, they breathed it in like the cool breezes or warm sun-filled air, the name was like a pulse in their bodies, giving them strength.

Galdr jumped. He realized that he was allowing his mind to wander. Silently he put down his spear and tiptoed over to the fire. He rubbed his wind-dried hands for a moment or two, crouching over the night fire, staring dumbly at the humps of furs which were his people. He found his mind wandering again as the warmth cradled him and his heart longed to rest with Injya's. How trusting and beautiful she was, how strong, how nurturing, how . . . Behind him a horse whinnied. Galdr froze. Silence . . . He held his breath. A footfall. Silence. Galdr did not move a muscle. Only his ears strained. Another footfall. Silence again.

Every sinew strained. Every nerve was alive to the sounds. Galdr's body was rigid, tensed for flight or fight. The only movement was in his eyes, seeking, searching the darkness for the faintest movement, the slightest shadow. Nothing. He could see, hear, nothing. He breathed a little more deeply, allowed his body to move a fraction. Slowly turning his head he looked around him -- again nothing. Suddenly Galdr felt an anger rise in him such as he had never known before. Before he had time to understand what he was doing he leapt to his feet and hurled himself around. There was no-one. The shadows still, the horses quiet.

The anger would not let him be. It grew inside him filling his body with heat. They were there -- he could sense them, feel them, smell them, but not see them. Rage filled his soul.

'Wake up!' he shouted in a voice which no longer seemed to be his own. 'Wake up! And see the faces of your hunters!' He ran to the huddle of furs which was Halfray and tore at his skins. 'The drum! Give me the drum!' he almost screamed at the sleep-befuddled Halfray. Seeing the drum under the skin which Halfray was using as a pillow he snatched it up. The rest were shouting, alarmed, crying as his words reached their understanding.

'See the faces of your hunters!' he repeated to the skies as he tore at his clothes in an effort to remove them. 'See the faces of those who would dare to hunt us Samoyja!'

'Galdr!' Injya screamed, disregarding Pentesh's cries of fear. 'What are you doing? What hunters? There *are* no hunters!' Galdr fixed her with a look which made her catch her words.

'Drum!' he shouted as if the word would make everything clear. 'I must drum – I will see them!'

As confusion reigned with children crying and horses stamping and whinnying with fright, Centill and Torben searched the copse – there was no sign of the hunters. Now all eyes rested on Galdr who was standing naked, arms raised above his head, drum in one hand, stick in the other. His whole body was shaking with anger and as he squatted down in front of the fire, oblivious to all, Injya suddenly came to her senses. She may not understand the drum as Halfray or Galdr did, but one thing she *did* know – if it was used with anger, then they were no better than Soosha! They would be using sacred powers to further their *own* ends, not those of the divine plan! Each slow, dull thud fell on Injya's senses like someone slowly cutting away a piece of her heart. She had to stop him.

'Galdr, NO!' The drumming stopped, Galdr's face, contorted with rage, lifted to hers. 'Not with anger – no. Give it to me – only with love must the drum be used.'

Galdr's mouth dropped open with surprise – how dare this woman take his drum from him – how dare she confront his power? Injya's eyes held his – he could find no insolence, no anger in them, only a steady outpouring of certain love. For a moment his masculine brain tried to reason – they were hunters, men – it was only right that he should protect his people, *he* should use whatever power he possessed to rid them of their adversaries; but as he gazed deeper into Injya's eyes, he knew that those thoughts were the thoughts of wounded pride. Suddenly the feelings of anger fled and he dropped his head. How much he still had to learn. When he handed Injya the drum it was with gratitude to her female wisdom. But there was no time to talk, no time to explain, time was of the essence – he *knew* that the hunters were upon them and as Injya took the drum from him with a little, sad smile playing on the corner of her mouth, he understood that Injya knew too.

'Please' – she began quietly – 'will all of you make a circle round me – I will need all the support I can get. The hunters *are* close, Galdr is right, and he is right too that the drum must be used – I do not know why, I just know it must. When I start drumming, think of those who have been hunting us with love – imagine them coming to us with gifts, not hatred.'

She stood for a moment longer, straightening her back, clearing her body, allowing herself to become a channel for the divine and then sat facing westwards, with Galdr's hands resting upon her shoulders.

With the first beat of the drum Injya felt her vision strengthen and clear. She let the stick fall on to the drum, let it find its own natural rhythm. She felt Galdr's hands warm upon her shoulders, felt his naked body close to hers and as the tempo of the drum rose, she felt that Galdr was giving her some of his power, as if their combined channels were creating a strong, clear course for the divine energy. When the drumming became faster, she felt it match her pulse as if it were a part of her, as if Galdr, herself and the drum were one. She closed her eyes, feeling the drum-beat coursing round her physical body.

Slowly she became aware of the vibrations affecting her spirit-body. It was as if the whole of her being – soul, spirit, flesh – was composed of tiny, minute particles, each one of which was vibrating slightly. Blue. The colour came upon her, she felt a deep purple-blue rise from the drum and pour, like liquid nightfall upon her being. She did not *see* blue, she *was* blue. When every atom of her being was moving within the liquid blueness, she heard the words coming from her, pouring from her mouth as if they were tangible entities. She knew that her physical body was shaking, knew that the people would be frightened and

401

alarmed, but inside herself, Injya knew that she was in a safe, connected place; that through her the spirits of the woods and streams, of the air and the fire were manifesting themselves. This was the real her.

'I know you are there—'

'I know that you are there!' she repeated herself in a deep voice, the voice of brother wolf. She felt the drumming become stronger as soon as she had spoken and now the particles of her consciousness were flying from her, tiny beams of light flying away from her, but somehow still connected to her. She felt her senses expand, as they flew through the trees, through the night – away, far away. She felt a sudden pain, a collision, as her blue self met with a yellow force.

Bright yellow threatening to bombard her. Her spirit form gathered strength, wrapped itself around the yellow, crystal-like entity and gentled its sharp edges, felt them converge with hers. She knew her physical body was speaking again, could hear the words coming from her body.

'I feel a sick seer – there is a sick seer among you – bring him to me, manifest yourselves and you will all be healed!' But she was not connected with her physical, the real Injya was here, among the ether of the spirit world. She could not see the physical forms of the men, only their spirits. It was on this plain of consciousness that her real work would be done.

The drumming increased in tempo as if guided by a will not her own to become stronger, clearer, more empowered. Now forms and lights were bombarding her from all sides: she waded through deep browns, sickly greens, violent reds and as each substance changed to hers, as each entity became part of her, she felt her senses expand once more. It was not necessary to change or confront, it was only necessary to bring, to guide, these entities to her. Her physical voice was speaking again.

'You are coming – I know you are moving, I feel your heartbeats, I feel you coming!' As inside, outside herself, she felt these atoms begin to move, gracefully now, easily now, the spirits following in the wake of her deep blue senses. She felt she was guiding them as slowly the hunters came towards her. She sensed the deep longing the animals they were riding had to be united with their kin, sensed the longing and the need the hunters had for this chase, this barbaric game to be over with and she sensed the one among them who, more than any, needed them.

Vronjyi had not wanted it to be like this. Right up until the words, 'I see a sick seer!', he had resisted the drum. When the wind first had brought the strange sounds of the drumming through the night, to the men who, sure of their quarry, were advancing on silent bare feet, they were sure that Galdr or whoever it was who was speaking, had gone mad. In muffled whispers they had decided to return to their horses, still catching the odd word on the wind. Pleased that the singing voice masked their approach, they had spread out in the copse, each sure of being able to surprise the group. They had planned this moment for three whole moons' passing and even though they were outnumbered they felt it was an even match; five men against five men – the women counted as nuisance rather than threat. With the hunted occupied by this strange singing, the hunters had surprise on their side, of that Vronjyi was convinced. But as they drew closer the words rang round in his head, as they did in the minds of each of them and each knew to whom they were addressed. It became impossible to unhear them. Once truth had dawned there was no going back and they came upon the hunted, not with terrifying whoops of war, but silently, as if the raised arms of Galdr were the comforting arms of their mothers.

The men stumbled forward, incapable of speech, as if walking in a dream. The people stood in a wide semicircle behind the naked figure of Galdr and the seated figure of

403

Injya. Their faces were smiling as if greeting long-lost brothers. Vronjyi found that he, too, was smiling. As if drawn forward by Galdr's open arms, he walked towards him. But it was not Galdr who spoke to him, but Injya, who whispered in a strangely deep, cracked voice: 'Bring me your sick seer.'

As if incapable of refusing her, Vronjyi motioned behind him, pointing at Rudju.

'I will heal him – then you will join us.' Injya's flat, slightly hoarse whispering continued as Rudju stumbled forward towards her. 'I will heal the sick seer and you will all be healed. Sit!'

As if robbed of his free will Vronjyi sat, as did Sopak, Kendosh and Tronüg, in the midst of these people whom he had been told were the sworn enemy of his people, watching intently every action that Injya made. When Rudju had stepped forward, Injya stood up, passed her hands over him and instantly Rudju had fallen to the ground. Vronjyi had wanted to jump up, slay the woman, slay them all, but something had stayed his hand and now he looked on, impassive as the rest, fascinated. The still naked Galdr picked up the drum and began hitting it, slowly and methodically, never taking his eyes off Injya and Rudju. Injya bound Rudju's many wounds and Galdr solemnly drummed. When Rudju was almost completely covered in strips of bark and scraps of furs and skins, Injya put one hand on his chest, the other on his temple, and began swaying and mumbling strange words, now low, now high and chattering.

Vronjyi kept shaking his head, trying to rid himself of this sudden and total loss of power. He knew that he should be despatching these people, this naked madman, this evil woman, but as the drumming and Injya's sing-song chattering grew, Vronjyi felt that it no longer mattered what he *ought* to be doing, what he wanted to do was to be with these people. He could not hold on to his rational mind – it had flown like an owl, swift and silently, away on wings of forgetfulness. He kept trying to think: 'What am I doing here? Like this?' but each time the question arose the answer would come to him – because it is right for you to be here, like this! He had a ridiculous sense of belonging, as if these people had somehow changed his heart, had taken away the moons of doubt, anger and frustration. He was not confused nor was he frightened – either the whole experience was a dream from which he would awaken shortly, or something had been done to him which had changed, utterly, his whole soul!

He looked round at the group of silent men and women, almost not recognizing his fellow hunters; Kendosh and Sopak who hitherto had been notorious for their cruelty both sat with eyes shining with joy, Tronüg, whose dark full-bearded face normally inspired fear, sat still as a stone, all traces of venom gone, watching intently the swaying figure of Injya, his weather-cracked face now creased with lines of smiling. And the group – the ones which had been his heart's sole desire to slay, now seemed as near and dear to him as his own kin.

Suddenly the drumming stopped and Galdr sat back on his heels. Injya threw back her head and gazed intently at lightening sky. A moment later, both Injya and Rudju began shaking. As if in great pain, Injya got up and walked unsteadily to Rudju's head. She fell on to all fours and stared into his face which was now also contorted with pain. Quite suddenly Injya leant forward, put both hands on to his belly and seemed to be trying to pull something out of it. Her fingers clenched tightly round something which Vronjyi could not see, as Injya's face grimaced in agony as if whatever it was that she was trying to pull out, caused her much pain. Sweat broke out all over her body as her arms began to shake with the effort and then with a force that seemed to rock the very earth upon which they were all seated, the 'thing' broke free and Injya fell back as if she had been pulling on a line which had suddenly snapped. Instantly two things happened: Rudju's quaking body became still and Injya, shaking her head slowly from side to side, got back on to her hands and knees and roared into the face of Rudju. The roar was that of a great bear in pain. Slowly Injya, still on all fours, her lower jaw gaping wide, her eyes creased against an internal hurt so profound that her shoulders hunched, made an attempt to move, swayed slightly, then with an almighty, blood-curdling cry, fell on to her side as if dead. Vronjyi was on his feet in an instant as were his compatriots, but their swift movements were stayed by a single command from Galdr: 'LEAVE HER!'

Stunned, the group obeyed, each standing as if frozen. All eyes turned to Galdr.

'She has removed the spirit which caused the sickness. Leave them both.'

As if these few words explained all that they had seen, Galdr slowly got up, picked up a fur cape and walked off into the copse with an attitude which defied further questioning.

' . . . You did . . . you still *are* practising magic! Deny that!' Tronüg's little black eyes shot a look of pure hatred in Halfray's direction. Halfray sighed quietly, not wishing to anger further.

'*You* may call it magic – we do not see it as that.'

'What is it then? What power have you got that can do this?' He pointed to Vronjyi who was sitting, quite quietly, watching him as he stormed up and down, his short hirsute body quivering with anger. 'Or that—' he pointed to Rudju who was still examining his scarless body as if he had never seen his flesh before.

'Tronüg, please,' Injya said quietly, 'we have explained it all to you – *we* are doing nothing, we are only allowing the divine to work through us.'

Tronüg snorted and sat down.

'All right, all right – so we all believe what you have said about Soosha – we know what you said about Igrat

406

makes sense – you have explained about the spirit of the bear taking his revenge on Rudju – but – but . . . '

'Does it matter?' Kendosh spoke for almost the first time that morning. 'Does it matter what they call it? My leg no longer hurts, my stammer has gone – can you deny the good of that?'

'Surely the *only* thing that matters is what we do now!'

Sopak shuffled his large body around uncomfortably on the ground. He raised his wide, brown face and stared at Vronjyi: 'The only question is – do we stay or do we return?'

Galdr and Injya, sitting close together, looked at each other then back at the men who were sitting hunched round their fire. They had not dreamt that it would be like this, had not known that this, too, would be asked of them. It was Halfray who spoke their thoughts to the men who, until so recently, had been their enemies.

'We have no will in this matter. We are at your mercy. We have hunting knives, that is true, but we will not fight you. You came here to kill us. We have healed you – no more. You are free to go, free to murder us if that is still your wish. You know the truth now – it is up to you to decide your fates and ours. Tronüg, you speak of magic – there is none – there is only the outpouring of the divine. Vronjyi, you spoke of us stealing your spirit – only the Shining Ones have the power to take one's spirit – not mere mortals such as we. You know our plans, know even the course we will take. For myself, I welcome you – we are all brothers – it will be difficult, but if it is right for you to come with us, you will. Also, if it is right for us to die here, then that also is for our higher good. We do not keep you here. *We* do nothing.'

Vronjyi looked across the fire at Halfray, the man who he had thought of as an imbecile. He stared at Galdr and Injya, at the faces of their tribe who had listened, without fear, to his words. His look was met by faces unanimated by smiles or fearful looks. The people looked at him – that was all, looked at him without malice or prejudice, just looked. As he looked at their almost childlike faces, their honest, clear eyes, he felt a twinge of pain and recognized that it was born of a sudden desire to weep. As he continued to look into each face in turn he felt a slow easing of tension, a gradual lessening of the grip of questioning doubt. His eyes came to rest upon Injya's face and as he stared into her shining eyes he knew that he had come home. For him there was no decision to be made.

CHAPTER THIRTY-FIVE

Galdr's words were prophetic: it took much work for the Samoyja people to accept those who had so recently hunted them. A great leap was required – a huge jump in consciousness – to admit these men into their hearts. Rudju was instantly accepted – he was such a personable young man it was difficult for any to understand how he could have willingly gone on such a hunt, although, as the trek got under way once more, his amazing ability for finding game made him indispensable. Torben, who up to the time that the hunters joined them, had found this task to his liking, was the only member of the tribe who felt a twinge of jealousy, but as the journey carried on and winter slowly turned into spring, he too took Rudju to his heart.

Tronüg's initial misgivings had been overcome as the adventure of the journey took hold of his imagination – he still found it difficult to accept the idea of the superbly natural – still found himself flushing when celebrations and prayers were offered; but although he did not understand with his mind what was happening to him, his good-natured openness began to shine through and before long, his fiery temper turned into unswerving loyalty. Kendosh, like Rudju, had been so overwhelmed by gratitude for his healed leg and the loss of his life-long stammer, that he unreservedly took the Samoyja people to his heart. Anything which could cure him – as easily and as naturally as his cure had been effected – could not be evil, of that he was convinced.

Sopak and Vronjyi alone still held on to misgivings. Sopak had left behind a woman whom he loved dearly.

Behind his big, bluff exterior, his hunter's hard heart was aching for her and for many moons, this sense of loss held him back from joy. Vronjyi also missed Kanshay, whose last tender caress had been so cruelly taken from him by the sight of Igrat's death-whitened corpse. Many things still troubled him, but the greatest of these was the effect Soosha had upon him when she had bidden him to go on this hunt. In his dreams he could still see Soosha, still feel her hands upon his shoulders as if her will was inside him. He, unlike Sopak, had the clarity of intelligence to understand with his head what Injya and Galdr and Halfray were doing, but the fact that these three seemed to possess a mutually exclusive right to something which he could still only term magic, frustrated him. He found that he could talk with Sanset and it was her admission that she, too, often felt excluded and somehow less than her mate because she did not possess this gift, helped him overcome these misgivings.

Vronjyi, like the burly Kendosh, was a big man. Taller than Galdr, thicker set and muscular with chiselled good looks and piercing brown eyes, had found that all his life he had had to fight. Smaller boys had taunted him and when manhood came, he found often men too would test his patience. Now Vronjyi felt as if he were battling with himself – his head was telling him one thing, yet a much deeper, indefinable knowing somewhere in the pit of his stomach, was telling him that all that Injya and Galdr and Halfray had told him was right – that Soosha was not only wrong in her interpretation of the facts, but motivated by something quite distinct from good. His feelings told him to allow the love to surround him – his mind did not and as the journeying took them into stranger and stranger terrain, he doubted that anything ever again would be straightforward and planned, knowable and certain.

Galdr knew. Galdr knew two things. His eagle-flight had been as accurate as a map and Vronjyi was, next to Injya and Halfray, perhaps the most important person in his life.

He had paid scant attention to Vronjyi while he had been growing up with him, but was unsurprised that it was he who had led the hunting team. Now, with Vronjyi beside him, he knew that he had a great opportunity to learn something from him – what it was, he had no idea, but as certain as he had been when Askoye had spoken to him, he knew that Vronjyi had a gift for him – possibly painful as all the best gifts are.

Without fear gnawing at their heels, spurring them onwards, the Samoyja people made slower progress. The winter, when it came, was milder than they had hitherto known and when the white rains did come in flurries and later, blizzards, the canopy of the dark forest through which they were travelling saved them from the worst effect. It took them two whole moons to cross this great expanse of forest, always steadily working their way south eastwards, but finally they were out of it and into a vast plain, stretching as far as the eye could see. Soon Aspar came to the land and they were able to ride many hundred of pchekts daily. They came to the fast-flowing river which Galdr had seen and which would lead them, eventually, to the vast high lake. They named this river the Vensyayei which meant river of many turns and as they followed its meandering course and later in the summer, its narrower, rushing rivulets, they knew that before long they would come to the mountains which Galdr insisted held the secret of the next part of their journey.

The wide treeless plain was abundant with all species of wildlife and as the sun became hotter than any season they had hitherto known, they finally saw the mountain range towards which they were now beginning to climb. With the unaccustomed heat, many of the skins they had been carrying were discarded and with the lightened loads, the grateful horses became frisky. Two mares were in foal and Sanset's wish was granted as she, too, was carrying a child – Halfray's first-born. Day after day they travelled, stopping frequently to hunt the game or

411

at Injya's behest, to pick the strange flowers and herbs that carpeted the plain. They looked often towards the mountain range which rose, blue-grey and majestic across the hazy, heather-dappled foothills. All felt exhilarated – all was new – all was exciting.

Now the course of the river was less meandering, often they lost sight of it as it cascaded through ravines. The foothills rose gently, but as the climb gradually steepened, the vegetation became less lush, the winds harsher. Now the Samoyja tribe made very slow progress for as they climbed steadily upwards the very air seemed to become thinner – less enervating. Peculiarly, everyone felt that although they had less physical energy, their senses were more alert, more alive than ever before. Injya, too, felt a similar response; she felt lighter, as if a great weight had been taken from her the moment they had left the plain and the forest. She felt as if all her life she had spent in dark sancars, black caves, little, low places where insects bit and snakes threatened – but here, she could feel her soul soar.

The sky was clearer and purer than any she had ever seen and in response her shining heart grew in love and understanding of Galdr. It had taken many moons for her to really feel that she could trust Galdr or even her own feelings. All through the long, dark winter she had been with him, but apart from him. Together they would lead celebrations, hunt, pray, cook, care for Pentesh, but not once during all this time had she allowed herself to feel close to him. Now, with the sun high, the skies clear, she allowed her feelings to rise, her hopes and needs to surface. Everything seemed to join forces to add to this rare feeling, the wonderful, high, cloud-scudding heavens, the brilliant sunshine or the sudden thunderstorms, the very air she breathed.

They rode up the soft purple foothills which emerged from the flat landscape like violet-blue cushions and as the weather began to turn cold once more, as the wind picked up, they gained what seemed to be the very top of the mountain range. Here there were only mosses and lichens, bleached and dead-looking, and flattened miniature trees clinging to life, but Galdr announced that they would make an encampment and that they would rest for perhaps a moon's passing, perhaps more. The news brought consternation from the people – why here in a tiny depression? Why here when they were totally unprotected from the elements? But Galdr would not be drawn, only saying that they would not move further until he had a sign that it was right to do so.

Grateful for the rest, even if unsure of the reason, the men set about making the sancars. As night drew on, Injya sat staring into the crackling fire, watching the sparks fly to the inky heavens. All around her were the familiar sounds of the people; Halfray's laugh, Sanset's response, Djyana's gentle admonition to the high-spirited Potyami, Bendula's soft singing to the sleeping Pentesh and the steady clap, clap of the sancar skins against the poles as the night winds caught some untethered corner. A soft touch on her head – Ullu passing by, her slender form silhouetted against the red fire – all around her, people, but inside a loneliness, an empty feeling.

When the sancars were finally made safe for the night, they ate, talking in hushed tones. Across the fire, Galdr was deep in conversation with Rudju, next to him, Centill and Toonjya were discussing something earnestly; Eabran and Torben, Oanti and Aywe sat giggling and laughing; Bendula and Sopak too were sharing secrets and Djyana, Tronüg and Kendosh were keeping Wa-Oagist and Potyami amused. Injya searched their faces for an answer to her loneliness and found none. Halfray and Sanset had left the group to sleep, as had Vronjyi, and as Injya looked at the sleeping Pentesh in her lap, she decided that perhaps sleep would take away this strange unease. She rose to leave the fire and no-one registered her movement. Suddenly, she felt like a little girl of whom no-one took any notice, very

413

vulnerable and very alone. Fighting back the tears which had welled up in her heart, she walked to the sancar in which Sanset and Halfray were sleeping. She looked at her cousin, surrounded by furs, wrapped in her brother's arms and felt a lump of jealousy rise in her throat. This was not like her – what *was* happening? She did not begrudge her cousin love, she was overjoyed that Halfray had found such happiness! She kissed Pentesh on her brow and laid her in the cradle by Sanset. She stood for a moment, watching the sleepers, examining her heart, but she could find no answer there. As she turned to go, she started – Galdr was standing in the entrance.

'I . . . ' she blurted out, flushing as if her presence required explanation. Galdr did not speak. Injya lowered her eyes. She felt her heart leaping inside her, her stomach knot in tension – what *was* this nonsense? As she moved to pass him, Galdr caught her by the wrist.

'Do not run away from your heart, Injya.'

The whispered words made her flush again. She turned towards him, prepared to fight, prepared to retort with something in the manner of: '*You* do not know what my heart wants!', but when her eyes met his, the anger that her head was telling her was the right response, melted away. As she stared into his deep brown eyes, she understood the truth in his words. In a voice tiny with anxiety, she replied: 'I do not know how to be, Galdr, I do not understand.'

He smiled at her and placing his hand upon her shoulder said gently: 'Heads do not understand love – only hearts, Injya.' He touched her face with his fingers, tracing the line of her jaw to her lips, then kissed her lightly on her forehead.

'Sleep well, beloved.' He squeezed her hand and left her, standing alone in the middle of the sancar.

She was lying on her stomach. The furs under her belly were soft and silky, warm from their coupling. Crossing her legs over her bottom she swung them to and fro, impatient for Galdr's return. One hand played with the long hair of the fur, circling round a pattern and in the dimness of the warm sancar she imagined his hands playing upon her flesh as she played with the furs. A streak of light shot across the floor of the sancar and was gone. Galdr was by her side once more. He offered the cup to her lips and she drank thirstily, not taking her eyes from his. When she had taken enough she pushed the cup away from her lips and rolled on to her side. She raised both hands up to him.

'Come to me – beloved – be with me once more.' She rolled on to her back, bending her legs, opening herself wide to him. It was hot, she could feel the perspiration running over her body, why did he not come to her?

'Galdr,' she implored, stretching her arms wide, her fingers taut, grasping at the air. 'Please – I want you inside me.'

The spoken words woke Injya from her dream. It was a black night. She was alone. It was cold, not hot – her arms, outside the protection of the furs were chill to the touch.

She stared into the blackness. There was no Galdr standing over her, only cold, empty night. She wriggled about, rubbing her arms, trying to make them warm again – such a dream – that she could imagine such a thing! She felt shocked yet curiously elated – perhaps the dream was a portent of things to come – perhaps one day she would welcome Galdr to her bed. No – she shook her head violently in the dark – such a thing could never be.

The dream had robbed her of her need to sleep – it was as if Galdr *had* lain with her, had given her fresh energy, fresh life. She lay for a long time, trying to go back to sleep, arguing with herself, arguing against the idea which, once thought, could not be silenced. As the blackness slowly gave way to a light grey she heard a rustle in the sancar. Sanset and Halfray were stirring. A bird began to sing – dawn was breaking – but inside the sancar it was still night. Another rustle and then slowly the unmistakable sounds began. The light rhythmic breathing of the couple changed, their breaths became shorter, slightly harsher. Injya pulled the furs around her ears, but the couple did not notice the movement and soon Sanset's whispered words of love filtered through the barrier Injya had put up. Unable to stop the sounds, Injya listened to the most secret and sacred act and as the sounds became more explicit, as the couple lost themselves in each other, Injya found her own body respond, her own blood begin its dance of need. She lay still as death until the sounds ceased and silence once more surrounded the people of the sancar. Now she knew she had no choice – she had to follow not only her heart, but her body's rhythm. She crept from the sancar and naked went to Galdr.

The day was gustily cold. Grey mist hung over the land below them like a blanket, but here, high up on the mountain, the wind blew bitingly from the east. The sancars which had been made in much haste the previous day were reinforced and much of the day was taken up with lighting and relighting the fire. Halfray, Kendosh and Vronjyi had gone at first light southwards to the next peak – something that Injya felt grateful for – why she should be embarrassed she had no idea, but she was pleased that Halfray did not witness her coming from Galdr's sancar later that morning. Her day was spent in a dream – she felt as if the pleasures of the night were still with her and although she performed all the usual tasks for the day, she felt as if part of her was still joined to Galdr. Often during that day, she would run to his side, touch his hand, stroke his hair, or simply stand in front of him, smiling. No words needed to be spoken, no secret smiles or loud exclamations needed to be made. When night fell once more, the Samoyja people left Galdr and Injya alone in a sancar, alone with their love.

'This is like my dream!' Injya said as she swung her legs over her bottom, 'just like my dream.'

'And what happened next in your dream?'

'Oh, you brought me a drink or something and then I turned over and called out for you, but you would not come.'

'What a silly man I was!' Galdr laughed as he kissed her shoulder. 'No – stay as you were.' Galdr put his hand on her waist as Injya was about to turn over. 'Have I ever told you how beautiful you are?'

His broad hand moved from her head, smoothing her tousled hair over her shoulders and back. She did not reply as his hand moved again, down her spine, round her buttocks, down her legs, right down until he cupped her heel in his palm. She sighed deeply as her flesh responded to his touch and she reached out for him.

'No – no' – he whispered – 'only let yourself feel, Injya – let me worship you!'

She giggled at his words – worship! But as his hands became stronger, as the flickering sensations of pleasure grew, she closed her eyes and allowed his hands to gentle her. Her feet suddenly became alive as his hands stroked her insteps and soles, his fingers separated each toe, his tongue licked the tiny valleys between them. She moaned and rolled over – that feet could feel so! He clung to her ankle, then brought his hands up the outside of her legs. How she wanted him! She reached out in the darkness for his head, but he shook her away as he touched her thighs once more. Nearer and nearer to her place of womanhood his fingers stroked, but always they circled round it. Now they pressed upon her hip bones, gently tracing the curve of her bones under her skin. Without taking his hands from her body he moved slightly and she felt him touch her breasts, her arms, her neck. When she felt as if she could bear no more, his mouth was upon her body, his tongue finding places of excitement that she did not know existed. Hands now – he was kissing the palms of her hands, sucking her fingers. She could feel his tongue beneath her fingers, a thing alive. How could these feelings have been so hidden from her all these years – how could

417

she have not known? She thought she would go mad with desire – her need of him was so great she thought she would explode.

'Galdr!' she cried out. 'Please!' But in answer he only kissed her breast. She felt his hand upon her stomach then with such relief, she felt the fingers part her lips of womanhood. Now surely, now, please – but his fingers only reached inside her. She could feel herself becoming tauter, could feel every muscle, every sinew in her body aching as wave after wave of pulsating passion coursed from her womb, down her secret place as her body responded to his hands. His hands now slid under her head, gripping her hair as he pulled her gently towards him and his mouth found hers. Her body strove upwards to meet his and she felt him enter her at last. His hand tightened on her hair pulling her head back to the furs, as he rose inside her.

Yes, yes, she wanted to say but her mouth was locked with Galdr's; his body responded to her unspoken wishes as stronger and stronger the waves of need manifested themselves. His fingers, caught in her hair pulled at the nape of her neck, her head fell backwards and she was finally able to cry out: 'Yes!' as she felt her body disintegrating.

'Yes!' his deep throated voice whispered in her ear, 'now, we are one!'

A long moment of ecstasy and Injya felt the urgency of her passion subside. She lay, cushioned in tenderness as if her world was only a soft, secret joy. Slowly she became aware of Galdr – he was still tense, still gripped with their passion. She brought him close to her, but he withdrew from her body and cradled her in his arms.

'But Galdr—' she began.

'We have a lifetime, many lifetimes – I can wait.'

He was stroking her thighs once more, hands wet now with love. She turned on her side, facing him, cradling his head to her breast and slowly, very slowly, she felt longing

418

rise in her once more. Gently she pushed him away from her until he was lying on his back, then she took him into her. It felt strange, her body above his, but as she felt his flesh beneath her hands, as the hot run of desire clutched at her belly once more, she knew again the urgency of his need. She leant over him, kissing his neck, his lips and shoulders, felt his strong hands on her back, guiding her, helping her, then opening her wider to him. And now she knew that his words were true – there was no hurry – they did have lifetimes together. She watched his face, saw the surprised look in his eyes, his mouth open wide as suddenly his fingers clutched at her hip bones and she felt his seed burst forth inside her. Now she did not feel as if she were disintegrating, now she felt as if each pulse of his body was matching one deep within hers, the pulse of love energy so strong that it seemed to fill her entire being, up through her secret place, through her belly, stomach and heart, up, up along her spine until she felt an ache on her brow – the same ache she experienced sometimes when she focused on the Goddess. She fell forwards until her forehead touched Galdr's and with the last rush of love felt her circle completing, knew that their spirits and bodies were one, one with each other and one with the divine source.

They were woken by the wind. The sancar was shaking and rattling as the wind tore at the skins. On the moaning air they could hear shouts from the other sancars. Quickly they put on clothes and ran towards the largest sancar – they had nearly reached it when behind them they heard the cracking, clapping sound of their sancar being torn to shreds by the wind. As if the furs were down and the poles no heavier than twigs, the sancar shivered once more, then lifted off the very rock itself. For a moment it looked like a giant dancing in a gargantuan cape or like a huge bird desperate for flight – then another gust filled it – and it was gone, up into the air and away, down the face of the mountain.

Everyone was running madly around, trying to find ropes and rocks with which to secure the three remaining sancars, but as the sun made a brief foray into the day, saw the clouds and retreated behind them as if hiding his face from the winds, another sancar blew away. By midday the people were reduced to lying upon the mountain – the wind had claimed the remaining two sancars and none dared to stand. The horses too had bolted down to the valley, but as the light faded, the wind too died down.

Exhausted and hungry, the men recaptured the horses and tethered them halfway up the mountain and the women made two large, low sancars, barely more than a pchekt high. Huddled together for safety and warmth, the people eventually slept and the next day dawned bright without a trace of the slightest breeze. As hot food warmed everyone's spirits, Halfray challenged Galdr's decision to stay in such a totally unsuitable place.

'Just beyond that next rise – Galdr – less than a day's travel – we have seen the caves – there is a good place to stay!'

Vronjyi and Kendosh nodded their agreement vigorously.

'That is as may be – but this is where I know I must stop, I know it, Halfray – we *have* to stop here!'

'But Galdr – think of Sanset – it is dangerous here – another night of storms and who knows what might happen!'

'Halfray – we stay – you go if you please, but I am staying!'

Halfray's piercing blue eyes met Galdr's unfathomable brown ones and he felt so annoyed with Galdr's dismissiveness that for the first time in his life, he raised his hand in anger. In the gasping moment that followed, Vronjyi was by his side, strong brown hand upon Halfray's slender forearm. Galdr could not speak with shock. That Halfray should raise his hand in anger! Dumbfounded he could only stare at the rocks beneath his feet.

420

Halfray recovered himself, and speaking very quietly said: 'Galdr, please, I must take Sanset away from here. I trust you – I know that you *have* to stay here – you have seen it therefore it must be, but Galdr, I will not put Sanset in any more danger – the baby is soon to be born and . . . and . . . ' His voice became broken with emotion, 'this is my first child, Galdr. I too have no option.'

For two days the weather was idyllic. Halfray, Vronjyi, Sanset and Bendula had gone to the caves, but the rest decided to stay with Galdr and Injya. The sancars were rebuilt with their skins weighed down with boulders and ropes were flung over the long, ovoid buildings and attached to the pegs to keep them secure. Two warm, sunlight days were spent catching the game birds as they made their way steadily southwards, two days of preparing food, mending garments, caring for each other, and their animals, but on the third night after the storm, the winds came again, tearing the skins from the boulders as if they were no more than cotton grasses, ripping the poles out of the ground and gusting them away like straw. On the morning of the fourth day everyone except Injya and Galdr left the high encampment for the safety of the caves which Vronjyi and Halfray had found.

For two days Injya and Galdr were alone. Two days of waiting, watching, for they knew not what. They delighted in each other, delighted in the freedom of being alone yet together. For Injya, each moment she spent with Galdr disclosed some new tenderness and as day merged into night as softly as their bodies merged into one, she finally understood the beauty of loving another not as well as oneself, but more. Now she felt complete – as if their love-making was fusing her very spirit to that of Galdr's – now she knew that she loved him utterly and would do so for the rest of her life.

On the sixth day, Injya awoke to find Galdr gone. Panic lurched in her stomach as she tore from the sancar. He was nowhere to be seen. She climbed the slight rise which gave their encampment what little shelter it had and scanned the landscape from south through west to the north. No-one. Shielding her eyes from the sun she stared into the east. Again no-one. Feeling as if she had just had half her being ripped away, she raced from boulder to boulder, desperation gnawing at her soul, rushing, panic-formed tears flying into the wind. She stared into the rising sun. Nothing – no-one. Hundreds of pchekts of barren mountain tops.

A cry of anguish came unbidden from her mouth. She thought her heart would break with the pain she now felt. Screaming his name over and over again she stared into the face of the sun. No-one . . . Nothing . . . Yet . . . There! Tiny, minute figures approaching – coming from over the mountains – no – an impossibility! She rubbed her eyes and ran to another ledge. With her heart crashing against her ribs, she saw again the figures, no larger than tiny brown dots, coming towards her. Without stopping to tie even her boots, she ran over the mountain top, calling Galdr's name to the thin white-wisped clouds, screaming his name, desperate for one of the little brown dots to be her beloved.

422

CHAPTER THIRTY-SIX

The tribe of the Samoyja people sat on the ledge, in front of the caves in total silence. The four men, dressed in brown shifts with hoods, sat with their backs to the setting sun. Shy smiles played upon their yellow-brown faces, their small, slightly slanted eyes seemed to smile too. Galdr had explained that these people were the ones for whom he had been waiting – they were the sign he had been looking for. He had not expected it to be in human form, but when he had woken, long before dawn on that sixth morning – he knew that these people were coming to him, that they had a message and, more importantly, that the Samoyja people had a message for them. The fates had brought these two tribes together – what for and how, he had no idea!

They established names; using only sign language they found out that the four men were from two tribes who lived in a high land far to the east. The two tribes, the Burya and the Chukis, lived at either end of a vast lake from which the river (the river which Galdr had named the Vensyayei) flowed. They were separate, but connected by marriages. The four men represented two from each tribe and they had been sent by the Burya Chen-Shun (which, the Samoyja people surmised, was their name for tribal leader or chief) to find the Samoyja people. Here, communications became difficult – pictures and sign language failed as the four desperately tried to show the Samoyja tribe something – something to do with why they felt drawn to them, why they had travelled for four days into the land which they called Sukhan – the land of the winds, a land into which they never normally travelled.

The four were offered food, which they refused and as night drew on, they were offered shelter in the cave. This too they refused vehemently, settling down to sleep, without covers, by the fire. As the first bird-song broke the air, the Samoyja tribe awoke to find the four little men already awake, eager to be gone. It was understood that they should travel with them to their home and as there was no reason why this should not be so, soon everyone was mounted on their horses, ready for the journey. To the Samoyja people's consternation, the four diminutive men refused horses – they ran ahead, easily keeping up with the trotting pace of the riders and it was the riders who tired before the runners!

Everyone was amazed at the four men's stamina – they had not eaten (or at least, not within sight of them) for almost two days, they had drunk only water and yet they were able to run, barefoot, for longer than they were able to ride! Halfray was particularly impressed – in this high land, he had found it difficult to breathe – let alone run – and yet these men ran on effortlessly.

Although it had taken the men four days to find Galdr and Injya, it took only two to reach their encampment. The journey was across a range of bare mountains which had looked to all as if it were below the one upon which Galdr and Injya had stayed. But as the journey progressed and they could all clearly see 'their' mountain far below them, they realized that they had not, in fact, seen these mountains before at all! It was as if something in the rarefied atmosphere had clouded their vision.

The encampment was unlike any they had seen. As they approached, the first sight that met their eyes was an enormous svarge, full of short, long-haired horses. Djyana was delighted – horses – so tiny yet so sturdy looking. Next came the encampment itself: this was arranged, not in a circle but in lines – four rows of identical round dwellings making a central square space which was bare earth. Each dwelling had smoke coming from their smoke-holes, which were tall, dried-mud cylinders which sat upon the roofs. The dwellings themselves were made out of rock or dried clay and the roofs were made from grasses and reeds. They were led past the first row of dwellings and slowly through the square. From these dwellings appeared women and children, small like the men, most, to the Samoyja eyes, quite fat – and all grinning broadly. Some of the children held flowers and waved them in greeting, though none would step forward. The women grinned and rubbed their hands together in what only could be assumed was their form of greeting. But stranger than their dwellings, stranger than their intricately woven patterned garments and tight-fitting caps, odder than their hand-rubbing welcome was the fact that though they smiled and grinned – all were totally silent!

The four motioned for everyone to dismount. On foot they were led through a gap between the furthest row of dwellings and into one large, low construction which was made partly from mud or clay, partly from wood and partly from skins and heavily embroidered woven material. As their eyes became accustomed to the darkness inside this dwelling (for there were no openings other than the entrance), they found themselves confronted with a long line of seated men. All were dressed exactly in the same manner as the four guides, all were seated cross-legged on the ground, all were smiling and all were silent.

The guide who had named himself Shesh-On-Yi then began speaking to one of the seated men – a man who looked so frail and old that the bones were nearly visible through his almost transparent yellowish skin. This was the first time – apart from single words – that anyone had heard the language of these people. Like the people themselves, who all appeared to be no taller than Bendula or Oanti, their language also seemed 'little'. It contained very many little words, some no more than soft 'shushing' sounds – and many of the words sounded only to be intakes of breath, as if their language reflected not only their stature but their high, wind-swept home itself.

Shesh-On-Yi's quiet, sing-song voice carried on for some time and then stopped. None had interrupted him. He, and the three other men, Hwaysaei, Tet-Shu-Satsum, and Sho-Unsho then proceeded to fall to their knees and prostrate themselves as the old man stood up; he said something to them, they got up from the ground and bowing low, they backed out of the dwelling. In the semi-darkness of the dwelling, Injya saw again the silent-walking of Askoye, saw in the old man's wizened face and tiny eyes something of the wisdom of the crone – could these people be Askoye's people? The old man stopped before Galdr and bowed his head. He touched Galdr's face with his paper-thin hands and nodded again. He lifted Galdr's long black hair away from his face and let it drop, nodding all the while – then he touched Galdr's chest over the place where his heart was and said, with some difficulty: 'You are The One.'

Galdr did not know which surprised him the most – the words, or the fact that the old man could speak his language! He was at a loss for words – did not know how to reply. He smiled into the lined old face and brought his own hand up, placing it over the old man's hand which was still resting on his chest. The old man seemed to tremble slightly at the touch, then turned to the seated, silent men. He said something in their language and, as if made of one body, they all stood up. Turning back to face Galdr again, he smiled, his face seeming to disintegrate into a thousand tiny pieces and then he removed his hand. The old man sighed deeply, then he looked along the line of people before him. When his eyes met Injya's in the darkness, she felt as if she was being drawn to him by an invisible thread, his eyes were hypnotic, powerful and compelling. She took one tentative step towards him. Instantly his hand shot up, palm towards her – a universal motion of 'come no further'. Injya stopped dead and stared into the old man's eyes; she felt that there was a deep level of recognition in

them, as if in some strange way, she was coming home –
she felt also that there was an acceptance of her which was
more than just polite courtesy, as if this man knew her and
everything about her. She smiled at him and bowed at him
– when she looked up again, his eyes had gone from hers
as he studied the long line of people before him.

A long moment passed then the old man turned to Galdr
once more, muttered something incomprehensible, then
took his arm and leaning on him heavily, walked out of
the building. In silence the other brown hooded figures
followed, leaving Injya and everyone else in open-mouthed
amazement inside the dark place. Should they, too, leave?
Would it be considered rude? As they were trying to sort
out what to do next, Hwaysaei came into the dwelling,
motioning them to follow him. As he led them from the
building and out into the central square the women and
children, as if having just been given the command, ran
from their dwellings, screaming with delight, throwing
handfuls of dried petals over them, hugging them, kissing
their cheeks, jumping up and down, suddenly very noisy
after their long silence.

That evening everyone crowded into the long building
which the Buryas called their Kurtsi – which by means
of drawn pictures on the earth and much miming they
found meant sky or spirit-home. The name for their
dwellings was kurt which they found by similar means
meant home and the lake they called Kaikal, a word
which meant world-home. They had found out that the
old man, the Chen-Shun (Wise Father) of the village, was
called Khoot-Omi. The Samoyja people suspended belief
– the Buryas were telling them that Khoot-Omi was over
two hundred tuns (winters) old!

Apart from his words: 'You are the One', Khoot-Omi
spoke no more that evening in their language – either he did
not know more or he was silent for a reason. The custom of
the people was that only one would speak at a time, each
would take it in turns to come over to every individual of

427

the Samoyja people, touch themselves, say their names, grin broadly and then try to explain something – perhaps it was pointing to an object and saying its Burya name, or pointing to another person, trying to indicate relationship. The women particularly seemed very curious and not a little distressed about the clothes that the Samoyja tribe wore, more than once they fingered their skins and pelts then touched their own clothes, showing them the embroidered cloth, the needlework and seaming needed to create their wide skirts and tight-fitting jackets. The women too seemed to be very much in awe of Sanset whose bulbous abdomen they were very inquisitive about. Each one would touch the mound of the baby, point to the sky and say 'Omi' or 'Omiruk' then point to Sanset and say 'Ome'. It was very confusing – were they telling her that she had the Moon Goddess in there? Omi and Ome was but a short step to Ahni Amwe – perhaps these people believed, as *they* had done many, many generations ago, that it was the moon that impregnated women – had they not yet discovered the part the men play in making children? It was strange indeed that these people who built kurts, who wove and embroidered cloth, who drank from intricately carved bone and metal cups could still believe in the power of the moon. Sanset tried to explain that she had a child about to be born, that her child came from her and Halfray, but the women laughed outright at this. It was confusing and very strange behaviour indeed, considering that many of the young women seemed to have two or three children clamouring around them and several were pregnant themselves!

When the 'introductions' were over and all forty or so members of the Burya people had examined, spoken, and touched those of the Samoyja, food was brought for them. The Buryas themselves ate in silence, not looking at anyone, seemingly concentrating hard upon each mouthful. The food was served to them on warmed bowls made from some strange material which Injya had never seen before – light in weight, yet hard as metal. When she knocked the sides of these bowls, they made a strange pinging sound against her nails. Not like the dull 'chock' sound of their own heavy clay bowls, nor the unmistakable sound of metal. The food itself was a mixture of strange white grains and shreds of meat and vegetables. It was very good and as the Samoyja people ate and discussed what they had learnt among themselves, slowly it came to Injya why she felt as if she was 'coming home' – slowly it dawned on her that these diminutive people were the people she had seen all that time ago when she had 'flown' to the World Tree – *these* were the people who had painstakingly brought fragments of the Arnjway Staff to the edge of the abyss – these were the people who safeguarded the old ways!

She felt the excitement of her revelation grow until she felt as if she could bear it no longer – she had to speak to Khoot-Omi – she had to ask him what had happened to the staff – she had to find out! But the moment had passed. As soon as they had finished eating, the Burya people got up, collected the dishes in silence, nodded to each – again in silence and trooped out of the kurtsi. As the last person left, Injya jumped to her feet and caught hold of the man – who turned out to be Hwaysaei.

'Please – Hwaysaei – stop. I need to talk.' She put her fingers to her mouth and brought them away again, indicating she wanted to speak to him.

'I need to talk to Khoot-Omi – please – you fetch him? Bring him here? Khoot-Omi – here.' She pointed to the long line of people now walking silently to their kurts.

'Please? – Khoot-Omi – here!' She pointed to the ground at her feet. Hwaysaei smiled at her blankly then touched her shoulder and shook his head.

'Net. Khoot-Omi drang.' He put his head to the side, resting it on his hands – drang obviously meant sleep! He smiled at her again, then he too left the kurtsi.

Once alone the Samoyja people talked over what had hap- pened. Injya explained why she so desperately needed

429

to talk with the Chen-Shun. She was convinced these people were still practising the old ways – her heart felt as if it would burst with happiness – this was why she felt so 'at home' – these people *were* connected to her somehow – they held the key, they *knew*! But when Galdr enquired, what, exactly, they were supposed to know, Injya could give no answer. Galdr too knew no reason for being where they were. He only knew that it was of the utmost importance that they stayed with these people – why and for how long, he, like Injya, could give no answer.

They talked long into the night but eventually they slept, huddled together for warmth as no skins or furs had been brought to them. Although it only felt as if he had slept for a moment, when Halfray woke, stiff from the floor and cramped conditions, he felt quite refreshed. Outside, he could hear morning sounds: children splashing in the lake, women chattering, men's voices low yet soft. Trying not to disturb the still sleeping Sanset, he crept from the kurtsi. The air outside was exhilaratingly cold: on the ground a frost, in the sky, a bright yellow, just-risen sun.

He walked across the square, smiling at the children and women who smiled back at him. He wandered between two kurts peeping in at their open doors – both were empty save for a low wooden pallet without any covering, but both had crackling fires. As he walked onwards, towards the rippling silver lake, he found himself wondering about these fires. Here, at this high encampment, there were few trees – did these people have to carry all their fuel from lower ground as they had to when they over-wintered in caves? Why did they not make their homes nearer their supply of fuel? Perhaps the forests, which he assumed were further down the mountain, were too dangerous – perhaps there were more ferocious beasts than even they knew about! Nothing would surprise him any more.

As he stood on the shores of the lake he saw the men – they were on the water in strange-shaped umiaks – which, unlike their umiaks which were capable of carrying only two at a time, were wider and much larger. But the main difference was that from the centre of these umiaks (or whatever the Burya word for them was), there rose a tall central pole, attached to which was a large skin or piece of woven cloth. This skin, filled with the morning breezes, propelled the boats around on the surface of the lake at great speed. As Halfray shielded his eyes against the brilliant dancing water, he watched in consternation as the men pulled up great nets from the water. They were far away, but Halfray knew that in those nets would be fish! So – *this* was the reason to make camp here – fish!

He sat on the water's edge, watching the men for some time, but as the sun rose higher in the heavens, he began to feel sleepy once more. He idly thought about returning to the encampment, thought he ought to tell everyone what he had found out, but the sun was so warm and soon, everyone would see for themselves. He allowed himself to lie backwards on the springy turf and folding his hands behind his head, allowed the morning sunshine, the bird-song, the soft lapping of the water, to gentle him into sleep.

He was walking through a green valley. Above him, the Burya tribe's homes, clinging precariously to the valley head. In his dream, Halfray knew that he had to be alone, away from the people who were wailing for him to return. He walked for a while, along the valley floor, by the side of a tinkling stream, until he came upon a strange looking tree; its roots in the banks of the stream, its overhanging branches almost touching the water. The people above him faded from view as he sat down under the tree, grateful for the shade and stared into the brook. The sparkling water mirrored the blue heavens: he crossed his arms on his chest and closed his eyes, but the water still seemed to be dazzling through his eyelids. He felt a shaft of sunlight penetrate the leaves overhead and dapple his forehead with warmth. He rested his back against the tree-trunk and sighed deeply, feeling utterly content. He crossed his legs in front of him, then, without knowing why, he drew them up so that he was almost sitting on top of his crossed calves. It felt very good to be sitting so, under this tree, in the soft dappled sunlight. The people had all gone, their wailing need of him over.

Dropping his arms to his knees he inhaled deeply. The air was fresh and pure, scented with heathers and pines. Halfray felt as if the air he breathed was reaching down to his very fingertips and he opened his palms and rested them, palm upwards, on his bent knees. This, too, felt very good. He was filled with a deep contentment, so deep, he could almost touch it. He raised his middle finger to touch his thumb and felt a rush of energy course through and round his body, as if each breath he took in was helping to complete a circle inside himself. Suddenly he felt compelled to open his eyes. On the opposite bank to him sat a man. He sat under a tree identical to the one under which Halfray was seated. His body was in exactly the same pose as his. This fact did not surprise the dreamer Halfray – he accepted him totally. He let his gaze fall from the broad, gentle face of the man and look into the brook. There was no reflection of the man, or the tree – only his own reflection rippled back at him. He looked again at the bank opposite. The sitter was still there, smiling at him serenely. Halfray examined his face; he was like many of the Burya people, he had the broad, flat nose and the half-closed eyes, the same high cheek-bones and square jaw, a man very much like any man in the encampment. But he was different. This man had a quality of light around him which was sublime. This man had a presence so serene, which radiated such compassion that Halfray knew that *this* one was the one for whom these people had waited.

The man stretched out his arms to Halfray and suddenly, behind him, all the people were there. It was as if the sitter's arms could embrace them all. The people began crying with joy, but the man began to fade from view and

432

their tears of joy changed to sorrow. Halfray felt stricken with grief that this beatific person had left his dream, but he knew, as certainly as he knew that he was sitting under a tree beside a brook, that, long though the wait would be, this shining, compassionate one would give these people the answer they were seeking. As if the keening people behind him could read Halfray's thoughts, they stopped crying and slowly, one by one, evaporated, leaving Halfray sitting, cross-legged, staring into the waters, looking at his own reflection.

CHAPTER THIRTY-SEVEN

'Enin,' Khoot-Omi pronounced, pointing at Halfray and Sanset and their tiny, new-born son. 'Long ago – *my* enin time.' He pointed to his chest, then again at Halfray and Sanset. Injya nodded – a long time ago, when his parents were alive. Injya pointed to her brother and cousin,

'Parents,' she said.

'Aah, yes, *parents* the word – forgot.'

The old man fell silent again, his mind lost in the mists of long ago. Injya tried not to fidget, but she was impatient. She had had to wait three moons for this audience with Khoot-Omi; three long moons when she had been instructed in weaving, embroidery, pottery, fishing, kurt-making, horse-riding – everything in fact other than her heart really wanted to know – the truth about her vision. In those three months, the Samoyja people had lived happily with the Buryas. They had visited the Chukis who lived at the opposite end of the lake, had learnt about marriage rites, birth rites, animal rites and many, many songs and dances to urge the spirits to guard their crop of long-grained grass which, with fish, was their staple diet. She had learnt all the words the Buryas used to name things, learnt some of the words which went to make up their strange language, but had learnt nothing of the Arnjway Staff.

It was with sadness that she had found out that, far from worshipping in the Old Way, the people were rather in awe of the moon, they did not worship her as the Gyaretz had done, instead they named her according to her thirteen cycles; Cold Udder Moon in the depths of their winter, Calving Moon at Aspar, Rubbing Antlers Moon in midsummer and Muscles of the Back Moon when again, before their shortest day, the meat and fish were limited. The Samoyja people had come to this land when they feared that winter would soon be upon them, but in fact, winter here brought only light flurries of snow – almost as if it was too cold to snow. The winds of this high plateau were dry, very cold, but dry. And now, apparently they were in the 'Genuine Moon' phase which preceded Calving Moon – their name for Aspar.

Injya stared at Halfray – imploring him with her eyes to remind the old man what he was supposed to be talking about. Halfray understood her look and said in a quiet voice: 'You were telling us about the time of your enin.'

Khoot-Omi nodded once and with obvious difficulty brought his attention back to Injya. He looked at her for a long time, then, as if suddenly changing his mind, started to rise, saying as he did so: 'Not words – forgot too much. Draw.'

Injya tried not to sigh out loud – he was going to draw one of his incomprehensible drawings again! As Khoot-Omi shuffled out of his kurt she frowned at Sanset.

'Have patience!' Sanset whispered, behind her hand. 'He is very old!'

'I know, I know,' Injya replied, trying to keep her voice level, 'but it is *so* important to me, Sanset.' She did not trust her voice not to divulge the tears which were rising in her throat – why must everything be so hard?

Once outside, Khoot-Omi slowly walked to the middle of the square and squatted down upon the earth. Taking up a stick he commenced to draw in the dust. He made a wide arc: 'Shoohar.'

He pointed to the sky.

'Sky – spirit-home.' The old man nodded – spirit-home.

Under this he drew a straight line.

'Por.' Por was the Burya name for earth – something which had confused the Samoyja people for quite some

435

time as in their language, of course, it meant the sun. Now it was Injya's turn to nod knowingly. Under this straight line he drew a wavy one.

'Beyen.'

'Land of the dead,' Injya said.

The old man patted her hand. On this wavy line he drew a stick figure in a boat.

'Khanyan-Ho.'

'King of the dead?' Injya suggested.

The old man shook his head,

'Ho!' he said somewhat crossly.

'Oh, *mother* of the dead!'

Khoot-Omi nodded again. He drew a cylinder lying on the straight line of Por, the earth.

'Lake Kaikal?'

'Yes. See. Two tribes' – he drew two waving lines coming from the ends of the crescent, down to the lake – 'Burya – Cow-Elk and Chukis – Bull-Elk.'

Injya nodded again. On either side of these two waving lines he drew two circles, one with rays, one without.

'Sun and moon?'

Khoot-Omi nodded his agreement. He then continued the waving lines down to where Khanyan-Ho was sitting in her boat. She understood the symbolism, the Cow-Elk and Bull- Elk peoples, two separate tribes, therefore two separate suns and moons. They came together in death. Next the old man drew a cross on the centre of the arc line and a straight line connecting this to the middle of the lake and down, to the middle of the boat.

'Xystus.'

Xystus, known to their people as the North Star, the star which never moved, the star by which they could always tell where they were. So, these people believed that Xystus was the centre of their universe, from where their power came! Khoot-Omi sat back on his heels, he had finished. Moving very tenuously, Injya took the stick from his hands.

436

'Bai Ulgan,' she said quietly as she drew, above the star but connected with the long, straight line, a crescent.

'Ahni Amwe?'

He shook his head at her. With mounting desperation, she thickened the line to where it joined the earth, then said: 'Arnjway Staff.'

Khoot-Omi looked at her as if she had taken leave of her senses.

'Net!' he repeated. 'Net Arnjway – Xystus!'

Injya tried again. She drew another picture, it had the arc, the straight line, the wavy line, but instead of Khanyan-Ho she drew a simplified Erlik. In the middle of the arc she drew again a crescent shape, then above this the sun and the moon together. Joining the crescent and the earth, she drew a tree with seven branches, under the tree she drew a straight line down to Erlik. Pointing to these symbols she named each one in her own language. The Chun-Shen shook his head – it seemed to make no sense to him at all. Keeping tears of frustration at bay, Injya drew a picture of the Arnjway Staff, then the Arnjway Staff broken up. Pointing to all the people of the encampment she mimed the actions of people picking up these pieces of the Arnjway Staff and then, pointing to the line down which Erlik was, 'threw' the fragments down to him.

'Ho (Mother) – moon, Ho – me, Injya, *my* Ho worship – pray – love (she pressed her hands to her heart), moon-Ho. Power (she pointed to the staff-picture), moon-Ho power.'

Again Khoot-Omi shook his head, then smiling at her somewhat sadly, he began to rise. Injya could have wept as she watched the old man amble off to his kurt, so all this meant nothing – the fact that he could speak some of their language – how, had never been explained: the fact that he could silent-walk – coincidence?: the synchronisities in belief systems, it was all for nought. None of it proved that they had worshipped the Goddess – ever!

437

As she lay, crying, in Galdr's arms that night, she struggled with the feelings of unfairness. Khoot-Omi had taken the vision of Halfray, as he had taken every other piece of news, with a faint smile and a faraway look. He had said that this *was* the sign he had been waiting for and now he knew that the man would come, he could now give his body to the earth with ease. But in return? He had given nothing! Injya could feel her bottom lip begin to tremble again – it was not fair!

Galdr gave her what little comfort she would accept; for himself, he knew that whatever his motives, Khoot-Omi was clearly saying that the Old Way was, just that, old. Galdr knew that Khoot-Omo *did* understand Injya's picture, *did* know exactly what she was trying to explain. Galdr had seen it in the old man's eyes that first night – had seen behind the yellowing whites and the pale, age-faded pupils, that he understood every word of their language. But more than this, he knew also that secreted behind this fact was one which he was concealing from himself – something that Galdr, too, was now hiding from Injya.

Khoot-Omi was Askoye's son. Galdr had sensed that the moment he had first seen him, had known the instant his withered hands had clutched at his shoulders. Galdr felt also that he was perhaps the only man who recognized this. He doubted that the Burya people themselves knew from where this sage had come, for he was so very old that no-one could remember any person who had known him in youth. Khoot-Omi *was* the last link with the old ways; and as surely as Galdr knew this to be true, he believed that to tell Injya would give to her and Khoot-Omi a burden too great to bear. Khoot-Omi would be robbed of his long-awaited physical death and Injya would be deprived of a future.

As he stroked Injya's brow and rocked her to sleep, Galdr felt the shadow of sadness settle on his soul. As he offered up thanks to the Great Spirit for keeping them safe for yet another day, he prayed fervently that he would not be called upon again to hide truths from his beloved and that soon they all would be freed from the claws of the past. He prayed also for strength, strength to take the sorrow from Injya's heart, strength to help remove the pain she felt so personally and to replace it with joy. But that, he knew, was a gift that only time, and the Great Spirit could give.

Injya left her sadness with the people of the Burya tribe who had stood, waving their farewells until they were no longer visible. One of their original guides, Hwaysaei, a strong youth of some twenty summers, came with them to act as their guide, and, as Injya surmised, to ensure that his three womenfolk, Sashaei, Neeho and Altai, were well treated. They had stayed with the Burya people until the end of the Calving Moon. The sun was warming the soil and Sanset and Halfray felt sure that Fonyek, their son, could stand up to the rigours of the travel.

They left the high plateau and travelled eastwards, down into the verdant valleys below. As the route became more tortuous and they left the clear, scented uplands and entered the sweltering shelter of the forest, Hwaysaei decided not to return to his tribe, partly because he was worried that they would not be able to endure the rigours of trekking through such a hot land and partly because of his feelings for Oanti. Hwaysaei had been married at fourteen summers; the marriage had been arranged, in accordance with the tribal custom, by both sets of parents when he had been born and until he had met Oanti, he had always felt that he loved his wife. They had four children whom he also fancied he loved, but the longer he spent in Oanti's company, the more he drank in her pretty mouth, her laughing eyes, the less the pain of leaving his wife and children hurt, the more the pain of leaving Oanti grew. Each day he promised he would return and each day he stayed. Soon he knew he would be unable to go back until after the rains and as each day became the next, his love for Oanti grew until he knew that he would never return.

The terrain over which Hwaysaei guided them was one which was totally new to their understanding. He led them through vast high forests interspersed with wind-swept plains, sudden rivers, marshes and more forests. Travelling through the forests, in which grew trees and plants in such profusion that they could scarce believe they were on the same continent, was at the same time the most frightening and yet the most awe-inspiring experience. Their progress was slow; in some places they had to cut a path through the dense undergrowth and the heat was as oppressive as the air was humid, heavy with the scents of flowers. Among the giant slimy tree-trunks grew great fleshy flowers, bright orange and red bursts of colour among the shining dark green of the forest – such a contrast to the pale, delicate flowers of their homeland. The air was thick with insects and musky with the smell of animals and decaying vegetation. When they had first come to this forest-land, Galdr was sure that this was the land to which his mother had guided him, so huge were the trees; but Sashaei, the girl whom Sopak had taken as his wife, insisted vehemently that this could not be true. This land had been given to the animal and plant kingdom, it was not for man, to live in it would mean certain death, if not at the tooth and claw of the animals, then through the sickness which every tiny insect, every drop of brackish water contained.

They travelled as fast as the soft earth and the cloying heat would allow. On the heat-shimmering plains, they saw an abundance of wild creatures, giant oxen and many horned creatures, like massive hairless bears, whose skins were so oversized that they wrinkled up into folds around their massive shoulders and haunches. On the muzzles of these slow-moving, pig-eyed creatures they carried two or sometimes three, vicious looking tusks. But these creatures of the plains were nothing compared to the animals of the forests. Cats, larger than the familiar snowleopard, more ferocious than the wildest wolf, blinked stealthily at them: great striped animals whose drowsy eyes belied their great speed or their rapacious appetite, vied for rank among long-limbed, long-haired tree creatures who swung, screeching overhead, disturbing the violently coloured birds who screamed their protests. Screams, screeches and roars filled their terrified nights. Sashaei was right – this was no place for man. In the swampy marshes they encountered long scaly snakes with short, clawed legs and mouths dripping with teeth, and the stunted trees were alive with bats and flying foxes, snakes and spiders, all living together in a seemingly endless battle for existence.

All through the humid summer they crossed the terrifying forests and treacherous swamps until cooler air met them. Feeling as if they had come through an initiation of heat, they descended steeply until before them, they came to a shore-line. This land was much closer to that of their forefathers: clear seas, high skies, and here they rested for almost a moon's passing. It was along this shore-line that the travellers journeyed, now heading northward to meet the white rains and the winds face on. Food was in abundance, the fishing was excellent, the hunting bountiful. When the first cold winds blew in from the sea, they built their sancars and stopped travelling. Galdr's people now numbered twenty-two adults and three children – too many to feed on scant winter supplies, too many people to put at risk simply because Galdr urgently wanted progress. This winter, although not as harsh as winters they had known before, still seemed to go on for ever, but as soon as the first buds opened they were off again. This time it was Aspar and not the white rains which covered their tracks as they advanced steadily northward.

It was not a frightened, straggling band of exiles who now joyfully rode towards their new home, it was the beginnings of a fine nation. The rest over winter had been good, it forged the bonds between them, broke down the barriers of language and as if to cement them further together, it had produced babies. Kendosh had been the first to tell in his fumbling, red-faced way that Neeho was with child; before another moon passed, Tronüg announced that his tiny child-wife, Altai, was also with child. And Injya, as she helped pack away the skins of their winter homes, knew that she, too, was carrying within her the fruits of her love of Galdr.

When they reached the land where the sky dripped with the glorious lights of their ancestors, Galdr saw the land across which they would have to travel to reach their new home. He stood on the shore-line, staring hard, surveying the barren, narrow band of black rocks stretching far to the east which he knew, was the beginnings of the land about which Patrec had spoken. As Galdr stared at the rocks, felt the cold wind cracking his face he saw two birds: one, a ragged old raven, cawing loudly, the other, a fine winter-white eagle, circling noiselessly. Feeling rather than knowing that haste was of the essence, Galdr urged his people onward. In the three winters they had been travelling he had told them often of the new land they would find beyond the rising sun, the land of high mountains and lush plains, the land of the soft golden metal, the true land of his soul. Now, as he looked at their weary, travel-worn faces as they surveyed the wilderness before them, his heart went out to them. The terrain across which they had to travel looked no more inhospitable than anything they had traversed before, but he had a deep sense of unease, which he knew was felt by everyone.

The islands which lay strung in a long line to the south of the land-mass were no more than rocky pimples cast in an angry sea. Some were conical, perfectly shaped, as if they had been whittled out of wood, others looked black and rough as if they had been poured out of the sky. The land itself was no more than a narrow isthmus beyond which, on the northern side, vast sheets of ice lay as if held back by the barren rocks. Few flowers grew on it, tiny stunted trees, no taller than a hand-span, clung to life and it supported no other wildlife save little grey-blue birds who burrowed

442

in the meagre earth and whose nightly pitapit calling was the only sound above the ceaseless moaning of the waves and the wind. It had been days since they had seen any game; it was as if here, on the top of the world, all known life stopped. Galdr tried to raise the spirits of his people by describing his vision of their new land, but the words stuck in his throat. He knew that first they would have to get across this bleak space and neither soft words nor pretty pictures would make them any stronger or protect them from the winds and the seas.

They travelled for a moon's quarter, covering a few hundred pchekts a day over the rough ground, stopping frequently. Sleep almost became a thing of the past as the nights were very short and the strange violet days long. To their right, frenzied seas sent an everlasting plume of white foam crashing on to their path; to their left, the tranquil green and white ice lay, as if waiting for release. Another quarter moon passed and ahead of them they could see a wider expanse of land, bare but definitely wider. By the time a further moon's quarter had elapsed, the sea to their right became calmer, the land stretched as far as they could see to the north and ahead was a dense forest, high mountains and . . . reindeer! They had arrived . . . their new home was here!

That night, exhausted though they were, the celebrations lasted until the violet night turned rose and the new day began. Ahead of them, their new land, behind them sea, ice, islands. Tronüg caught a hare and Injya, giving thanks to the Great Spirit which provided for them, was quietly engaged on skinning it. Around her the bustle of the people getting ready for the day, before her, her pretty child, Pentesh, now a clear-eyed beauty of nearly three summers, stood, finger in mouth in wide-eyed amazement at her mother's skill. Injya looked at her child, then down at the soft animal, still warm upon the earth – both gifts of the Great Spirit. With the sun warming her back she smiled up happily as a very wobbly Fonyek held firmly by the hand of Sanset tottered over, clenching and unclenching his tiny fist in greeting. All was well and happy, Injya thought, as she gazed at the pretty children and the face of her beloved Sanset, this new land, the land of their dreams. She felt a stirring in her belly and flushed as if Sanset could sense it too. Sanset could not feel the movement but caught the flushed look.

'What is it?' Her face puckered into a slight frown of unease.

'My son, waking up.' Injya grinned at her then resumed her task.

'As long as that is all it is.' Sanset looked at Injya's bowed head.

'Of course – what else could it be?' Behind her she heard Djyana cry out: 'Woa – woa there, boy!' as she struggled to calm one of the horses.

'The horses seem very restless today,' Sanset remarked looking over to where Djyana and Vronjyi were struggling to load the beasts.

Injya agreed, somewhat abstractedly. It was not until a long time later that Injya had time to rue her careless murmur – perhaps if she had turned around, perhaps if she had looked, but it was useless.

The horses *had* been very restive all the previous night. They had not settled, but had constantly whinnied and pawed the ground while everyone was singing and rejoicing. It had taken them a long time to get them packed that morning, the horses kicking and one even taking a nip at poor little Wa-Oagist, but eventually they were mounted and the last part of their journey commenced. But after a short while the horses stopped, ears flat against their heads, eyes wide as if some unseen foe forbade further movement. They resisted cajoles, threats, entreaties and even whips. They would not move.

The horses had felt the earth tremble long before the humans did. And when the low rumble first happened, when the island they could see far below them blew apart in a great roaring flame, the shock to the earth upon which they were standing was still imperceptible to humans. Only when the solid black plume of smoke rose straight into the air and the sea round the shattered island began to boil as molten rock hissed into it, did the humans feel the first shock rise up out of the earth. Aywe's horse shied, throwing her to the ground; horses and people screamed in terror as the shock quivered through the earth as if it was no more than water. Animal and man alike fell upon the earth, screaming and wailing, as through their bodies the shock waves trembled and the black stench-filled smoke reached their senses.

All day the rumblings continued. A day in which most of the horses escaped, galloping over the shaking ground in terror. A day when the sky was filled with the awful smoke of the island which they could still see glowing red in the murk, a day when the wailing of the children could not be hushed and when the fear of the adults was profound. This earth, this new earth, moved and shuddered as if she were a mother heaving with the pangs of childbirth.

Night fell and with it the rain. By morning all were drenched and covered in filthy black slime. The raging red sun showed the people that the land over which they had ridden now was rent in two. An angry fissure in the black rocks opened wide, like a gaping mouth, from which spewed jagged ice. The sea, where they had caught their fish and swam, was now filled with gargantuan mountains of ice, cracking and crashing on the spuming waves. The island-mountain, which had blown apart their world, had disappeared. Only an occasional bubble showed the place where once it had stood, unremarkable and unreliable.

Injya lost her son. With the first violent shock she felt her child dislodge from the safety of her womb. Throughout that terrible day and night where there was no safety anywhere, her pains, like those of the great mother earth, grew and somewhere in the sooty rain-filled night, her child had slithered into the violent world and died without taking breath. Lying, with Galdr's hand so comforting on her temple, all Injya could say was: 'I should have cared, I should have known!'

Although Djyana kept telling her that it was useless, there was nothing anybody could have known or done, Injya was inconsolable, as if the loss of her child was inextricably linked with the loss of that tiny fire-filled island or the great chasm the earthquake had caused in the slender causeway between one world and another.

Somehow during that awful day and night, they had managed to drag themselves up on to higher ground. Both Aywe and Injya had to be carried, Aywe moaning pitifully from the deep gash in her head, Injya bleeding profusely and only semi-conscious. The torrential rain, the terrible thick blackness, suffocating and life destroying, seemed to cling to their very souls. A grey light, filtered by the sooty water-filled atmosphere, told them another day had dawned and shivering and exhausted, they made their way on foot to yet higher ground. Why they did this, none knew, but a deep instinct drove them further and further uphill. On the second day, the rain became less angry and a fine grey mist seemed to creep over the land. On the third day the sun shone pale now, as if in awe of the mountain's fire and almost stealthily illuminated the scene, allowing the people the first glimpse of the havoc caused by the island's death.

Before them the land was covered in grey ash, behind them the sea had risen alarmingly in depth. The fissure in the land-bridge caused by the first quake was now a gigantic lake, the rocks up which they had scrambled non-existent. The line of tiny islands along the shore-line had submerged and in their place giant chunks of ice sailed on the glassy sea like massive arctic geese.

Now they felt once again like a frightened, straggling band of exiles as they faced the enormity of their actions. Supporting each other they staggered towards the shelter of the giant red-barked trees of Galdr's vision. That this was the promised land, there was no doubt, but none felt like rejoicing; ahead of them lay only ash-covered trees and mountains – gone were the herds of reindeer, gone also were all but two of their horses. Gone also was Injya's child, the first child to have been born on this new continent. A deep sadness filled the hearts of the people, a soft regret, as fine as the ash, clung to their spirits as each accepted that there could be no return. As if Hoola could sense the people's depression and was trying to take away the offending ash, in the middle of the fourth night she covered herself in a soft blanket of white rain. When the sun rose on that fifth morning, they found it very difficult to give thanks to Bai Ulgan, but Injya, weak as she was, insisted that everything, no matter how painful, was, ultimately, for their own good and with Galdr supporting her they chanted together.

'Great Spirit of us all, if it is your divine will, help us to survive and bring to fruition your great and glorious plan. Show us how to live on this, your creation, and give us the strength to carry out your purpose. You have helped us so much already, do not desert us now.'

For a moment the white rains ceased their dancing, for a split second the sun shone upon the people but then, as if He had only been teasing, the wind blew harder and the white rains fell thicker and once more, despair filled the hearts of the people.

Soosha too had felt despair. Often during the three winters' turning since Galdr and Injya had escaped, she had briefly felt despair; briefly because as soon as she felt it, she would censor it. Despair was allowed no room. Occasionally, she would have liked to give in to the luxury of tears, occasionally she would have liked to give in and cry, raw to the night, why me?, but as hardship followed hardship for herself and her people alike, Soosha's heart became inured to suffering. She had given birth to a girl-child, an agonizing blood-ridden birth which had lasted two

447

days. She took no solace from the child which eventually wailed its protest at leaving the comfort of the womb one rain-swept night in late autumn. Staring at the wizened red scrap of life she had felt nothing, as if this gift touched her not. Later, as the depths of winter once more shrouded her people in white stillness, she continued to look at her child as if it belonged to someone else – seeing in her child the failure of her plan. Xynon had impregnated her, but Erlik had deserted her. The impregnation had occurred and Xynon still lived.

For two summers the people of Skoonjay had travelled, south and westward, eventually coming to a land where the sun was hotter but the nights longer, a land of steeply wooded mountains and swift flowing rivers. Here in a broad valley, lush and green, protected by the mountains on either side, they made their new home.

They, like the Samoyja people, had come across other settlements of people, but unlike the Samoyja, they had not learnt, had not respected, and driven by greed and lust, had chosen instead to take slaves and wives. But, as if their new land brought forth a renaissance, ideas flowed from the people as freely as the waters flowed from the mountains. Gone were the sancars, the life which revolved around the migrations of the animals and the vagaries of the elements. Gone also was a sense of freedom which roaming people feel. But in the rush of ideas, the reckless yearning for the new, the people did not realize that their freedom was slipping away with each house they built, each tree they cut, each piece of earth claimed as theirs. Like a child who, excited by the first day of school, does not comprehend that this first day will grow into a thousand days and that for years, school will be his life; the Branfjord people did not understand to what they were binding themselves. So, willingly, they cut and built, dug and hoed; happily they caught and tamed animals, bred from them and slaughtered them; and joyfully, they sowed the seeds of their own spiritual destruction.

Of Anfjord, she knew little and cared less. During that first, ice-bound home, she had dreamt of him often, seeing him and his band, crossing great plains of ice. When she had lain, heavy with child, she sensed him in her dreams, no longer struggling across vast plains of snow, but settled in verdant valleys. For many moons her dreams were haunted by visions of her father, as he cut the tall fir trees to make the long, low houses which his people lived in, but when her child had been born, the visions stopped.

That Anfjord had survived his exile, that he had found the home of which he had spoken, far to the north, did not surprise her. She even contrived to take pleasure from his tenacity – it showed her that she, too, would survive – unlike . . .

She had never, in three winters and four summers, dreamt of Galdr. Never had a vision, a presentiment, a vague feeling even. Galdr, Injya and the rest were dead to her, as dead as if they were no longer inhabiting the same earth.

CHAPTER THIRTY-EIGHT

With most of their horses missing, with nearly all their skins and provisions gone, they had no option but to make their homes where they could. Injya had fallen senseless after her prayer to Bai Ulgan as if the act had robbed her of her strength. For days she had lain semi-conscious and feverish, barely able to drink the healing infusions Sanset and Halfray prepared for her. Aywe, too, had fallen ill, the gash to her temples deep and in the cold, reluctant to heal. It seemed to Galdr that all their efforts were in vain and that without Injya and the strength she represented, they would surely perish.

Rudju had no such misgivings. As he saw Galdr, the man who had saved him from insanity, seem to shrink before his very eyes, he became stronger. The men with whom he had hunted, Sopak, Tronüg and Kendosh, seemed far away from him – busy as they were with their new women. Only Vronjyi and Halfray seemed close to him and as he was sitting with these two men, watching Vronjyi idly tease a tuft of grass with a stick and listening to Halfray who was bemoaning the fact that his drum had been lost, he was suddenly struck with an idea. He had been picturing Halfray's drum, lost somewhere, covered in white rain, and imagining how grateful the insects of the earth would be to have such a snug sancar, when as clear as daylight he visualized them, too, living in an upturned drum covered with white rain. He interrupted Halfray.

' . . . sorry, but I have just had an idea! Look, if we can – as we all have done when we have had to – survive in holes made from the white rain – why cannot we make, not holes, but sancars out of white rain?'

Halfray guffawed unkindly and Vronjyi laughed outright.

Rudju frowned but continued, 'But what is to stop us trying?' he urged. 'Surely anything would be better than this?' He waved his arm around indicating the huddled group.

When the white rain had first fallen, hoping that it would be just a squall, branches had been pulled from the trees and roughly tied together – what few scraps of skin they had left had been thrown over the outside. Now, three days after the white rain had first started, they were still crouched together in a tiny soot-filled hovel, the ground under their feet trodden into a quagmire.

'Because it will blow away – like the white rain itself – it will simply blow away in the wind!'

Vronjyi stabbed at the earth with his stick, angered at the seeming stupidity of the idea. He was hungry and hunger made him bad-tempered. Everyone was hungry and bad-tempered apart from Rudju who seemed incapable of grasping the notion that if they could not move soon, or at least catch something to eat, they would all perish.

'But it does not!' Rudju replied hotly. 'It does not blow away – did those vast sheets of ice blow away? No, they stayed solid and floated away. They would melt, of course, when the sun warmed them, but they were solid – as solid as this ground. The white rain turns to ice – all we have to do is make it solid!'

'But that ice has been here for hundreds of seasons' turnings – it is not one winter's white rain, it is countless winters!'

'Precisely!' Rudju's eyes gleamed in triumph. 'Precisely! It has turned hard because it has had more white rain piled on top of it, pressing it into ice, then more white rain has fallen and then that has turned to ice too. We could do that – we will not have to wait hundreds of winters – oh – look . . . !' He got up suddenly as if exasperated by the inadequacies of speech and his friend's stubbornness, dashed outside into the blizzard and came back covered in white rain, clutching a big fistful of snow.

'Now, Vronjyi – now tell me that we cannot make sancars out of it!'

He moulded the fistful, pressing it between his palms until it had turned into a hard ball. Placing it on the ground he rolled it near the fire. The outside of the ball glistened as it began to melt. Snatching it up, he took it outside for a moment then brought it back for them to examine. On the outside of the ball had formed a skin of ice. Rudju scraped at it with his fingernail.

'Look – almost as hard as rock!'

Vronjyi looked first at Rudju, then down at the ball of ice, then up at Rudju again. Of course! Thunderstruck at the simplicity of the idea he banged his forehead with the palm of his hand – how simple – how utterly childlike and how utterly practical!

The men, shouting like excited children, went outside into the freezing wind. Within a very short time they returned, fingers reddened, eyes streaming, dithering with cold. First one, then another looked guiltily towards Djyana and the women, then down at the ground. Slowly, as if speaking with a great boulder on his chest, Galdr spoke: 'We cannot make our winter homes without food. We cannot survive out there – we have not got the energy to make our new homes. Djyana, we are all going to die.'

Djyana looked up swiftly – why was he speaking only to her? Galdr looked at the ground, coughed uncomfortably, then said quietly, 'We have to take the life of one of the horses.'

The atmosphere in the sancar turned as cold as the weather. Djyana looked at him, her face expressionless and dumb with shock. Oanti and Bendula looked at each other with tears in their eyes, then quickly looked away, preferring to stare at the muddy earth than admit the truth of Galdr's statement. Ullu, suppressing a sob, rushed over to an open-mouthed Toonjya for comfort and

Sanset turned her back on the men and concentrated on Injya's sleeping face, glad that Injya had been spared the awfulness of Galdr's words. Sanset knew them to be true, she knew that they would all die if not from cold, then hunger, but kill the horses? She shook her head and drew Fonyek close to her – a murderous idea.

'Djyana . . . I . . . ' Galdr began, trying to stop himself shivering as great drops of ice fell from his cloak.

'I . . . ' He fell silent. It was Sashaei who saved him from further embarrassment and who broke the awful, deathly silence.

'In my old home we worshipped our horses,' she said gently, her soft sing-song voice, lisping slightly as she fought for the right words. 'In my old home we believed that the horse would take our souls to the Creator. Horses are our brothers. As one brother would lay down his life to save another, our brother horse would not blame us for using his body – he would be proud – he would think it an honour.'

She stopped abruptly and looked towards Galdr, her narrow eyes glinting, her heart pounding – she had never said so many words all together before – she hoped she had them right.

Slowly Djyana rose and in the darkness her eyes shone into Galdr's as she stretched out her hand.

'Give me your knife,' she said quietly, not taking her eyes from Galdr's. 'I will take the life of my brother.'

None dared look after her as she walked from the sancar. None spoke as they listened to her footsteps crunch away in the white rain or heard her whispered greetings to the two shivering animals. In silence the men crowded round the fire, not looking at their women and as they sat on their haunches with their downcast eyes, Djyana slit the throats of both horses, weeping silent tears of treachery. She bathed her arms in their warm trusting blood. She felt their life-force freeze on her skin as she watched the gentle creatures fall down, one after the other, on to the soft earth.

She felt as if she were slaying not just her animal-brother, but her spirit-father. She stood for a long time watching the blood stain the white rain, as her brothers succumbed to death. When convinced that they were no more, she threw the instrument of their death upon the innocent white carpet and walked away from the ramshackle sancar and the hungry people inside it.

Vronjyi and Centill had hunted for three days for Djyana. When they returned, alone and dejected, they heard that it had taken only two days to make five ice-homes. Two days of battling with the blizzard, two days of cracking fingers packing white rain hard into ice, of carrying fire to the low-domed buildings only to find the flame extinguished when they got there, two days of frustration and frozen-fingered pain, but finally the ice-homes were habitable. They were small, not big enough to stand in, barely wide enough for four adults to sleep crammed side by side in, but they kept out the wind and kept in some heat. Frozen horse flesh was eaten raw, as daily the temperature outside their houses fell. But neither men had the stomach for frozen horse flesh. Djyana had sacrificed herself along with these animals and that left a sour taste in their mouths which could not be washed away.

The blizzard stopped and the men hunted. Some days they were lucky, catching a careless bird or a curious seal, most days they were not. When the blizzard first stopped, larger ice-homes were made and now they had a cluster of eight, all tightly packed together in a circle, their low entrances pointing outward like the long legs of a white, fat-bodied spider. And so they lived, in semi-darkness, in ice-houses filled with sooty smoke from the blubber candles. When they thought that summer would never come, Neeho had her child, a tiny yellow-skinned boy with fierce brown eyes and jet-black hair. The joyous parents called him Do-Ashook, son of white rain, and now all attention was turned on Sopak and the waiting

Sashaei, but Sashaei's child was born without a breath and they buried her in the hard ground under the tall trees on the mountainside, Sashaei calling to the earth long into the night the name of her child born without a breath, Pa-Paydoh, a name for sadness and tears.

As soon as Sashaei was well enough to move, they left their ice-homes. In the bright spring, with the waters of the mountainside rushing crystal clear, with the game returned to the uplands, they travelled easily. They followed the route of a river which flowed into a lake so vast that when they first saw it, they imagined it to be a sea. On either side of this river mountains rose, towering over them, some covered in white rain, some densely forested with the straight red-barked trees of Galdr's vision. On the banks of the rivers grew graceful larches and willows, their vivid new-green buds and yellow catkins dancing in the wind, shaking and laughing at the gaunt, pale people. The rivers were alive with water-fowl and fish and as the sun turned their pale faces a deep bronzed tan, the plentiful food plumped out their winter-withered frames and made them strong once more.

As spring turned into summer and summer began to fade, they found themselves in a high valley. From either side the mountains rose, red and grey; cascading waterfalls fed the many lakes and rivers and it was in the bed of one such river that Galdr saw the golden soft metal, shining out at him as prettily as an opened buttercup. They had decided to make their winter's camp by this river, everyone suddenly aware that they had been travelling virtually non-stop for seven moons' passing, everyone suddenly expressing the need to make a shelter more permanent than they had on the long walk from the frozen mountains. There was a quality in the wind which suggested that winter would soon be upon them again and they had spent the day cutting new saplings for sancars and testing the ground for a good encampment place. The air was alive with bustling people and when Galdr first saw the metal, two things happened in quick succession: he stared into the water and saw the dancing, liquid metal and Centill shouted away ahead of him one word: 'Horses!'

Tearing himself away from the bank of the river he ran towards Centill, following his pointing arm. Shielding his eyes from the sun's last glaring rays he searched in the direction Centill indicated. Further down the valley, tiny – far away, but unmistakable – wild horses – an enormous herd! His heart sang – horses! Now they would find it, now they would get there. Suddenly he stopped. Find what? Get where? They had found the trees, he had seen the metal, what more was there to do? There *was* nowhere else to go – this place was where he was meant to be, this was the end of his journey.

He took scant notice of the men running wildly up to him, their voices excited, the air alive with vibrant hopes. All he could feel was a sense of defeat. This *was* the end of their journey – but was this all? Was this all there was? Over and over again he heard his mother's voice: a land, far to the rising sun, full of tall red trees: a land shining with soft sun-metal, the land of your futures – but what futures? It suddenly seemed to him that they had spent all this time travelling, struggling to get to this point, and now they had reached it – all had been for nought! He had not known what he was expecting from this metal, but he had always felt that it, like the drum, would open his soul to a new depth of understanding, but now, having seen it, he sensed its transience. He knew he no longer knew.

Suddenly overcome, he sank to the ground. Centill, not expecting this response, thought he had suddenly been taken ill and called to Injya. Injya struggled through the press of people gathered round him, and putting her hand on Galdr's neck, closed her eyes. The crowd immediately fell silent as she breathed deeply, focusing her attention on Galdr's spirit-body. She felt Halfray's hand touch her shoulder and sensed his thoughts: sun-metal, he seemed to be saying, again, sun-metal. She ran her hand down his spine, feeling the vibrations of his spirit-body, no, he was not ill, not physically, but something . . . there it was, just there – a hard nugget of pain – just below his left shoulder-blade, as if something was stuck. Opening her eyes and squatting in front of him she pulled his face towards her.

'Galdr – what is the pain in your heart?'

Galdr stared at her silently, then shook his head as if shaking away a memory.

'Galdr, I can feel a hard little knot, like a crystal or a lump of metal, attached to your heart – what is it?'

When she said the word metal Galdr's eyes looked frightened. He closed them as if closing his eyes from the consciousness of the words and then, speaking falteringly he said in a whisper: 'Injya, I have found the gold metal Patrec told me about – in the river, chunks of it, all gold and gleaming – but I am afraid.'

He fell silent and stared dumbly at the earth.

'You are afraid of the metal?' Injya prompted, eyes searching Galdr's for an answer.

'No – but – something that is in the metal – or perhaps, not in it, but around it – the answer to a question – but I do not know what that question is!' He dropped his eyes from hers and stared at the ground. When he looked up again his brow was furrowed with pain.

'Injya – I have brought all of you here, to this new land – and now we are here – I do not know what to do. Before' – he stumbled over his words, his anguished eyes searched the crowd, then he rushed on – 'before, I thought I knew what I was doing – and why . . . not completely of course, but I have always *known* . . . and now – *is* there anything to do? *Is* this it? Our life? What *do* we do?'

Galdr's eyes had filled with tears and, as Injya drew him close to her, he began weeping. The people stared at the two crouching figures with disbelief – Galdr crying? As Injya rocked him to and fro like a child, she whispered with a voice thick with emotion the words Askoye had said so often to her: 'When it is right – you will understand – you cannot hurry the universe.'

The people made their home in this wide valley, with its sun-metal river dancing by, with its massive mountains sheltering it. They made tall sancars: one for each family; one large sancar for daily prayers and meetings; a sturdy svarge for the horses they caught; and a smoke-house for the game they killed with reverence. They cared for the earth with as much love as they gave each other and when the leaves turned russet then orange, when the wind blew its final warm blast from the south, they put their trust in Bai Ulgan and his mother, Hoola, whom they had served so well and they prayed that winter in this new homeland would not take their lives.

Winter did not take their lives. It gave them one. On the morning of the third day of the season, when the sun had just risen and the moon still hung on a gossamer thread, they were woken by the sounds of the horses whinnying and a far-off calling.

Oanti was the first to reach the half-starved wreck of the one whom they had all thought dead. Djyana was greeted with yells of surprised rapture, bone-breaking hugs and showers of kisses. She was pulled from her horse, bombarded with so many questions that she could not answer until finally, gasping for breath, choking on her tears of joy, she had to push the people away from her.

'You are going to kill me with love! You could at least feed me first!'

The seven moons which had passed had changed Djyana beyond all recognition. Apart from the fact that she had obviously had little to eat and consequently had become leaner and healthier looking, her hitherto cropped hair had grown long and wild and now framed her handsome face, turning the once bovine woman into a beautiful maiden. Now, she seemed more like a young colt than a mother-mare as she laughingly made light of one danger or another and talked animatedly of trapping bears single-handed; of a fight with a mountain lion; of her catching and taming a horse only to have it break its leg under her; of nights spent in holes in the white rains or of days sailing down fast-flowing rivers, every second fearing that she would be dashed to death.

The celebrations lasted long into the night and when Galdr woke the next day he found that he knew, that with the return of Djyana, he could now leave his people. He had not been aware that he had been waiting for an omen, but all the time spent in this valley he had felt that soon he would be shown the way to unlock the secret of the sun-metal. Now he was sure. He would go back – back to the mountains – back to solitude and silence. He would find himself as Djyana had done, not surrounded by people, not being guided, he would find his answer alone.

As the first rays of dawn the next day turned their world pink, Galdr left his silent, tearful people. He left, taking with him nothing, no water, no covering save the clothes he was wearing.

'I have to be as a child,' he had said to them proudly, already the light of distance showing in his eyes. 'To understand I have to leave behind my man-frame and become one with the mountains and the skies.'

As the bright red sun rose unsteadily over the horizon, Galdr walked up the mountain, heading straight into the path of the sun. The Samoyja people watched him silently, a lone figure silhouetted by the carmine rays of the sunrise and their hearts went out to him.

As Injya watched silently the figure of her beloved became no more than a dot, she put behind her her doubts and fears. She closed her mind on the memory of the previous night when Galdr and she had talked, when they had both wept, when they had fallen asleep after making sorrowful love. She knew deep down that what Galdr was doing was completely right, but that did not stop the pain of parting. She had a dreadful presentiment that he would not return, but she also knew that even to consider the unthinkable could alter the course of events. She *had* to rid herself of that fear – she had to ensure that all of them only looked towards the hopeful. Now, with Galdr gone, she knew that she had to be mother and father to the people. And she had to show them nothing but trust in the divine.

As they were all turning away, heads bowed, an air of gloom shrouding each, Injya stopped them and with eyes bright with unshed tears she cried aloud:

> 'Great Spirit of the plains,
> Great Spirit of the forests and waters,
> Care for your son, Galdr.
> Beloved Por, warm him,
> Silver Goddess Ahni, cherish him.
> Great Hoola, bear your son with tenderness.'

She stopped, arms upraised to the heavens and gazed at the faces of the people before her: their despondency was lifting as their faces became flushed with the rays of the living sun.

'Pray with me – now – all, pray with me!' The people stood round her in a ring, arms and heads raised with hope:

> 'Great Spirit of the plains,
> Great Spirit of the forests and waters,
> Help your son – guide him and protect him.'

She felt the air vibrate as the hearts of those gathered before her responded to her plea.

> 'Great Spirit of the plains,
> Guide and protect us.
> We trust and love you.

460

Protect your son, Galdr, and bring him back to us.
We are your children, you have breathed life into us.
In return, we care for your body, Hoola.
Take care of our brother, Galdr, and if it is Your will
Return him to us, Great Spirit, return him to us.'

Return him to us, she whispered to herself, as she drew
Pentesh close to her as her tears splashed on her daughter's
curls. Great Spirit – return him to us.

CHAPTER THIRTY-NINE

Galdr prayed for death. High above him the death-birds glided silently, their scraggy necks craning as they strained to see if his prayers had yet been answered. High above them the sky was white, the thin autumnal azure paled to bleached-bone colour. The clouds which the cutting wind had brought, the menacing snow-filled clouds, were gone today. Gone too was his resolve. For fourteen nights and long days Galdr had neither eaten nor drunk, he had prayed continuously, using all his powers, calling upon the spirit to give him strength, calling upon his eagle-self to take flight, calling upon his mother and, when the hunger maddened him, his father also. Now as he lay, enfeebled and scarce-breathing, staring into the high white sky, he welcomed death – urged for death's gentle arms to enfold him – pleaded with his living body for respite.

The sun-metal would give him no peace. It burnt in his soul as it burnt in his palm. At the beginning of his journey while he was still looking for the right place to be, he had done all that he could to gain clarity: prayed for guidance, looked into the sun-metal, watched for visions, listened to the small voice inside which always had guided his head, but nothing would come. It had taken him six searing days to find the ledge upon which he was now resting. Driven by a half-formulated picture in his mind, he had wandered through the vast canyons of red sandstone where his only companions were the desert lizards and the sleek snakes of the caverns. Eventually he had scaled one of the high red mountains and found this place to rest. Now, alone for eight days, he had given up. He did not possess the strength to return to his people nor did he have the heart.

He had failed. All the journey had been for nought – this land was as any other – there *was* no great secret here waiting to be uncovered. There was simply this: sun-metal, high mountains, pretty streams, vast landscapes, trees and lakes. No more. There was no secret.

Galdr felt as if there was a barrier between him and the gold – an invisible wall which made the metal impervious to the strongest thaumaturgy he possessed. More than once he had wanted to hurl the sun-metal from him, but always something stopped him, checking his hand, forcing him to place it calmly back upon the bare rocks.

Tears smarted his wind-cracked face as he stared at the white sky and the hovering birds.

'Come on!' he cried to them, 'why delay? I am as good as dead now! Here! Come here! I am waiting!'

But the birds carried on wheeling overhead, ignoring his angry shouts, biding their time.

Galdr struggled to his feet and unclenched his fist. The nugget lay accusing in its innocence in his palm. He stared at it, loathing its brilliance and its all-too familiar shape. Giddy, no longer knowing what to do or how to be, he shambled about on the dusty rock, kicking at the pebbles, watching with satisfaction as some rolled over the edge of the ledge. Far below him was a stream, busily rushing through rustling trees, above them the dense trees of dark green clung to the mountainside and then the dry rocks began. Perhaps if he threw himself down into the stream the sun-metal would save him or produce something that would break his fall? He no longer cared. He sat down heavily among the pebbles and dust and leant back against a boulder.

'Go away!' he shouted now at the birds, 'leave me alone!' – oblivious to the fact that only a moment before he had called to them to come.

He gazed at the sun-metal then at the ground. Tiny shards of crystal, pink, grey and clear, lay all around him, forming, to his mind, a perfect circle with him at its centre. He laughed weakly at himself and his need to make order out of chaos. He picked up a handful of crystals absent-mindedly and began turning them over in his hand, feeling their sharp edges, weighing them, enjoying the pinpricks of pain as he closed his fist over them. He smiled as he remembered Halfray and his 'no water – no man' revelation – perhaps this would be the same: no crystal – no sun-metal!

As if the thought suddenly invigorated him, he began feverishly picking up crystals, looking at them, discarding some, wiping others, sorting the crystals into piles, now of shape, now of colour. He did not understand why he was doing this or what the outcome would be, he only knew that this stone collecting, this manic sorting held the key. Now scrabbling about on all fours, he combed his ledge for more sharp stones, even trying to pick pieces out from the rock-face, desperately seeking for the right stones. What constituted right from wrong he did not know, but he dared to hope that he *would* understand something at the end of it. The first wind of night had blown long before and the sky was already turning magenta when Galdr was sure that he had collected enough crystals. Exhausted, he sat back on his heels and looked at the various piles of stones in front of him. They meant nothing to him. He wanted to stop, wanted to cry, wanted to die – anything to take him out of this hell, but something urged him onward.

By the light of the full moon he continued his work; now, in moonlight, the crystals seemed luminous, his sun-metal dull. He held each crystal up to the moon, searching for unflawed ones, oblivious to their colours. As if taken over by a power which defied reason, he arranged the crystals in a complicated format. Choosing the four largest, most perfect ones, he laid these on the cardinal points – one facing towards where the sun would rise, one to where the sun had long since disappeared, one to the north and one to the south. Joining these four he carefully placed twenty-eight lesser crystals in a wide ring. From each of these twenty-eight he placed a line of smaller crystals with nine crystals in each, all pointing to the middle of the circle. In the centre, he placed his piece of sun-metal.

Weakened by his exertion, he sat back and looked at his work. Now he felt curiously distanced from it – as if the thing no longer belonged to him or had anything to do with him. Leaning against his rock, with a deep sense of well-being, he closed his eyes and fell instantly asleep.

That night, the night of the full moon, Injya had been unable to sleep. Leaving Pentesh asleep in the sancar with Halfray, Sanset and their child, she stood for a long time looking upwards at the mountain where she had caught the last glimpse of Galdr. It looked dark and sombre in the white light of the moon. She walked swiftly over to the fire and stood stock-still listening to the sounds of the night. All around her insects were rattling their strange love calls – here and there fireflies winked and a far way off she heard the sound of a wolf. She felt very alone. Gazing into the face of the moon she wondered if She could see her daughter and an old longing filled her soul. On such a night as this the women of her old country had danced, invoking the power of the Goddess to come unto them; on such a night as this wonders would happen, children would be born or conceived – now her life felt sterile. But it was the same moon, the same sky and stars, the sun was warmer but it was the same sun! Shaking her head as if to rid herself of her gloomy feelings she began to sway, holding her arms up to the moon, allowing herself to respond to the rhythm of the moon as she gentled the tides of her body. Soon swaying was not enough and she began dancing, slowly at first, keeping her hands outstretched to the light, her head thrown backwards, her eyes on the moon's face.

Beyond the moon was a circle of lights, a halo of the faintest, purest pinks, ambers and amethysts and as Injya danced, she imagined these lights coming to the earth and becoming matter in a perfect ring of the purest crystals; she imagined how wonderful their life would be if they

465

were all protected by a magic circle of moon-lights and as the idea took hold she began to dance round the fire, then out, round the encampment, willing the lights of the halo to gather around the encampment, sheltering them forever from harm, keeping them always in the light. The halo had faded long before Injya, finally fatigued, dropped her arms and walked slowly back to her sancar. She was tired, but she felt purer, more invigorated than she had done for many a moon's passing. How silly she was not to do this every moon – what a lazy, stupid woman she had become. But, as she remembered the long journey, she forgave herself – fording raging torrents and walking hundreds of pchekts a day was not conducive to moon-worship! Once inside her sancar she vowed that when Galdr returned she would tell him of her vision, share with him the happiness she now felt, and who knows – perhaps they could make a ring such as she imagined. Like Galdr she fell instantly asleep, dreaming of luminous rings of power, circles of light which purified and healed anyone who stood in their centres.

Galdr awoke with voices whispering inside his head. He opened his eyes and looked at the stones before him. He shook his head, trying to rid himself of the voices and to make sense of what he had done the night before. Dawn had not yet risen and in the light grey that heralded the sunrise, Galdr stared at the almost colourless stones. Inside his head the voices were now all speaking together, the high cackling of old women, soft whispering of the young ones and interspersed with these the voices of the animals, brother fox and wolf, brother bison and deer. He found the action of putting his hands to his ears in an effort to stop the noise crippling, his arms tingling and shaking as his dried-out, malnourished body tried to carry out his commands. His hands did eventually reach his ears, but putting them over them, made no difference to the voices still talking away. Behind the voices he could hear his blood rhythmically beating upon his ear-drums and behind the beating, felt the dry rasp of his tongue. His parched throat screamed for water, but on this ridge, on this little platform high above the land, there was no water – only the sound.

He tried to rise, but his body no longer obeyed him and he fell heavily backwards against the rock which had supported him throughout the night. He felt himself lose consciousness, felt his senses swirling around in his brain with the words which now filled his head. For a long time all was blackness, then slowly the voices came into his head again and the dryness hit his throat. He tried to hear what the voices were telling him, but he could not and the effort turned his world black once more. He slowly became conscious of sitting on a hard rock, the pale light turning rose and the voices and drumming in his ears.

'So, this is death!' he thought, wishing that his last sight could be of the high sky and the sunrise, but knowing that he lacked the stamina to raise his eyelids.

'How curious!' If he had had the strength, he would have laughed, but merely taking breath after breath seemed like too much effort, too much work. He sighed deeply, welcoming the thought that this curious occurrence was at last about to be experienced by him. The voices in his head had ceased, now only a low booming filled his ears. He took another breath and heard his lungs rattle as if they, deprived of water like the rest of his body, were now dry, no longer flowing with the liquid essence of life. The rattle seemed to go on for an age and again Galdr felt a sense of curious anticipation. The rattle ended and his body was still for an age. He felt the sun burst from the horizon, he felt the sudden heat wash over his body and behind his eyes he saw a bright orange glow grow larger. Another breath, so cool in this morning of his death, and again came the creaking rattling of his lungs, like seeds being slowly shaken inside a dried gourd.

He felt the sun grow stronger but only wished that he could open his eyes to witness the glory of the morning, once more. His last wish. He sighed again and felt his head fall on to his shrunken chest. A deep sense of calm expectancy filled his heart. He no longer wished for the sunrise, no longer wished for anything. The secret of the sun-metal would be for others to discover.

Ahh, the sun-metal, he thought. Yes, I am doing something important with that – I wish I could remember what it was – but never matter – I have done my best. Deep orange glow, that must be the sun – how warm, how gentle; but no, I am mistaken, or is it changing? Deep pools of purple and beyond . . . ? White light! Yes, the white light, the white light of power and love . . . Love . . . Injya . . . Pentesh . . . Halfray! . . . Love . . . Ah – a pain! A pain in my heart! No – I will not have pain! Only the white light, please Great Spirit, give me no pain! It is creasing me, pulling my heart out, please Great Spirit, no pain – only the white light of love. That noise – what is it? Croaking, creaking noise – the wind? The wind of breath – my breath. Aah, it has stopped – that is good, the pain too, gone, all gone. Colours swirling, a great ring of colours wheeling round, drawing me into them towards the white light. Like the crystals illuminated by the sun-metal, translucent rose and clear petal-yellow, warm orange sun, purest blue and Aspar green, shining violet and deepest amethyst swirling round, whirling into pearl-white light. Oh, beloved Bai Ulgan – you have answered me – you have taken away the pain and brought back the white light. Allow me to come into that love, allow me to fall into your arms of pure love. Accept your son. You have answered! I feel wings take my soul! I feel myself flying towards You! Spirit, all is spirit, all is white. The joy is boundless, to be flying to the white light! Sing my soul – sing in ecstasy. Hear the songs all around, the songs of the spirit-world, the songs of the animals and trees, the whispers of the insects, the melody of the air. I am no more. I am the White Spirit. I am. I am the trees. I am the animals. I am the wind and the sun and the waters. Bai Ulgan – I AM!

High in the sky Galdr soared. Below him lay mountains and valleys. In the rose glow of the sunrise he saw the circle of stones on the bare rocks with the sun-metal at its centre sending rays of love shining out to the world. The golden light passed along each pathway of stones, lighting up the crystals until they glowed with such transcendent beauty that it filled his soul with joy. The circle radiated light, a pure incandescent white light, rising straight up to him and beyond into the furthest heavens. Now he understood the secret of his workings – the moon crystals and the sun-metal fusing together to bring white healing light to the world. And he knew, as his soul soared further towards its source, that his brief life on earth had not been in vain – that everything he had done and strived for was to bring him to this understanding. The understanding of I am. Once he understood – there was no more reason for life. Galdr was free.

CHAPTER FORTY

Halfray felt that he had spent half his life looking for Galdr. He was tired, his horse was tired, Centill and Rudju were tired. He had wanted to stop a long while before, but each time he did, the cawing of the bird urged him onward. The three climbed steadily up this latest mountain, the horses quivering with exertion. In the last moon's quarter they had covered five mountains, sometimes on foot, sometimes riding, resting little, eating less. He did not know which was worse, the constant combing of the lowlands through trees and dried river-beds, or this steady plodding up dry mountain peaks. At night they scarce felt the frost numbing their aching bodies, only on rising did they feel the effects of the previous day's travelling and the hard night's cold. As he slowly followed the flight of the familiar raven, Halfray thought of Injya as he had last seen her; her pale face upturned to his, her worried eyes seeking his, her lips trembling as she fought with her emotions.

'Find him, Halfray, bring him back to me,' she had whispered and then hurriedly turned away, ruffling Pentesh's hair, anxious not to frighten her child. He sighed and looked up at the bird, doubting that he would be able to fulfil her wish and hating himself for that doubt.

The raven cawed again overhead. Upwards, always upwards. The ground became too steep to ride and once more they dismounted, aching legs and backs screaming with the change of position. Grasping his horse's reins he struggled on, eventually gaining a rise from which he could view the valley below and scan the plateau of mountains which stretched out behind him like a craggy man lying sleeping in the sunshine. There was no sign of Galdr.

They rested for a while, silently eating, each occasionally turning round, looking at the mountains and the valleys, then turning slowly back to face his compatriots, smiling weakly and resuming his eating morosely.

'How much longer?' Centill dared to ask, his voice faint and cracked.

'Do not ask,' Halfray sighed back as he rose stiffly and went over to his horse, and silently Centill and Rudju followed him, each wrapped in his own world of doubt and fear.

Late on the evening of the ninth day they came upon Galdr's body. He was still sitting, propped up against the rock, his head fallen on to his chest. In the rose glow of the setting sun his naked body gleamed as if it had been polished. His skin, dried by the winds and the sun, looked as if it had been burnished with gold. The sun and the winds had caressed his body, saving it from corruption and as if in awe of this, the birds of death had not feasted upon his remains but still flew overhead, gliding noiselessly as if caught in a magical airstream of light. For the second time in his life, Halfray saw the radiance of death and was not afraid.

In complete silence, as if they had previously arranged it, as if coming upon his body was no surprise, they gently, almost tenderly covered Galdr's body with skins and tied it to the baggage horse. Unbidden, Rudju collected the stones, placing each one with meticulous care into his riding bag, strapping it back on to his body with the air of a lover caressing a beloved. Centill alone was moved to tears and begged to be left upon the ridge for the night to mourn. Halfray and Rudju began descending the mountain in the light of a high half-moon, a moon lying on its back, cut completely in half, as if it too, had lost a loved one.

Centill did not sleep that night but had a series of waking dreams. He imagined himself in the centre of the ring of stones, feeling all the while that his body was being transported by light to the highest realms of love. When

471

the dawn broke he skittered down the mountain feeling lighter and happier than he could remember in his whole life. If he had ever been sure of anything, he was now sure of this – the stones which they had collected were sacred and powerful, so powerful that their image was still held by the bare rocks. The place of Galdr's death was a sacred place, the first sacred site of their people.

Injya stood tall feeling the warmed water being gently rubbed over her arms, hands and face. Sanset worked quietly and quickly, bathing her cousin not just in water but in love. Once dried, she deftly oiled Injya's skin, palm-warmed oil over rounded belly, finger-gentle oil down Injya's straight back and legs. Silently Bendula raised the gown over Injya's head then dropped it over her unmoving form. In the firelight of the sancar Injya's eyes glistened as her body shone. Stepping back Bendula looked into Injya's eyes and saw only the reflection of her own staring out from them.

Sanset brushed Injya's hair, combing the oiled hair until it glistened. Taking a strand between forefinger and thumb she began to plait the hair, watching in silent satisfaction as she tamed the curls into a long shining rope which hung thickly down her straight back. On the ends she entwined the beads of mourning and then the strips of red-dyed material, the signs of a mourning heart. The plait reached Injya's waist – a thick black ladder of grief running from the centre of her being to the roof of her head. Neither woman spoke. Neither needed reminding that the last time Sanset had washed and dressed Injya had been when a quaking fourteen-summer girl, recently orphaned, was about to be butchered by Kraa. The similarity was too poignant for words, Injya, now a twenty-four-summer woman, now widowed, once more losing a beloved.

Her task over, Sanset left the sancar, walking into the hushed night on silent feet. Even the noisy insects were quiet. She looked into the heavens – it was the time of the death of the moon – blackness was total. The central fire was out, doused upon the return of Galdr, not to be relit for three days and as the frost pinched her arms she rubbed them vigorously, feeling guilty for feeling so alive when all around her death wept. She crept into the sancar where Halfray, Centill, Rudju and Bendula were seated. Crossing over the fire, she caught sight of the two children, Pentesh and her own Fonyek asleep with their arms around each other, oblivious to the night and the sadness.

'She is ready,' she said quietly to Halfray who only lowered his head in response. After a long time he nodded, as if agreeing with some thought and then rose, somewhat unsteadily.

'It is time.' Without looking at each other, the men all got up and left the sancar. Bendula looked at her mother, tears swimming in her eyes.

'Not now, Bendula,' she said gently, 'a time for mourning tomorrow – now the tears are for Injya alone.'

Vronjyi had prepared Galdr's body. Washed and oiled, Galdr still looked as if he was sleeping. He had dressed him in the softest skins, laid him on a wooden platform and put beside the body the symbols of his soul: in one hand a single silver-eagle feather, in the other a small sharp knife, below his feet lay the pelt of a wolf, above his head a single rose-quartz crystal.

He stood for a long while, staring at the impassive, radiant face, trying to understand what this death meant for him. He had seen death many times but had only seen this face once before. This had been the face of Igrat – Igrat, the soft-man – and here it was again on Galdr. He thought of Soosha and her dire warnings and wanted to laugh – no man would die looking so peaceful if fear had entered him at the last. As if he needed a final reminder that what he had done was right, he looked again into the face of Galdr and wondered. Before him was a man who had been dead for how long? Three – four – eight days before being discovered? And it had taken them six days to return and yet there was no mark, no sign of corruption – it was truly as if Galdr was sleeping. Now no-one could tell him that Galdr was evil, he had seen for himself that this man was as pure as the wind and as good as the summer sun was golden.

The entrance flap to the sancar was lifted and the three men entered. Silently they each took hold of one corner of the platform and walked with it out of the sancar. They halted before Injya's sancar, and left, leaving only Halfray beside the body of Galdr. The entrance skin moved as Injya bent to come out. Halfray turned away from her, facing inwards to the dead fire and the rest of the circle of sancars. He crossed his arms on his chest and stared into the black night. Behind him, he knew that his sister was walking, unfalteringly, head erect, towards the body of her husband. He heard her gown rustle over the dried leaves as she approached, slowly and silently. Still facing the dead fire he heard his sister drop on to her knees and place her hands upon the pallet. He knew that Injya would kiss the cold mouth once and though his heart was breaking inside him, he stared – still and silent – at the dead fire and the black outlines of the hushed sancars.

Her scream of mourning when it came shattered the very air. The next made each hair on his head stand on end and his blood chill his soul, but as the screams grew, as the very ground shook with Injya's grief, Halfray stood stock-still, arms crossed, guarding the right of his sister to mourn, keeping her safe in her thredony from the spirits of evil who are always watching for a crack in the armour of love. All night he stayed thus and when the women of the tribe came to weep in the first rays of the morning he still stood guard, listening to the wailing, keening women, feeling his own heart wrung with the rain of sorrow.

At sunset Halfray, Centill, Vronjyi and Rudju, following the now silent figure of Injya, carried the wooden pallet away to the place for the souls of the dead. Behind them walked all the people of the tribe, silent now, their weeping and fasting done. Among the trees near the head of the valley they had erected a high platform, facing east – the pathway of the soul – and here they left the body of Galdr with the goods he would need on his journey to the creator, the eagle feather of flight, the knife of clarity and truth, the strength and cunning of brother wolf and the guiding spirit of the crystal.

For another two days and nights Injya sat alone, not eating, not drinking. Once his body had been removed to the place of death she cried no more. To cry now would hold his soul back on earth. She sat, silent in the blackness of her sancar, aware of the great sadness of her people but feeling apart from it. The returning of Galdr's body had been merely a formality, which she had kept custom with, because custom brings comfort in death, but she had wanted to utter that cry of mourning a long time before. She had known on the morning after her full-moon dance that Galdr was dead. She had woken that awful morning and felt half of her wither away and die. The feeling in her heart was as tangible as the feeling she had in her belly when her child had come too soon and had died. Half of her soul had died, half of her reason for living had perished. The only thing which stopped her taking her own life that morning was feeling Galdr's life stir within her. She was carrying his child – she had no right to die too. But as she sat in the darkness, she wished that she could join him – life without him could only be a half-life.

She allowed herself a little pride. She had not run screaming to Vronjyi or Halfray that first morning, she had kept her composure all that time, waiting for the men to come to her, willing them to come; but it had taken seven days before they became worried and it had taken them another seven days to find his body. She suppressed a sob, choking it back in her throat as she thought the word – body. His beautiful body, bronzed like metal, glistening and healthy-looking. A miracle. She tried to shut out the picture of Galdr, as a vision of his face came unbidden to her mind, but she failed and she felt her heart pulse with pain. Perhaps it always will lurch at the thought of my beloved, she thought to herself, as she rocked herself in the gloom of the fireless sancar, perhaps it always will.

On the third morning the fire was relit and slowly at first, the sound of humans talking was heard over the crackling of the wood and the hissing of the bark. A child laughed and was hushed, but before long an adult laughed and Injya heard a voice sing, stop abruptly in remembrance, only to resume its song a moment later, having forgotten itself. As the tribe came to life again, Injya began to allow herself to feel nurtured, cosseted with the child's laughter and the lone singing, taking heart that in the very celebration of life we also celebrate death. She stopped rocking and walked over to her bed. Stretching out for the first time for three days, she took a sip of water, covered herself with furs and fell into a dreamless, healing sleep.

It was with a supreme effort of will that Injya left her sancar when she awoke the next morning. All around her the people came, a kind glance here, a comforting hug there. It had been Sanset who took her to the brook that cold, white-sunshine morning and showed her the reason for her shocked look. In the three days' mourning, Injya's raven hair was turning white. Along the central parting of the oiled hair, still kept in place by the plait of widowhood, the new growth was showing white. Injya touched her hair in wonder – how strange – but it was Injya who comforted Sanset with the softly spoken words: 'I am glad – for now I wear the mark of the alone one – it is how it should be.'

Injya was now concerned with more than her hair. When Rudju had ridden in to the encampment a whole day before Halfray and Centill returned with Galdr's body, he had not only chokingly told her of Galdr's death, but also of the stones. The link between his death and the stones was of the greatest importance. After seeing for herself the miracle of Galdr's death, she was even more convinced that he had found the secret of the sun-metal and that the secret was held within the pattern of the stones themselves. Now she called the people to her and bid Rudju explain everything he had found at the site.

The stones were laid out in exactly the same manner as he had found them and Halfray and Injya, working together, tried to divine what their secret was. It was not until the next full moon that Injya, seated at her now usual place beside the strange circle of crystals, found the same luminosity that had so empowered Galdr.

In the light of the full moon each stone glowed at her, almost speaking to her, telling her where it should be placed. Injya knew that she was dealing with an energy at once divine, but so powerful that it had taken Galdr's life. She woke the whole encampment, urging them to be with her, needing the strength of many as she moved first one, then another, winking crystal. Soon the circle and the lines were complete, the sun-metal placed at its centre. Open mouthed the people waited, a ripple of excitement running through them as they stared at the ring of light. But as the night wore on and nothing seemed to emanate from the circle they fell asleep one by one, until only Rudju and Injya were left awake.

They were the first to see the sun-metal come to life by the rays of the rising sun. It was they who woke the sleepy people and bade them look, as along each line of crystals the light played, the sun-metal reflecting the light of the sun and turning the whole circle into a shimmering shining. Suddenly Injya knew what it was. It was the core, the very heart of her work and Galdr's. It was a living synthesis of the sun and the moon. From the combination of the sun-metal and the moon-lighted crystals came the essence of healing light, the pure white light of love. They had created a channel through which Bai Ulgan Himself could manifest. Now, she finally understood the words spoken so long ago, in such a different place; the words of Askoye: 'When you fully understand the symbol of the two moons, then your terror will leave you.' She turned her face to the sun and through tear-washed eyes saw an eagle fly. She opened her mouth to call but no words came – he was beyond her words now.

It was a short step from that first circle of crystals to the making of a healing circle. As if guided by unseen hands, Rudju and Injya moved the stones, one by one, until the circle became three times the original size. Now the circle covered an area of some five pchekts – a sacred area where anyone needing the strength of the divine could come and obtain nourishment. At first everyone had felt a little in awe of the circle, but as the days turned colder and the nights longer, one by one they came to the stones to receive their blessing and went away again feeling renewed.

In the stillness of the midwinter with the white rains lying cold upon the ground, one place on earth remained uncovered. It was the place of the crystals, the sacred circle of power. It was to this circle that they brought Toonjya's son, Potyami, when he fell ill with a fever and cough that kept the women by his side for nights on end; it was to this circle that they brought Oanti when the first pains of childbirth were upon her and it was in this circle that Hwaysaei sat all that long night while his wife struggled to give birth to their daughter. His prayers, like Toonjya's, were answered and Lafayla became the second child to be born upon this new land. Injya sat often at the centre of the circle, meditating upon the turning world, listening to her child calling within her, hearing Galdr's voice in her heart. She knew she would deliver his son safely, knew that the Samoyja people would grow into a fine race and knew that however slowly, however falteringly and unsurely, she was walking her path, the path of the Divine Will.

Far over the oceans a silver-white eagle flies. He half-expects to see the old raven, his spirit-friend for many a moon's passing, to suddenly appear before him, urging him onward; but he knows that the old spirit is resting now, enjoying at long last the companionship of his one great love, Mensoon. Below him the world spins, little dots of light emanate from the tiny groups of humans living within her gentle folds. He feels drawn to one small group and freed from the constraints of time and place, flies effortlessly over the frozen wastes of the north until the narrow mountainous isthmus of land lies before him, like a knobbly finger pointing southward.

Surrounded by the deep greens of the trees and the blues of the seas, silver-white eagle sees a small band of people, living like limpits on the seashore, their stout wooden houses clinging to the foothills like old, gnarled snails. He flies down and comes to rest on top of a bent old pine. Yellow eagle-eyes sees an old man, bent double with age; around him are young girls and men, some twenty souls in all. The old man is talking with them in an age-cracked voice – he summons one whom he calls Törhilde to come before him, kneels, and receives the old man's blessing. Törhilde rises and one called Amjund also comes to sit at the old man's feet. The silver-white eagle has seen enough. He takes flight again and sees the old man look up suddenly. Yellow eagle-eyes meet misty brown and both know that before long, the bull spirit of Anfjord will be free to roam the world once more.

The silver-white eagle flies away, away on warm air, away over high mountains and rushing rivers, away to a wooded glade surrounded by gentle mountains. He circles twice the home of his sister, weaving in and out of the lights coming from this large group of humans. They are faint lights, pale yellows, delicate roses with only here and there a spark of pure white shining like stars in the mists of dawn. He feels a sadness begin to pull him to the earth and senses that there is one among them who is calling him – only one among so many.

He lands with difficulty on a slender birch waving gracefully in the Aspar winds. Below him is a lone figure, watching his every move. Silver-white eagle twists his head and staring through bright eagle-eyes looks straight into the soul of Xynon. He sees the man's shame, his weakness, he reads the times when he was unable to shout 'NO!' to his wife's cruelty, he understands the wretchedness of one who has watched his wife take lover after lover in an attempt to make a 'perfect' child; he knows the heart of one who loved his wife so greatly that Erlik, no matter how much she tried, could not gain possession of her. And as he looks he becomes aware that this man has within him a spirit as gentle and soft as his eagle-spirit is strong: for behind Xynon's head stands the spirit of Igrat, the soft-man, his one true love. He gains the upper air and turns to take one last look: he sees Xynon hesitate and then sadly turn away. He knows that Xynon understood what he saw and as he flies upwards, into the very heart of the sun, he hopes Soosha one day will also understand.

Xynon had watched as the eagle took flight. He knew he had looked into the eyes of love and he was no longer afraid.

THE END